Sacred Mountain

Robert Ferguson

Matador
9 Priory Business Park
Kibworth Beauchamp
Leicestershire LE8 0RX, UK
Tel: (+44) 116 279 2299
Fax: (+44) 116 279 2277
Email: books@troubador.co.uk
Web: www.troubador.co.uk/matador

ISBN 978-1783061-891

British Library Cataloguing in Publication Data.
A catalogue record for this book is available from the British Library.

Typeset in Aldine by Troubador Publishing Ltd
Printed and bound in the UK by TJ International, Padstow, Cornwall

Matador is an imprint of Troubador Publishing Ltd

To Fiona, Isabelle and Jemima.

PROLOGUE

Tibet, 1953

The moon lit the monastery in a light that was clear and pure.

It magnified as it reflected off the snow-capped peaks surrounding him, glistening on the tumbling glaciers that fell towards the valley. Philip could smell the air, the rock, the snow and vast space, tainted by the odour of sun block and days' old perspiration.

His body ached with cold, his joints grating as he moved stiffly along the side of the building. Each breath seemed to chill the furthest recesses of his tired lungs, drawing the raw, thin air deeper inside his body. He hadn't had any feeling in his toes for days and now the bones in his fingers throbbed just like when, as a boy, he used to play in the snow for too long.

Far away he could hear the distant roar of fast-flowing water; small rocky streams joining the larger torrent of freezing snow melt that cut its way down the barren valley. Above it came the occasional howling of wolves as they searched for stray goats in the higher pastures, and the ferocious snarling of guard dogs, chained near the animal pens to protect the many rather than the few.

He edged his way along the rough stone-wall, its whitewash stained and cracked by the bitter weather it had endured over the centuries. As he walked he placed his hand against the stones, reassured by their solidity and texture that made everything feel more real.

Stooping down as he passed the only window, he turned to ensure the men who followed did the same. Noises tumbled out from the opening, a babble of murmuring voices and the groans of injured men smothered by the wooden shutters and thick woollen hangings that protected the interior from the biting winter winds. He grunted to himself satisfied. Any noise they made would be muffled by these and the echoing acoustics inside.

At the end of the wall he stopped and looked at his watch. Its enamel dial glowed back at him in the moonlight, a reassuring face that had been through so much with him. He had twenty seconds. He turned and mouthed this to the three men who were crouched close behind, each with a curved bladed knife grasped in their hands.

He reached inside his coat for the grenade. Its casing felt smooth after the roughness of the wall, its metal warm to the touch, heated by his body. His mind flashed back to the small charcoal pocket warmers he'd been given by his mother as a boy while out on the salt marshes in winter, beating through the tall grasses to drive wild duck towards the waiting guns.

He pulled the grenade out into the night and glanced down at it. Panic shivered through him, bile pushing into his mouth. He felt his legs weaken and leant against the wall, clenching his fists to prevent them from shaking and squeezing his eyes closed. The distant roar of water transformed into a background chorus of cicadas and frogs; the wolves into shrieking monkeys as they crashed through thick jungle canopy. A smell of cordite and burning filled his nostrils, mingling with the pungent, metallic aroma of blood.

Rifle shots rang out from the far side of the courtyard, pulling him back to the present. Philip heard the bullets slamming into the stone frame and heavy wood of the door around the corner, ricocheting away into the darkness. Ten seconds. Cautiously he peered around, forcing his memories away. He could see several rifles poking from the doorway about ten yards away, their muzzles flashing as they returned fire.

He pulled himself back and looked down at the grenade once more, visualising what he had to do. He would pull the pin and release the trigger. It was a five second fuse so he'd throw it on two. It would slowly tumble in the air, its shallow arc bringing it down onto the stone paving with a dull, metallic thud. It would probably bounce, catching the edge of a flagstone and deflecting slightly one way or the other. It wouldn't settle, its oval shape gradually rolling it around until it hit the wooden door with a gentle tap. Then it would explode. Faces flew at him. Long dead people crying through ripped eyes, women screaming over broken bodies, hair burning, gaping wounds. He shook his head, trying to dislodge the images from his mind, trying to control his breathing.

He glanced again at his watch. It was time. Time for redemption.

CHAPTER 1

Nepal, 1953

It was like a journey back in time. The Dakota banked steeply and Philip looked out of the small window at the medieval city below. Winding streets snaked between tiled roofs and the occasional glint of gold reflected from the gilded decoration of a hundred temples. Wispy columns of smoke rose lazily into the sky, while a river of crystal blue cut through the city, its sandy banks covered with the dazzling colours of washing drying in the sun.

He caught his breath as the plane dropped, lurching to the right and depositing the dregs of his drink onto his lap. He hated flying and this journey had been worse than most, the turbulence, as they'd flown through narrow mountains passes, tossing them around like a flimsy paper plane. Nausea dried his mouth, whiskey burning the back of his throat. For the first time in years he craved a cigarette, biting at his nails instead.

He looked out of the window again, taking long, steady breaths. He could now see people in the streets below. There were women squatting beside piles of vegetables and porters bent double by huge loads balanced on their backs. He glimpsed a child driving a herd of sheep and a column of monks in bright purple robes. As they heard the noise of the propellers they all stopped and looked up, shading their eyes from the bright afternoon sun, to marvel at the silver machine roaring overhead.

The houses and streets changed to the vivid green of verdant countryside and the plane glided lazily over a grassy field, its engines throttling back. There was a small bump as the wheels silently kissed the turf and he relaxed back into his seat as they rolled to a stop up a gentle slope. He'd made it. "Welcome to Kathmandu," he said to himself, raising his empty glass in a mock salute.

The airport terminal was little more than a bamboo shed at one end of the field. Philip and the other passengers, all of whom seemed to be Indian businessmen, stood in the warm sunshine as their bags were unloaded onto the grass. An immigration official walked over to him and politely requested, in broken English, to see his passport. He handed it over and watched as the man solemnly held it upside down and copied his inverted name into a blue school exercise book, returning it with a small bow. He was just walking forward to identify his cases when a man dressed in lounge suit and tie came hurrying towards him.

"You must be Armitage," he said through half opened lips that clamped a cigarette. "I'm Arthur Hutchinson. Call me Hutch."

Philip reached out to grasp the proffered hand. "Delighted to meet you," he replied. "Philip, please. Thanks for coming to meet me, it really wasn't necessary."

"Think nothing of it," Hutch answered with a dismissive

wave of the hand. "Anyway, they said you'd be bringing out some scotch and I didn't want this lot," he nodded towards a group of customs officials circling the bags, "relieving you of any before I'd the chance to savour some of it."

He slapped Philip on the back and strode off, waving a piece of paper he'd pulled from his jacket. Philip followed and listened to a confusing stream of English, Hindi and Nepalese that was being directed at the officials. Whatever it meant seemed to work because within minutes his cases were being loaded onto the back of an ancient jeep.

The jeep had seen better days. Its bumpers were gone and there was no sign of the windscreen. The bonnet restraints were broken and as the driver turned the ignition it bounced up and down in time with the misfiring engine. Hutch saw the look on his face and laughed, swinging himself into the passenger seat.

"This is as good as it gets over here I'm afraid," he said with a shrug, gesturing to the back seat. "There're no roads into Kathmandu from the outside world so every vehicle has to be dismantled in India and carried through the mountains by porters. There's only a couple of hundred in the whole country." He shook his head. "Even the petrol's carried in. Expensive too and these damned drivers really try to rip you off over it."

Philip clambered into the back and they juddered off in a cloud of black fumes, turning a lazy circle on the airstrip before picking up a rough track towards the city. Philip looked out, enjoying the feel of cold air after the stale cabin of the plane. They were driving through rice paddies and meadows which stretched away on either side across a wide valley that rose in the distance into thickly forested foothills. The colours were so bright, the air so crisp that for the first time since leaving London he smiled.

"So what've they told you?" Hutch shouted over his shoulder. "We only asked for an extra pair of hands last week so they must've dispatched you pretty damn quick."

"They said you were having problems with the *Daily Mail*," he yelled back. "Told me I was booked on the flight out of London the next day and to go pack a bag." He paused. "That's about it. I've been either flying or sitting in airports for the last three days and that was quick apparently. They managed to get me on a Comet jetliner rather than one of the old Constellations."

Hutch nodded. "I know. It's the back of beyond. Further! Less the Forbidden Kingdom, more the bloody Forgotten Kingdom." He shifted in his seat and turned to face Philip. "There's hardly any electricity, other than that produced by generators. No telephones either. And the local tipple. Christ, you could pickle rats in it!"

Philip laughed. "Just as well I bought that scotch then." There was a pause. "So what's the issue with the *Mail*?"

"Well, they're here for a start, although that in itself wouldn't be a problem." Hutch scratched lazily at a mosquito bite on his cheek. "The *Telegraph's* sent Colin Reid but he's happy enough to stay in town and forage for news. The *Mail* guy, Izzard's his name, has hired a guide and disappeared into the hills." He stopped talking to light a cigarette, inhaling deeply and then thoughtfully picking a piece of stray tobacco from his mouth. "If he's got a radio transmitter in all the baggage he took with him then he could cause us a few problems. I sent James a message by runner telling him what was happening and decided we could do with someone checking up on him properly. Trouble is James is stuck with the expedition and I'm stuck here relaying his reports to London." He shook his head. "Wish we'd brought our own transmitter now, although last year when I was working with the Swiss Expedition on Everest they were adamant that it would've been a complete waste of time. Too many big mountains in the way blocking the signal."

They drove on in silence, Philip enjoying the warm sun on his face. James Morris was the Special Correspondent from *The Times* who'd been sent to cover the British Expedition to Mount Everest. The paper had paid for exclusive rights to the story but no one could prevent the other papers trying to scoop the news. Morris' dispatches took nine days to reach Kathmandu, sent by runners who had to cover 180 miles of rough trails, river crossings and steep climbs. There was, Philip realised, a lot of scope for interception and bribery, and if this Izzard had brought a radio transmitter with him, he could get the news to London days before their runners had even left the mountain.

Hutch flicked the butt of his cigarette out into a paddy field. "Not much time to rest I'm afraid," he said, looking at Phillip. "Izzard left a few days ago and the expedition should have reached Everest by now. We'll need to set you up with a guide and porters and get you going. You need to catch him and find out just what he's up to." He paused. "If he gets the story to London before we do, I don't want to be first back in the office. Guts for garters, I reckon."

They entered the city. It was like crossing an invisible line, the country lane transforming into a bustling street hemmed in by high, closely packed houses of brick two or three stories high. Narrow alleys and shadowy side streets disappeared off through small gaps between them. The ornately carved doorways and gates of houses stood open, revealing tidy courtyards and built into every threshold and street corner were small shrines containing statues of various deities, decorated with garlands of marigolds and daubs of vibrant paint.

Philip was overwhelmed by the fetid smell of sewage and decay, of pinewood smoke, stale sweat and livestock mingling with exotic spices and sweet incense. He shuddered, his mind travelling back to places from his past he tried hard to forget.

Despite entering the city the driver hadn't slowed down and Philip found himself thrown back to the present as they swerved violently around pedestrians, frantic shouting from the driver and a dilapidated horn serving as warning to their approach.

They emerged into a small square, at the centre of which stood a towering pagoda, its tiered roof soaring into the sky, and guarded at each corner by a large stone griffin. The square was packed, mainly by women out buying fresh vegetables, all dressed in colourful saris and many with flowers tucked into their hair. They looked up, curious as to the occupants of the vehicle, and smiled shyly as they saw Philip staring back. Stalls covered the square, most just blankets or baskets on the rough paving on which vegetables and fruits were arranged in piles. Elsewhere were heaps of firewood, tied into equal bundles by hemp twine, which were being examined and haggled over. Around its four sides were small shops, rough wooden shutters pulled back to display their merchandise. Whole sides of meat hung on hooks in clouds of swarming flies. Sacks of spices with their sides carefully rolled down and their contents arranged into pointed cones of brilliant colour. Bolts of materials shimmered in the sunlight with gold and silver braid flashing as shop owners unrolled them for prospective clients.

A sacred cow wandered out in front of them and for the first time the driver used his rather ineffective brakes, swerving narrowly around its hind quarters. Philip turned to watch it start feeding unperturbed on some rotting leaves in the gutter, its forehead anointed with orange paint. Behind it an old woman brandished a stick at three monkeys who'd jumped from the pagoda roof and were skulking towards her stall of beautifully polished apples.

The scene disappeared as the jeep dived off down a dark, narrow street and after only a couple of minutes, they turned sharply left through a tall, stone archway. They emerged into a sweeping courtyard of sun-bleached brick and looking up Philip saw the grand but dilapidated edifice of what appeared to be a large Palace. They rolled to a stop in front of a grand central flight of steps, scattering a brood of scrawny chickens pecking lazily at weeds. A small man dressed in a tight-fitting waistcoat, white cotton pantaloons and traditional Nepali cap scuttled down the steps to meet them. He bowed, holding his hands together.

"Welcome to Kathmandu Sahib!" he said, a serious look on his face. "Welcome to your stay at the Royal Hotel."

That evening Philip sat in the hotel bar as the conversation washed around him, exhausted from all the travelling. The room was dark, lit only by a single flickering light bulb and the glow of three hurricane lamps that hissed and spat on nearby tables. The walls were covered with moth-eaten tiger heads baring yellow fangs, dusty eyed rhino staring sadly back at him and the faded photos of Maharajas and Kings standing proudly over fallen prey. Everywhere smelt of wood smoke and decay, a blazing log fire making the animals shadows dance in its flickering light to the music of a jazz quartet who were playing disinterestedly in the corner.

Hutch leant forward and picked up the half-empty bottle of whiskey that sat before them on a fraying elephant's foot table, pouring a generous measure into his glass. They were discussing Hunt, the leader of the expedition.

"He seems a reasonable enough bloke to me," Hutch stated, collapsing comfortably back into the depths of a sagging leather armchair. "I guess the last thing he wanted was a journalist tagging along." He chuckled. "Especially one who'd never even been on a bloody mountain before."

Another man spoke up. "James will be all right. Your editor made a good choice in sending him." It was Colin Reid, special correspondent of the *Daily Telegraph*. "I see his runners have already started arriving with messages from the mountain." He paused, glancing up at Hutch. "They must be doing well?"

Hutch laughed. "Nice try, old man." He wagged a finger in Reid's direction. "You'll have to get me drunker than this if you want any free information. You'll just have to spend more time on that radio receiver of yours, seeing if you can intercept the Embassy transmissions."

Reid shook his head. "It's useless. There's so much chatter going on I can't understand anything that's being said."

"What sort of chatter?" Hutch asked, raising an eyebrow.

"There's hardly enough electricity in this country to run that light bulb," he pointed towards the ceiling, "let alone a transmitter." He paused. "Don't suppose you've heard anything from Izzard have you?" he asked, shooting a glance towards Philip.

Reid shrugged. "I don't think so but, to be honest, it's hard to make anything out." He stopped, rubbing his eyes as a billow of smoke rolled into the room from the narrow chimney. "It's certainly not English but it doesn't sound like Nepalese or Hindi either. More like Mandarin, but the Himalayas should, in theory, block out any broadcasts from Tibet." He paused again. "Sometimes it's so weak I can hardly make it out through the static."

The conversation lulled, each lost in thought and relaxed by the warmth and whiskey. The expedition should be camped at the foot of Everest by now. Another runner from the base camp was due any day. Philip closed his eyes, enjoying the luxury of being still after all the travelling. In a few days he'd be out in those hills, looking for Izzard, no doubt cold and tired.

"So Armitage," Reid asked, pulling Philip back from his daydream. "What's your plan?"

Philip sipped his drink. "First thing tomorrow I'm meeting a man who's going to sort me out. Apparently he helped James arrange his trip."

Hutch nodded. "I know the one, seems very good. Poor old James had to organize all his own staff and food for the whole trip as Hunt didn't want to add his stuff to the expeditions." He chuckled. "Should have seen him when they set off, it looked as if he was going to climb the mountain himself. He'd got two men just to carry the money with which to pay all the rest!"

They laughed. "I intend to travel lighter than that," Philip continued. "I'll need to travel fast if I'm to catch up with Izzard." He yawned. "I also have to call at the Ministry to pick up my permit to get to Everest. Without it the authorities won't let me out of Kathmandu." He pulled himself wearily to his feet. "Now, if you'll excuse me gentlemen, it's been a long day."

He walked slowly down the dark corridors to his room, guided by a young Nepali holding a lantern up in front of them. When they reached his room door he was presented with the lantern and the man vanished into the shadows. Philip unlocked his door with an impressively large key the size of a serving spoon. After quickly changing and splashing his face with some scalding water that clunked its way out of the tap, he climbed into a creaky wooden bed that sagged badly in the middle. His body ached from the travelling, but his body clock hadn't yet adjusted and he found sleep was slow to come. His stomach tingling at the prospect of heading into the mountains of this mysterious Kingdom he'd heard so much about but had never expected to visit. Only a few hundred westerners had ever been given visas to enter Nepal and of them, only a handful had been allowed to leave the city.

He turned, pulling the thick covers up to his chin against the cold night air. It had been strange hearing Nepalese again, listening to snippets of conversation at the airport and hotel. It had brought back memories, phrases and words that had once been so familiar and which for years he'd tried to forget.

CHAPTER 2

Burma, 1943

Philip tried to concentrate, but the smell of blood was making his mind wander. Its rich, salty odour flooded his mind with the image of rare roast beef. He forced the thought away and looked down to where their right hands were clasped together, wondering whether the trembling was coming from him or the injured man.

He looked him in the eye. "We've left you a chagal with about two pints of water in it and some chocolate. I've also left one of the letters in Burmese explaining that you need help. We'll push on but in an hour or so the burrif will go into the village and tell them where to find you." He paused, forcing himself to maintain the eye contact. "I'm sure they'll come and get you."

The wounded man nodded weakly, his head scarcely moving.

Philip waved his free hand towards the thick layer of flies that covered the blood-soaked dressing, but they didn't pause from their frenzy of feeding. He could see fresh blood oozing from beneath it, dripping half-congealed onto the sodden ground.

“Anyway, good luck,” he said, trying to sound confident and giving the hand a final squeeze before placing it on the prostrate man’s chest. “You can tell me all about it when we next meet up in Calcutta.”

The man smiled up at him, his eyes revealing the futility of the words.

“Thank you, Sir,” he whispered, a soft bubbling coming from his lungs. “Get the men home.”

Philip stood and looked down at the broken body of the man he’d relied on for the last few weeks. It had always seemed indestructible, never showing fatigue or hunger, always in control. Always clean and tidy, for Christ’s sake, even in this hell hole.

Sergeant Gurung had been injured two days before, in a fleeting skirmish with an enemy patrol. No one had realised he’d been injured until there was too much blood to miss. A bullet to the upper chest that they’d initially thought, or at least hoped, had passed through and missed anything vital. That morning he’d coughed up blood and they’d known it hadn’t.

It’s what Philip had dreaded most from the start of the operation. Any injured man who couldn’t walk was to be left in the care of local villagers. He hadn’t told the men at first, he and the other junior officers had thought it would be so bad for morale; it was best for them not to know. Word soon got out, however, but the Gurkhas had taken it in their usual stoic way. No fuss. No discussion.

Philip walked back to the small streambed where the rest of the platoon was waiting. He looked around until he saw the burrif. “Maung,” he called in a low voice. “Here please.”

The small, squatting Burmese stood up and scurried over.

"Go and sit with Sergeant Gurung. Keep a look out and try to keep him comfortable." He looked at his watch. It was ten past three in the afternoon. "Give us until four and then go into the village. If it's clear, find the headman and lead the villagers to Gurung. If there are Japs about, you'll have to wait until the coast's clear." He scratched irritably at a swollen insect bite on his cheek. "You know the bearing we're taking. We'll expect you after nightfall." He looked at the small man. "And don't get followed by the bloody Japs."

The man nodded and disappeared silently into the bush, a legacy of his upbringing in the Karen tribes of Northern Burma. Every platoon had been assigned a local guide to act as liaison with the local population, and Philip counted his blessings that Maung was still with them. It was a dangerous job as the Japanese shot any they caught as traitors. He was replaced by the squat, muscular frame of Corporal Prem who saluted him crisply.

"Corporal," Philip acknowledged irritably, having wanted some time to get his thought together. "I'm going to be relying on you now that Sergeant Gurung is ... indisposed." He chose his word carefully, wanting to appear calm in front of the experienced Gurkha. "We're going to have to work together if we're to get out of this." He nodded towards the resting men. "Fall them in, we'll move out in five minutes."

The Nepali turned and headed off, and Philip watched as the Gurkhas roused themselves as Prem walked past, preparing themselves for the march. They'd been out for six weeks, the same routine every day so that now they knew what to do without thinking. But there'd always been Gurung there before, chiding them on, encouraging them. He'd have to see how things went now he was gone.

The terrain was straightforward at first. Their bearing of north-west took them up the stream course they'd been resting in. It meandered slowly up into the hills but was much quicker than trying to cut a straight path through the jungle, especially with the men so weak. Beyond the hills lay the Chindwin River and India.

Philip felt the sweat running down between his shoulder blades, viscous trails that plastered his shirt to his back. Reaching behind, he caught his water bottle and pulling it round unscrewed the top and took a long draught, savouring the sensation despite it being as hot as tea and tasting of purification tablets. How things had changed. Only a year ago he'd been sitting in the snug bar of the Coach and Horses in Cambridge, a pint of Adnams in front of him, warming himself by a log fire.

He'd been on leave, the last he was to have before shipping out. It had all seemed so exotic and exciting. Off to India to take up a commission in the Gurkhas. He'd just completed his first year at Cambridge University when he'd received his call-up. His friends had joked that Ancient History was hardly an essential profession and at heart he was pleased to be going.

He'd loved archaeology ever since his father had taken him to a lecture by the great Egyptologist Howard Carter, returning in triumph to his childhood town of Swaffham, with golden statues and treasures from the tombs of the pharaohs that had dazzled his ten-year-old mind. When he'd discovered his posting he'd been even more pleased, imagining opportunities to explore the ruins of the great Indus civilization and the forts of the Moguls.

It hadn't worked out as he'd hoped. He'd only been in India for a couple of weeks when his Regiment, the 2nd Gurkha Rifles, has been assigned to special operations. For months they'd trained in jungle survival, river crossing and, worst of all, mule handling. Rumours abounded as to what they were being trained to do.

It was generally agreed that they were to spearhead a counter offensive against the Japanese in Burma, who'd routed the allied forces there the previous year. Then, at Christmas, they'd been told that they were going to be operating deep behind enemy lines, sabotaging railway and road links to the Japanese front line. Three months later and here he was. He glanced back at his men and felt a surge of pride. Their faces were pinched with hunger, uniforms that had fitted perfectly a few weeks before now hung loose around them, often ripped and holed by the sharp undergrowth they spent most of their days cutting through.

The pride was replaced by a wave of hunger, followed by a weakness that threatened to take his legs away from under him. They hadn't had a food drop for five days and he'd already put the men on half rations. They'd managed to buy some rice from a local village a few days before, storing it in their spare socks, but with so many men to feed it was soon eaten. He reached into his chest pocket and took out a packet of acid drops. He hated them. His face winced as he popped one in his mouth, its sourness making his mouth tingle painfully, but he felt some strength return as the sugar ran down into his stomach.

The streambed was now down to single file, and turning a bend he saw one of the scouts standing at the foot of a small waterfall. He held up his hand to halt the column and the men disappeared instantly into the undergrowth on either side.

He looked up at the waterfall. It was about twenty foot high, its rock face rounded and polished from the flow of water that must rush down it from the hills at certain times of the year. Now only a gentle trickle fell from its lip, which seemed to have vanished in a fine spray by the time it reached the bottom.

Philip drew a deep breath and momentarily closed his eyes. It seemed endless. Rivers, swamps, impenetrable jungle, mountains, snakes and insects. Whenever they seemed to be making progress something always stopped them and that didn't even include the enemy who harried them constantly.

"Is there a way around?" he asked, his eyes wearily sweeping along the low cliff.

The rifleman nodded. "Yes, sir." He pointed. "If we follow the ridge north for 100 yards we can get up."

Philip wiped the sweat from his face, squashing a mosquito and rolling its body between his fingers. He turned and signalled the men. They re-emerged and walked wearily forward. Philip looked at his watch. It seemed to be getting dark but was impossible to be sure under the thick jungle canopy. It was time to make camp if the men were to have time to find fodder for the mules and firewood for themselves. He turned to Prem who was at his shoulder.

"Follow the scouts up and then make camp at a suitable place up stream." He nodded towards the waterfall. "This'll give us some protection if we've been followed. Station a sentry up there tonight."

The Gurkha nodded and moved out, signalling the platoon to follow. Philip watched as they passed. He could see hunger and fatigue etched on their faces, and yet many smiled as they passed before disappearing into the undergrowth.

At the rear came the mules, driven on by their handlers who walked silently behind. They were sorry looking creatures, heads down and little more than skeletons. They hadn't had any hay for weeks, surviving on freshly cut bamboo when it was available and foraging for anything else they could find. At least their weakness had solved one problem. In the beginning their angry braying had constantly threatened to give away their position to Japanese patrols. Now they were silent, trudging resignedly along behind the men.

Once they'd passed, Philip stood for a few moments looking back down the streambed. It all seemed quiet. The sound of the crickets and frogs had returned, and looking up he could see a small patch of evening sky just starting to glow orange as the hidden sun sank lower.

He turned and felt his spirits sink as he was swallowed once more by the damp, darkness of the jungle. The six weeks they'd been there felt like a lifetime; slashing through the undergrowth, lacerated by branches and bamboo. Uniforms so rotted by the humidity that pieces are left hanging on brushing twigs. The constant smell of corrupted flesh and loose bowels, flies swarming on open sores and mosquitoes and ants tormenting their nights. He sighed, wishing again he was at home, on a crisp, winter morning, walking over frosted meadows with the dogs playing and friends laughing. God it would be good to feel cold.

It only took a few minutes to reach the place Prem had chosen to camp and he glanced around approvingly, the men having already lit several small cooking fires. Now that dusk had fallen their smoke wouldn't be seen so they were busy boiling water drawn from the small stream. The flow was weak but it was moving, as their training had instructed them to leave all stagnant water alone. He smiled grimly to himself. Whoever had written that would've been shocked if they'd seen where they'd drunk from during the last few weeks.

He checked the mules, finding them hobbled and chewing unenthusiastically on some tough looking bamboo that had just been cut. Walking through the camp he tried to give a few words of encouragement to the men, before arriving at his own fire where he gratefully dropped his pack on the ground. He untied his groundsheet from where it hung and unfolded it, collapsing down onto it and leaning against the trunk of a large teak tree. Reaching across to the pack he unstrapped a side pocket and pulled out a tattered map, dropping it by his side as he unlaced and removed his boots. As his feet slipped out he groaned with relief, peeling off worn and bloody socks and exposing his feet to the air. They were white and shrivelled, the result of weeks of being wet, with painful blisters on each heel.

A quick inspection revealed only two leech bites, thin trails of blood still running from them. The leeches crawled into his boots through the lace holes, latching on and gorging on his blood until they were too fat to escape. Philip always knew when one had popped, a warm sticky sensation on the sole of his foot as the blood oozed out of its ruptured body.

Picking up the map he laid it across his drawn up knees and carefully worked out their position, taking into account the bearing they'd been on and the length of time they'd marched. It was six days since they'd initially tried to re-cross the Irrawaddy River, a night of total confusion that had seen them cut off from the rest of the column. The crossing had started fine. The burrifs had found some local fishermen who'd been willing, in exchange for silver rupees, for them to use their boats. They'd only been big enough for twelve or so men to cross at a time so after three hours they'd still been at it when a Japanese patrol had turned up.

All hell had broken loose and as a result Philip had found his platoon, who'd been operating as the vanguard, stuck on the wrong side of the river. He'd been the only officer left but at least he knew the orders from High Command. The mission was over and they were to return to India but they were now marooned with the enemy searching for them. He'd head south, hoping the Japanese would least expect them to move away from the rest of the column.

The Japanese had ordered all local craft to be moored on the west bank to prevent their use. If they hadn't stumbled on a battered old dug-out canoe hidden in some elephant grass next day they might still be walking. As it was, under the cover of a dark, moonless night, they'd managed to cross over, four men at a time, with the mules swimming behind. They'd almost lost some men when a mule had panicked and hooked its hoof over the canoe's side, struggling to get out of the water. It had taken the sharp blade of a kukri to dispatch the animal and prevent three nervous Gurkhas from joining it on the riverbed.

At least, Philip thought, they were still largely together. If half of the platoon had already crossed when the attack had come on the initial crossing it would've been a disaster. The Gurkhas had a bond that gave them an almost telepathic understanding of each other, working seamlessly as a team that only men who'd grown up from boyhood together could have. If they'd been ripped apart and this intuition destroyed Philip dreaded to think what their chances of survival would have been. They were grim enough as it was.

He put his finger on their position and sighed. They'd made reasonable progress, considering the terrain and their physical condition. They were now high in the Mangin Hills, about three hours walk, give or take, from their next food drop. It was due at midday the next day so they had enough time he hoped to get in position and recce the area first. He felt the urge to get the radio out and call HQ to confirm the drop but knew they only had enough power left in the batteries for a minute or two of transmission and needed to conserve them. He had to hold his nerve and trust that the RAF would be there.

He glanced up as a soldier arrived with a mug of tea, the steam rising into the air as if it was a chill winter's morning. He took it and carefully placed it on the jungle floor beside him to cool. He lifted up his right foot, resting it on his left thigh so he could inspect a large ulcer that had formed on his shin. It had started as an ant bite but, like most cuts and scratches in this climate, it had quickly become infected and now formed an ugly crater the size of a Crown piece.

Gingerly he peeled away the small piece of field dressing that covered it, wincing as it pulled pieces of dead flesh and crusty discharge with it.

He waved his hand to keep an excited fly from landing and in the fading light tried to examine it. It looked white and puffy, a little blood seeping into it but with no sign of a scab forming. At least he couldn't see the bone and there weren't any maggots. He picked up his tea, drinking the bitter brew quickly and feeling strength come back as the liquid ran into him. The last mouthful he left in his cup, added a couple of drops of iodine, and braced himself.

The pain as the liquid ran into the ulcer on his leg was excruciating, as if a knife was being dragged across it. He forced himself to keep still, trying to keep the liquid in it for as long as he could bear, before straightening his leg and letting the foul fluid run down his foot and into the forest floor.

Glancing up he saw Corporal Prem standing respectfully a few yards away and sitting up stiffly he beckoned the Gurkha over.

"Is the camp secure?" he asked, trying to keep his voice authoritative.

"Sir," replied the soldier with a nod. "Teams of two on sentry all night, changing every three hours."

Phillip nodded. "Good. Get the men to make enough tea and boiled parnee tonight for the morning, we'll be breaking camp early. Canteens need to be full. Then get the fires out and everybody resting."

He looked around at the men, sitting exhausted around the small fires, their faces lit by the pale flickering light as thousands of insects swirled around them. "They'll need their strength. At least hopefully they'll get a decent meal tomorrow night."

The corporal saluted. "How far to the drop?"

"About three hours if the terrain stays like this, then we'll need to have a good dekko around and secure the drop zone."

The corporal turned to go. "Oh, and send the burrif to me when he gets in please Corporal," Philip added, "I want to hear how things went back there."

Philip ate his food in silence, cutting cheese straight from the tin and then chewing half-heartedly on some dried dates. He popped some rock salt crystals in his mouth and sucked unenthusiastically. They'd run short of salt a week before, a serious problem given the sweltering heat in the jungle, but the burrif always somehow managed to find natural deposits of rock salt. It was gritty and course but kept them going, each man having to suck two pieces a day to supplement his meagre ration.

Having tidied everything away he took a small tin from the side of his pack and lay back, using his pack as a pillow. He could see a few stars through the canopy of trees high above, the branches motionless in the still night. Some thin shafts of moonlight sliced down to the forest floor, forming tiny pools of silver white in the otherwise dark jungle. The fires were out and with the lack of cigarettes it was the only light. The night was filled with the sound of lizards and frogs, a chorus that drowned out the fidgeting and coughing of the men. It was a harsh sound, but a comforting one as it would stop and warn them if anybody tried to approach.

Opening the tin he removed a folded letter, carefully sliding the thin sheets of paper out of a grubby envelope. He held it towards one of the small pools of light but could still barely see the neat hand writing, his eyes no longer working well in the dark. It was of little consequence, since he'd received it in an airdrop just over two weeks earlier and had read it so often he knew it by heart.

5th January 1943

My Dearest Philip,

I pray that this letter finds you safe and well. I hope you received the Christmas card we sent. I wanted to send you a fruit cake but your father said that it would be eaten by the ants before it reached you. I rather think he was more concerned with his dwindling brandy supply than the insects of India.

Old Peters managed to get us a rather scrawny goose for Christmas dinner, I suspect from the marshes rather than the butcher, but as there were so few of us at the house this year it sufficed well enough. Kim was unable to get leave, his ship is goodness knows where and Mary was busy driving her ambulance around London. She did get to come up at New Year and sends her little brother a big hug.

Our Christmas was rather spoilt by the news that young William Spalding had been killed in North Africa. I'm sorry to have to give you such bad news, I know you were friends and remember you running wild together across the estate, lost in whatever game you'd invented that day. It's got everybody quite upset, as if the war has finally arrived in our little world in North Norfolk.

His mother was trying so hard to be brave at the WI but she quite fell to pieces when we were clearing up at the end. I felt so guilty, trying to comfort her but at the same time so relieved that you are in India.

The Reverend Fisher and his wife came round for drinks at New Year and he kindly blessed the enclosed St. Christopher medal. Please wear it, it's only tiny and I'm sure would slip around your neck unnoticed. It would be such a comfort for me to know you had it with you, keeping you safe on these travels that I cannot accompany you on. Mrs Fisher burst into tears when I asked, remembering you from her Sunday School lessons, and saying she couldn't believe you were away fighting a war. A sloe gin seemed to revive her spirits.

We are now nearly halfway to our Spitfire! Fund-raising has been rather slow of late, what with the winter weather keeping people inside. I've been busy however chasing the tenants and it's amazing how much scrap metal you can find in some of the farmyards. Some things seem to date from the time of the Ark.

Your father sends his best regards and says that he hopes your aim has improved since the last shoot you attended. (He's only joking dear, that's his idea of small talk.) He's been busy organising the Home Guard and I doubt you and your friends could march better than the poor old souls he has out in all weather. Still, it is keeping him busy and he is pleased to be doing his bit, even if he finds it hard some days. Too many memories.

Stay safe, my love. Wear the St Christopher as with it come our prayers that you be kept safe and well. I hope Christmas in Calcutta was bearable and beware of the local food. Your great grandfathers digestion was never the same after his time out there.

With all my love,
Your Mother.

He slowly folded the letter and carefully returned it to the tin. His stomach still twisted every time he read about Will's death. It seemed impossible that the ball of energy he'd grown up with, searching for treasure, racing Bentleys and building dens on the estate, was dead. He'd been Philip's one true childhood friend. The son of the local blacksmith, neither had cared about the size of the others house or the reputation of their school. They were friends of choice, not circumstance.

Will would have known what to do to get these men home. He'd always been the one with the clever schemes, admittedly ones that usually landed them in trouble. He wished he was alive, that he was with him right now to help him out of this mess.

He lay back and looked up, noticing that another shaft of moonlight was lighting a small patch of branch high up in a nearby tree, spotlighting a tall orchid that grew in a mossy crevice. It was a pale purple, a thing of such delicate beauty that it seemed completely out of place in such an unforgiving habitat. His mother had one at home that was almost identical, which she tended lovingly most days in her conservatory. It was part of the collection she'd grown from seeds and cuttings brought back on her father's trading ships from the East when she'd been a girl. He'd always loved helping her water and trim them, mesmerised by their dazzling colours and sweet aromas, as she told him stories of the lands they'd come from. He lay for a few minutes staring up at it until the mosquitoes got too bad, making him pull his blanket up over his head and hiding himself from the hell of his existence.

CHAPTER 3

Nepal, 1953

Philip woke in the dark, completely disorientated. He was dripping with sweat, his pyjamas clinging to his skin. He could hear a chorus of insects and frogs providing a backdrop of noise that merged with the soothing sound of a fast-flowing stream. On his back was a heavy canvas back-pack and in his hand a mountaineer's ice-axe, its sharp point glinting in the light of a half-moon.

He heard running footsteps and swung around. "Who's there?" He heard his voice but knew his cracked lips hadn't opened. There was a burst of radio static and the indistinct sound of Chinese or Japanese fading in and out. He felt a hand on his shoulder and a strong voice yelled in his ear.

"Khabaradāra!"

There was an explosion, a blinding flash of light that physically knocked him backwards. The ice-axe had changed in his hands to a gun, its grey metal icy to the touch. The explosion dulled as something grew to eclipse it. It was a body of a young woman flying towards him, tears falling from her black, intense eyes that were fixed onto his.

He fell to his knees. "I'm sorry!" he screamed, dropping

the gun. The girl's spinning body exploded, her head, her mouth flying straight at him. He woke with a start, bolt upright in bed, dishevelled covers on the floor and the first rays of dawn forcing their way in through the old, warped shutters. He sucked in long, deep breaths of the cold morning air and ran his hands through his hair, scraping away thick sweat.

Philip didn't really feel like breakfast. He wandered into the deserted dining room and sat at a table overlooking the rather overgrown garden. "Just coffee and toast," he said to the waiter. While he waited he watched a bald peacock pecking forlornly at the dirt on the patchy lawn.

The toast, or rather toasted naan, arrived, together with some greasy butter and apricot jam. He took a bite and chewed half-heartedly for a few moments before dropping it onto his plate and pouring himself a large cup of thick black coffee. It was piping hot. He stirred in a large spoonful of sugar and sat back, feeling his mind focus as the caffeine entered his system.

Fresh coffee always reminded him of his mother. When younger, she'd taken him with her on her travels to Europe; to Rome and Naples and many other places he hadn't appreciated or cared about at the time. As they dined together she'd often let him sip at her wine or coffee, making him feel very grown up and important.

His father always stayed on the Estate in Norfolk and he'd secretly been glad he had, giving him his mother's undivided attention as she told him stories of his grandfather and great-grandfather, both in turn merchants from Kings Lynn and their colourful voyages to the Eastern colonies.

He often wondered how his parents had ever married.

His father was quiet and reserved, a product of old style public school and club. His mother was independent and strong-minded. Had it not been for his father being thrown from his new hunter as he tried to break him in it would probably never have happened. It was his mother who'd fearlessly caught the horse as it ran through the surf on Holkham Beach, there swimming with her sisters. Ever since then his father had been devoted to her. When he'd returned from the war they'd married, her strength helping him through the hard years that followed.

Throughout his childhood he'd known not to disturb his father in his study when thunderstorms rolled in from the Wash, once spying on him through its window and seeing him motionless at his desk, body shaking so violently that the whiskey barely made it in the glass to his mouth. It was never spoken of, his father staring icily ahead if a visitor should ever mention the war and often stalking from the room. Now Philip understood it was too late. His father was gone and it was his turn to face demons that others couldn't comprehend.

He made himself focus, running through the day ahead. The first task was to organise his trek into the mountains. It had been arranged by the *Times*' London office, a telegram had been waiting for him the previous afternoon with details of where to go.

Twenty minutes later he walked out of the hotel gate, following a young boy he suspected to be the son of the hotel manager. It was a beautiful morning, the sky deep blue and the air crisp. Ahead of him, above the terracotta rooftops and golden pagoda tips, he could see the Himalayas, their jagged peaks glistening white in the morning sunshine. They were so clear he felt he could reach out and touch them, a stark contrast from the choking smog of London that often hid the far side of the street and only a few months before had killed thousands in one night.

With the absence of cars he was able to walk along the middle of the street, avoiding the stagnant puddles that gathered at the sides. These were fed by small trickles of water and waste that ran from side alleys and doorways. Along the road walked a tide of people, carrying loads of firewood, potatoes and vegetables from the countryside to sell in the markets of the city. Soon he had a crowd of followers, all silently walking a few paces behind and watching his every move. When he turned to look they smiled at him without breaking stride. Stalls started springing up, further congesting the way and on a couple of occasions small groups of Tibetans, with their distinctive clothes and long braided hair, accosted him and tried to sell him some battered trinkets. By the time they'd reached his destination they were hardly moving, such was the crush.

The British Embassy was an imposing building which looked at first glance as if it had been plucked from the countryside of Surrey and dumped into the heart of Asia. Two guards stood in front of a white sentry box, set beside large wrought iron gates. As Philip approached they turned to face him, scaring away his young guide who ran off at full tilt back towards the hotel.

"Good morning," he said, smiling and touching the rim of his hat. The soldiers nodded back, staring at him enquiringly. "I've an appointment here with Mingma Sherpa." He paused, looking at the soldiers. "I'm Philip Armitage from the *Times* in London. It's to do with the Everest expedition."

"Certainly, sir" the taller soldier replied, pointing towards a small side door that stood open beside the gates. "The remaining expedition staff and equipment are housed in the tents on the rear lawn. If you report there, I'm sure you will be able to locate Mr Sherpa."

Philip thanked the soldier, walking past him into the grounds. After the bustle and clamour of the streets it was like walking into an oasis. The lawn was a deep green, hand-trimmed to a length suitable for the croquet equipment set up on it. Thick bushes of red rhododendrons grew against the tall perimeter wall, from which a small flock of sunbirds emerged, squabbling noisily as they flew past him and disappeared into the thick purple bougainvillea that covered the house.

"Armitage sahib?"

Philip turned around to see a young man striding towards him.

"Yes, hello," replied Philip. "Mingma?" He held out his hand.

The small Nepali held his hands together in front of him and gave a small bow before straightening up to take Philips hand.

"You are very welcome to Nepal sir," he said, his smile beaming. "I hope it was correct of me but I went ahead and made the necessary arrangements for your trek. I was told by the officer who brought the message from the *Times* that we had to be quick about it." He glanced at Philip nervously. "I have employed five porters for the camping equipment as well as a cook and four porters for your food." He paused and pointed back in the direction from which he'd come. "I have them here for inspection if you would like to see?"

Philip followed Mingma towards a row of stables that ran along the back of the grounds and as they walked he studied the Sherpa. He was, like most Nepalese he'd so far met, short, not even reaching up to his shoulder. His features were, however, distinctly different from the citizens of Kathmandu, looking more Tibetan in origin. His hair was jet black, covering his neck and held back from his eyes by a thin red cord that ran over his head and behind his ears. He was dressed in old mountaineering clothes, a western appearance that looked rather incongruous with his features, a vast woollen jumper hanging off his small, sinewy frame. Despite his youth, early twenties Philip guessed, his face was burnt a deep brown. It was wrinkled and lined, the result of living a hard, outdoor life at high altitudes where the air was dry and the sun unforgiving.

Turning a corner Philip saw the trekking staff huddled in a group, crouching on their haunches. The porters all stood as he approached, and after a few sharp words from Mingma they put their hands together and bowed. Philip returned the gesture before turning as Mingma introduced an ancient Sherpa.

"This is Old Gompu," he announced proudly. "He's the best camp cook in Nepal and has agreed to come with us."

Philip stared at the old man, doubting whether he'd manage to reach the outskirts of Kathmandu let alone Everest. He looked back up at Mingma. "Us?" he asked, "are you accompanying us?"

Mingma looked awkward, shifting his weight from one foot to the other. "Indeed sahib," he replied. "Now the expedition has gone and Mr James has also departed there is nothing more to be done here." He glanced at Philip anxiously. "I'd like to visit my family who live near the mountain, in the town called Namche. We would pass through it."

Philip broke into a smile. "Excellent," he replied, slapping the Sherpa on the back. "I was worried how I'd get on alone in the mountains." He laughed. "My Nepalese is a bit rusty to ask directions all the way to Everest!"

Mingma looked back at him in apparent surprise. "You speak Nepali?" he asked in a quizzical voice.

Philip silently cursed, annoyed with his indiscretion. "Oh, just a few words and phrases," he stammered. "It was a long time ago." He turned back towards the Embassy gate, keen to get away. "I'll leave you to purchase the necessary equipment and supplies on the *Times* account held by the Embassy. You'll know our requirements much better than I do. I must get to the Ministry to get the permit for Everest or none of us will be going anywhere." He strode off towards the gates and soon found himself back in the bustle of the city.

Hutch had given him directions the previous night of how to get from the Embassy to the Government Ministry where he was to pick up his permit, but in the maze of streets and alleyways he soon found himself lost. He tried retracing his steps and had just stopped at a junction to decide on which way to go when somebody spoke. Turning towards the voice he saw a young man, hair cut in a western style and looking somewhat out of place in casual slacks, leather shoes and collared shirt.

"Good morning," the man said with a smile. "Can I be of any assistance? You look as if you may be a little lost?"

Philip nodded. "Thank you," he replied. "I'm trying to locate the Ministry of Foreign Affairs but seem to have taken a wrong turn."

"I'm not surprised," said the man, "finding your way around Kathmandu can be very confusing even for those who know it well. First time I was here I goofed up and was lost for hours." He looked Philip up and down. "And I suspect you're not from around here either?"

Philip laughed. "You're right." He looked at the man, surprised by his excellent English, and studied his face. Whether he was from Nepal, India or Tibet he couldn't tell, his features were soft and further confused by his western appearance and distinct American accent. He held out his hand. "I'm Philip Armitage, from the *Times* newspaper in London."

"Tashi Banagee," the man replied, shaking the hand, "from Calcutta." He pointed up a small street that ran away to the left which Philip hadn't even been considering. "I'm heading that way myself, so please let me accompany you there," he said, starting to walk.

"You seem to know the city very well," Philip said, catching him up. "Do you spend much time in Kathmandu?"

Tashi nodded. "I'm often here on business, so have a reasonable knowledge of the city. I must admit though," he added with a shrug, "I do still get lost on occasion."

They walked on, making slow progress along the busy street. "What line of business are you in?" Philip asked as they walked. "There doesn't seem to be a great deal going on here for foreigners?"

Tashi looked at him and smiled. "Oh, I trade in this and that, just try to keep my eyes open for an opportunity to make a bit of dough. Since Nepal was only opened to foreigners a couple of years ago, there're plenty of things that they still need from the outside world."

Before Philip could ask anything further the crowds of people made it necessary for them to walk in single file and they lapsed into silence. After a couple more turns they emerged on to a wide boulevard and there, on the opposite side, stood an tall stucco-fronted building with a huge official red sign outside.

"Well, here we are," said Tashi, turning to Philip. "I hope you get what you need."

"I hope so too," Philip replied," I'm meant to be off to Everest first thing tomorrow. My editor won't be too pleased if the permit isn't ready."

He thanked him and after crossing the road climbed an elegant flight of steps that led to a large ornamental door. Once inside he gave his name to a man at a large desk who wrote something on a slip. This was given to a small boy who ran off down one of several long corridors that radiated from the central foyer. He stood waiting, looking up at the high plaster ceilings and large chandeliers that hung down on golden chains. It would have been very impressive had there been more than a single bulb in each of them. After several minutes a man, neatly dressed in waistcoat and cotton jodhpurs, emerged from the same corridor and invited him through.

The office of the Secretary for Foreign Affairs was large and airy. Light streamed in through three large windows that overlooked a central courtyard, lighting up a huge desk behind which sat a small man wearing a thick pair of spectacles. As Philip entered, the man dropped the paper he was reading and rushed around his desk to greet him.

"Good morning, Mr Armitage," he said enthusiastically. "Please, take a seat while we get you some tea." He said something in Nepali to the man who'd shown Philip in, who nodded and left the room. "My name is Dixhit, the Minister for Foreign Affairs and please," he said with a small bow. "You have nothing to worry about. Your illustrious paper sent the request via your Embassy a few days ago and we have prepared the necessary permissions for you." Turning to his desk he picked up a sheet of thick paper that was covered in Nepali text and several large official-looking stamps. "This," he said proudly, showing Philip the sheet, "is your permit to visit the Khumbu region and this…" he paused and pointed to a hand-written note at the bottom, "is my own personal endorsement allowing you to visit the mountain itself, right up on the Tibetan border."

He gave the permit to Philip who sat studying the incomprehensible writing while the tea, which had just arrived, was served. "This really is most kind of you," Philip said at last, as they both sat in comfortable armchairs. "I do apologise for the short notice."

Mr Dixhit shook his head and waved a hand, sloshing some tea into his saucer as he did so. "It is not a problem. We all hope that this expedition is successful on Sagarmartha." He carefully poured the spilt tea back into his cup and smiled at Philip, "That, I'm sure you know, is our name for Everest. Getting the news out to the world is vital if we want to Nepal to be on the global map at last." He paused again. "It was wise that your London office cabled us however, as we're having to currently restrict all travel to the northern borders."

Philip looked up at him. "Really? Is there a problem there?"

"It's the refugees from Tibet," Mr Dixhit replied, shaking his head. "Ever since the Chinese invaded their homeland a couple of years ago, there has been a steady stream of Tibetans fleeing. In the last few months," he shrugged, "it has become much worse. When they get here they have to sell their valuables to survive, jewellery and the like. But now the monasteries in Eastern Tibet are being looted by the Chinese and priceless artefacts sold to unscrupulous traders. They smuggle them into Kathmandu posing as refugees." He looked out of his window. "The city is awash with dealers from India trying to get their hands on the finest and they even started travelling into the mountains to try to get the best pieces. Therefore, we've stopped all foreigners leaving the city and do our best to control what is sold here. His Majesty has just this year created a Department of Antiquities to help deal with the problem but..." he shrugged, "it is early days."

He turned and smiled again at Philip. "But please don't worry. With this permit you will travel unmolested and on your return I must insist you to visit me again for tea to tell me of your great adventure and, I hope, its successful conclusion." He leant forward, adding with a mischievous glint in his eye. "Although I must admit to a bias. I hope it is our own Sherpa climber Tenzing Norgay about whom you bring me good news!"

A few minutes later and Philip was once more out on the

streets of the bustling city. The preparations had all gone much more smoothly than he'd anticipated and he found he'd some time on his hands to explore the city. While Mingma was getting the main supplies for the trip, he thought he'd try to pick up a few small treats to brighten up what he thought might be a fairly monotonous diet.

The Ministry of Foreign Affairs was near to Durbar Square, the ancient heart of Kathmandu. This array of old palaces, pagodas and shrines was packed with traders shouting out their wares, haggling with passers-by over the cost of their produce. Beggars stood in corners chanting prayers, hands outstretched for alms. Holy men sat beside the statues of mythical animals, some in meditation, others reading cards covered in strange symbols. Their hair was wild, unkempt and dirty, some with ash rubbed through it. Their foreheads were smeared with bright paints, their robes a brilliant orange and copper bowls were laid beside them in which to receive offerings of food.

Philip had to stop as a bull walked out in front of him, intent on reaching a pile of rotting vegetables that was being thrown into the gutter by an old man with a small stall. Two skeletal dogs raced over to it, quickly grabbing hungry mouthfuls before scampering away from its tossing horns.

The roofs and spires of the temples sparkled gold in the warm morning sun, the brick buildings and their terracotta tiles glowing a warm red. With no car engines to drown out the noise of the square, Philip seemed able to hear everything. Shoemakers sat on the pavement, hammering fine nails into the soles of well-worn shoes. Monks walked around the temples, spinning prayer wheels that were mounted in the walls and chanting prayers. Children chased each other, screaming as they leapt from statue to statue, the angry yells of the stallholders following them as they upset their carefully displayed produce.

Philip walked over to a small shop that opened onto the square, drawn by the stacks of tinned food on the paving outside. Ducking his head under the low lintel, he cautiously walked inside. It was tiny, only a few yards square and crammed from floor to ceiling with tins. At the bottom the tins were large, more like small barrels, tapering to smaller, household sizes at the top. Many were labelled in Hindi but some were in French and English and after a couple of minutes perusing he left with five tins of peaches, tinned in the US and which, he'd a sneaking suspicion from the design of the labels and condition of the tins, were left over from the war.

He emerged once more into the square, almost colliding with a barber's chair in which a man was receiving a shave with a cut-throat razor. Slowly Philip's eyes readjusted to the brightness. Looking around he noticed a large sign written in English on the far side announcing the "Rangana Café – tee, cakes, cofee". He glanced at his watch and seeing that it was nearing lunchtime, crossed the square and sat himself at a small, rather rickety table outside.

A young man appeared, dressed in the white jodhpurs and jerkin that seemed to be the clothes of choice for men in Kathmandu, but embellished with a bright green sash and traditional multi-coloured Nepali cap. After much pointing at the menu, which seemed to contain words that fused English and Nepali together, he disappeared again, Philip hoped, to fetch a large omelette and some tea. He leant back in his chair, closing his eyes and letting the sun bathe his upturned face, looking forward to food that until a few months ago had still been rationed at home. Even now actually getting hold of extra eggs was virtually impossible.

"Good afternoon," came a voice from the next table. There were two of them, both dressed in lounge suits and smoking cigarettes while drinking from a large pot of coffee.

"Please excuse us disturbing you, but westerners are such a rarity here I'm assuming you must be something to do with the expedition to Everest?"

Philip nodded cautiously. "That's right, I am, in a way of speaking." He stopped, taking in the two men, unwilling to divulge too much information until he knew who they were. The man who'd spoken leant over and offered his hand.

"My name is Navel Gupta", he said, "and my companion is Rajiv Mehru. We're here to cover the climb for our papers. I work for the *Times of India* while Rajiv is from the *Hindustan Times.*"

"In which case," Philip replied with a grim, "we are sworn enemies. I'm Philip Armitage from *The Times* in London." He could see their interest pick up, instantly more alert.

"Ah, *The Times,*" Navel replied with a shrug. "Then you are the cause of our problems. We have editors in Delhi demanding a constant stream of news and yet the expedition tells us nothing." He carefully stubbed out his cigarette before looking at Philip. "I don't suppose you have anything you could pass onto us, information that you've already sent to your paper but which we are yet to hear?"

Philip shook his head. "I'm afraid you've cornered the

wrong man. I only arrived yesterday and haven't really caught up. You'll have to ask Arthur Hutchinson if you want the latest."

"Hutch?" the Indian replied, shaking his head. "We have more chance of climbing Everest ourselves than getting a crumb of information out of him. You know he lives in Delhi so we know him well, but when he did the communications for the Swiss expedition last year we got absolutely nothing out of him, despite a lot of whiskey being consumed."

Philip laughed, looking down at his food which had just arrived. "In which case I don't think I can help," he said picking up a battered fork with only two prongs and giving it a good wipe with his handkerchief. "Now if you'll excuse me."

Navel nodded courteously and turned back to his table, allowing Philip to pour himself a glass of tea and cut into his omelette. It tasted wonderful, rich egg stuffed with a pungent cheese and slivers of sliced vegetable. He was feeling more settled, memories of his nightmare the previous night fading away in the warm sun. Hearing the language spoken again after so long, seeing the people all around had made him anxious as to what memories it might bring back. But now he was in a different place in happier times. People were going about their normal lives, there was laughter in the square and a relaxed atmosphere in the city that made him feel calm and safe.

His food finished, he downed the last of the tea and put some rupees on the table to cover the bill. He was just standing to go when he saw Navel. He'd been leaning forward talking quietly to his companion for much of the time. Now he turned and offered Philip a piece of folded paper.

Philip glanced at it and then looked at the man's face. "What's this?"

"It's the address of the hotel I'm staying at in case you think of any information that you might be able to spare us."

Philip shook his head, leaving the man's arm outstretched. "I'm leaving Kathmandu tomorrow for the mountain so I won't be around to help even if I could."

The Indians eyes didn't leave Philips. "Perhaps an occasional dispatch could be sent to this address instead," he replied, head angled enquiringly. "Nothing exclusive, just a little general information on what's going on. I'm sure," he added slowly, "it would be made worth your while. Say ten pounds per dispatch?"

Philip returned the man's stare before shaking his head slowly and turning away. "I'm afraid not," he said coldly and strode off.

"Fifteen, Mr Armitage, but we would require a little more specific information at that price."

Philip continued walking, calling over his shoulder, "You can have all the information you want for free. Just buy yourselves a copy of *The Times* and read what James has written."

He was soon lost in the crowd and relieved to be so, disconcerted by the experience at the café. If he'd bumped into two journalists so quickly, there must be plenty more in Kathmandu all circling around for the story. It was going to be trickier than he'd thought keeping James dispatches a secret, especially if people were prepared to pay such good money for it. He wandered on, following the main street from the square, enjoying the freedom of just meandering along with nowhere specific to go.

He drifted down another street and then turned into an alley that caught his eye because of the hundreds of prayer flags, small colourful squares of cotton with Buddhist mantras stamped on them, that hung from all its ornately carved balconies and window frames. He stopped to look at a small shrine to the Hindu God Ganesh that adorned the doorway of one house, its elephant head garlanded with a chains of dried flowers and sprinkled with rose petals.

As he stood admiring it a young Tibetan woman came towards him, her head bowed and hands held together in greeting. Her woollen clothes were brown and a deep purple, covered at the front by a colourful striped apron on which she now wiped her hands. She reached up to her forehead on which hung a disc of beaten gold, a polished coral stone mounted at its centre. It was hanging on a band of Tibetan turquoise that ran around the crown of her head, keeping her long, shining hair tightly held in a bun. She carefully removed the headdress, some of her hair falling free as she did so, and grabbed Philip's hand, trying to press the jewel into it.

Philip froze, unable to move as her dark eyes locked onto his. In them he saw a desperation he'd witnessed before, a plea for help that brought back terrible memories; ones he longed to forget.

"No, please …" Philip stammered, "please, you keep it."

Undeterred she continued, trying to force his hand open while leaning forward slightly and indicating over her shoulder with her head. He could see the fine hair of a tiny baby strapped to her back.

"No," Philip said again, desperate to get away. He reached into his trouser pocket and pulled out some loose rupee notes, pressing them all into her hand while holding her other one tightly closed around the gold.

She looked at him, as if puzzled as to why he was so frightened of her. Quietly she said something in Tibetan, gently reaching out to take his hand and slowly placing the back of it against her forehead. She seemed to study him as she replaced the headdress, carefully tidying the hair that still drew Philips eyes, before holding her hands together once more and continuing past him up the alley.

Philip stood, his hands now clenched by his sides to stop the trembling. He wanted to turn and stare after her, to check she was real and not a figment of his mind, but he couldn't summon the courage to do so. He strode forward, suddenly desperate to get away and hurrying round a sharp turn at the bottom of the alley found himself emerging into a sun-drenched square.

At the centre stood a huge Stupa, a Buddhist shrine that to Philips' eye resembled a giant bell. Its base was a large plinth of stone on which sat a huge white dome. From this a tall, stepped tower climbed into the sky, crowned with what looked like a huge, golden umbrella. Long lines of prayer flags ran from this down to the outer walls of the square, themselves embedded with hundreds of copper prayer wheels. The tower had large eyes painted on each side, gazing down over the square which was crowded with Tibetans. There was hardly any space remaining without a flimsy hut or makeshift tent on it. Smoke filtered through the roofs, goats bleated from their tight tethers by doorways, while a crowd of women waited with wooden buckets beside a stone water trough.

Philip found himself surrounded by smiling children, all with hands held out and shouting for his attention. He smiled, shaking his head but to no affect, until a young Tibetan man, his thick woollen coat hanging free from his upper body but still tied around his waist, came over waving a short leather yak whip at them. They scattered, screaming with excitement. He looked at Philip suspiciously, before turning and gesturing Philip to follow. They walked through the hovels, in places the path not wide enough for two people to pass. Finally he ducked under a makeshift door made from a hanging blanket and held it up for Philip to follow.

His first impression was of how tidy it was. Despite being little more than fabric and skins on a wooden frame tied together with flax, it felt homely and warm. Wooden stools sat around a small hearth made of nothing more than three flat stones. Philip coughed as smoke caught in his throat and eyes, but when the man pointed to one of the stools and they sat, the air got cleaner and less of an irritant.

"Thank you for rescuing me from the children," Philip said slowly, not sure whether the man would understand. "They're very friendly but rather persistent!"

The man nodded, waiting until a girl no older than nine or ten had served them each a glass of thick, greasy looking tea. "They are excited," he replied at last. "They are always hopeful of a sweet or pencil."

Philip smiled back, and cautiously sipped his drink. He

tried not to gag. The taste of strong, stewed tea, rancid butter and salt filled his mouth and he quickly lowered his glass.

The young man laughed. "I've heard that it's a taste you have to get used to. To those of us brought up with it, it is what we like. In a Tibetan winter it keeps us strong so we drink up to fifty glasses a day."

Philip blew out his cheeks. "Well," he replied. "I think I'll stick to just the one if that's acceptable to you." He looked down, gently blowing on the drink before continuing. "You're from Tibet?"

The man nodded. "We all are here. When we get to Kathmandu there are few places to go so we stay here in the protection of the great Bodnath shrine. Here we are safe, as the land around it is viewed as Tibetan land where even the King of Nepal has no authority. "

Philip looked at the man. "How long have you been here?"

"Myself, only a few months, but some have been here for over a year, ever since the Chinese invaded." He scratched at a flea bite in the side of his neck. "It is hard in winter."

Philip nodded. "How do you survive?"

"Many walk to the foothills every morning and collect firewood to sell in the bazaars. Other work as porters or any other job they can find."

"And you?"

The man sat still, looking hard at Philip, before reaching down and pulling over a stout wooden chest from the edge of the shelter. He opened it and took out one of several pieces of rolled cloth. Holding it up, he released one edge and it unrolled to reveal a beautiful painting. It was made of silk. In the centre, beautifully embroidered, sat the Buddha, picked out in golden thread on a rich blue background. Around him were a series of concentric circles, each with tiny scenes of places and portraits of people sown in.

"It's a Thanka," the man explained. "It is very old, maybe two or three hundred years. I buy them from the people when they arrive, before they are sold to the foreigners and lost. The best ones we store in the Great Shrine. The others," he shrugged, "we sell to get money to be able to afford the best. It is sad but necessary."

Philip nodded. "And you thought that I might be a buyer?"

The man looked back and smiled. "You didn't look like a buyer but westerners always pay more than the Indians so I thought it was worth a try."

Philip laughed. "Well, it's bad manners in England to argue over a price, so I'd have made you very happy."

The man smiled. "The perfect person to do business with. To be honest I don't know why I asked. I knew you were not here for antiquities and treasures. Something just led me to fetch you."

The Tibetan finished his drink and stood. Back outside Philip turned and faced the young man. "Thank you for the hospitality." He glanced up and down the alley, looking for a landmark. "If I wanted to find you again, do I just come back here?"

The man looked at him thoughtfully. "You can ask at the shrine for Zigsa. They will know where to find me." He bowed politely and walked off, vanishing into the maze of alleyways.

CHAPTER 4

Philip sat on a low stone wall, drinking deeply from the metal water bottle that hung on a leather strap around his neck. It was still only mid-morning but now the sun had risen over the surrounding hills sweat ran down his face, his shirt sticking to his back. He looked back down over the valley, the roar of the fast flowing river below now no more than a distant rumble.

He felt more relaxed now. The first few days had taken them through a dark jungle, tangled forests vying with thick bamboo thickets that seemed to hem the trail in. Monkeys had called in the shadows and leeches had reached out from the foliage, blindly searching for an ankle or leg to attach onto. The porters had been nervous, walking together in case of meeting a hungry leopard.

He found himself starting at the rustle of the undergrowth, convinced there was somebody following and often instinctively sniffing the air. Once he stopped short, heart pounding as his nostrils flared at the smell of tobacco. Edging forward he turned a corner to find his porters resting on a Mani wall, rough, hand-rolled cigarettes hanging from their mouths. He'd walked on in silence, head down, intuitively avoiding soft ground so as not to leave footprints as he tried to hurry along as quickly as possible. Mingma had initially been impressed with his pace, complimenting him on his fitness but it seemed he'd somehow sensed there was another reason behind it and Philips quiet, edgy state of mind.

His mood wasn't helped by his fatigue from all the travelling, the physical exertion and a lack of sleep. His nightmares had returned, triggered by the sounds and smells of the damp, fetid forest.

They'd slowly improved since the war. At first, back home, he'd often woken at night, screaming and trembling, calling out to the long dead. By the time he got his job as a junior correspondent with *The Times* and moved to a shared house just off Covent Garden he'd learnt to control them better, and they only re-emerged when he was in unfamiliar places or something triggered them. It could be anything. He'd taken his last girlfriend to the cinema to see the latest film *Peter Pan* one evening just before he'd left and had woken later that night screaming in Japanese. She'd ended their relationship, calling him damaged if he reacted like that to a ticking, cartoon crocodile. He'd sat on the bed long after she'd left with his head in his hands, despairing and embarrassed by his inability to control them.

The Everest assignment had come up the following week and he'd been so desperate to get away there'd been no time to dwell on it. But an unease had been growing ever since the wheels of the plane had left London Airport and now he'd no choice now but to confront his fears. Like it or not, he knew that if he wanted to be able to live a normal life, it was something that had to be faced.

Slowly they'd climbed out of the tropical zone, entering the foothills where sharp ridges from the high Himalaya reached down towards the plains. They'd emerged from the jungles gloom into valleys of vibrant colour, azure blue rivers and brilliant green fields that dazzled in the clear mountain light. To Philip, after the hell of the previous few days, it felt like an awakening. After the sooty drabness of war-scarred London, the crisp colours were almost too much for his senses.

Despite its remoteness the countryside was full of small, neat villages and pretty farmhouses that dotted the hill sides. The valleys weren't wide, their sides plunging down to rivers before climbing away again on the far bank. Yet every piece of land that could be used was covered in crops of barley, maize and potatoes. Terraces climbed the hillsides, some no wider than a couple of yards, others the size of tennis courts. The houses were brightly painted in white and orange, thickly thatched, with wood piles against the walls and ricks of hay and maize beside them. The bleating of sheep and goats carried across to him, as did the shouting and laughter of children, larking around as they helped their parents in the fields.

He carefully screwed the top back on his bottle and walked back to where his heavy rucksack stood balanced on a large rock. He turned and pushed his arms through the shoulder straps, shuddering as he stood and the pack pushed his cold, damp shirt against his skin. His shoulders were sore, not used to carrying so much weight over a rough terrain that constantly shifted the straps. He sighed, blowing out his cheeks. Five days they'd been walking, probably another ten or so until they caught up with James and the expedition.

They were making good progress. Mingma was everywhere. Taking the tents down and loading the porters in the morning, cajoling them along the trail and ensuring that the camp was ready when Philip arrived in the evening. Already Philip had fallen into the daily routine as if he'd never been away from it. Up at dawn with a cup of tea, he walked for a few hours until the sun had risen and the warmth grown. He then stopped for a large breakfast at a place Old Gompu had gone ahead to select, usually beside a river or stream so that he could do some washing of either himself or his clothes. They then trekked on until the middle of the afternoon when camp was reached and Philip could relax by reading or writing until supper was prepared.

They normally stopped near villages so that his porters had somewhere to shelter, staying in basic guest houses that offered a simple meal and place on the floor to sleep. There were no roads outside Kathmandu, the only way anything got in or out of the mountains was on the back of the sturdy porters who were paid per load. Philip watched as several walked towards him, veins standing out in their necks from the weight of the loads they carried on a strap that ran across their foreheads. Their legs were bowed, calves like balloons and muscles bulging as they slowly edged their way down the path.

Philip continued up the trail, its worn surface smooth from centuries of use. It switched-back several times as it climbed towards the top of the ridge, each hairpin marked with a small shrine either carved into the rock or made from roughly piled stones, all adorned with prayer flags. Finally the path flattened out and passed through a small notch in the rocks. As he stepped through it was like entering a different world as a new valley lay stretched out before him.

He stopped, forgetting his fatigue. Before him rose a towering range of mountains, their steep lower slopes covered in a thick forest that tumbled to a twisting white river far below. Occasional waterfalls cascaded through the trees, great plumes of spray drifting down the valley where they smashed onto the rocks below. The summits were jagged, black, naked rock silhouetted against what he initially took to be cloud. He caught his breath as his eyes continued upwards and he realised the whiteness was snow, the icy slopes of a continuous chain of mountains that lay beyond, so high they appeared like a row of towering storm clouds.

Just as they framed the foothills, so their white outlines were pin clear before a deep blue sky, plumes of snow blasting from their summits. He stood, spellbound, wondering what the mountaineers had thought when they'd looked up a few weeks before. Excitement? Apprehension? His thoughts were interrupted by a voice.

"It sure is quite a sight."

Philip recognised the American accent immediately. "Unbelievable," he replied, his eyes still on the mountains. "I thought they were clouds."

Tashi threw the butt of a beedi cigarette away and hauled himself to his feet. "I remember the first time I saw them, near Darjeeling." He smiled at the memory. "I was a child with my father. I thought he was jerking me around when he told me they were mountains, that he was making it up. That's why when I was older I walked in to see them close up. Just to be sure."

Philip looked at him. "Where did you go?" he asked.

"First I walked to Kanchenjunga, a mountain on the eastern end of the Himalaya. I remember looking up at it from its base, glaciers tumbling down its side, sheer rock faces swept by avalanches and wondering if anything could be more beautiful." He took a long drink of water and wiped his mouth dry on his sleeve. "Eventually I reached Lhasa, the capital of Tibet," the Indian continued. "It was easier then, it was before the Chinese had invaded. In those days you could come and go with the trading caravans." He stopped and looked at Philip. "Well, I could anyway. I grew up in India but my family was from Tibet so I had the look of a Tibetan and after a few weeks of not washing on the trail no one came too close to investigate." He guffawed and slapped Philip on the back. "It'll be like us in a few more days."

They continued together along the path, now descending into the new, steeper valley. There was less cultivation; Philip could see a few fields far below but much of the valley was covered in thin forest.

"So what brings you into the mountains this time?" he asked. "Still not convinced they're real?"

There was a short pause. "No, I know they're real now." Tashi replied with a smile. "I trade in precious stones that are found by the nomads on the plateaux and brought over by traders. Corals, turquoise and red jade mainly, which I exchange for money. They use this to buy food which they bring back to Tibet with them. I sell the rocks in Calcutta to jewellers and make a good profit. It works well for us all." He shrugged. "And all this walking keeps me fit!"

Philip laughed. "Well, before you get too thin, join me

for some breakfast, I can see Old Gompu down there and as usual he'll have cooked far too much."

Tashi gave a small bow. "I accept, thank you, but I mustn't stay too long. I need to make the next village by nightfall or I'll be sleeping in the forest."

They arrived at the breakfast spot, and Philip dropped his bag to the ground and sank gratefully into a canvas chair that had been set up for him in the shade of a rhododendron tree. He took a cup of chai offered to him by a young porter who seemed to have become Old Gompu's assistant. He carefully sipped the scalding drink, the sweetness of the condensed milk kicking energy back into him. Tashi had settled himself on a large stone that protruded from the soft green turf and was lighting another beedi, holding out the pack towards Philip.

"Not for me thanks," Philip replied with a small shake of the head. "I lost the taste for them during the war when we ran out of tobacco and resorted to smoking anything we could find." He wagged a finger jovially towards Tashi. "Mind you, I read an article in the *Reader's Digest* a couple of months ago suggesting there was a link between smoking and cancer. My friends all thought it ridiculous but who knows."

There was a short pause as both men relaxed in the warmth of the day, enjoying the tranquillity that seemed to envelop them.

"Were you visiting Darjeeling when you saw the Himalaya for the first time?" Philip asked, gazing out at the view.

"No," Tashi replied, shaking his head. "It was where we lived. I remember arriving there after fleeing from Tibet. It seemed so sophisticated with electricity and cars."

"And why did you have to flee Tibet?"

"We were driven from our lands. We lived in the East of Tibet, my father had a small farm that had been in our family for generations." He smiled, staring vacantly down the valley as he remembered his old home. "It was in a small side valley, leading off the main open steppe. A small stream ran through it in which there were trout, and the head of the valley was covered in thin forest where we hunted small deer and hares. It was a good place to live." He laughed. "I had three sisters and two brothers, and as the youngest I always managed to escape the work. I spent most of my time riding the young ponies, pretending I was training them but really I just loved to ride.

"But we lived near the border, in an area that China had claimed for centuries and there was often fighting nearby, in the larger villages and towns." He stopped, looking down to study the glowing tip of his beedi, gently wafting the smoke away from his eyes. "This time soldiers came to our lands, burning the buildings and taking our animals. My brothers were killed defending our home. We had nothing.

"For months we lived in a rough yurt, living by hunting and scavenging for food." He paused again, his face sad. "Everything was destroyed. All you could smell was ash and rotting flesh. The winter that year was so cold people were freezing in their tents so we went to the Chinese authorities in the town and begged to be allowed to settle again. They drove us down the streets, whipping us with leather lashes, keeping my two oldest sisters as slaves." His voice cracked. "I never saw them again. My father decided our only chance to live was to flee to India, to get away from the turmoil in Tibet completely."

Philip nodded, for a moment too shocked to respond. "That must be where you learnt your English? It's very good," he replied at last.

Tashi looked up and smiled. "It was my father who made me learn. He worked hard and sent me to a missionary school, travelling into Tibet to trade in gems. It was very dangerous. Sometimes he was away for months and returned not far from starvation. But he became renowned as the best source of Tibetan stones and when I was old enough sent me to work for one of the best jewellers in Calcutta, with whom he did business."

He paused as he was handed a plate piled high with egg fried rice and started to hungrily shovel the food into his mouth.

"I was lucky," he continued, chewing as he talked. "I learnt quickly. People were worried about Indian Independence and the possibility of war, wanting something they could pack quickly and take with them if they had to flee." He shook his head as he ate. "We made a lot of dough."

Philip looked up. "You were in Calcutta during the war?" he asked, a spoonful of rice poised before his mouth.

The Indian nodded. "All through it. Things got even better when the Americans arrived; they wanted souvenirs for their wives and girlfriends and paid in dollars. They were flying supplies to the Chinese over the hump, that's what they called the Himalaya. They were known at the Flying Tigers." He shook his head. "They were incredible pilots but so many of them died. I went with them on several trips, flying into Kunming, hoping there might be gem stones to trade but the authorities usually managed to stop me." He put down his empty plate and smiled. "Luckily the pilots were very well paid and never argued over my prices." He chuckled. "It must have seemed cheap to them but to me it was a fortune. I spent a lot of time with them, doing business, hanging out. That's when I picked up this accent, to help fit in. My father would have hated it. He wanted me to speak like an English gentleman saying it would help me get on. Trouble was that in Calcutta many of the colonial English gentlemen didn't want a Tibetan Indian to succeed or socialise with them, so I found myself mixing with the Sammy's."

Philip nodded. "I did wonder how you'd got your accent. I spent some time in Calcutta around then so I know what you mean," he said, putting his untouched spoon back on his plate, his appetite gone. "I was only there a few weeks on leave so I didn't get to know it that well, but I do remember the old boys at the club complaining at such a junior officer being let in."

"That must have been the 300 Club," Tashi said, looking at him. "That was where everybody used to socialize. There may have been a war on but jeez did they know how to live. I think more tigers were shot than Japanese considering the number of hunts the officers went on. Who knows, I might have even seen you there. Your face doesn't ring any bells but there were so many soldiers coming through Calcutta in those days it's hardly surprising." He shook his head sadly. "Many of them never returned."

There was a silence as both men continued eating and then helped themselves to some fresh fruit that had been laid out for them. Philip thoughtfully peeled a small milk banana that Old Gompu had bought from some villagers that morning.

"I haven't thought of Calcutta for years. It seems a lifetime ago." He bit the banana and chewed. "I spent so little time there and yet the memories of it were once very important to me. I lived them over and over and what I would do if I ever got to return." He finished the banana and tossed the skin into the undergrowth. He looked back at Tashi. "What happened after the war? Did business dry up?"

The Indian shook his head. "Not at all. There were the British leaving before Independence and then the partition with the Muslims fleeing to East Pakistan. They all needed jewellery to carry their wealth with them." He looked at Philip and winked. "When that died down I contacted some of my old American buddies from the war. They helped me out by flying some of my goods to the States where there is a good market for my stones. It helps cut out the … the red tape shall we say."

Tashi stood, brushing some spilt rice from his lap. "I must be heading on. Thank you for the food, no doubt we'll see each other again soon." Picking up his bag he turned and walked off down the trail.

Philip watched him go. He liked the Indian, even if he didn't trust him. It certainly hadn't been the coincidence that they'd both happened to be on the same path out of Kathmandu at the same time. Philip knew it was the attraction of his permit that had drawn Tashi there rather than his company, but as there'd been no problems at the small police check point near the mountain pass out of the valley, he'd been happy to let it go. Although they weren't camping together, they covered similar distances every day so naturally came across each other frequently on the trail.

Philip had twice passed Tashi as he sat talking to Tibetans, a steady stream of whom were heading towards Kathmandu in the opposite direction. With their long hair pinned up under a colourful headdress, and their distinctive black clothes and colourful bibs they were easy to spot against the poor Nepali peasants working in the fields. They were always polite, putting their hands together in greeting, although the younger children tended to run off or hide behind their mothers in terror, having rarely, if ever, seen a large white man before. If they were camped they would often stop to look at his tents, table and chairs in wonder, accepting a drink of strong Tibetan tea from Old Gompu.

That evening, after they'd made camp and eaten supper Philip was sitting beside a large camp fire, lost in thoughts of Calcutta. He started, aware suddenly of being watched and instinctively reached for a non-existent revolver. He could make out dark figures standing just out of the glow of the firelight, silently watching him. Mingma, who was boiling the kettle, looked over to where Philip was staring and called out, having a quick conversation with the mysterious figures.

"They are from the East," Mingma explained, beckoning a group of twelve or so Tibetans to the fire. When they'd settled he talked to them some more, the language alien to Philip who was able to understand little more than the occasional word. "Their village was burnt by the Chinese so they fled to Lhasa for protection." He shook his head. "The Chinese are there too, rulers in all but name. When they ordered all Tibetans to disperse home they decided to flee to Nepal." He looked at a young woman with a small baby strapped to her back. "To come over the high mountains passes to a country you've only heard about, they must be very desperate."

The Sherpa talked some more with the oldest woman in the group, resplendent in a large felt hat the point of which curled over to almost touch her wrinkled forehead. It reminded Philip of a Punch and Judy hat from shows he'd seen at the village fete as a boy.

"They have no food," Mingma said at last, glancing up at Philip. "They've sold everything they brought but the little money they got has been spent. They will have nothing now until they reach the Buddhist shrines in Kathmandu. The local farmers and villagers here have little to spare and there are now so many refugees."

"What did they sell?" Philip asked curiously, looking around the group.

"All their jewellery and two old silk thankas", the Sherpa replied, shaking his head. "They should have received a lot more for them but they were desperate for the children and baby."

Philip looked at the old woman. Her face was deeply lined with age, the skin leathery from the bitter climate of the Tibetan plateau and a life of cooking over smoky fires. Her hair was flecked with grey, several of her teeth were missing and the others stained brown. He could now see the hunger; the prominent cheekbones and sunken eyes, the thin wrist protruding from the heavy cuff of her tunic. She was looking at him, pride trying to hide the desperation that lay behind them.

He looked around at the group. The men were all thin and weary, the children watched him silently through huge eyes too large for their faces, reminding him of other children from years before. He breathed deeply, trying to control his emotions. "Tell Gompu to cook dhido for them all. They can sleep by the fire. Tomorrow give them rice for the day when they leave." He turned to the old woman. "Mingma, can you tell them that tonight they're our guests."

Mingma did so and the Tibetans bowed to Philip, mumbling their thanks. They sat close to the fire in an exhausted silence, disturbed only by the crackle of the burning wood and the clanging of pans as Gompu prepared the maize paste. When they were eating Philip excused himself, retiring to his tent. He lay on his camp bed, the hiss of the storm light and murmur of conversation slowly lulling him off into a deep, exhausted sleep.

Everything was dark. He smelt rotting leaves and felt something crawling through his hair. He didn't move. He could feel sweat sticking his clothes to his body, his feet squelching in tightly tied boots. His stomach ached. Not a grumble or hunger pang. It hurt. It was so constricted it felt stapled to his spine. His intestines kept going into spasm, waves of pain flowing through his chest to the back of his patched throat that throbbed with hunger. All he could think of was scones; raisins and sultanas peeping through the sides, thick butter topped with strawberry jam. He scratched absent-mindedly at the lice that infested his shirt. Damn it, he'd go for the cream too. It wouldn't kill him.

He heard a voice and sat up. There was the porter with a cup of bed tea in his hand. It was morning. He could see the blue light of dawn behind the boy, feel the cold air on his warm skin as he reached out for the mug. Sitting up, he ran a hand through his hair, rubbing at the growth of stubble on his chin.

"Tato Pani," he said to the boy, who, delighted at hearing his own language smiled and raced off to get the hot water. Philip quickly dressed and walked from the tent. The camp was deserted.

"Mingma," he called, nodding as the Sherpa appeared from the cook tent. "What happened to our guests?" he asked. "I thought they'd be staying for breakfast?"

Mingma shook his head. "They left at first light. The temperature dips at dawn so they need to walk to be warm. They will rest in the sun later."

"Did you give them rice?" he asked.

The Sherpa nodded. "They took it. Enough I think for two days if they are sparing." He pulled something from his pocket. "They left you this." He walked forward and handed Philip a small leather pouch on a strap, looking down awkwardly, as if not sure what to say.

"They wanted to thank you for your kindness. They respect you greatly for it. They also…" he shuffled awkwardly from foot to foot, "… they also wanted to help you with your night terror. They heard you shouting in your sleep. The old woman says that this charm is powerful and will keep the demons away when you are resting."

There was silence. Phillip reached out and took the pouch, feeling its contents grating as he gently rubbed them between his fingers. He didn't know what to say, touched that the old woman with so little should show such concern for a stranger with so much.

"Thank you," he replied at last, "for sorting out the food. Poor devils. What a journey to have to make." He reached up and tied the strap around his neck, tucking the pouch inside his shirt. "We'll head straight off," he said, sitting to lace up his boots. "I'm not hungry this morning."

Over the next week Philip became more aware of the steady stream of refugees heading towards Kathmandu. Some stopped to look at the strange man and talk to Mingma, while others trudged on, heads down as if already defeated by the journey. On several occasions he came across Tashi, usually sitting in a tea shop or porters lodge along the trail, talking to the Tibetans. The Indian invariably waved, cheerfully gesturing to Philip to join them but he always declined, uncomfortable with what he was doing.

The journey settled into a routine, his body adapting to the hard physical day and uncomfortable nights. After the jet-lag and bustle of Kathmandu and the initial days in the jungle, he enjoyed the clean, cool air and aura of peace that the mountains brought. The trail had turned north now, no longer endlessly climbing and descending the ridges and valleys that ran off the main mountains. The valley they were following had a large river raging down it, the trail often crossing the white water on rickety bridges. At the start of the trip these bridges had been suspended from sturdy steel cables but as Kathmandu fell away they became less robust, sometimes made of local hemp rope, other times of two tree trunks rested on piles of stone and covered in turf to allow yaks and dzos to cross.

The villages got fewer, the fields smaller as the valley

sides steepened and the altitude got higher. What didn't change were the children who still came every night to sit in silence and watch Philip as he sat in his Mess tent eating his supper or writing his diary. They would start a safe distance back, serious eyes following his every move. At some point he'd usually sneeze and pull a large silver rupee coin from his nose, at which point the children would laugh and edge closer. Small magic tricks he'd learn to idle away boring hours years before now became a language with which he could communicate with them. They would try to teach him their games, especially a local form of chess which involved tigers chasing buffalo around a board, at which he always lost spectacularly. Their spontaneity and joy, despite their hard lives, made Philip enjoy their company as he hadn't done with anyone in years.

One morning Philip found himself lying on a huge boulder that jutted out from the bank into the frothing torrent of the river, letting the sun warm his aching muscles. He'd seen his porters pass by an hour or so ago while eating his breakfast on a small sandy beach, and was letting them get a head so that camp would be ready upon his arrival in a few hours.

As he lightly dozed he became aware of voices above the roar of the churning water. Sitting up and shading his eyes against the sun, he saw Mingma talking with a tall young Sherpa. He looked over at Philip and beckoned him over, still deep in conversation. Philip jumped down from the rock onto part of the dry river beach and made his way over to where the men were standing.

"This is Ang Sarkey Sherpa," Mingma said, the young

man nodding with hands together in greeting. "He is working for Mr James as a messenger. He left Thangboche with a dispatch two days ago."

Philip looked closer at the young Sherpa. He could see why he'd been selected as a dispatch runner. He was tall for a Sherpa and lean, but the muscles on his legs, which could be seen below the filthy trousers he'd carefully rolled up to the knee, were well defined and strong. On his back he had a stout canvas rucksack.

"Is everything well with James?" he asked, glancing at Mingma in case there was the need for him to translate.

"He is fine," came the reply, the young man speaking slowly and with a nervous smile. "The climbers are at Thangboche and everything is going well."

"Excellent," Philip replied. "When you reach Kathmandu make sure to give your message to Mr Hutchinson, won't you? Nobody else. There are plenty of other newspapers there who will be trying to get the news you have. He will give you the rest of your pay."

The young Sherpa nodded and started to move away when Mingma caught his arm. "Wait." He looked at Philip. "Sarkey had other news." He looked at the Sherpa who nodded. "He's seen another European on the trail. He thought at first it was you but realised when he spoke to his Sherpa's that this was not the case. It was a man called Ralph."

"Izzard?" interrupted Philip. "Was his second name Izzard?"

The young Sherpa nodded.

"Where was this?" Philip asked, "And how long ago?"

"It was yesterday Sahib," the Sherpa replied. "He was

camped two hours below Thangboche, in a small clearing in the forest."

"And did he seem to have much equipment with him?"

The Sherpa nodded. "He had a very big tent set up, but the door was tied and I could not see inside."

Philip nodded his thanks to the man, who turned and headed off down the trail at a pace that Philip could only marvel at. Two hours from Thangboche. That was the village where the expedition was planning to stay while they acclimatized to the altitude. As one of the last places of habitation before the glaciers and moraine of the mountains, they'd hoped to get themselves rested and ready and the equipment sorted in the grounds of the large monastery that dominated the village. If Izzard was camped so near he'd be able to watch and report back to the *Mail.* That, he thought, wouldn't make his bosses at *The Times* very happy and if that large tent contained a transmitter, and their rival was getting updates ten days before they were, they'd be apoplectic.

He looked at Mingma. "We must go. I need to get to Thangboche as soon as possible, and I need to pay Mr Izzard a little social call on the way past."

Mingma picked up his rucksack. "If we walk hard we can reach Namche by sunset. We can stay there with my family as the porters will not be able to travel so far with the baggage. Then tomorrow we can make Thangboche." Philip nodded and quickly dropped back down to the river to retrieve his bag. In less than a minute they were striding off up the trail.

It was a punishing walk. The trail rose and fell as it crossed small tributaries and mountain spurs, often uneven and eroded by the monsoon rains. Mingma kept up a furious pace, skipping over the ground with a fleetness of foot that Philip struggled to emulate. After a couple of hours he was starting to lag behind, when they entered a small village perched on a long, wide ridge that protruded out into the valley, and he caught sight of his camp. Mingma was already there, giving instructions to the porters.

"This young porter is the strongest," Mingma explained as he arrived, collapsing into a camp chair. "He will take a light load that just contains your important items and should be with us tonight. Old Gompu will get the rest of the camp loaded onto the others and they will catch up at Thangboche."

Philip nodded, gratefully taking a mug of chai. "How much further to Namche?" he asked between small slurps of the boiling brew.

"It's not so far. This village is Lukla which is the nearest village downstream." He pointed up the valley. "It's about five hours, but it is all uphill so very tiring." He glanced up at the sky. "When you finish your tea we must go if we're to make it there by nightfall."

He gulped at the drink, burning the roof of his mouth in the process, and pulled himself to his feet. "Let's go," he announced with more enthusiasm than he felt. "If I stay sitting any longer you'll never get me standing again."

Mingma smiled and turned, leading him through the small village. There was only one street; a muddy track lined on either side by small squat houses made of thick, grey stone. Elaborately carved doors and shutters were open, allowing smoke from the cooking fires to escape. Young children stood in the doorways watching them pass, hiding their filthy faces behind the door jambs. Cockerels strutted around, scratching at the mud in search of scraps of food and a skeletal looking dog slunk off down an alley when he saw the young Sherpa approaching.

Almost as soon as they'd left the village the trail started to climb, slowly at first as it crossed gently sloping fields. When these were left behind it quickly rose above the river, switching back on itself in a series of hairpins. It was hard going and Philip had to stop frequently to catch his breath. It wasn't just the climb making him breathless but also the altitude. They were heading north, into the High Himalaya and were quickly gaining height. The thin air left him panting after walking only a few hundred yards. Philip noticed enviously that Mingma hadn't even broken a sweat, but waited for him patiently at every turn.

"Why don't you go on ahead," Philip said irritably as he recovered from a particularly steep climb. "It's a good path so I can't get lost. You can get things organised for our stay tonight in Namche."

Mingma reluctantly agreed, torn between the logic of doing so and the possibility of losing Philip. "Keep on the main trail," he instructed. "I will send back my youngest brother to meet you and bring you to our house." With that he was gone, disappearing at what appeared to Philip to be a jog.

Philip looked out over the valley. The river he'd been relaxing beside only a few hours before was now no more than a winding ribbon of churning white far below. Its rushing waters created a distant roar that bounced off the valley walls to give a feeling of vastness.

He started off up the trail again, walking at a slower speed than the one he'd felt obliged to keep up with the young Sherpa. In this steady rhythm he felt better, mechanically pacing forward and finding less need to stop. His mind was able to wander away from his aching legs and think about what James Morris would be doing. It must have been much harder to do this trek with fit mountaineers snapping at your heels. He also thought about Izzard and what he was going to say when they met. If the truth be known he was rather looking forward to it. After two weeks out it would be good to chat with someone from his own world, even if that person was, in theory, a rival.

The climb seemed to go on and on, but at least the trail was well graded and much of the climb was in shade. After a couple of hours, during which time he'd only had to stop twice for a drink, he saw a small boy of about eight skipping towards him down the trail. The boy stopped and greeted him solemnly, two large, apprehensive eyes peeping out from beneath a mop of unkempt hair.

Philip tried to smile and waved a tired hand towards the boy, who immediately turned and fled back up the trail, stopping whenever he reached a corner, but always keeping as far ahead as possible. The light was going. The sun has set behind the jagged skyline of the western valley several minutes before and the light of dusk now silhouetted the ridge in a warm orange glow. Looking up he could still see the evening sun playing on the summits of the peaks on the opposite side, but it was getting increasingly hard to see where to put his feet on the broken trail.

The boy had sped off and disappeared into the gloom,

but when Philip finally reached the place he'd last seen him and turned the corner he was met by the sight of lamp and firelight. A small town of maybe eighty houses was clustered together in a small natural amphitheatre where two valleys met. As the last rays left the mountain tops and a sea of stars appeared in the thin strip of visible sky, he saw Mingma hurrying towards him, fetched by his young brother, and holding aloft a hissing hurricane lamp.

CHAPTER 5

Burma, 1943

It wasn't going to come. Philip glanced around the faces of those nearest to him. Their eyes were intently scanning the small patches of sky that could be seen through the thick canopy, ears straining to hear the faintest drone of aircraft engines. He rubbed his eyes. They ached from fatigue and from staring up into the unaccustomed light for so long; the jungle had got them used to living in a constant twilight. It had been a tough day.

The burrif had arrived at camp just before first light to report that the villagers had been too scared to help Sergeant Gurung. They'd sent food and drink but wouldn't take him in. He'd died just after midnight. Then the terrain on their march had been harder than he'd anticipated, the undergrowth so thick in places they'd had to detour to the south. It had rained the whole time, a tropical downpour that sliced through the canopy and meant every branch they touched showered them in water. They were still steaming now as the midday heat sucked the moisture from their still damp clothes.

Reaching into his bag he pulled out the dog-eared map

and studied it, glancing up occasionally at the landscape laid out in front of him. There was the river and the two small hills behind. There was the confluence downstream of the small tributary. They were definitely in the right place. Bloody RAF. He turned as he heard somebody approach, his hand instinctively dropping to the butt of his holstered revolver.

A Gurkha appeared through the foliage and stopped by Philip. "Message from Corporal Prem, sir," he said in a clear but accented voice. "Should he light the fires to guide in the pilot?"

Philip glanced out over the riverbed, hand running through the itchy stubble that covered his chin. He shook his head but before he could say anything caught his breath, ears straining. A faint drone intermittently drifted towards him. The sound of a plane.

"Yes please, Rifleman," he replied, relief washing through him. "At the double."

The rifleman scurried off, vanishing back into the thick vegetation. He turned and strained his ears again. It was closer, now a constant whine only a couple of valleys away.

Looking down towards the riverbed he watched two men running from the cover of the forest to crouch beside two small bonfires, one on each side of the confluence. After a few moments of fanning, smoke and some tall fingers of flames licked up into the air and the men darted back into cover, leaving the fires to leap skyward. It never ceased to amaze him how the Gurkhas could get anything to burn so quickly in this sodden jungle, but they were able to boil water and produce a cup of piping tea within minutes of a stop being called.

Smoke was now climbing into the sky, clearing the tree line and raising straight in the still, dank air. White against the lush green forest, Philip felt sure the pilots would be able to use it to guide themselves in for the drop.

He turned to listen to the plane again, angling his head to pick up its engine. It seemed to be taking an age to reach them. Normally when they heard engines the Dakotas would almost instantly roar overhead before banking round to return on a drop run. Perhaps they hadn't seen the smoke and were flying up and down the neighbouring valleys looking for the signal. He listened again at the constant, steady hum.

"Shit!" Leaping to his feet he put his hands to his mouth. "Extinguish the fires!" he screamed down into the valley.

Instantly four men ran out, kicking the flames apart and throwing handfuls of silt onto the embers. It was too late. The pall of smoke still hung thick over them as a small spotter plane skimmed over the ridge and flew straight through the cloud. Banking hard to the right, it circled overhead, its pilot starring down onto the riverbed as the soldiers dived for cover. The cockpit glass gleamed in the sun as it made another pass before flying over the ridge on which Philip and his men were standing. As it flashed overhead Philip saw the burning red markings of the Japanese Air force.

He turned to one of the riflemen. "Tell the corporal to gather his men and return here immediately."

The man nodded and ran off down the slope.

Philip brushed the rotting leaves from his legs, his heart pounding. Glancing up, he saw the men looking at him. "Stand down everybody," he ordered. "There's not going to be a drop now."

Philip could feel the disappointment. Tense bodies sagged, eyes were downcast. It's was no wonder if they were as hungry as he was. He picked up the map from where it'd fallen. While waiting for the plane he'd marked the compass bearing that would lead them back towards India. Near this route lay a large, isolated village and their only real chance of finding food if he couldn't organise a new drop. Christ, he hoped there was some life left in the radio batteries. No more than three inches on the map. Perhaps fifteen miles as the crow flies, more like twenty-five through the thick vegetation and skirting mud-sucking swamps. They had, he estimated, half-rations left for another two days.

He looked up as the rest of the men started returning through the trees. Soon they were all gathered and he turned to face them.

"We need to move out. That was a Jap plane and they'll have seen us down here."

And he'd just ordered two large fires lit to show them. "There must've been a problem with the drop. Most likely the plane got intercepted by fighters, poor sods." He glanced around the men, looking them hard in the eye. "Which means that the Japs now know exactly where we are so we need to get going."

He held up the map and pointed to a place on it. "First we need to put some distance between us and here. There's a decent sized village a couple of days march away. We'll head towards there and if it looks clear, we'll buy food." He didn't mention the radio, not wanting to raise hopes.

The men looked up, some nodded, some smiled, relieved at the prospect of food.

"Corporal," Philip continued, looking over at Prem, "form up the men and send out scouts. We'll leave in two minutes."

Philip watched as the men prepared themselves, tying loose kit and water bottles to their battered Everest frames before pulling them onto their backs. He shoved the map back into his bag, checked the bearing once more on his compass and dropped down to the edge of the riverbed. He couldn't see the scouts but knew they were there, keeping his ears alert for any signal they might give.

Behind him he could hear nothing but knew he was being followed by the men. It was unbelievable how quietly the Gurkhas moved over rough terrain, a legacy of childhoods spent living in the Himalayan foothills. The river course swung westwards and he continued due north, plunging into the thick undergrowth. Without needing to say anything two soldiers walked past him and started wielding their khukris to clear a path.

Bloody idiot, he thought to himself. Rule one of air supply. Identify aircraft before giving any ground signals. If he hadn't lit those fires so early there was no way they'd have been spotted. Now they'd have the whole bloody Japanese garrison chasing after them. He shuddered, despite the heat. He was uneasy. They'd been too lucky over the last few weeks. Three times they'd blown up rail tracks and each time had managed to slip away before the Japanese could reach them. This time felt different. The Japanese knew they were trying to get back to India and therefore which way they were heading. They'd be able to set an ambush and simply wait for them to walk into it.

Two more soldiers took over the trail blazing, their relieved comrades dropping back dripping in sweat. Progress seemed painfully slow, the jungle itself hindering them. In the gloom of the forest it was impossible to keep track of time. For several hours Philip kept them moving, carefully checking the bearing every few minutes before they finally crossed over a wide, rolling ridge and started slowly dropping out of the hills.

At last he held up his hand and gave the fall-out signal. He could hear it ripple down the line, groans of exhaustion as men dropped their loads to the ground and collapsed beside them. He wanted to do the same but waited until Prem had appeared beside him.

"We'll rest for thirty minutes. Tell the men to eat but no fires." He mopped sweat from his face, his forehead stinging as the dried salt on his handkerchief rubbed against the open pores. "I want to push on for another couple of hours while there's still light, to get more distance between us and the drop site." He swatted a mosquito biting the back of his neck. "We'll be reaching the Mu River soon. I want to get across as soon as we can as it's the obvious ambush point."

The corporal nodded and head off to tell the men.

Philip sat on a moss covered boulder. It lay at the base of a small cliff that made up one side of the small valley they were now following down towards the river. Dropping his pack to the ground he took out a packet of hard biscuits and took a bite, chewing unenthusiastically, his mouth clogging with the dry crumbs as they stripped his mouth of what little moisture it contained. He reached for his mug and after crumbling two biscuits inside it, added some tepid water from his bottle and a few small pieces of dried fruit. After stirring it for a few moments he swallowed it down without chewing.

He watched as some of the men opened tins of meat and carefully divided each can between two. He was pleased to see they'd learnt their lesson. Initially when put on half-rations they'd eaten half a tin and saved the rest for the next day. In the tropical heat the tinned mutton had gone bad and incapacitated half the platoon. This was not the time or place for a recurrence.

Philip settled down, taking out his penknife to work at a painful splinter he'd picked up in the ball of his thumb. Already it looked red and angry and he didn't want it to infect his hand. He heard footsteps and looking up saw one of the sentries running towards him.

"Enemy, Sir," the soldier reported. "Coming this way, about half a mile away."

Philip nodded, closing his knife and slipping it into his pocket. "How many?"

"About twenty," the man replied, "maybe one or two more. They are following the small stream that runs past about thirty yards to our south."

"How long until they reach us?"

The soldier thought for a moment. "About twenty minutes."

Prem had joined them and was looking at Philip for orders. Philip swallowed a flicker of panic, gripping his mug hard to prevent his hands from shaking.

"There's water running in the stream so they won't have heard us." He said, thinking aloud. "They'll have sent patrols up all the tributaries of the Mu, trying to flush us out. If we take them on we'll we'd give our position away and have the others swarming all over us."

He looked at Prem. "Tell the men to move as far from the stream as they can, up against this cliff. I want the mules taken back a few hundred yards and given all the remaining fodder. That should keep them quiet. If they do start braying at least they won't give away our exact position and it'll give us the chance to slip away."

The men had seen the scouts return and were on edge, ready to move. Philip watched them quickly pack their things away, checking they'd left no trace on the ground before falling back to where he was. They settled themselves behind rocks and fallen trees, lying on the damp jungle floor with their weapons trained towards the stream. A few minutes later Prem returned.

"The mules are in position," he reported in a whisper. "They are well hidden and fed."

Philip nodded. "Excellent." He looked out into the undergrowth. "Now we wait."

Silence fell. His stomach rumbled angrily and he hoped the food he'd just consumed would stay in long enough that he wouldn't have to sprint for the bushes. The same went for many of the men, whose bowels had been loose for weeks.

Looking straight ahead Philip found it possible to believe he was there all on his own. Not a sound could be heard from his men. It was disconcerting and he had to stop himself from glancing sideways to check they were still there. He could hear the sound of running water coming from the stream, a gentle bubbling as it gently flowed over small pebbles. Insects buzzed around him, drawn by the sweat that drenched his head. Mosquitoes whined past his ears and it took all his resolve not to swat at them when they landed and fell silent. All around was a chorus of frogs, mingling with the rhythmic calling of lizards. Some red breasted parakeets landed in the trees overhead, squawking noisily as they searched for wild berries.

Philip froze as he saw movement to his right. A small, plump pheasant emerged from the undergrowth and made its way slowly through the forest, scrapping at the leaves on the floor searching for bugs to eat. His mouth started watering, as he guessed had every mouth in the platoon. His mind slipped back home. As a boy he'd often beat for shoots on the Norfolk marshes, thrashing through the undergrowth with a stout beech stick to put up pheasants for the guns. He smiled to himself. He used to complain to his mother that he got scratched by the thickets and brambles in the copses and hedgerows. If he'd only known. The taste of game flooded his mouth, rich, strong meat served in thick, greasy gravy.

His mind snapped back to the present, his body tensing. He could hear something new. The water in the stream was now making a different noise that was nothing to do with the rhythm of its flow. It was irregular, sometimes abrupt, sometimes gentle. After a few seconds it became clearer, distinct footfalls moving slowly up the channel. They stopped and Philip heard the murmur of voices, indistinct words but recognisable as Japanese.

The enemy seemed to have stopped directly opposite their hiding place. Philip forced himself to breathe slowly and deeply, his mind alert. Had they left something down by the water? Perhaps some of the men had been down by the stream had left a sign. A footprint, a wet patch on a rock?

He strained his eyes, cursing the thick foliage for blocking his view while thankful for its cover. He just wanted to know what was happening. A new sound came, the regular slash of a machete cutting into the jungle, coming towards them. If they reached the place they'd been sitting they might realise they'd been there. He heard voices again, and then laughter. The sound of machetes stopped, replaced by one voice speaking clearly. A buzz of static filled the air, followed by the voice again. They were radioing in.

The call lasted no more than a minute, and when it finished the voices started again. They seemed to be resting, perhaps drinking before moving on. The jungle had gone quiet. He could hear water sloshing in bottles as they drank from their canteens. The rustle of paper as food was unwrapped. A belch was greeted with groans and laughter.

Philip's nostrils flared as the odour of the Japanese reached him. It was a pungent, heavy smell of humans. He'd always wondered how his dogs at home smelt out game from the undergrowth, his own sense of smell seemingly reserved for food and the perfume of beautiful women. Now he knew how they did it. It was the stench of stale humanity, of overcooked rice, concentrated sweat, tobacco and shit. It seemed incredible to him now he'd never noticed it before as it seemed so powerful. He could detect the smell of cigarette smoke from hundreds of yards and for hours after it was extinguished. Even before they'd run out of supplies he'd been tempted to ban them. Thank Goodness the Japs were smoking and eating. God knows what they smelt like after all these weeks in the jungle.

He tensed as he heard foliage being disturbed, the sharp snapping of stalks and rustling of leaves. A man burst into view, no more than ten yards away. Philip help his breath, finger tight around his pistol trigger. It was a Japanese soldier.

The man was smaller than one of his Gurkhas, perhaps just over 5 ft tall. Philip's first thought was how fat he looked, before realising that he'd got used to living with half-starved men. Apart from large sweat stains under his arms the man looked spotless. No rips or tears in the uniform, no bites or sores on him. He'd taken his pack off but had his rifle slung over his shoulder. His head and neck were protected by the standard Jap jungle hat which had a protective cloth hanging down to his shoulders. He had a half-smoked cigarette clamped in his mouth and after fumbling with his fly he started to relieve himself.

He was looking directly at Philip. Philips heart was beating so loud he felt sure the man must hear it, certainly must see him. He waited for realisation to spread over the soldiers face, but he just stood staring at him. Occasionally he lifted his head up, tilting it to the side, until he finished and turned away with a satisfied grunt. He took the cigarette from his mouth and rubbed his eyes, smarting from the smoke, before turning and vanishing back into the jungle.

CHAPTER 6

Nepal, 1953

Philip sat on a hard wooden bench, leaning back against a wall with his legs stretched out in front of him. His whole body ached after the exertions of the day and he rubbed his eyes, trying to ease the headache that throbbed gently behind them and clear the smoke that was making them ache. They had, he knew, climbed up too quickly, and his body hadn't had time to acclimatize to the increase in altitude. He took a sip of the drink he'd been given, a type of local beer made from fermented millet and hot water. It tasted bitter and initially had been rather unpleasant but now, half way through his second mug, he was starting to feel its affect as the weak alcohol warmed him and dulled the aching.

In front of him was a cooking fire, logs pushed into the embers just far enough to generate a flame without wasting wood. Hanging above it, on a rickety wooden tripod, was a large iron pot from which steam rose. The light from the fire was supplemented by two lamps that gave the small room a cosy feel. It was certainly warm, a welcome sensation after days of camping, as the fireplace had no chimney, the smoke slowly filtering through the stone roof and leaving much of its heat behind.

He'd been led through the narrow streets by Mingma and on their arrival at a squat, stone house he'd been welcomed with great ceremony by the Sherpa's family. Mingma's father was dead and it was his mother who ran the household; a small, squat lady with whom, Philip decided, it would be best to keep on the right side of. Two of her sons lived with her, responsible for the family's animals and fields, and their wives and children seemed to fill the house to capacity.

"What do they grow?" Philip asked, enjoying the warmth of the fire on his feet. "It seems so barren up here I can't believe that anything would survive."

"Potatoes", Mingma had replied proudly. "Life was very hard before, but somebody brought potatoes here that had been taken to India by the British. They grow very well."

Philip looked around. "You must have plenty of land to feed all these mouths," he said, giving up counting the endless number of children who stared at him with a mixture of fascination and fear.

"There is not enough," Mingma said, shaking his head. "My mother runs this house as a lodge. The porters and traders who come to trade with the Tibetans stay here while they are bartering their goods in the bazaar. She is famous for her cooking and is usually full." He pointed towards a small door at the far end of the room. "Later we will go through as we will be sleeping there too."

Philip looked up as one of the brothers wives came up to refill his empty mug. He smiled and nodded his thanks. He looked at Mingma.

"Have they heard any news of the expedition?" he asked. "I'm sure the Sherpa's who work for it must pass through occasionally."

Mingma nodded. "One of them is here now, a cousin of mine. He was allowed back for the night as his wife has just had a baby. The preparations are going well. Everybody is safely at Thangboche and some of the climbers have gone up to the ice flow to get fit and look for possible routes."

"I don't suppose he's seen any western journalists wandering around has he?" Philip asked hopefully.

Mingma shook his head and drained his drink. "No one. He said nobody has visited the expedition other than James."

They fell quiet as Mingma's mother served them bowls of small boiled potatoes, tossed in some kind of wilted green leaves, chilli flakes and butter. His mug was topped up yet again with fresh chang, and as he ate he watched as one of the younger women carefully poured more boiling water and millet into a large wooden churn and started making the next batch.

Mingma took his mug and downed it in one, smacking his lips when he'd finished and holding it out to be refilled. "Nobody makes Chang like my sister-in-law," he pronounced, smiling happily at her.

They ate in silence, Philip only realising how hungry he was as he chewed his first mouthful. Within minutes his bowl was empty and he was gratefully accepting more. After some dried fruit the meal was over.

"I'll take you through to where we will sleep," Mingma offered, hauling himself to his feet. "We have an early start tomorrow.

Philip thanked Mingma's mother and followed the young Sherpa through the roughly made door. They entered a large room that looked as though it occupied the rest of the building. At the far end there were bunks, rough wooden platforms three tiers high that comprised the sleeping accommodation. Already it looked full. The porters who carried the enormous loads into the mountains would need to be up before first light to tout for a load to bring down to the lowlands.

Elsewhere a few latecomers sat in the dark gloom eating their evening meals. The food was included with the accommodation, but the millet beer or fiery spirit made from potato peelings was extra. Glancing around Phillip realised with an inward groan that there were going to be a few drunken snorers later that night.

Mingma initially insisted on sitting with him by a small low fire in the corner of the room but eventually Philip managed to get him to go and spend time with his family. It had, he'd finally got him to admit, been nearly a year since his last trip home. He was content sitting in silence, letting his mind gently wander as his body warmed up and relaxed.

He jerked up and realised that he'd been starting to doze. He'd dreamt he'd heard his name. He was just settling down again when it came again.

"Lieutenant Armitage?"

It was strange, he was sure he was awake but he couldn't be. Nobody had called him that for years. He glanced round and saw a face, indistinct in the gloom. It seemed familiar so he turned to face it and leant forward, trying to make it out more of its features. The face moved towards him and became clearer as it moved into the light of the fire.

Philip froze. He must still be asleep. Memories flooded his head that had been locked away years before. It was impossible, he felt his body trembling, his headache starting to pound again. This man was dead.

The man spoke again, this time with certainty in its voice, mixed with incredulity. "Lieutenant, sahib! It is you. I thought it was when you entered but couldn't believe it. After all this time and why would you be here? It seemed impossible that it could be!"

Philip gasped a breath, his mind dizzy. "Prem? Corporal Prem?" He stood up shakily, keeping one hand against the wall to keep himself steady. "How the hell did you get here?"

The small Nepali quickly snatched his hat off his head and stretching himself up snapped into a smart salute. Before Philip could tell him to stop he was bowing with his hands together. Straightening up, he was smiling, his face glowing with joy.

"I'm working, sir," he laughed. "I live in the lowlands in a small town called Okhaldhunga. We come up here to trade with the Tibetans. We are all still together. After we left the army we returned to our homes but didn't want to settle back onto the land. Trading was the only way we could earn money." He shrugged. "With our profits and the army pensions we live well."

"We?" Philip queried. "Who else is here?"

Prem laughed again. "There are ten of us in total, all from the old platoon. Look," he said, indicating towards the bunk beds. "They are all here."

Philip looked over and saw a group of shadowy shapes get to their feet. Several saluted him. He smiled and raised his hand weakly, overwhelmed by the appearance of so many familiar faces from so long ago.

"Why are you in Nepal?" Prem asked. "I am guessing it is something to do with the British climbers on Everest?"

Philip nodded, relieved to be able to talk about something else. "That's right," he replied, "although I work for a newspaper, *The Times* in London. I'm reporting on it rather than doing any of the climbing." He smiled weakly. "At the moment I'm chasing about after another Englishman from a rival paper who we think has got a radio. Bit silly really."

The other men had come over and one by one Philip greeted them. It was like a dream, perhaps induced by all the alcohol, but the hands he shook were real. Faces he'd long shut from his mind stood before him, glowing in the weak light of the fire. The warmth of their greeting made him giddy, their joy at meeting him palpable and he struggled to cope with their undisguised happiness. He felt it but fought the emotion down, scared that it would overcome him. After all these years of not knowing, it was too much.

He turned to Prem, trying to anchor his mind in the present. "So what is it you trade with the Tibetans?" he asked in as steady a voice as he could manage.

"We bring tea and rice with us which are grown around our town. We trade them for salt that they bring from the plateau and also their thick wool. We can sell this back in the lowlands for a good profit, although the Tibetans are hard barterers."

"When did you leave the army?" Philip asked, so many questions forming in his mind. "Straight after the war?"

Prem shook his head. "No. We stayed until the regiment

was transferred to the Indian Army when there was Independence. After our time together the platoon was rebuilt but it was never the same. We decided it was time to spend more time with our wives and children, to build a life here before we were either too old or were killed."

Philip smiled weakly. "You have a wife?"

Prem nodded. "And three sons," he added proudly. "Life has been good to me since my return."

A silence fell, Philip conscious that the Nepali wanted to know about his life but was perhaps too polite to ask. He couldn't bring himself to reply and a silence fell, so one by one the men said goodnight and returned to their sleeping places. Soon only Prem was left and he too raised his hands together in a parting gesture.

"I've often prayed to see you again. During the last Sakela festival I gave offerings for you for allowing my life to continue." Slowly he reached out his hand and placed it on Philips arm. "We often wondered what happened. We would talk around camp fires during the war and our hearths when back home. We never stopped hoping."

"Christ, Prem, I don't know whether to laugh or cry." He rubbed his face with his free hand, and cleared his throat. "I, I never knew what happened, whether...whether you made it back or not. I'm so pleased that you did." He stopped, unable to find any more words.

"It's an honour to see you again sir," Prem said quietly. "I hope you are happy."

Philip took the hand into a handshake, trying hard to keep it steady. "Thank you, corporal," he replied, trying to think what to say. "I'd no idea I was travelling so near to your homes. I hope you have a successful trip." He turned quickly and sat down on the bench, trying to hide his tears. He held his hands to the flames, but quickly clasped them together when he saw them trembling. He closed his eyes, head hanging down when he felt a hand laid gently upon his shoulder and a voice whispering in his ear.

"You did the right thing sir," Prem said, so quietly it was hardly audible over the hiss of the lamps. "There was no other choice. We lived because of it. Balbir Rai has five children now because of you and we thank you for it."

Philip closed his eyes, the memories flooding back, panic welling up and forcing him to take deep breaths. When he opened them again Prem had returned to the shadows and he was alone, the whole episode like a dream. He stood and walked unsteadily to the door, needing to be alone. Outside the air was cold and crisp, clearing his head as he breathed long, slow breaths. He walked to a small terrace and undid his fly, staring out across the valley as he relieved himself into a drainage gutter. In the freezing air he felt calmer, the shock of the meeting numbing.

When he'd finished he walked to a huge boulder that lay half embedded in the edge of a terrace and leant back against it, staring up at the stars. He didn't remember any stars, mainly he guessed because they were hidden by the jungle canopy for so much of the time. The moon always reminded him of his men but the stars, no.

It had been over ten years since he'd last seen Prem and the others. He'd thought they'd died. Ten years of believing that their deaths were down to him. Tears ran silently down his cheeks. A sob racked his body which he tried to stifle by hugging himself tightly with his arms, squeezing it inside himself. He sank down the boulder until he was sitting on the ground and silently let the tears flow out of him. He'd never dared to ask when he'd got back and he'd been discharged so quickly. All ten of them. He covered his face with his hands and wept.

When Philip woke next morning it was still early. Mingma's mother was making up the fire, using dried dung that Mingma was stacking by the hearth and the first hint of dawn was shining through the cracks in the rough wooden shutters. He sat up, his body stiff after the exertions of the previous day and a night sleeping on the stone floor cushioned only by thick woollen blankets and oily sheep skins. Glancing over at the bunks on the far side of the room he saw that Prem and the other ex-soldiers had gone. Mingma followed his gaze.

"They left a few minutes ago," he said. "They wanted to get to the bazaar at first light to do their business."

Philip nodded. Now he'd recovered from the initial shock, there were so many questions he wanted to ask.

Mingma must've sensed this. "They will return later, they left their travelling things here. I doubt they will buy everything they require in one day. It can take a week to fill up their loads and those of their porters and animals." He stood up. "I'm afraid we will miss them however if we wish to make Thangboche today."

Philip nodded again, rubbing his face vigorously in an effort to wake up.

"Of course," he replied at last. "I'll just go and splash my face and then I'll be ready."

By the time he returned a few minutes later he found Mingma ready to go, both their rucksacks packed and ready by the door. After saying goodbye to Mingma's mother they walked out of the smoke-filled lodge into the crisp air of dawn. He could feel it reach the extremities of his lungs as he gratefully sucked it in, vaporising in great clouds around him as he blew it back out.

It was his first look at Namche in daylight and it looked to him like a larger version of all the villages he'd passed through over the last couple of weeks. The houses had flat stone roofs and would have looked fairly drab had it not been for the bright colours of the doors and shutters, and the prayer flags that adorned many of the buildings. Being built in a natural bowl the houses tumbled down the steep slope so each doorway has higher than the roof of the house in front. The main street was paved with large flagstone, its surface worn smooth by the feet of countless animals and men on this important trading route.

They passed a wall of prayer wheels, large copper drums covered in sacred scripts that could be spun by the devout to send prayers to the gods, all draped in a layer of fluttering flags. Philip moved to one side as a column of yaks ambled calmly past, the bells around their necks ringing in time with their lumbering gait. Each was carrying a towering load that swung wildly from side to side and threatened to spill at any moment. Tibetan handlers kept them moving with a range of guttural calls and by brandishing thin wooden sticks near the animals' wary eyes.

After they'd passed by they continued, the smell of the animals still pungent in the air. Smoke occasionally drifted around them from one of the chimneys of houses lower down the slope and more people were emerging as the light grew stronger. Women walked by with leather pails full of water from a stream that cut through the centre of the settlement and children with armfuls of firewood stopped to watch them pass.

After only a few hundred yards the track became a trail that started to climb towards the top of one of the adjoining ridges. It didn't look far but it took nearly forty minutes until they were standing on its crest and looking north up the valley they were to follow. The path fell away in front of them, entering thick rhododendron forest and not reappearing until it crossed the river far below on a small suspension bridge. You could then follow it as it zigzagged steeply up the far slope until it arrived on a large spur that jutted far out into the valley. Here, surrounded in a patchwork of small, stone-walled fields lay the small village of Thangboche, a huddle of stone houses and piled wood sitting under a pall of wood smoke. Its monastery stood to the side of the houses, a large building painted dazzling white and topped with a large stupa, the tip of which gleamed gold as the first rays of morning sun struck it. In the clear morning air Philip felt he could reach out and touch it, but he knew that it would take all day to get there. Looking further up the valley he saw vast forested spurs giving way to alpine meadows and then walls of glacial debris. At its head an imposing wall of rock and ice created a seemingly impenetrable barrier, and peeping over the top of this was a small triangle of black rock, a plume of white blasting from its summit.

"Sagarmartha," said Mingma, following Philips gaze. "Mt. Everest. It's lucky the climbers are not there today. Look at the snow being blown from its summit. They would not be able to even stand up in a wind that strong."

Philip stared at the summit, unable to comprehend how any man would get to such a place. He pointed to the wall of rock and ice before it. "Do they have to climb over that first?"

Mingma shook his head. "They climb up a glacier that runs around to the west. It's this ice flow they then follow onto Everest itself."

Philips eyes dropped down to the monastery and then into the valley. Somewhere in there was Izzard. He needed to find him and discover whether he had a transmitter or not. It felt strange in such a beautiful and remote setting to be thinking about work.

"Do we know where Izzard is camping?" he asked, making himself concentrate.

Mingma pointed down into the valley, to just over half way up the far slope. "There is a spring about half way up from the river. It is in a small clearing used by the trading caravans to water their animals. That is where the runner said he was." He looked at Philip. "That was two days ago. I asked in Namche and he has not returned there but he may have moved further up the valley."

Philip sighed. Izzards permit had only allowed him to go as far as Namche, but who was there to stop him? Since the checkpoint at the head of the Kathmandu valley nobody had asked to see his permissions. He'd initially hoped that he might be able to get the local authorities to keep the *Mail* journalist away from the expedition, but now he doubted that would work. There was a small police post in Namche and Philip made a mental note to call in there on his next time through.

He watched spellbound as a Golden Eagle soared down the valley, effortlessly floating on the warming morning air and passing only a few feet below them. It swung out over the valley and within moments was no more than a speck disappearing over the distant monastery.

"I wish we could travel like that," Philip remarked with a wry smile.

Mingma nodded and started walking down the trail. "Whoever returns as an eagle must have lived very devoutly in this life," he said, smiling. "After all that time I've spent in Kathmandu I think I will be coming back as a yak."

They laughed and Philip followed. For the next few hours they descended, steadily dropping down to the river. Philip felt as if he was descending an enormous staircase; the path was a constant progression of rough stone steps built over the years to allow laden porters and pack animals to negotiate the steep gradients more easily. His knees started to ache from the constant pounding, but at least it was easy on the lungs so he and Mingma could talk.

"One time when my brother and I were looking after the goats we were high up in a meadow where the winter snow was just melting." He stopped and turned to Philip, holding his hands wide apart. "We saw huge footprints!" he exclaimed, eye wide. "They led off across the slope and then climbed high into the mountain. We followed them for a while but we were young and got scared. Everybody knows what Yeti's do to you if they catch you." He pointed back up the slope. "In the village of Khame a Sherpani was found bitten in half after she went out at night to get some firewood. No scream, nothing!"

"And has anyone actually seen one?" Philip asked.

"Of course," Mingma replied, waving an arm dismissively. "Many people have. My uncle has seen one on this very trail when he was heading to the monastery to make an offering. It was early morning when he saw some musk deer run across the trail, taking no notice of him in their fright. Next thing, a yeti crashed from the trees and dived into the forest after them." Mingma shook his head. "He ran straight back home. I still remember the look of fear on his face as he burst into our house."

Philip was silent and Mingma, clearly sensing his scepticism, spoke again. "Anyway, you can see the head of one for yourself if you wish."

Philip looked up, stumbling on an uneven rock as he did so. "Really? Where?"

"There is a scalp of one at the shrine in the village of Pangboche." He pointed up the valley towards the mountains. "It was brought there as an offering many years ago from herders who killed it as it tried to attack their flocks. They said it was old and weak which was the only reason it didn't kill them all first. We will pass there on the way to the mountain." He sped off down the trail. "Then you will believe for yourself."

At the valley floor they rested for a few minutes by the river. Philip splashed some icy water over his head, his hands going instantly numb in the freezing melt water. They shared some food that Mingma produced from his bag, cold potatoes and dried fruit and Philip opened a bar of chocolate. Soon they were off again and their progress slowed considerably. It was now all uphill, easier on the legs but much harder on the heart and lungs. The sun was high in the sky and despite being in the shade of the forest Philip could feel its rays burning the back of his neck. He tried to get into a rhythm, steadily counting off the steps until he allowed himself short breaks and a swig of water. After a time he stopped and looked back, pleasantly surprised at how far they'd already climbed up from the river. The rhododendron trees gave off a delicate smell, the colours of the flowers vibrant in the sun. Near the river their flowers had been a deep red, but as they climbed and the air temperature fell with the altitude they'd faded to a pink and finally a pure snow white. Thick clumps of lichen hung from their twisted boughs, while the floor was carpeted in vivid green mosses and clumps of small alpine flowers clinging to crevices in the rock. They continued on to a sharp switchback and looking around the corner Philip could see a clearing up ahead.

"This is where Izzard was camping," Mingma remarked, following Philips gaze.

As they climbed towards it, it became increasingly clear that he wasn't there anymore. When they arrived at the small meadow it was deserted, the only noise a trickle of water that ran from a rough stone trough tight up against a rock overhang. They walked over to it and Philip could see where a small spring seeped from the rock and filled the trough.

"Well," said Philip at last. "He's certainly not here now. He must have moved higher into the mountains."

Mingma had walked over to the remnants of a camp fire that lay on the far side of the clearing and reached out to touch the stones that surrounded it.

"Cold," he remarked. "They must have left yesterday."

"Is there anywhere else he could go?" asked Philip, looking around the clearing. "Are there any other trails around the valley?"

Mingma stood and thought. "There is only this trail. The valley is too steep for him to have climbed out of it." He pointed up the trail. "He must have either continued higher to Thangboche or returned towards the river. It is the only crossing place. If he returned that way he must have taken the trail to the upper villages, as he has not been seen in Namche." The Sherpa scratched at his hair. "But I don't know why he would want to go up there as it is away from Everest."

Philip nodded. "Well, we'll soon know. Let's push on to Thangboche and see James. He'll know if he's been there or not."

They set off again, climbing up through thinning trees which soon became a rough juniper scrub. His mind was distracted by Izzard, trying to work out what he could be doing, and he fell into a steady pace. In what seemed like no time they suddenly crested a ridge and found themselves in small fields, divided by rough stone walls. In them grew a few small potato plants and some thin looking barley.

Two skeletal dogs ran out to meet them, baring their teeth and barking angrily. A couple of stones thrown in their direction by Mingma, together with a few choice words, soon drove them away. They passed two tall chorterns, painted white and standing like gate posts at the entrance of the village. Prayer flags hung between them, limp in the still afternoon air. The village itself comprised of squat stone houses all built together in a huddle, piles of firewood stacked in every available nook.

The only street was roughly paved, set lower than the surrounding houses, with ledges and low stone walls running down either side. Three small children sat on a doorstep, a green mucus oozing from their noses and dribbling down undisturbed off their chins. The eldest, herself no more than six or seven years old, had a baby strapped to her back that contentedly slept with its head resting on her shoulder. Their faces were grubby with soot, a consequence of sleeping in houses with no chimneys to keep in warmth during the freezing nights. Philip smiled and waved but was met only by large watchful eyes.

Looking up Philip could see the roof of the monastery, its three tiered roof topped off in the small golden spire he'd seen from the other side of the valley that morning. The street opened into a wide meadow, from which the monastery entrance, a large arch, ornately carved and covered in prayer flags and wheels, led to a wide flight of stairs. This space, Philip guessed, must be used for ceremonies and dancing during festivals. At its far side was a small band of trees and behind these he could make out a long line of tents. Most of them were small sleeping tents like his own, but a couple of larger ones were obviously designed to hold a lot of people and would only be here for one thing. The Expedition.

They started walking across the meadow, its gently sloping grass sprinkled with a covering of primulas. Philip could see people wandering around the camp, some carrying boxes and crates. He stopped and starred as two men appeared from the biggest tent, a large dome, with oxygen cylinders on their back and faces covered by full masks, slowly walking off towards the valley walls. As he got closer he noticed a group of three tents pitched by themselves, some fifty yards from the main expedition. Outside one of them sat a man at a small collapsible table writing in a large notebook, a large mug beside him from which he took frequent sips. He glanced up and Philip recognised him, changing his direction towards him.

After a few moments the man jumped to his feet and strode towards Philip, stopping only when they grasped each other's hands.

"Philip!" exclaimed James Morris, *The Times* Special Correspondent to the Everest trip. "You've made it and in good time. I wasn't expecting you for another week."

Philip smiled. "We pushed on a bit over the last few days because we had some reports about Izzard." He nodded over towards the table. "Get me a comfortable chair and I'll tell you all about it."

That evening Philip and James sat around the table in the small Mess tent, their empty plates pushed back. Each had a small mug of whiskey and took occasional sips as they filled each other in on what had been going on.

"I haven't seen or heard of him since we left Kathmandu," James replied, when Philip had enquired about Izzard. "I got a note from Hutch saying you were on your way to help but after that there's been nothing." He scratched the light stubble on his chin. "If he was camped just below Thangboche then he must've been up to something, probably trying to intercept my runners. I'll go and see Hunt tomorrow and make sure he reminds the climbers not to speak to any other reporters. To be honest I'm more concerned about the expedition porters. It he manages to talk to them, a few dollars will go a long way." He shook his head. "I can't believe he came through Thangboche and wasn't spotted by anyone. Sherpa's are like hawks for gossip." He took a mouthful of whiskey. "I've met him before you know. We both followed a story in Egypt last year. Lovely chap, excellent company. I think he'd have dropped in to say hello if he had passed through since he knows I'm here."

Philip nodded. "What I need to discover is whether or not he's got a damned radio transmitter. That'd give him a big advantage in getting news back to London."

"I know," James agreed. "We made a mistake there. The Swiss told us that they didn't work so we didn't bring one. And now I know that's not true." He stretched, arms held above his head, "When we were passing through Namche I found out that an Indian Army post has just been established there with a radio link to Kathmandu. They want to monitor the border apparently. Something to do with worries that that the Chinese are using the refugee situation as a smokescreen to send spies over into Nepal and India." He smiled. "It's run by a charming Indian called Tiwari, who actually sent a quick dispatch for me. It went to the Indian Embassy in Kathmandu who sent it round by runner to Hutch. He's kindly agreed to send any urgent messages for me, so we do have a way of speeding things up if push comes to shove. I also got him to shake on only doing it for us, so in theory no other papers can use him. Mind you, I wouldn't trust them in Kathmandu as far as I could throw them so," he sat forward, leaning on the table, "I've also been working on a code that only we'll know. That way, if the other hacks do manage to get their hands on the message, they still won't be any the wiser!"

Philip smiled. "Good idea. I'll be heading back towards Namche in a couple of days to find Izzard. If you have the codes ready by then I can take them with me and give them directly to Hutch when I'm back in Kathmandu. That way we'll know they're secure."

The conversation turned to the progress of the Expedition.

"I saw a couple of them earlier walking around with oxygen cylinders on. Training I assume?" Philip asked.

James nodded, gently swilling the contents of his mug. "They've been practising with the breathing apparatus since we left Kathmandu. Some have slept in it, others wear it while walking during the day." He laughed. "Scares the hell out of the locals I can tell you. Since we've been at Thangboche, Hunt's had them out doing a bit of climbing in the masks as well, seeing how they get on. Apart from getting hot and sweaty, they seem to work fine." He took a drink. "Spirits seem high anyway. They're all fit and well and cannot wait to get started on the mountain."

Philip nodded, watching at the man opposite over the top of his mug. He'd often seen him around the Times office in London, although as he was a more senior Staff reporter they'd never really socialised. With short black hair and the shadow of a beard, he had a youthful face, friendly eyes with a confident gaze looking out over a prominent nose. For a young reporter this was the assignment of a lifetime. Many of the staff at *The Times* had been envious when they heard he'd be assigned to it and yet nobody had begrudged Morris his opportunity. Philip could see why. He was modest and unassuming, with an easy manner about him that made you want him to like you.

The story of how he was invited by John Hunt, over lunch in the Garrick Club, to join the expedition as the Special Correspondent had already been often recounted, normally with much amusement as Morris had never actually done any mountaineering before and was now expected to write reports from high on Everest itself. Looking at the man Philip had no doubts that he would manage.

"Anyway," James continued, "You've arrived at an excellent moment. The abbot of the monastery has invited us all to a blessing ceremony tomorrow to wish the expedition a safe climb. You can come along and meet everybody."

They chatted a bit longer but Philip soon excused himself and wandered back to his tent. A few minutes before dusk Old Gompu had arrived, followed by his weary porters, carrying all his camping equipment. It was amazing what the promise of double pay could do. Mingma had wasted no time in getting the tents erected and everything unpacked and it felt luxurious to be back on his old camp bed rather that the hard floor and greasy woollen blankets of the previous night. He had a slight headache, a consequence he thought of the altitude rather than the whiskey, and lay there thinking, warm in his sleeping bag.

Seeing James had been good, the chance to clarify exactly what he was here to do and to catch up on the expedition's news. But it was to Prem and the other Gurkhas that his mind kept returning, still finding it hard to believe that they'd actually met. It had been just over ten years since he'd last seen them. For the first two he'd been driven almost insane by not knowing what had happened. Then he'd learnt to block it out, to forget and get on, as best he could, with his life. That they'd survived made him feel a sense of relief so overwhelming that he couldn't linger on the thought without becoming dizzy. But there were other memories he wasn't sure he was ready to face.

CHAPTER 7

Despite not having to be up at dawn, Philip was awake early and upon emerging from his tent found it to be a beautiful, still morning. Smoke from the village fires was rising straight up into the sky and Sherpas were scurrying around the expedition camp. Old Gompu came over and handed him a large mug of breakfast tea which he gratefully took, cupping it in his gloved hands and enjoying the sensation of the heat through his woollen gloves.

Turning towards the monastery he could see that things were busy here too. Monks in their distinctive purple robes were hurrying to and fro, while a group of village women had arrived with heavy loads of firewood that they were piling by the entrance.

"Morning," he heard from behind and looking over his shoulder he saw James emerging from his tent, boots unlaced. "Time for a quick breakfast then off to the monastery." He rolled his eyes. "I've been told by Tenzing that these ceremonies can go on for hours so better get some food inside us. I dread to think what they'll be giving us afterwards."

Gompu and James' cook had combined to provide an excellent breakfast of pancakes with honey and some boiled eggs they'd managed to buy from the village. After polishing these off Philip felt much better and he was just finishing a large mug of Camp coffee when he heard the most extraordinary noise, making him jump and spill some down his shirt. It was a low pitched moan, a noise that seemed to make his heart vibrate inside him. He looked up at James in alarm who'd started laughing.

"Christ, the look on your face," he said through guffaws. "Don't worry, it's just the horns from the monastery. Bloody great things. It must mean they're ready for us. Come on, we better get going."

They walked out of the Mess tent and crossed the meadow towards the monastery. Philip could see a large group from the Expedition already there, standing beneath the entrance arch, and happily spinning the large prayer wheels embedded in its walls.

"Gentlemen," James announced formally when they reached them, "and New Zealanders. May I introduce Philip Armitage, another humble scribe from my illustrious publication. Please be nice to him as he's just arrived."

Several of the men smiled or raised a hand towards him, but before much else could happen the door in the archway opened and two monks appeared, beckoning them inside. They all shuffled forward and started climbing a wide flight of stone steps. Philip found himself walking beside a tall young man with a large smile.

"George," the man said, holding out a hand. "George Band."

Philip took the hand and smiled back. "Philip. Pleased to meet you."

"Looks like you've arrived just in time for the fun," Band said, looking around as they entered an inner courtyard. "I've been trying to get in here for the last week."

The two monks indicated that they should remove their shoes and then beckoned them forward, giving each a small stick of burning incense. When everyone was holding one they led them off, walking around a large Golden statue of a seated Buddha with outstretched arms. Everyone had gone silent, the only noise the repetitive chant of several monks sitting before the statue and the chiming of small hand-held chimes that swung rhythmically in their hands.

It was dark inside, the windows covered by intricately carved shutters and with only a few lamps and candles lighting the way. Philip could see that the walls were painted red and covered in thankas, larger and more intricate than the ones Zigsa had shown him back in Kathmandu, depicting scenes from the Buddha's life. Gold and purple statuettes lined the walls in a procession of small niches and hanging down from the beams were rough wooden masks he guessed were used by the monks during the various festivals held every year.

When they'd circled around and were back at the front door the monks took the incense sticks and pushed them into pots of sand that stood before the statue. There was a loud ringing of a bell, or at least that's what it sounded like until Philip looked up to see a monk standing on a balcony beside an empty oxygen cylinder, hanging from its nozzle. The monk struck it again with a small brass hammer and everyone fell silent.

Everybody's attention fell on an ancient monk who was standing on the lowest steps of a small staircase that climbed to the upper floor. He held his hands outstretched and with a warm smile spoke for over a minute, talking a dialect Philip didn't recognise. When he finished a young woman, who had been standing in the shadows beside him, stepped forward and started to speak in a quiet but clear voice. Philip stared at her.

"Our Abbot of Thangboche welcomes you to this monastery, the most important in the Sherpa lands. He is honoured that you have visited and assures you that the monks have said prayers for the safety of the men on your trip." She looked down as if carefully choosing the correct words to use. "He says you are welcome to pray in his monastery. He says that a feast is prepared for you in the main room and you are all to join him there to celebrate the new friendship."

She turned and bowed to the old Llama, walking backwards to one side, and as she did so Philip saw one of the mountaineers walk forward. He recognised him immediately from photos he'd seen in the newspapers. It was John Hunt, the expedition leader.

Hunt turned to face the assembled crowd, bowing first to the abbot. "We all thank the Llama for his welcome and his blessing. His monastery is situated in one of the most beautiful places I've had the privilege of visiting anywhere in the world. I can think of nowhere better to stay to inspire us for the task ahead."

He turned once more to the Llama and gave a small bow, before stepping forward and placing a wad of rupee banknotes, tied together with a boot lace, before the main statue as an offering. The abbot held his hands together and returned the bow, before leading Hunt up the rickety staircase, shafts of daylight cutting down it and lighting up wisps of smoke rising from the burning incense.

Everybody started to shuffle towards the stairs, taking their time to study the magnificent statue as they passed. Philip was still slyly looking at the young translator, trying to make out her face in the poor light. She was a Sherpani, probably in her early twenties and with large, expressive eyes. Her long black hair was tied back in a tight pony tail, but leaving two long locks, one falling each side of her face. A small nose wrinkled slightly every time she smiled and bowed at a passing climber.

As he approached the bottom of the stairs, a few yards from where she was standing, she glanced over and caught his eye. A jolt of panic hit him, his mind flashing back in time; large, dark eyes framed by long black hair, the smoky interior dredging up terrible, long-suppressed memories. He shook his head in an attempt to dislodge them.

"Hello," he mumbled, his tongue feeling like a splinter of wood. For a moment he hoped that he hadn't been heard above the repetitive chanting of the monks which had started again now the speeches were over.

Her eyes remained on him, head tilted quizzically to one side as she calmly watched his face. "Namaste," she replied at last, stepping forward into a patch of daylight that shone down the stairwell. "Welcome."

Philip forced a smile, acutely aware that it must look like a painful grimace. "Thank you," he replied at last, making himself look at her again. Now she was in the light he could see her features more clearly and the images in his mind dissolved. This face was fuller, the cheekbones higher and with a smile that fell easily upon it.

"Wh … where did you learn such good English?" he stammered, trying to cover the embarrassment that burnt at his cheeks. "You seem very fluent."

"From my father," she answered slowly, "and it's not so good." He could see her working through in her mind what she wanted to say. "He worked with the English in Tibet many years before. When he returned he taught all his children the language he had learnt from them. The rest we took from a book he had been given. It was by a man called Rudyard Kipling and told of animals who lived like men." She giggled shyly. "How strange we thought England must be."

Philip relaxed a little and caught her infectious laugh. "Sometimes I think animals would make a better job of running things that we do." He looked at her. "These Englishmen, what were they doing in Tibet?"

"They were climbing," she replied. "The English always climb. They came many times to climb Everest. Some died, some vanished but they never got to its top." She stopped and glanced out of the open door through which the mountain could be seen, towering over the valley. "He believes that those who died are at peace on the sacred mountain with the spirits who live there." She looked back at Philip. "Maybe this time you will succeed."

Philip smiled. "Let's just pray everybody comes back in one piece." He stood transfixed, not knowing what to say next but not wanting to move away. He was acting just like a schoolboy. "So how did you come to be working in the monastery?" he continued quickly. "Seems a strange thing for a young woman to be doing?"

She laughed again. "I speak your language and can write.

The monks need my help here rather than collecting their firewood."

Their eyes were locked. "I don't blame them," he answered in a voice little more than a whisper. They were motionless. The pungent incense filled Philip's senses, sweet, thick and sensual. The monks chanting seemed to drown out the world. A new beam of sunlight burst down the stairwell as another window was opened on the gallery to light up the upstairs rooms. Its rays fell on the girl, bathing her in red, her face shimmering crimson as if blood was running down her face. The smell in his nostrils became cordite, the chorus behind him one of moaning and weeping. He looked away from her, tearing his eyes up towards the light and gradually they focused on long red hangings beside the window, billowing in the wind and filtering the sun as if fell down upon them.

He tried to compose himself, embarrassed by his behaviour and desperate not to seem like a complete idiot.

"I … I would very much like to meet your father," he said at last. "I'm a journalist and would love to write about some his memories."

"He would enjoy that," the girl replied after a thoughtful pause. "He would like to see an Englishman again before he dies. Come to the monastery gate this evening at sunset. We will walk to his house."

She took a step backwards and added, "You can tell us about how animals in England really behave," before turning and disappearing into the shadows of the shrine.

He leant against a carved, wooden column, greasy and black from years of lamp smoke. He felt breathless, legs weak, trying to calm himself. He couldn't go through that again.

After a few moment he straightened and followed the rest of the expedition up the stairs and, after following a narrow corridor, into a large hall, windows set high in its walls through which daylight slanted in. Statues again decorated the walls, of many different sizes and materials and set in niches at the far end of the room were a line of impressive looking urns.

"Apparently they're the old abbots' ashes," James whispered to him as he settled down. "Once they've been cremated they are put in those urns to be venerated." He smiled. "That's what you call a job for eternity, let alone life."

The ceremony did, as Tenzing had warned, go on for hours. They were fed a constant stream of Tibetan tea as the monks chanted their mantras, talking quietly amongst themselves. Philip found himself next to George Band again and the young mountaineer began telling him about the expedition.

"I'm still amazed I got chosen to come, if the truth be told," he'd confessed after they'd been talking for an hour or so. "Apparently they were impressed with all the climbing I'd managed to do in the Alps last year. It was a lot more than anyone else and showed how dedicated I was." He chuckled. "I didn't tell them that my old man had got me a rather easy job in Switzerland so I had plenty of time and a bit of cash. All the other poor blighters had to try to survive on £20 because of the currency restrictions."

Philip nodded. Since the war the amount of money you could take overseas when you travelled was restricted to £20 per trip, which made long holidays all but impossible. He'd checked with his editor about this when told about the assignment but was informed that he'd be able to draw money through Hutchinson in Kathmandu as he was there for work.

"Plan is to move up to the ice flow in the next few days and establish the Base Camp." Bands eyes sparkled with anticipation. "That's when the fun really starts. Hillary and Westmacott will go first with a group of Sherpas, bringing up the first of the supplies and looking for a good place to position it. Somewhere near to where the serious climbing starts but out of the path of avalanches. After that we'll all start shuttling up the supplies while they head off into the ice flow itself and look for a route up the mountain." He smiled ruefully, "We all want to help but hands up, it's fair to say that they're the best at ice work."

He was interrupted by a long blast on the huge horn which had now appeared in the hall and the level of the chanting rose as more monks entered, many with hand-held prayer wheels flashing in the sunlight as they spun around. They stood along the far wall, bowing low as a final group of monks entered. These monks looked thin and lean, their faces drawn and tired. They seated themselves on some rugs opposite and food suddenly appeared, carried by boy monks who giggled excitedly as they approached and served the climbers.

Philip kept glancing across at the young Sherpani who was now sitting behind the abbot, translating the conversation between him, Hunt and another monk who was dressed in a different style of robe. On one occasion their eyes met and she smiled shyly before he looked away in embarrassment.

When the food was eaten, a meal consisting of potatoes and vegetables, with jugs of millet chang that the monks seemed particularly partial to, Philip followed the expedition members as they slowly filed before the abbot to receive a personal blessing. Bowing his head, he stood with his hands together as if in prayer and felt a silk prayer scarf being placed around his neck. With a slight bow, he turned and walked away, examining the wood block print writing that covered the fine material.

Outside the monastery, he walked slowly back to his camp, enjoying stretching his legs after sitting cross-legged for so long. Glancing up he could see clouds building up and obscuring the high peaks, as often happened at this time of year prior to the arrival of the monsoon. James had returned to the expedition tents to try to get some quotes from Hunt and the others about the ceremony, so Philip got out his leather document case and pulled out a map. He'd been presented with them by Hutch on the morning of his departure, a whole sheaf of them that had come from the Forestry Department in Kathmandu. He hoped they might give him some indication of where Izzard may have gone.

If he'd headed back down the valley he would, as Mingma had said, have had to cross the river on the same bridge they'd used. It was the only crossing point below Thangboche and although only a few miles long at that stage, the river was already a raging torrent of icy, white water, not the kind of thing you'd want to ford on your own. Mingma was also right in that as there were no trails branching off near Thangboche, but if he'd climbed back towards Namche there was the trail that climbed to a village called Khumjung and the other villages of the upper meadows. Looking at the map Philip realised that these villages sat high up in the valley, on a small plateau well away from any of the tallest mountains and the obvious place from where to try to transmit a radio message.

He worked out a plan. At first light they'd retrace their steps down the valley and head for Khumjung. If Izzard was there he'd talk to him, if not they'd return to Namche and see if they could find out anything there. He'd also pop into the police post and see if he could get them to do anything about Izzard.

He called Mingma, who'd been lying on the grass on the far side of the clearing chatting to some other Sherpa's. Once he'd explained everything and ensured that the necessary arrangements would be made, he head back to his tent for a rest, still tired after the exertions of the previous few days.

Lying on his camp bed, however, he couldn't sleep. He was nervous. An excitement was running through him that he didn't really understand or know how to deal with. It had been a long time since he'd felt so apprehensive about meeting a woman. Some of it, he knew, was a worry about making a fool of himself again, like he had back in the monastery. But there was more.

He'd never been very comfortable around girls, a result, he thought, of not really coming across them much in his life. His boarding school had been boys only and during the holidays on the estate there just weren't any around. A brief dalliance aged fourteen with his friend Will's elder sister had resulted in a few chaste kisses and awkward embracing, but had ended in humiliation when she'd started ignoring him on his hopeful visits to their family forge. Soon after she'd become engaged to a farmer's son a few villages away and had disappeared from his world.

There'd also been his sister Mary's constant parade of visiting school friends, but their attentions seemed firmly fixed on his older brother rather than him, something he'd been very grateful for at the time. A relationship with another Classics student at Cambridge had been cut short by the war and after his return he'd struggled to keep relationships going, despite a desire to settle down to a normal life, as illustrated by the latest break-up just before his departure.

Whenever he managed to get into a relationship, a glance or gesture, even a smell would fill his mind with memories that made him recoil and turn away. He knew he had to face up to them. Perhaps a friendship in such an isolated place, away from his normal world, would help heal and banish the images from his mind, letting him move onto better relationships when he returned home.

He sat up and tried to write his journal but found he couldn't concentrate on that either. Eventually he walked over and asked old Gompu for a bowl of hot water he then used to shave with. A brush of his rather long and none too clean hair and as the day started to fade he emerged from his tent and head off towards the monastery gate.

When he arrived there was nobody there. He felt relieved, although at the same time disappointed. Perhaps she'd forgotten about their brief conversation or that he'd already missed her. He made himself wait, chastising himself for his initial thought of returning to the Expedition Mess Tent. The sun had disappeared and the temperature had dropped considerably, so he stood with his hands pushed deep into his pockets, collar up and stamping his feet in an attempt to keep them warm and steady his nerves. After a few minutes he heard the creak of the monastery's heavy wooden door and glancing up saw her silhouetted against the yellow lamp light coming from the smoky interior. She closed the door and glided down the flight of stone steps towards him.

"Good evening," she said, the shy smile just visible again in the last light of dusk. "I'm sorry if I kept you waiting." She took a breath but paused as if searching for the correct words. "There are some important guests in the monastery and I was needed to help make them comfortable."

"Please, don't worry," Philip replied, "I've only just got here. Let me introduce myself properly. I'm Philip, Philip Armitage." He looked at the girl's face. It was perfect. Her large hazel eyes dominated it, a warm smile now making him feel as if she really did want to see him and wasn't just being polite. He suddenly felt very pleased he'd made himself wait.

She gave a small bow, hands together which Philip rather clumsily copied. "My name is Lhamu Sherpa," she replied in a quiet voice, her mouth opening to continue. There was an awkward silence. "You must excuse my English," she said at last. "Sometimes it is hard to get the correct word. I sometimes have to think in my own language and then try to remember the English. You have so many words."

Philip shook his head. "It's excellent, honestly, and it's been a very long day for you. What with the Expedition and these other guests, the monks must be exhausted!" He smiled weakly.

She laughed, a contagious giggle that lit up her face.

"That's true. We go weeks without seeing anyone up here in the mountains and now suddenly everybody is here." She leant in towards him and whispered. "The Abbot is very happy. The climbers left an offering of money that is enough to pay for the repairs to the roof, while the other guests are important Tibetan monks carrying with them a sacred artefact. It will give the monastery great status to have had it there."

They started to walk, skirting around the side of the monastery towards the village.

"The abbot didn't know they were coming until they arrived last night. Their mission was a secret as they didn't want the Chinese intercepting them and taking what they have. Since they invaded a few years ago much damage has been done to the monasteries in Tibet and many sacred things have been stolen or destroyed."

They'd entered the village by now, and before Philip had time to reply she walked up to a weathered wooden door of a small house on the main street. She put her hand on the latch but before lifting it, turned towards Philip. "My father is very old. I sent a message to say I was bringing an Englishman tonight and he is very happy. You will have to talk loudly as his hearing is poor."

Philip nodded and he followed Lhamu through the doorway, ducking under the low wooden lintel. They entered a large room, lit by the cooking fire in the centre and two small lamps on stone ledges that jutted out from the walls, lined with gleaming copper pots he assumed were full of food. Philips eyes started to sting from the smoke and he felt the urge to cough growing at the back of his throat. There were six people already in the room and they all turned to look.

Sitting on a wooden stool by the fire was an old man, wrapped up in a thick padded jacket despite the warmth of the room. As his face creased into a smile, his few remaining teeth becoming visible. Lhamu crossed to him and standing behind him put her hands on his shoulders. "This is my father, Karma Sherpa," she said loudly. She then said something into his ear in a language Philip didn't understand, although he did catch his name. The old man pulled himself to his feet, using Lhamu as a support. Philip stepped forward and took the outstretched hand.

"It's good to see an Englishman again," he said in a surprisingly strong voice, looking Philip up and down. "They seem to make you all giants in that country!" He started to laugh, a chuckle that turned into a chesty cough and made him sit down on his stool. Lhamu introduced two of her brothers Tshering and Lhakpa, both also sitting by the fire, and a young woman called Chiki, who was the wife of Tshering and was stirring some pans that hung over the hearth. Lastly she dragged forward two young children who were hiding behind Chiki. "And these are Dali and Sarkey, my niece and nephew," she said holding each by the upper arm so they couldn't run away. "They are a little frightened to have someone so white in their house."

Philip smiled at them reassuringly, making them go wide-eyed in terror, and then squatted down. "I'm pleased to meet you," he said quietly, holding out his hand. With encouragement from Lhamu the children quickly touched the hand before retreating behind their aunt, faces buried in her long skirt.

"Please," said the now recovered Karma, "take a seat by me so we can talk."

He stood, crossing the room to a stool that Lhakpa had vacated and sat down. It was better when seated, the smoke rising to the rafters and leaving cleaner air lower down. Philip felt both his eyes and throat clear. Chiki came over and with a shy bow gave him a bowl of rice and lentils. The others were also served and soon everybody was eating, except the children who still stared at Philip suspiciously. Little was said until the bowls were cleared away and the men were all served with a large beaker of the strongest chang Philip had yet tasted.

"It's been many years since I've had the opportunity to speak to an Englishman," Karma said at last. "I often think of my friends from there who must now be old and useless like me." He stared into the fire. "At least we got to live our lives. Sometimes I wonder what drives a man to risk his life and the prosperity of his family for one brief moment of glory."

Philip nodded. "I'm afraid I agree with you. I shouldn't really admit it but I think the climbers camping out there are mad." He paused, glancing at the old man. "When was it you met these other Englishmen?"

Karma looked at him with a smile, enjoying the chance to reminisce. "It must have been thirty years ago. I was living in Darjeeling in India at the time, as that was where all the big climbing trips started. In those days Nepal was closed to all foreigners so to get to Everest the only way was through Sikkim and then Tibet." He paused. "It was a long hard trek. But I was young and we were paid so much money it was hard for a young Sherpa to believe."

"Do you remember any of their names?" Philip asked, a feeling of excitement growing.

The old man chuckled. "I remember their names better than I remember what I had for breakfast today. Three times I went with them. The first was just to make maps, but the other two times they tried to climb to the top. On the first trip it was run by Howardbury. He was a fine man but we were all a little bit scared of him." He stopped and waited as Chiki came round and refilled their cups. After taking a long pull he continued. "It was the next two trips that I knew the men better. My English had improved and the younger climbers were keen to learn some Tibetan. I taught them. In the evenings we sat in the Mess tent and talked. A man called Bruce taught me to read English."

He paused again, his voice now quieter and strained with emotion. "Many of my friends died on these trips. On the first I survived only because I was snow blinded and stayed in camp. Seven Sherpas, including my replacement, were swept away in an avalanche. The last time two of the sahibs vanished." He pointed up in the air, as if seeing images from years ago. "They were climbing near the top and then we never saw them again. I like to believe they reached the top and the mother goddess of the mountain kept them with her because they were such brave men."

There was silence. "That must have been Mallory and Irvine?" Philip asked at last. "I've read the book about it. It was 1924. It's become something of a legend in Britain now, did they or didn't they make it to the summit!"

Karma shook his head. "They were not a legend. They were my friends. It was Irvine sahib who leant me books to read."

He gestured towards a battered wooden chest in the

corner and Lhamu got up and walked over to it, lifting its creaking lid and reaching inside. She took out a package wrapped in a white silk cloth, from which she pulled a book and passed it over to Philip.

Just So Stories by Rudyard Kipling. He read, the words embossed in faded gold letters on a green cover. Carefully he opened it and looked at the title page. There, written in strong copperplate handwriting was the name Sandy Irvine.

Karma looked at the book and laughed. "It's only a tattered old book but it means more to me than the Kanjur next door!"

"Father!" Lhamu said. "I told you that was a secret. Nobody is to know."

The old man dismissed her words with a wave of his hand. "Everybody knows. It's the talk of the village. What do you expect if they turn up here in such a big group with those heavy boxes on their yaks?" He looked at Philip with a twinkle in his eye. "We all thought it was gold!"

"Am I missing something here?" Philip asked, raising an eyebrow towards Lhamu. "What's a Kanjur?"

"The Kanjur is very sacred to all Buddhists," she replied quietly. "It is the word of the Buddha that was translated and written down many centuries ago by the first Dalai Lama. They say it is written in gold on paper as dark as night. The book is so sacred it has been decided to bring it to safety away from the Chinese. It has been in Lhasa but now even there is too dangerous."

Philip nodded. "So those monks eating with us today are the ones carrying it?"

"That's right," Lhamu replied. "They are very senior

Llamas. They have brought with them some young, strong monks to help protect them and look after the animals. They are at the monastery for two nights recovering from crossing a high pass through the Himalaya. It was very cold. Tomorrow they leave early to continue their journey with the Kanjur to Kathmandu." She sat down again by the fire, warming her hands. "They are very nervous. Even their most senior Llama was constantly glancing around today, always on edge. He was very angry when he found out that the climbers were coming to the monastery but it was too late to change it. I would have thought that now they are out of Tibet they would be able to relax but he said to my abbot that until he has passed on his responsibility he will allow himself no sleep."

"Typical monk!" exclaimed Karma. "They sit all day praying and eating and when they actually have a proper job to do they think it's the hardest thing in the world." He shook his head, looking up at Lhamu. "They are lucky to have you working there. If it wasn't for you getting them organised they wouldn't have enough firewood in the winter or food to live on."

He turned to Philip. "Her mother was the same. She died when in childbirth with Lhamu otherwise I'm sure they would together now be running the whole village. I remember her as a little girl, always the one who got my sons to do what they were told. She was always the clever one, unlike this lot," he nodded towards Tshering and Lhakpa, "who never understood your language and are happy to live in the village. That's why I brought her with me on my trips." He stopped and took Lhamu's hand, squeezing it. "I always knew she'd get out into the world, that our valley would be too small for her. I've had many requests from families as far away as Namche for her to marry their sons but I've turned them all down. She's not going to be tied here." The old man kissed her hand and yawned.

Philip caught Lhamu's eyes and she smiled, nodding almost imperceptibly towards the door. He stood and turned to face Karma. "You must excuse me sir, but I have an early morning. It's been a privilege to meet you," he said, as they shook hands. "I'd like very much to visit you again when I'm next in the village. Perhaps I could take some notes about your memories of those trips."

The old man smiled. "I'd like to do that, young man, and look forward to our next meeting." He glanced across at his daughter and winked at her. "But not as much as Lhamu is looking forward to it I think." He sat down chuckling, leaving Philip and Lhamu to head towards the door, faces burning.

CHAPTER 8

Burma, 1943

Philip scrutinized the far river bank with his binoculars, idly scratching at an itchy rash he'd developed the previous night from a large hairy caterpillar that'd crawled up his arm. It looked clear. They'd been there for about thirty minutes. Philip, Prem and two rifleman had crawled from the fringe of the jungle into the thick elephant grass that ran along the river bank. From where he lay he looked out over a silt beach of probably twenty yards to the water's edge. The river itself was slow and languid, like thick, warm chocolate running from the pan.

He'd chosen this spot as there was no sign of any habitation either up or down stream, allowing them the opportunity to cross without being seen. If they could do so they might just fool the Japanese into believing they still had them trapped on the eastern bank. That, he hoped, gave them a chance. During their vigil they'd seen or heard nothing. No soldiers, no people, no engines, only a small shell duck dabbling for food in the shallows.

Philip lowered the glasses and rubbed his aching eyes. He felt exhausted. There'd been little sleep the previous night. After the Japanese patrol had retreated down the valley, he'd waited until he'd thought it was clear and then taken the men north-east out of the ravine. It had been quite a detour before they'd finally dropped down to the river. They'd camped, exhausted and hungry, in teak forest a few hundred yards from the bank, plagued by aggressive red ants that had crawled over them and nipped at them all night. At first light he'd been relieved to get up and made his way to the water.

Judging by the large trunks of driftwood caught up midstream the river didn't look deep. He hoped not as most of the platoon couldn't swim. That was one problem with the Gurkhas, they didn't swim and didn't like water. Unfortunately they'd lost their ropes in the confusion at the last crossing so he'd nothing to rig up to help them across. There certainly wasn't time, and the men didn't have the energy, to build rafts. If the worst came to the worst they'd have to hang onto pieces of wood and kick their way over. He crawled back from the edge of the grass, beckoning the others to follow. In a couple of minutes they were back at the camp.

"Get the men prepared," he told Prem, deepening his voice slightly to make it more authoritative. "All weapons and ammo must be rolled in ground-sheets and tied high out of the water, everything else packed away."

Prem nodded. "Rifleman Rai has asked for you to inspect the mules. They have a problem."

Philip nodded and walked back through the men to the rear where the mules were tethered. As soon as he saw them he knew they were finished. One was lying on its side, sucking in great juddering breaths. The other two stood with their noses touching the floor, legs splayed out to keep their balance, ribs and pelvis painfully visible through their worn hides. Large sores stood out a vivid red on their backs, crusty with discharge and covered in flies.

He looked at the three Gurkha handlers, all of whom understood the situation and looked to be on the brink of tears. They'd been through a lot with these animals and although they'd often been a nightmare to control they'd always made it through. It was time to put them out of their misery, but he couldn't risk a shot being heard. "Turn them loose," he said at last, fighting to keep his voice steady. "They'll never get over the river in this state."

He turned quickly and walked to where the baggage panniers were piled. There was little left, dwindling food supplies, some water containers, ammo and the radio set. The last radio battery had died the previous night as he'd tried unsuccessfully to reach HQ. There was no way to recharge it. Before, new batteries had been delivered in the air drops or charged by a small generator. That had gone with the main column. Without the radio there was no way of organizing a new drop but without batteries it was useless and would slow them down. It would be a pain to get it dry across the river anyway without any boats.

He nodded towards the pile of equipment. "Split this lot up between the men. Dump the water containers and the radio. The rest needs to go." The men nodded and started unpacking the panniers.

He returned to his own pack and was just finishing preparing it when he saw Prem hurry over. He looked at him. "Everything OK, corporal?"

The Gurkha nodded but stood there, something obviously on his mind.

"What is it?" he asked after a short silence.

"The mules sir," came the reply. "I was thinking we could kill them and take some of the meat."

Philip turned and looked at him. "It's going to be inedible, tough as boots."

The corporal shrugged. "It's still meat. The men need something."

Philip nodded, realising Prem was right and annoyed that he hadn't thought of it himself. How could he have overlooked such an obvious bloody thing considering they were all starving? "They'll need to be dispatched silently," he said. "Drive them apart first. I don't want them braying in panic when they smell blood. And be quick. I want to start the crossing in ten minutes."

Prem turned and strode off through the camp, drawing his khukri as he went.

Philip took twenty rounds of ammo and some food from the soldier who was distributing the mules baggage and tucked it in the top of his pack. It had felt heavy before, nearly fifty pounds of kit. Now he could hardly lift it off the ground. Leaving it standing on a tree stump he finished his mug of tea and then put his last piece of chocolate into his mouth. He closed his eyes, savouring the burst of sweetness that made him feel light-headed. He remembered a shop in Kings Lynn that made the most divine chocolates he'd ever tasted. His mother had always bought his Easter eggs there when he was a child and he vowed to head back there on his next leave.

When he opened his eyes again he saw the men had fallen in. He beckoned them closer.

"The Mu is one of the last big barriers between us and home," he announced, trying to sound encouraging. "When we get across this we're only eighty miles from India and there should be less Japs crawling around."

He looked around the faces of his men, none betraying any emotion.

"I'm going to cross first with 1st squad to check the depth and current. Once we've make it and are in position, we'll signal and you all follow. Single file, well spaced. And don't stop to admire the view."

A chuckle of nervous laughter ran through the group. That's as good as it's going to get, Philip thought, so turned and slipped into his pack, trying to make it look effortless as he straightened up. The three surviving members of 1st squad followed him as he walked towards the river, trying to keep his legs from trembling from a combination of weight and fear. He never liked these crossings, always convinced that here was something horrible lurking in the opaque water. Reaching the edge of the tall grass, he held up his hand.

"Wait here. Don't enter the water until I give you a signal."

He emerged onto the sandy riverbed at what he hoped would be a run, but under the weight of his pack and his weakened state was barely a jog. Glancing up and down the shore he checked it was clear and entered the river. He felt water seep into his boots, initially through the ripped seams and holes in the sole. It was rather pleasant, soothing the aches. As he waded further he felt the current starting to tug at him and as the bottom of his pack entered the water he found it necessary to turn slightly upstream in order to keep his balance.

He walked on, carefully edging his feet forward through the water, heavy with silt. The riverbed was firm, his feet sinking in no more than an inch or so, but a couple of times his boot hit submerged debris which almost tripped him. Looking forward he realised he was already in mid- stream. The water was up over his waist and he walked with his revolver and map held high above his head.

He reached the stump of an enormous teak tree that sat grounded, the current breaking around it and stopped, gratefully hanging onto an exposed root for a rest. He was breathing heavily from the exertion of trying to stay balanced. After a few seconds he pushed out once more into the current and found that the river shelved up quickly, making the going much easier.

When the water was at his knees he turned and waved the rest of the squad forward. He saw them run into the water and set off determinedly towards him. He turned and waded on, soon reaching the far bank and gratefully dropping his pack into the fringe of the forest that ran down to the water's edge. He turned to check on the progress of the men and was surprised to see them almost with him. The look on their faces was of grim determination. They hated water and seemed to have decided that the best way of crossing was to get it over with as quickly as possible.

Looking to the far bank he signalled for the rest of the platoon to start their crossing. Almost immediately the first Gurkha appeared, scurrying into the water. He turned to the men with him, pointing at the nearest two. "You and you, I want one twenty yards upstream and one twenty yards downstream keeping watch. If you see anything, let me know. And you," he pointed to the last man, "Recce the jungle behind. Make sure there are no tracks or houses nearby."

The men nodded and disappeared. Philip turned back towards the river. There was now a line of soldiers crossing, one approximately every ten yards. They bunched closer as the water deepened and the progress of the front ones slowed. He saw it reached chest level on many of the men but they still appeared unaffected by the current.

It took the first man a minute or so to get across and when he looked at the far bank he saw that Prem was now in the water at the end of the line. He glanced up at the sky. No planes in sight, no spotters or worse still a Zero diving down to strafe the exposed men.

"Boat!" came an urgent cry and peering upstream Philip saw the man he'd positioned there pointing to a dark spot on the river, a large white bow wave showing that it was indeed a boat and heading towards them fast.

"Bloody hell," he cursed under his breath, jumping up and wading a few steps into the water.

"Get over here, at the double. Enemy boat," he yelled, hands cupped around his mouth.

He saw the men look up in the direction he was pointing and then try to run. The ones nearest the shore kicked up sheets of water as they lifted their feet from the river and ran. A couple stumbled and fell. Philip ran towards them, crouching as he went and grabbed them by the collar. Heaving them up he pushed them towards the bank.

Small plumes of water were now kicking up around him, and for a moment he thought it was raining. Then the clatter of a machine gun reached his ears and he ran for the bank, diving headlong into the undergrowth. He turned, keeping low behind some tangled roots. Two bodies were drifting slowly off downstream; the muddy waters around them turned a burnished copper as blood mixed in with the silt. The four soldiers nearest the bank were lying, just their heads above the surface, crawling to safety. Further back he could see that several of the Gurkhas, including Prem, were sheltering behind the tree stump mid-stream. A couple had gained a footing and were trying to shoot back with their rifles.

"Return fire," Philip yelled, and immediately there was the crackle of rifle fire around him. The boat veering sharply towards them, making itself a smaller target and he could see the muzzle of the machine gun flashing yellow flame. Bits of bark and vegetation showered down on them as the bullets slammed home in the jungle above their heads. After a sustained burst that kept the Gurkhas pinned down, it abruptly swung towards the stranded men. Philip heard the sound of bullets ricocheting off the hard teak stump and realised that as soon as the boat got down river of them they'd have no cover.

He could see the boat clearly now. About thirty feet in length it was a local boat that had been commandeered. It had heavy wooden planking, off which their rifle rounds seem to deflect harmlessly. Inside he could make out six soldiers, two in the bow where the machine gun was set, its barrel peeping over the prow and surrounded in sand bags.

At the stern three other soldiers were shooting with rifles and the last was crouched low, looking forward, steering the vessel.

"Aim for the stern," Philip ordered. "Go for the man on the tiller."

The shooting picked up and Philip smiled grimly as he saw one of the soldiers on the boat pitch backwards and disappear from view. He cursed to himself. If they hadn't lost their Bren gun they'd have been able to return fire. When they'd been split off from the main column their platoon gun had already crossed the river, leaving them with only light arms.

The boat passed them, firing a broadside as it did so that had them again pinned down to the damp forest floor. It smelt of decay and rot. He heard a stifled yell as a bullet hit home into one of the Gurkhas near to him. Raising his head he peered out through the tangled roots and watched as the boat turned up stream, its guns swivelling round towards the driftwood stump.

A flash of movement caught his eye, accompanied by a crash of undergrowth and the sound of splashing water. Philip looked up in surprise, before screaming "Cover him!" and repeatedly firing his revolver in the direction of the boat. A Gurkha had burst from the trees, jumping into the shallows and was now running towards the enemy boat which had slowed right down as it closed in on the stranded soldiers. Philip saw the soldier pull the pin from a grenade and after a small pause throw it high into the air, diving into the water as he released it.

Time slowed. Philip watched the grenade arc through

the air, trying to judge its flight and the movement of the boat. It was going to fall short, he was sure of it. The Japanese had seen the grenade coming and one of the soldiers in the stern tried to swat it away with his hand. It was too low for him to reach, clipping the gunwale and disappearing into the boat. He could see the panic spread, with several of the Japanese making to jump overboard. As they launched themselves clear there was a dazzling flash of flame followed by a deafening explosion. The body of the soldier nearest to them was thrown upwards with pieces of fabric and flesh flying away. It landed with a belly flop in the river and didn't move.

The boat itself was ablaze, the wooden hull a cauldron of fire. Ammunition was exploding, popping in the extreme heat, and now the engine's power had gone the current slowly took it and started pulling it downstream, gathering speed as it went.

Philip pulled himself up and jumped into the river, splashing to where the Gurkha had thrown himself into the water. Hauling him to his feet he quickly scanned his body for signs of wounds and it was only when he looked into his face that he relaxed, a large grin fixed to the man's face.

"That was very brave, Rifleman Balbir," he said, resting a hand on the man's shoulder and squeezing. "Bloody stupid but very brave."

He glanced over his shoulder and was relieved to see movement from behind the teak stump.

"Get over there and help them," he yelled.

Men piled down the bank and waded back into the water, assisting and dragging the rest onto the beach. Philip walked over to where Prem was sitting panting in the shallows, blood running down his face from a wound high on his forehead.

"Two dead with me," he panted between breaths. "And another has a bad wound in the arm." He stared down at the fine silt of the river bed that sucked at his feet. "They were from my village. We grew up together. One was my cousin."

Philip nodded and tentatively reached his hand out towards the corporal's shoulder, unsure what to say. Prem pushed himself up, composing himself, so that instead Philip quickly pointed towards the corporals own wound. It was met with a dismissive shake of the head. "Nothing. Just a graze."

He shoved his revolver back into its holster and glanced around at his men. They looked dazed and exhausted. No wonder. He knew that the Gurkhas were a close-knit group, but if they'd all grown up together then these deaths were going to hurt badly. Best, he thought, to keep them distracted. "Five minutes. We'll dress the wounds and then head off. We'll have every Jap between here and Mandalay coming this way after that little explosion."

He turned and walked over to where his pack lay abandoned in the jungle. Christ. Four more dead, another two injured. If it hadn't been for the heroics of Balbir they'd have lost five more. He rubbed his face, pretending to scratch his stubble but trying to keep his jaw from trembling. He should have waited, waited until nightfall or made them cross the previous night, however exhausted they'd been. He was a bloody fool.

CHAPTER 9

Nepal, 1953

The next morning Philip was woken at daybreak and after a mug of bed tea he got dressed and went out to join James in the small Mess tent. He was feeling rested, having slept deeply, undisturbed by nightmares. He didn't know why, but after his evening with Lhamu and her family, it felt like a break through.

"Nothing new," was James reply when asked if he'd learnt anything of interest from Hunt the previous day. "I'm pretty sure he knows which of the climbers he's going to use for the summit attempt but damned if he'll tell me. Don't really see what harm it could do and the climbers must know themselves by what they've been told to practise. I've noticed Bourdillon and Charlie Evans practising together so I reckon they've got a shot at it."

He paused as he finished off the last of his eggs, wiping his plate clean with a piece of flatbread. "I wanted them for the code I've been working on. Here." He pulled a piece of paper from his leather notebook that lay beside him on the table and slid it across to Philip. It was a list of names and phrases. "A radio message is quick but not secure. The transmissions from Namche go to the Indian Embassy in Kathmandu where anyone could get hold of it. A bit of baksheesh in the right palm." He took a gulp of coffee. "Even my runners might get tempted to hand over a dispatch bag if they're offered silly money. I couldn't really blame them as £50 is more than they earn in a year."

He leant across the table and pointed to a name on the list. "So, if my message contains the phrase "Ridge Camp untenable" it means that Charlie has got to the top. It is reads "Advance Base abandoned" it means that Hillary's made it. This way, it'll only make sense to you, Hutch and the office in London. Nobody else will be any the wiser, just thinking it's a normal update." He smiled at Philip. "Not bad, eh?"

Philip nodded, running his finger down the list.

"That copy's for you," James continued. "Take it with you and keep it safe. If you take it to Kathmandu and give it to Hutch then we'll know for sure that nobody else has the code. He'll then decipher the message and send on the real message to London."

Mingma entered the tent and smiled at both men. "We are ready Philip," he said. "The equipment is packed and the porters are just leaving."

Philip nodded and stood, offering his hand to James. "I'll let you know what happens when I finally catch up with Izzard."

"It's been a pleasure having you here," James replied, shaking the hand. "Hopefully next time we meet we can share a cold beer and toast the success of both the expedition and our exclusive report."

It was a cold morning. Clouds were sitting on the mountains, keeping out the morning sun and a breeze moved the leaves of the nearby larch trees. Mingma picked up Philips rucksack and held it for him as he slipped his arms through the leather straps and secured it onto his back.

"How long until we reach Khunde?" he asked as they walked through the village, waving as he noticed the boy Sarkey staring at him from the doorway of Karma's house.

"It will take about five to six hours," Mingma replied. "You are fit now and starting to walk like a Sherpa."

Philip laughed. "I don't think I'm quite that fast, but at least I remembered not to ask how far it was!"

At the start of the trek he'd always want to know how far it was to the next camp, a concept that meant little to Mingma. He'd grown up knowing that the mountains were so vast that you could be climbing up to a ridge one day, and then dropping to a valley floor the next. The distances were the same, but the ascent took twice as long. That was why distances were measured in time.

They passed the rough stone wall of engraved mani stones that marked the edge of the village and the trail immediately fell away on the long descent to the river far below. Prayer flags flapped in the wind and glancing back at the village before it disappeared from view he saw Sarkey cautiously raise his hand in a timid wave before turning and fleeing back down the street.

They continued in silence for an hour or so, moving quickly down the well maintained path. They soon overtook Old Gompu and the porters, who'd stopped to adjust their loads to get the balance even. Without the sun it was a comfortable temperature and with the steady descent Philips thoughts wandered back to Lhamu. He'd wanted to pop in to say goodbye as they'd passed her house, but he realised that she'd be at the monastery, helping with the guests. He felt confused. He'd only met her the day before and yet already he felt at ease with her, something he hadn't experienced towards a woman since he'd returned from the war.

They came to a switchback in the trail where a stone ledge had been built into the upslope for passing porters to rest their loads and take a break. Leaving their rucksacks there, they stood on the edge of the trail above a sheer drop as Mingma pointed out to him the route they were to take.

"From the bridge you can see the path climbing up towards the top of the ridge opposite." He pointed across the valley to almost the same level as they were. "By that large rocky outcrop the trail splits. The trail to the south is the one we came along. It traverses the ridge before dropping to Namche. If you climb past the boulder to the right it leads to Khunde and the other upper villages. It's very steep and used..."

He stopped, interrupted by a strange noise rising up from the valley below. It came again, a hollow popping, then again and finally a burst of sound that bounced back off the mountains until it filled the valley with a continuous rumbling.

Philip recognised it immediately. "Gunfire," he said, more to himself than Mingma. He removed his hat and ran a hand through his hair, taking a moment to gather his thoughts. "Is there much hunting up here?"

Mingma shook his head. "None. We are Buddhists and do not kill animals."

"Of course," Philip mumbled. "I forgot, sorry. What about a festival or a funeral? Perhaps someone's letting off a few firecrackers?" He knew it wasn't. He'd heard gunfire many times and even after all these years he still knew its sound. It had been rifles; he guessed two or three of them and a then a couple of short bursts of automatic fire. He tried to think. James hadn't sent out a courier that day so if couldn't be anything to do with the expedition and anyway, surely the other newspapers weren't so desperate for the story they'd kill for it? He looked down the valley, trying to fix the point from where the shooting had come.

"It came from near the bridge," he said at last, pointing down towards the river. "If you wanted to ambush someone then that would be the best place. Everybody has to cross the river there, there's no other option."

He turned and returned to his rucksack. "Come on. We'd better go and see what's happened."

They walked on in silence, moving quickly and sure-footedly down the trail. The forest had engulfed them once more so that the only noise was the gentle rustling of the leaves in the breeze and the sound of their boots kicking out loose stones as they hurried on. Even at this pace it still took them the best part of an hour to reach the bottom of the valley. Here the trail flattened out and followed the river for a few minutes, contouring along its bank as it approached the bridge.

They slowed down, walking cautiously and keeping their eyes fixed ahead. The roar of the river drowned out everything. There was a rush of movement ahead and Philip threw himself into the thin scrub beside the trail, Mingma landing heavily beside him. Carefully raising his head he looked cautiously up and saw a yak ambling down the trail towards him, stopping occasionally to graze at the plants growing on the bank of the river. They pulled themselves up, brushing dust and leaves from their clothes. Philip laughed, a release of the tension that was racking his body. He was about to walk forward when Mingma grabbed his arm.

"Wait," said the Sherpa, sounding alarmed. "I recognise it. It's one of the yaks belonging to the Tibetan monks. They set off first think this morning."

Philip nodded. "Perhaps they've stopped to rest by the river and are letting them graze..." His voice tailed away as the creature wandered nearer. As it turned to graze the other side of the trail its other flank came into view. The animal's long, shaggy coat was plastered to its side by a large patch of congealing blood.

Without speaking, they slowly moved forward. The yak stared at them dolefully, its heavy load still balanced on its back, and when they got closer it was apparent that the blood didn't belong to the animal. They moved on and edged around a bend in the trail. Philip could now see the bridge ahead, a couple of hundred yards downstream. It was a large suspension bridge, built of heavy ropes supporting a floor of rough wooden planking, covered by a thin layer of packed earth. It looked deserted but he couldn't see where it joined the bank they were on, its end hidden behind a small rocky outcrop.

It felt wrong. They'd dropped out of the breeze and the air felt oppressive. With the exception of the river, everything was still. There were no birds flying in the thick foliage or perched on the rocks. Thick clumps of lichen hung down from the boughs of the rhododendron trees, making the woods look dark and sinister. Philip turned to Mingma and held his finger to his lips, before slowly moving along the trail, staying close to the fringe of the forest.

He could now feel an updraft of cold air coming from the icy river water as it roared past down the valley, the chill adding to his sense of foreboding. He kept his eyes forward, fixed on the furthermost point he could see. Another yak wandered past, almost knocking Philip over in its enthusiasm to reach some grazing in the forest behind.

Philip's mind was still trying to work out a plausible explanation for the gunfire. Perhaps it had come from a group of porters or traders from the Hindu lowlands who'd been out looking for game. Prem and the other Gurkhas might well have guns and would be happy to eat fresh, free meat. That didn't, however, explain why there were blood-stained yaks wandering around. His mind sharpened as they reached what he thought was the last corner in the trail before the bridge.

He felt his senses heighten, aware of every noise and movement. He could smell something. It was triggering something in his mind, something that was telling him to run. He sniffed the air again, his eyes scanning around for anything that looked out of place. A mantra he'd long forgotten flooded back into his head; *never tread on what can be stepped over. Never cut what can be broken. Never bend what can be moved.* He could sense that something wasn't right, wasn't natural. He just had to see it. He glanced down to the water, wondering if anything had been dropped or fallen from the trail and his eyes fell on something in the rushing water.

At first it didn't really register what he was seeing, just knowing that something wasn't right. Dropping his rucksack to the ground he crossed the path and scrambled down the steep slope to the river's edge, a narrow strip of boulders and silt that had been deposited there during the summer floods. Crouching down he put his fingers into the icy water and immediately realised what had caught his eye. The water here wasn't crystal clear. It had a pink tinge to it as swept past where he was kneeling, before quickly diluting and vanishing as it entered the main flow of the river.

He turned and slowly worked his way up stream, climbing on top of a large boulder that jutted out into the main river. Looking down he saw that behind it a small pool had formed where water from the main current got trapped, eddying around. In this, floating face-down, was the body of a man. The water around it was bright crimson, spiralling in the current and a small hint of this was being dragged out by escaping water into the main stream. It was this that Philip had noticed.

He slid down the rock, beckoning to Mingma to follow. The pool wasn't deep, reaching to just over his knees but he gasped as its icy temperature made his legs go numb. He grabbed the man's clothes and dragged him to the bank, trying to roll him over to get his face clear of the water. Mingma took hold of an arm and between them they dragged him onto a small silt beach.

Philip recognised him at once. It was the Llama, the Tibetan monk who'd been sitting next to the Abbot at the feast in Thangboche the day before. His distinctive yellow and purple robes clung to his thin body, a silver ring with a large piece of engraved coral still on a white, shrivelled finger. A neat hole, still seeping blood, showed where he'd been shot in the head, just above the ear.

Philip and Mingma looked up at each other, too shocked to speak. Mingma glanced up towards the trail, fear in his eyes and Philip, realising the danger they were in, grabbed his arm and pulled him over the body. They scrambled backwards until the large boulder hid them from view, sitting on the beach, leaning up against it.

It was Mingma who spoke first, shouting above the roar of the river into Philip's ear. "It's one of the Tibetan monks," he said, shaking his head in disbelief.

Philip nodded grimly. "Somebody certainly wanted him dead." He nodded towards the body. "That shot to the head was done at close range; you can see the burns from the muzzle flash. It looks as though he was executed and his body thrown down into the river."

Mingma looked shocked. "But who would do it? He was a holy man, a higher incarnation."

Philip shrugged. "I don't know but it wasn't robbery." He pointed to the ring. "Whoever did it knew exactly what they were after and didn't hang around afterwards to loot anything." He glanced around. "We cannot stay here; we're sitting ducks if whoever did this is still around." He pointed up the slope. "We need to get up above the trail. That way we can approach the bridge in the forest without being seen. We need to find out what's happened to the other monks, see if there are any survivors."

Mingma nodded, following Philip as he climbed cautiously back up to the path. After a quick glance in each direction they sprinted across and threw themselves into the undergrowth. They lay still for a few seconds, ears straining to hear anything above the water, before Philip slowly pushed himself up and started to scramble up into the forest.

The slope was steep and the thick undergrowth kept snagging on his clothes. Philip swore silently as one branch scratched a painful cut in his forearm. After about thirty yards the gradient eased and a thin ledge, formed where a softer stratum of rock had eroded away, seemed to run off parallel to the river. Crouching, Philip examined it and realised it was used by animals as a pathway, probably deer which he'd seen quite frequently crossing the trail. He beckoned Mingma to follow him up before turning and carefully setting off along the game trail.

It was slow going. The surface was loose and they had to tread carefully, trying to avoid sending small stones bouncing down the slope onto the path below. The forest got thicker, low branches obstructing their way and the hanging curtains of lichen blotting out any view. Frequently they had to climb over or duck under boughs or push through thick foliage. At least, Philip reassured himself, the river would drown out the racket they must be making.

After a couple of minutes the path started to descend and as it did so the trees thinned. Philip slowed, his body tense and eyes constantly scanning ahead. Something moved, catching his eye and he stopped, holding up his hand to

Mingma and then pointing down. He could see movement through the leaves, but didn't have a clear view it. He crept forward, stopping when a small break in the undergrowth revealed a man, his back turned to them, searching the body of a monk that lay sprawled across the trail in a pool of blood. The man stood up and walked further down the trail, kneeling again beside what Philip assumed was another body.

Philip edged forward, the path dropping until it ran parallel with the main trail, about ten feet above it, along the top of a small bluff that was a continuation of the rocky outcrop. Looking down he could see the man was still absorbed in searching the bodies which lay all around. He beckoned Mingma to join him and they looked out over the carnage. He counted seven dead monks, some lying on the trail, others half hidden in the undergrowth. Most had been shot, while others seemed to have been beaten or slashed with knives. Philip felt nausea rise inside him, the smell of blood and sight of death making him dizzy.

He felt a hand on his shoulder and spun round, fist raised to strike out. It was Mingma. He'd forgotten where he was and shook his head, spitting the taste of bile from his mouth.

"He is not armed," whispered the Sherpa, looking down the trail. "When he comes up the path we'll wait until he is passed the rock and then jump on him. He will not hear us over the river."

Philip nodded, the words sounding distant and cumbersome. He took several deep breathes, trying to regain control of himself. Mingma squeezed his arm, nodding towards where the trail emerged and glancing up, Philip saw a shape walk below them. He felt Mingma's body explode past him and instinctively followed, flashing from the dark of the undergrowth into brilliant sunlight.

The man had no idea what was happening. Mingma hit him full on the shoulder with his knee and sent him crashing to the ground. Before he could draw breath Philip landed on top of him as well, knees slamming into the small of his back. They pulled his arms back, which the man had instinctively raised to break his fall, and roughly tied them behind him with the silk scarf the abbot had given Philip the previous day. Philip quickly frisked him for weapons and finding nothing, stood up. Mingma gripped the man's shoulder and rolling him over. The man was gasping for air, still recovering from being winded in the attack, face dirty and bloodied where it had slammed into the rocky ground. It took Philip a few moments to recognise him but as realisation dawned he found himself looking down into the terrified face of Tashi Banagee.

Philip stared at him, speechless. Tashi rolled onto one side and spat a mouthful of blood onto the ground. "Don't kill me," he pleaded, still breathless. "I'll say nothing..." He paused, desperately sucking in air and squinted up into Philip's face. "It's you," he spluttered, confusion sweeping his face. His head fell back onto the ground, his body relaxing. "Thank God. I thought the soldiers had returned and were going to waste me." He rolled himself up into a sitting position and rolled his neck painfully."

Philip studied him in silence, perplexed as to what the Calcutta trader was talking about. Tashi's eyes fixed on him and realisation swept his face. "You think this was me?" he asked, incredulously. "That I shot these people and then decided to hang around for someone to turn up?"

Philip continued to stare, trying to understand something of the chaos. Finally he replied. "These monks were carrying a priceless Tibetan artefact. The kind of thing an antiquities dealer would," he raised his eyebrows, "kill for."

Tashi shook his head vehemently. "No. You are wrong. I was camping a little way downstream from the bridge," he said, flicking his head down the valley. "I arrived here yesterday and decided to stay. There is a small beach about a hundred yards downstream that's soft to sleep on. An overhang in the bank gives me shelter. I thought it would be a good place to meet refugees as they cross the river. I brew some tea on a small fire, offer some food and buy what they have to sell." He looked Philip in the eyes. "Precious stones. Some old Thankas, maybe some jewellery. That's all."

He spat more blood from his mouth, wiping his chin on his shoulder. "I heard the shooting from my camp and stayed hidden in the rocks. After an hour or so, when everything was quiet again I came out and found this." He shook his head. "I was trying to help, seeing if anyone was still alive, when you jumped me." He looked around, shaking his head. "If you want my two-cents worth, whoever did this knew what they were doing and were packing some pretty serious fire-power."

"Did you see anybody?" Mingma asked, distrust bristling in his voice.

Tashi shook his head. "Whoever it was were long gone by the time I arrived." He nodded down the trail. "But the monk I just left is still alive, although not for long. You could try asking him. I was just going to get him some water."

Philip dragged Tashi to his feet and pushed him ahead of

them, letting him lead them to the body of a young monk. He'd been badly beaten. His robes were soaked in blood which ran from wounds that covered his body. His face was almost unrecognisable; his nose smashed, an eye bruised and closed and with blood trickling from an ear. Mingma kneeled beside him and pulling round his water bottle from where it hung, carefully dribbled a little water into the monk's mouth. For a few seconds nothing happened, then the young man's eyes flickered and he gagged, the water running pink from the corner of his mouth.

Mingma said something to him but there was no reply, just the laboured rattle of the man's breathing. The Sherpa leant forward and said the same thing again. The monk looked surprised and then relaxed as his eyes focused on the young guide's face. Philip saw the man's lips move, more watery blood running down his cheek.

"Rinpoche," was the only word Philip could make out, the rest was too quiet to hear.

Mingma leant down until his ear was almost touching the man's lips. He listened intently, waiting patiently as the man spluttered and gasped for air between words. A couple of times he asked what sounded like questions. Both times the young man gave hardly perceptible nods.

After less than a minute Mingma slowly sat back up, and Philip could see that the Sherpa's body was shaking. With a trembling hand he reached forward and gently closed the eyes of the monk which were now staring vacantly at the sky.

"Could you make out anything he said?" Philip asked.

The Sherpa nodded and got slowly to his feet. "It is very bad," he said, his voice cracking.

Philip was confused. He'd never seen Mingma so shaken, his face ashen grey.

"I'm sure the authorities will be able to recover this Kanjur," he said, trying to sound reassuring. "They've a long way to go to smuggle it out of the country. We'll send a message from the transmitter in Namche and get the authorities in Kathmandu to be on the lookout." He stopped and rubbed at the stubble on his chin. "From what I hear it's fairly large and distinctive to look at, so will be pretty hard to hide."

Mingma shook his head. "It's not the Kanjur." He paused, trying to compose himself. "That was just a decoy. The real treasure they were escorting wasn't a sacred book, it was a person."

Philip stared at the guide, not understanding what he meant. He looked back up the trail towards the body of the Llama they'd found in the river. "But who would want to kill a Llama, however important?"

"They didn't," replied Mingma. "He was only outwardly in charge, for appearances sake." He took a deep breath. "Whoever did this knew exactly what they were after." He shook his head. "It was the Rinpoche," he continued, "they've captured the Rinpoche."

There was a pause. "I'm sorry," Philip said, confused. "I still don't understand. Who's the Rinpoche?"

It was Tashi who answered. "He is one of the highest incarnations in Tibetan Buddhism. The Rinpoche is the Llama who is the public voice of the Dalai Lama, their sacred leader. Most importantly, he is the one who leads the search for a new Dalai Lama when the old one dies." He looked at

Philip and obviously seeing his confusion continued. "They believe that when the Dalai Lama dies he is reincarnated into the body of a baby or child. It is the Rinpoche who leads the search for this child, bringing with him the favourite possessions of the old one to see if any child recognises them. Without him it would be impossible to replace the current Dalai Lama when he dies."

Philip nodded slowly. "So what the hell was he doing here?" He rubbed his eyes. "Why was he trying to escape from Tibet?"

Mingma shook his head. "I don't know," he replied. "The monk died as he was trying to tell me."

Philip shook his head and walked off towards the bridge, trying to think amidst the slaughter. Bodies littered the path, making him tread carefully around sticky pools of congealing blood. One young monk had obviously put up a strong fight. His knuckles were bloody and raw from the punches he'd thrown but his skull was caved in from a heavy blow. He lay across one of the wooden crates they'd been carrying, about the size of a small suitcase. Its lid was ripped off, hanging by one hinge and lying open. Philip rolled the dead man off it and looked inside.

A cloth of shimmering yellow silk had been ripped aside to reveal a magnificent book. Philip reached forward and pulled the silken package out, the cloth falling smoothly away as he did so. He could feel a jagged edge where the front cover had been ripped off and turning it over saw that it had originally been bound in silver sheets, embedded with garnets and other jewels. A text of beautiful characters was written in sheet gold on parchment that had been dyed jet black. He flicked through, spellbound as intricate pictures and illuminations flashed past. It was the Kanjur, and other than being looted for its gem-encrusted cover, it had been left to rot.

Philip stood up, still holding the book, and was turning to return to the others when something else caught his eye. There was something lying partly covered by the broken box. He pushed it aside with his foot and bent to pick it up.

It was a cap, sticky with concealing blood. It was green, with a soft green peak above which was embroidered a large red star. He turned and brought it back to the others. Tashi, who was still sitting on the ground, took one look at it and spat on the ground.

"Chinese," he said. "It's part of the uniform of the Red Army."

Mingma stood up and snatched the cap. "They cannot just come over into our country and kill people."

Tashi shrugged. "From what I know of the Chinese Army, they do whatever they want. And this is important to them. If they have captured the Rinpoche they can make him talk to the people, even put their own Dalai Lama in charge instead of the old one. Then they'll have all Tibet under their control."

There was silence again. Philip looked around at the broken bodies and drying blood. A ray of sun broke through the clouds, bathing the valley in a warm light. He glanced up, captivated by the beautiful canopy of red flowers that covered the rhododendron forest. His eyes moving higher, to the meadows and glaciers of the upper valley and then to the soaring white peaks of the Himalayas themselves, glimpsing their wind-blasted summits high above the breaking layer of cloud. How could such terrible things happen in a place of such beauty? Scenes like this were understandable on a battlefield, after the desperation of battle. But here?

He'd looked down at the bodies of innocent victims before, at carnage beyond description or understanding. The last time he had been responsible for it and powerless to rectify what had happened. He wouldn't let that happen again.

He put his hand on Mingma's shoulder. "We need to get going. If there's to be any chance of them being caught we need to tell the authorities." He looked at the Sherpa. "You return to Thangboche and tell the abbot what's happened." He glanced back up the trail. "Take the ring from the dead Llama to show him. He will know if the Rinpoche really was among them." He nodded at the bodies. "Get the monks to come and fetch these bodies. At least they can be given proper funerals." He shook the Sherpa's shoulder and gave him a gentle push. "Go on, go. And hurry."

"Where will you be?" Mingma asked, looking at Philip.

"I'm going to the Police post in Namche to report it. I'll also try to get a message sent from the radio transmitter there to warn the authorities in Kathmandu."

"You-must-be-careful," Mingma stammered. "They-must have gone that way. We didn't meet them and there are no other ways." He looked at Philip. "If they are trying to get back to Tibet they must be taking the trail through the upper villages. That is the quickest way to the pass through the mountains." He paused, his mind starting to work again.

"How will you manage to communicate without me to translate? I doubt the police will speak any English."

"Don't worry about that," replied Philip, nodding towards Tashi. "I'll have our friend Mr Banagee here to keep me company. Now go."

Mingmo head off up the trail and when he was out of sight Philip reached into his jacket pocket and pulled out a penknife. He walked over to where Tashi was standing and turning him around, cut the scarf that still bound his hands.

The two men stood looking at each other, Tashi rubbing the circulation back into his wrists.

"I'm going to need your help." Philip said calmly. "You're lucky I didn't find you with this in your hands," he held up the ripped remains of the Kanjur, "or I'd have killed you."

The Indian looked at him, his eyes steady on Philips. "I make my living by trading things." he said, a steely edge to his voice. "Maybe I sometimes take advantage of people's desperation, maybe I just give them the money they need to survive, but that doesn't make me a murderer."

Philip returned the gaze and slowly nodded. He didn't trust the man, but realised he couldn't have killed all these men on his own. Nor would he have hung around so long afterwards when the Kanjur had obviously been discovered. "You're got five minutes. Go to you camp and get your things. Then we're off to Namche."

CHAPTER 10

The climb up from the river went on forever. Tashi had quickly returned from collecting his belongings and they'd set off in silence. If he felt insulted by the treatment he'd received he didn't show any ill-feeling, more concerned that they might catch up with the soldiers. At every switchback and turn in the trail they slowed and carefully checked the way ahead was clear before proceeding. Although the soldiers had a good two hour start, Philip was worried that some of them might have been injured during the ambush and had stopped, once clear of the scene, to dress their wounds. These fears, however, were unfounded despite spotting the occasional drop of blood on the ground.

Finally they passed the junction with the trail to the upper valley and soon after reached the small stone chortern that marked the top of the ridge. From here it was an easy descent into Namche. Everything was normal. People were going about their everyday business, women carrying firewood or fetching water. Children ran along the streets, playing and shouting loudly at each other. Some sheep grazed a small field, hemmed in by a gateway of thorns and two dzos walked along the main street, driven by an ancient man leaning in a thick stick he occasionally used to prod them.

Striding through, Philip dropped down some rough stone stairs to the street below and arrived at the house of Mingma's family. The door was wide open, as were the shutters on the windows, dusty bedding hanging over the sills to air. He entered, leaned his pack against the wall and looked around, his eyes taking several seconds to adjust to the darkness.

The lodge looked empty and he'd just started walking towards the door that partitioned off the families living area when he heard the bunk beds behind him creak as someone climbed off. A small man jumped down and held his hands together in greeting, his teeth visible in the half-light in a large smile. Philip stared through the gloom at the face.

"Ram," He said, recognising one of the Gurkhas and returning the greeting.

The Nepali bowed. "Sahib," he replied. "We did not expect to see you again so soon."

Philip grunted grimly. "And I didn't expect to be here." He ran his hand through his hair which was slick with sweat after the hard climb. "This might sound a bit strange but have you seen or heard any reports of any soldiers being seen today?"

The soldier looked confused but shook his head.

Philip nodded. "Good, now listen. I need your help. Can you take me to the Police post? I need to see the District Commissioner. I've got something urgent to report."

Ram nodded and turned, picking up his hat from the bunks before darting out into the bright sunlight. Philip followed him out and beckoned to Tashi who'd been waiting outside.

They hurried off after Ram who was waiting for them

beside a small alley that ran down the hillside to the lower town. In less than a minute, but after navigating a warren of small streets, they stood outside a large stone building with a bright blue sign nailed over the door. Carved into it was an impressive insignia.

"This is it, sahib," Ram said, pointing at the doorway as he backed up the track. "I must now return to the others. They will be sorting out the loads as we have bought all we can and are going to leave in the morning for home." He gave a small bow and hurried off.

"Thank you," Philip called after the disappearing Gurkha, before knocking on the door before him. There was no answer and it was only on the third attempt, which was more of a battering, that the door finally opened. In front of them stood a tiny man, obviously just woken, squinting blearily out at Philip.

"Good afternoon," Philip said. When there was no reply he continued slowly. "Do you speak English?" Again silence. "Tashi, I think I need your help," he said over his shoulder and the Indian walked forward.

"Namaste," he said in greeting, before starting a conversation with the rather bemused policeman who, during the course of it, ushered them through to a large bare room and indicated to them to sit on a rough wooden bench. The policeman sat behind a large desk, behind which, on the wall, hung a large portrait of the King, and opened a heavy, leather-bound ledger. In this he started to take details as Tashi spoke.

After a few minutes of what Philip could tell were questions the man stood and went to another door. Opening it, he yelled something and moments later two young policemen, both dressed in rather worn and dirty uniforms, came hurrying through.

Tashi turned to Philip. "He says he cannot do anything until the felony has been confirmed. He's sending these two men down to the bridge to check our story. I've told him it will cause too much delay but he insists that it's the correct procedure." He shook his head. "He says it's too late to go today so they'll head off at first light."

"Damn it," Philip spat out. "I should have brought the army cap with me. At least that would've been some evidence. Can't he see how important this is?" He blew out his cheeks. "The Chinese will have at least a two day start by the time they get back from the river tomorrow and get themselves organised. There's no way they'll catch them."

Tashi nodded. "I've told him as much but what else can we do. He's in charge and I think the story sounds so nuts he doesn't believe us. Normally the worst crime they get here are disputes over sheep ownership and drinking too much Chang."

Philip was silent. "OK, thanks," he said at last. "Can you stay a little longer and see if you can persuade him to send the men tonight. At least they'll be ready quicker then. I'll meet you at the lodge in twenty minutes and then we'll go to find the radio transmitter. I need to get my Expedition accreditation as James said they'll only send messages for *The Times*. That'll serve as proof of ID."

Tashi nodded and resumed talking to the policeman as Philip excused himself, ducked out the front door and quickly retraced his steps to the lodge. As he approached he could see Prem and the other men standing outside, talking quietly together. When they saw him approach they fell silent, looking at him quizzically.

"Lieutenant," Prem said, tilting his head enquiringly. "Ram told us you were agitated." He looked at Philip. "Is there something wrong? He said you were asking about soldiers."

Philip looked around the familiar faces and nodded. "Bad news I'm afraid. We'd better go inside as I don't want too many people finding out or it could cause panic."

They filed after him through the door and sat quietly in as he told them what'd happened. It took some time as he had to pause occasionally to let Prem translate some of what he'd said to some of the Gurkhas who were was less fluent in English. They shuffled uneasily when he told them about what the dying monk had said. When he'd finished he sat while they discussed it in Nepali.

When they fell quiet Philip shrugged and sat forward. "The police aren't going to do anything until they've got proof but by then it'll be too late. My guide Mingma has gone to the monastery in Thangboche to confirm the story about the Rinpoche. If it's true, then God help the Tibetans."

He stood and walked to his bag, starting to untie the straps. "I've just come for some ID and them I'm off to the Indian Radio Station to try to get a message to Kathmandu. God knows what I'll say but there's little else I can do."

There was a silence as the men took this in, followed by a brief conversation. Philip pulled his wallet from his bag and turned just in time to see Prem stand and turn to him.

"What can we do?" he asked in a steady voice.

Philip stared at him. "What do you mean?"

"While we are waiting for the police, there must be something we can do to assist."

Philip nodded. "Well, to start with they'll need information. The soldiers must be heading back to the Tibetan border. As they didn't come through here or go to Thangboche, they must have taken the trail to the villages above Namche. There's no way that they could've gone that way in daylight and not been seen. The police will need to know when they were there, how many there were and which way they were going. That way they'll be able to work out where they're headed."

Prem said something to the other nine men in Nepalese. They got up and quickly filed out of the door. The corporal followed and Philip heard him give some brisk orders and watched through the open windows as the men set off in pairs up the street. Philip followed them outside and as the last ones disappeared around the corner Prem turned to him.

"I've sent them up to the villages. They will be quick and be back by sunset. We will know then if the soldiers have passed that way. Is there anything else we can do?"

Philip shook his head. "Thank you Prem, I can't think of anything. We'll just have to see what we find out and then pass it on to the police when they finally confirm what's happened."

Prem looked at him inquisitively. "What of your own job? Will this not interfere with your work with the newspaper?"

Philip shrugged. "It's not ideal, but what can I do? A

couple of days shouldn't matter too much. It'll be at least three to four weeks until the Expedition will be ready to attempt the summit so there shouldn't be any news of note to transmit back to Kathmandu. I'll just have to hope that if there is, his radio blows up."

Prem nodded and turned, heading off in pursuit of his friends. Philip looked at his watch. It was half an hour since he'd left Tashi at the Police station. Perhaps he'd thought they were meeting at the Indian Radio Station. He checked his ID letter was in his wallet and set off, before realising that he'd no idea where the transmitter was located. Working on the assumption that the higher the aerial was placed the better the signal, he began climbing up through the small town. The sun, which had briefly appeared in the middle of the day, was now hidden again behind a blanket of white cloud, the wind blowing an icy chill through the narrow streets that soon had Philip shivering.

After twenty minutes of wandering he was about to give up when he noticed the tip of a tall mast peeping above the roofs of the nearest houses and finding a flight of steps that climbed in that direction he set off. Soon he was standing outside a large stone enclosure that seemed to consist of a high wall surrounding an open courtyard. From its centre rose the tall aerial, anchored by four long wires which ran from the corners of the enclosure to half-way up the mast. Beside a large double door was nailed a sign, written in both Nepali and English. It read "The Government of India. Radio Communications. Namche Bazaar Branch. Director: Mr A. Tiwali."

Philip pushed at the door but found it locked. He was

just lifting his hand to knock when he heard someone calling his name and turning, saw Tashi struggling up behind him.

The Indian caught him up, standing with his hands on his knees as he panted from the exertion. "Sorry I'm late," he gasped. "The policeman offered me tea and I thought it prudent to accept and not appear rude. I tried to convince him to send off the men but he refused. I then requested that he radioed for help but he told me it wasn't possible." He shook his still lowered head, waving a hand towards the closed door. "Apparently the operator has gone away for a few days. He's had to return to the road head to pick up some delicate parts for the radio that he didn't trust the local porters with."

Philip looked at the doors again. "Damn it!" he said, turning and kicking at a loose rock that lay on the path. "Can anything else go wrong? Looks like we'll just have to wait for the local police to check it out."

They walked in silence back to the lodge. They found Mingma's mother had relit the fire to cook supper and Philip sat wearily beside it. He yawned and stretched, trying to straighten out some of his tired muscles. He felt exhausted, a combination of the exertions of the day combined with the shock of what he'd seen. He couldn't get the massacre by the bridge out of his mind. Whoever had killed the monks had done a ruthless job. He guessed that the younger monks were picked for their strength and martial art skills. For them to be brushed aside so easily meant they must've been seriously outnumbered and outgunned.

He smiled and nodded his thanks as the old lady handed him a bowl of rice and lentils, a sprinkling of chilli on top.

He started to eat, his mind still down by the river. He winced as the chilli stung his dry lips, the spice burning into the open cracks in them. He heard the door open and a blast of freezing air swept into the room. Glancing up over the rim of his bowl he saw Mingma enter and hurry over to warm his hands by the fire.

The door was still open and Philip had just got up to close it when he came face to face with another person entering, silhouetted by the evening sky. It was Lhamu. His mouth dropped open but nothing came out. She looked at him and nodded, closing the door behind her without looking away.

"Namaste," she said, her dark eyes flashing in the firelight. "I'm pleased you are safe. I am sorry it is not for happier reasons that we meet again."

Philip smiled and gestured for her to join them by the fire. They were both given Tibetan tea by Mingma's mother and started telling Philip all that had happened.

"I climbed back to Thangboche; I was almost running because of fear. When I got there I went straight to the abbot and showed him the ring." Mingma shook his head. "He went pale and collapsed. Fortunately Lhamu was with us and we managed to catch him and carry him to a bench."

"The monk was telling the truth then. The Rinpoche was with them?" Philip cut in impatiently, looking at the Sherpani.

She nodded slowly, appearing to be translating in her head what she wanted to say next. "He was. It had been decided in Lhasa that he must go to the United Nations and ask for help against the Chinese. The Dalai Lama and the other Tibetan leaders are watched constantly and kept prisoner in their homes. The Rinpoche was allowed to travel to Shigatze for his father's funeral and his escape was planned. With the help of the Head Lhama and monks from the monastery there he managed to slip away and cross to Thangboche." She stopped and looked into the embers. "There have been reports that the monastery at Shigatze has been destroyed by the Chinese when they found out, with monks lying dead in the streets."

She sipped her tea. "They were very tired when they arrived at the monastery as they had been travelling very fast. That is why they rested for a day. They believed they had escaped and were safe. The story of the sacred book was a way to explain their journey without making people suspicious."

Mingma pulled the blood-stained hat out of his pocket and held it up in the firelight. "I showed them this. They recognised it immediately as several of the monks went to Lhasa to visit the Jokung Temple last year. It's definitely Red Army."

"Did the abbot know where they'd crossed the border when they came?" Philip asked, taking the hat. "If they were being tracked then you'd expect the Chinese to return by the same route."

Lhamu nodded. "They crossed the Nangpa la. It's a high pass through the Himalaya that is used by Tibetan traders. There are no checkpoints or police there. It is so high that it's impossible for most people to climb over it. Only the hardiest will do so." She looked at Philip. "This is where the Chinese lost them. After crossing the pass the monks took a short cut to Thangboche over a smaller pass. The Chinese missed this and went straight down the valley towards Namche. They must have realised their mistake and turned back, waiting by the river to ambush them as they came down the other valley." She sat up straight. "That is why I've come. I travelled over the Nangpa la on several trading trips with my father so I know the route. I will help guide the rescue."

Philip looked at her and shook his head. "That's far too dangerous," he said. "These soldiers are cold blooded killers. They wouldn't think twice about shooting you or the Nepalese police. I can't let you take such a risk. I'd never forgive myself if something happened."

Lhamu stared at him, narrowing her eyes in annoyance. "Luckily for you it is not your choice. The Head Llama at Thangboche has blessed me for this trip and it is my duty. You need not worry. It is not your responsibility so you have no blame to take if things go badly."

"It's irrelevant anyway," Philip replied, looking away from her glare. "The police won't believe us without proof and they won't check the story until tomorrow. By then the Chinese will have all but escaped and there won't been the need for a guide.

Lhamu stood up and reached inside her apron, pulling out the abbot's ring. She held it up and took the soldiers cap from Mingma. "In which case, I had better take these along to the police now. Perhaps with them I will be able to convince them." She turned towards the door but before she could move was stopped by a voice.

"Let me take them." It was Tashi, who'd be quietly sitting in the corner of the room, drinking chang. He stubbed out a beedi. "After my brown-nosing this afternoon I seem to now be on good terms with the commissioner. Perhaps with these items I can get him to act or at least send for reinforcements. That way you can eat your food while it's still hot. " He smiled. "If necessary I'll come and fetch you if he wants to hear your evidence."

There was a pause as Lhamu studied him suspiciously, before glancing quizzically across at Philip as if not exactly sure what the Indian had said.

Philip nodded. "Good idea. Tashi was there this afternoon with me. Give them to him and he can go. You rest and eat after your walk."

Lhamu gave the two items to Tashi, who drained his cup and strode out into the night.

They all ate hungrily, Philip gratefully accepting a second helping. A bowl of boiled potatoes was put in front of them, together with a small plate of salt, for them to take, as well as some dried fruit. They chatted as they ate. The monks had returned to the river with Mingma as soon as they'd been told what had happened and gathered the bodies. Each had been sewn into a heavy cloth that was then tied to a long pole. As he and Lhamu had started the climb to Namche, the column of monks started carrying their burden in the opposite direction, the mournful sound of ritual chanting echoing through the valley.

They'd just finishing their meal when the door opened and looking up Philip saw Prem and the Gurkhas enter. He stood and beckoned them over to warm themselves by the fire. Soon they too were seated, eating the meal and drinking greasy butter tea.

In between large mouthfuls Prem told them what they'd discovered. "As soon as we arrived at Syanboche we could tell something was wrong. There was nobody about. Everybody was shut up in their houses." He nodded towards one of the other men who Philip recognised as Lal, one of his old lance corporals. "Fortunately Lal has done business there with one of the local traders so we went to his house." He shook his head. "It took several minutes before he would even let us in."

He looked at Philip. "You are right. The soldiers were there. They must have passed at night when they went through the first time. The dogs barked but the villagers assumed it was a bear or yeti. But they returned today, travelling fast. They pointed their guns at the children and told everybody to go into their houses and stay there until dark."

"Did they say how many there were?" Philip asked, his face grim.

"He thought around twenty, but was not sure. Other people we saw later said more." Prem put his bowl down on the floor. "But they did agree that they had a prisoner with them, a young monk whose face was swollen and bloody. His hands were tied in front of him and he was being pulled along by a rope tied to his belt."

There was silence.

"Did the villagers see which direction they were going?" asked Lhamu, gazing at the ex- soldier intently.

Prem nodded. "They were heading west. We left the village and made our way to Khunde village where we discovered the same thing. Here the soldiers had stolen chickens and rice." He looked down. "We also found the body of an old man who'd been shot trying to stop them. They are heading to the Nangpa La."

"What time did they go through Khunde?" Philip asked.

"The villagers said it was early afternoon," Prem replied. "By now they will be approaching the Nangpa Glacier. They will follow this up to the pass and into Tibet."

A silence fell, everybody lost in their thoughts. The room was warm, everybody was full after their meal but there was a tension that kept them alert.

"When do we move out?" a voice said. Glancing up the dark room Philip made out the squat, thick-set outline of Balbir looking at him expectantly. He'd been little more than a boy when he'd served in Burma and still looked fresh faced now.

Philip looked around the faces of his old platoon. They all stared back at him and he recognised a determination that had helped them survive before. He tried to breathe calmly. He'd sworn never to take responsibility for people's lives again. He looked at Lhamu, her eyes locked onto his, hope gleaming from them.

He took a deep breath and cleared his throat, wanting his voice to sound strong. "This isn't our fight," he said looking round the men. "You're no longer in the army. I'm no longer your officer."

There was murmuring amongst the men and Prem shook his head. "We will always be Gurkhas." He looked around at the others, several of whom were nodding to urge him on. "There was a reason we survived and a reason why you came back with us. We cannot escape our destiny. We live with

Sherpas, we trade with Tibetans. They are our friends, and we will help them now."

He turned and spoke to one of the men called Lalit. "We'll need shelter for the high mountains. See if you can find something."

Lalit stood up but before he could leave Mingma spoke. "We have shelter." He looked at Philip. "Old Gompu has arrived with your equipment. If we take the Mess tent we can all sleep in it. It will be warmer all together. We can split it between us to keep down the weight each of us has to carry."

Philip looked around, realising the decision had been made. "But we have no supplies. And what are we going to fight them with? Snow balls?"

A discussion started amongst the men, ending with Lalit and a young Gurkha called Giri hurrying out of the door. Giri, Philip remembered, had always been the best shot in the platoon.

"They will find some," said Prem calmly. "And we still all have these," he added, drawing his khukri from its battered wooden scabbard.

Philip leant back against the wall, resignation washing through him. He looked at Lhamu and smiled weakly. "I suppose you still want to come?"

She looked back at him, her face serious. "I have always felt envious of my father for the adventures he had when he was young. Distant places, strange peoples, excitement." She looked back at him. "Now it is my turn."

"Once we head off from Namche we'll be all on our own," Philip said in a firm voice. "We can hope that the

Nepalese police, maybe even their army, come to help when they've finally worked out what's happened but there's no guarantee." He glanced around all the faces in the room. "We could be ambushed or stuck in a storm with no way of calling for help."

He stopped as he heard someone chuckling and looking up saw Prem beaming back at him.

"That's not strictly true," said the Gurkha. "There was something else I hadn't got round to telling you. We found something else at Khunde. It was the camp site of the Englishman you spoke about. From the newspaper that is not yours."

Philip felt his body tense. "Christ! Izzard. Was he OK?"

Prem nodded and gave a dismissive wave of the hand. "He was fine. He was locked in the house of the village headman for safety. So we took the opportunity to look in his tents and Parul found something of use." The corporal said something in Nepalese and a stocky man Philip remembered having been his Radio Operator stood up and disappeared across to the bunks. After a few seconds he returned with a radio set.

Philip stared open mouthed.

"So you see," continued Prem happily, "we do have communications and at the same time your Englishman has none."

CHAPTER 11

Burma, 1943

He pointed at the tattered map that lay unfolded on a moss-covered log. "The village is about 400 yards ahead. You can see the river bed through the trees over there." He pointed to a small gap in the foliage through which white boulders, bathed in sunlight, could be seen. "It's to the north, on the western bank." He looked around the drawn faces, smeared with grime and streaked with sweat. "Corporal Prem, take two men and the burrif and approach the village. If it looks clear, go in and find the headman. Send a man back for us."

The corporal nodded.

"The rest of you, at ease. No fires though. That's all."

They moved off, slumping down where they could find space, too tired even to remove their packs. Philip wearily pulled out his groundsheet and after dropping it still folded to the ground collapsed on top of it. He leant against the log, his head resting back on it and closed his eyes. He didn't know whether he was more hungry or more tired. Christ, he hoped this village would sell them something.

They'd been lucky at the start of the expedition. The Burmese had been happy to see British soldiers, and they'd often been given the food they required. Recently it had been a different story. The villagers were scared. The Japanese checked on them frequently, staying in their villages and threatening them with execution should they help the enemy. For three weeks they'd got nothing, the burrifs returning empty-handed each time, despite silver rupee coins and parachute silk being offered in payment. With the failure of the supply drops and no way to arrange any more they were on the verge of exhausting their supplies. They were starving anyway. Philip reached inside his shirt to examine a painful bite on his side and felt his fingers running up and down his protruding ribs.

The bite was from a large bull leech that had attached itself to his side. Bloated to the size of a large, ripe plum, he took out a match and carefully burnt it until it released its grip. The last thing he wanted was to rip it out and leave its jaws still attached to him, as they'd fester and quickly become an infected sore. Could have been worse he thought to himself grimly. Earlier in the expedition one of the other junior officers, now dead, had found one attached to his testicles.

He dozed, the ache of his constricted stomach no match for the exhaustion of his body. It was Christmas. In front of him as a table covered in a starched linen table cloth, silver cutlery and bone china. A goose was being carved, he couldn't see by whom as his eyes were transfixed by the slices of succulent meat falling before the knife. The smell flooded his senses and looking down he saw his plate was piled with thick wedges of meat, drowned in rich, dark gravy. He knew it was bad manners but he reached out to grab his fork but it vanished as his fingers closed on it. He didn't care, he shoved his hand into his plate but the food had gone.

He woke confused, ripped back to the present. Gunfire. His mind cleared instantly. It was rifle fire, no more than seven or eight rounds. All around his men were alert, crouching, staring outwards into the surrounding jungle with raised rifles.

Philip called over his shoulder as he peered towards the river. "Is the corporal back?"

"No sir," the nearest Gurkha replied, coming to kneeling beside him.

Philip rubbed his eyes, trying to get the last of the sleep out of them. Damn it. There must've been enemy in the village. He tried to think, attempting to shake food from his mind. After the river crossing the previous day they'd pushed on hard to get away from the river. All day they'd had no contact with the enemy and Philip's hopes had slowly grown as the day had worn on that the burning boat had drifted far enough downstream to confuse the Japs as to their exact crossing point.

As dusk had fallen they'd stopped. The men had been exhausted. He'd ordered them to light fires and boil water so they could drink and clean each other's wounds and injuries. He'd also let them cook the strips of mule meat they'd taken earlier. Better, he thought, to eat it while it was fresh than have it go rancid in the stifling heat and humidity. The smell of roasting meat would carry a long way but he'd just have to risk it. The men needed something or he thought they'd might just lie down on the dead leaves of the jungle floor and sleep. God knows he wanted to.

With some mule meat inside them, accompanied by hot tea with some of the remaining milk powder and sugar, their spirits had risen. The mule meat had been a revelation, quite tasty when roasted rather than boiled. Philip suspected that this judgement may have been influenced by the fact that he was starving, but he certainly preferred it to boiled python and the unpalatable bull frog.

They'd bivvied on a small knoll in the middle of a large area of jungle bog. The security it offered meant Philip took the risk of setting only one sentry at a time, allowing everybody to get a decent rest. He'd spent the evening delousing his clothes with the help of burning twigs from the fire and the blade of his knife, which he'd scraped down the seams. Every time the flame hissed and spat as it incinerated one he'd chuckled to himself happily. When he pulled his shirt back on it felt like new; dry, crisp and much less itchy.

That morning they'd moved on to their current position, near a large but remote village in the hope they'd have food to sell. He'd looked at his maps, piecing together what remained of some of the sheets that had been packed away and damp for weeks. Another eight days he reckoned, given no enemy encounters, until the Chindwin River and home. Given the state of the men it was probably nearer ten, especially as they were going to have to scavenge for food as they went. He scratched idly at a weeping scab on his neck, wincing as he accidentally pushed the clasp of his small St. Christopher into the raw flesh. In a burst of anger he ripped it from his neck, throwing it down on the maps.

"Bloody thing," he spat out, not caring who heard. "At least a fruit cake would have been useful."

Philip checked his watch, a present from his sister on his eighteenth birthday and still working beautifully after all it'd been through. It was late afternoon, a couple of hours until sunset. After being caught by the Japanese the previous day he didn't want to be attacked in daylight again. He tried not to think about what the Japanese would be doing to his men if they'd been captured.

"We'll move a few hundred yards back into the jungle and wait until dusk," he ordered. "Then we'll move in on the village."

He gathered together his gear and led the remnants of his platoon back into the thick undergrowth. He couldn't settle but sat fidgeting with his compass, checking and rechecking the bearings of their next march. When and if the moment came, he wanted to be able to get away quickly. They'd been give strict instructions when they'd received the order to return to India to avoid all engagements with the Japanese. Yet here he was, preparing to attack a village where he knew the enemy were. Sod it. His men were there. Surely that order wasn't meant to include situations like this? Anyway, he thought grimly, if they succeed no one will care, if they fail, no one would know.

He tried to calm himself, leaning back against a teak trunk and closing his eyes. Taking deep breaths, he imagined he was being called through into the treatment room, the chiropodist removing his boots and gently massaging his feet with ointments and creams. They felt great, the skin clean and unmarked, no blisters, sores or rotting flesh to be seen or smelt. He sighed. His first stop on leave was there. Not a pub, not a restaurant but there. As the light began to fade he stood up and stretched, popping his last acid drop into his mouth. Its sour taste made him wince and sharpened his mind. It was time to go.

He led the men to the riverbed, turning north when he reached it but staying concealed in the forest. They got to a bend and Philip indicated for the men to remain there while he crept forward. A small paddy field appeared on the far bank, then others climbing back up the shallow slope of the valley where the jungle had been hacked back. Soon he was back.

"Leave your packs. We'll move quicker and quieter without them. Take guns, ammo and grenades."

The packs were piled behind the stump of a rotten tree and a couple of the men cut some large leaves with their khukri to cover them with. When they'd finished, Philip got them together.

"We'll move together until we reach the edge of the village." He said, looking around the faces of the seven remaining men. "Then we'll fan out to offer a range of fire should we need to open up. Tarun and Giri," he nodded at two of the men, "stay with me. You're good with your knives and I suspect they'll be needed. Chances are there are going to be more Japs than us so we'll need to use surprise, hit them quick and then get out again. I want the rest of you to cover our escape. Is that understood?"

The men nodded.

"Good. Best of luck everybody. If you get separated from the rest then rendezvous back here."

He turned and set off across the riverbed, the men falling in behind. It wasn't far, perhaps thirty yards, with only a small stream flowing down it, but to Philip it seemed to take a lifetime to cross. He kept his eyes upstream, looking for any sign of movement, but saw nothing.

Once over he kept by the bank of the river, pausing in a crouch when he arrived at the fields. The crops were high but not tall enough to give cover to a full-grown man. There was no sign of any houses but he decided to stay in the forest as long as possible. By circling to the west, keeping in the scrub that had been thinned by the grazing of the domestic animals, they could move quickly and quietly. They passed behind a small plantation of bananas and Philip fought the temptation to eat a few of the green fruits. Finally he saw the village no more than fifty yards ahead and he dropped down into the grass, gesticulating to the men where he wanted them to go. He was joined by Giri and Tarun and, heads raised just above the grass, lay quietly surveying the village.

There was little sign of life. He counted a total of fifteen huts, each built several feet clear of the ground on stout teak stilts. They were constructed of rough wooden planking and then thatched with a thick layer of dried grass. Chickens scraped at the dusty yard around them and from the dark spaces beneath several of the huts came the grunting of pigs. From the centre of the village rose a temple, a building that resembled a large stone bell about fifteen feet tall, standing on a three- tiered dais of worn bricks. A niche in one side housed the small statue of a deity, daubed with bright orange paint and garlanded with flowers.

Philip's eyes were drawn to a large discarded rattan mat on the far side of the clearing. It was crumpled, covering something that lay on the ground. He went cold as he made out a scuffed and battered army boot protruding out from one side. He watched as a cockerel strutted over to it and started pecking enthusiastically at its laces.

He focused his mind. If that was one of his men, the others must presumably still be alive or they'd have been dumped outside as well. The silence of dusk was abruptly rent by a scream that echoed through the village clearing. It was followed by muffled laughter that emerged from a large hut near the centre of the clearing, a thin trail of smoke rising through its thatch. As he watched, a figure stood up from the shadows of its veranda. There was a brief flicker of light that subsided to a tiny patch of orange. It was enough. He'd seen the face of a Japanese soldier lighting up a cigarette, presumably to while away the boredom of sentry duty.

He turned to Giri and without speaking pointed towards the sentry, drawing his other finger across his throat. The Gurkha was gone, moving silently through the village. Philip waited, hardly daring to watch. The sentry had descended the ladder – no more than a tall log with foot holes hacked into it – from the veranda and was slowly ambling around the clearing. A smudge of darkness appeared behind him and the speck of orange fell to the dirt. Within seconds Giri was back, wiping his khukri on a large leaf.

As dusk faded, a thin line of light could be seen around the hut door. He couldn't see any other guards in the shadows. Another scream pierced the evening.

"OK," whispered Philip. "We're going in." He checked his revolver. He advanced cautiously across the clearing, watching carefully where he trod. He could now hear muffled voices, Japanese and the occasional word of heavily accented

English. It was unintelligible. He glanced at the two Gurkhas and, satisfied with their positions, slowly climbed the ladder. Every footfall seemed to echo around the village. He reached the door and slowly stooped to look through a tiny gap in the wooden planking.

The hut was lit by a central fire and a hurricane lamp that hung hissing from a rafter. Also hanging from it was Prem. His hands were tied above his head and blood ran down his arms where the rope cut deep into his flesh. His back was raw and lacerated. Philip could see three Japs, one holding a bloody lash that hung from his hand to the floor, two others sitting on a wooden bench drinking from wooden cups. He could see their rifles leaning against the hut wall to their left. He heart was pounding so hard that his hands twitched with every beat. This was their chance. They were off guard and unarmed. He gently took hold of the latch and beckoned the Gurkhas up to his side. After a final glance through the crack he opened the door and stepped in.

The soldier with the lash was the nearest to him but had his back turned. One of the soldiers drinking tea had just turned to refill his cup. The third soldier glanced up at him, his eyes dropping to the strange uniform and revolver which at that moment exploded and sent him flying backwards into the fire. The man with the lash turned but before he could act Philip swung round and fired straight into his face. The back of his head erupted in a plume of blood and brain.

From the corner of his eye Philip saw that the third soldier had dived for his rifle. Everything seemed to slow. He started to swing his pistol but realised that he wasn't going to make it in time, the barrel of the Japanese rifle was already rising to his chest. There was an explosion of sound and Philip staggered back. He opened his eyes to see the man lying prone against the wall, flung there like a ragdoll. He glanced round and saw the grim face of Tarun staring down the smoking barrel of his rifle.

Giri drew his khukri and cut Prem down. The corporal grimaced as he took the weight on his bruised legs and gingerly massaged blood back into his arms.

"Can you walk?" Philip asked.

"Of course," replied the Gurkha. "I'm not hurt."

Rana had released another Gurkha who'd been left tied in a corner, presumably waiting his turn to be interrogated. Both he and Prem recovered their weapons from where they'd been stacked and turned to face Philip.

"What happened to the others?" Philip asked grimly.

"They shot the burrif as soon as they caught us. He went in first and was told the village was clear by the headman. He came back for us but as we approached we were ambushed." The corporal shrugged. "There was little we could do against their machine gun. Their Sergeant," he stopped and nodded towards the dead soldier who'd been using the lash, "walked straight up to him and shot him in the head. He said he was a traitor."

Philip shook his head. "And Balbir?"

"They tortured him first. I think because he was young they thought he'd be the easiest to break." Prem shook his head. "He said nothing, which is why they thought we were alone and were not expecting to be attacked. Then he passed out. He was so covered in blood they made us drag his body to the hut next door so their uniforms stayed clean. He must be in there, but whether he's alive or not, I don't know."

"How many are there of them?" Philip asked.

Prem shrugged. "I counted six. They seem to have been stationed here for the few days. They also have a radio which I heard them use. They will have told their HQ that we are here and will have requested reinforcements."

Philip nodded. "OK. Time to get moving. Keep low and spread out when you hit the ground. Make your way towards the hut you took him to. And be careful. We know there's at least a couple more of them out there and after all this noise, they know we're here too."

He took a deep breath and flung himself out of the door, to be met by the deafening evening chorus of frogs in the paddy fields, a noise disturbed only by their lumbering footfall's and laboured breathing.

CHAPTER 12

Nepal, 1953

Philip couldn't settle that night. Whenever he closed his eyes he smelt blood and saw the despair in the eyes of the dying monk. When he did finally doze he dreamt of being lost in a never ending jungle, never being able to find the right path out. He was woken on several occasions by loud snoring and coughing caused by the pungent smoke from the yak dung fire. He was also aware of Lhamu sleeping on the other side of the fireplace, almost invisible in a heavy woollen blanket.

He'd wanted to talk to her after the discussion had broken up but had been kept busy with the preparations. During one lull he'd glanced across but she'd already made up her bed on the floor and had settled down for the night. Soon after, the men returned from their search for weapons and it was obvious that it hadn't been very successful. Philip looked at the five guns they'd manage to locate. Four were flintlocks so ancient that Philip doubted their barrels would survive another firing. The only serviceable weapon was a revolver from the Second World War. It was dirty and only had eight rounds of ammunition but at least it was more likely to kill the target rather than the shooter. When Prem had finished examining it he'd walked over to Philip, holding it out. Philip paused, looking the corporal in the eye, before nodding slowly and taking it from him.

The Gurkhas didn't seem at all discouraged by their lack of firepower and spent a good twenty minutes sharpening and oiling the evil looking knives they all carried. Philip shivered as he watched the dull blades glinting in the firelight. Memories came back of these very blades slashing through skin and sinew, silently dispatching enemies who'd died drowning in their own blood. He'd rather have these men with knives on his side than any others with rifles. Where they were going, in the terrain and conditions they were going to be fighting in, with the Gurkhas knowledge and skill, they had a chance.

He'd just fallen into what he thought was his first deep sleep of the night when he felt his shoulder being shaken. It was Mingma. He sat up in his sleeping bag, rubbing his eyes and yawning, grunting a greeting to the Sherpa. The room was dark, lit only by the fire embers and a lamp Mingma was now hanging from a ceiling hook. The others men were stirring, heading out into the dark and cold morning to relieve themselves. He glanced across the hearth and saw that Lhamu had gone, the space where her bed had been now just an empty patch of floor.

Getting up, he quickly rolled his sleeping bag and shoved it into his rucksack. He then helped Mingma mix his own expedition food with supplies from the lodge, making twelve equal piles. When they were satisfied that they all weighed the same he picked one up and called the others over.

"Here's the food. Take a pile each so we have some rations

with us. I don't want to take any more as it'll slow us down and we need to travel quickly. We'll try to buy more as we go."

The Gurkhas took the food, stowing it away in their packs. When Lhamu came over Philip stepped forward and held out a small canvas bag.

"There's no food for you to carry as I want you to be in charge of this."

She reached out and tilted the package to see it better. On its side was stamped a large red cross and the words "First Aid".

"As I'm the one with the gun I think it's best that I don't carry this. They'll most likely shoot at me first."

Lhamu nodded and took it, her hand brushing Philips as she did so. Their eyes briefly met before she turned and walked away.

Blankets were folded and stowed, boots laced and a quick breakfast of boiled eggs and chapatti eaten. As the first hint of morning silhouetted the eastern peaks, they walked from the lodge out into the deserted street. Their breath blew out in front of them in white clouds as they began the climb to the upper villages in the freezing dawn air. The whole valley lay silent except for the distant roar of the river and the occasional crow from a disturbed cockerel. Philip stopped and looked back over the silent town, wondering when he'd next get to sleep under a proper roof. He could hardly believe what they were setting out to attempt, slowly shaking his head and sighing as he turned and resumed the climb.

Everybody seemed to be thinking the same thing. The column climbed quickly and quietly towards the first ridge.

It gave time for Philip to try to work out a plan for the next few days. He kept his thumbs tucked inside the straps of his rucksack, worried that he might be betrayed by his trembling hands. Old fears pushed their way into his head and he tried to steady his breathing, despite the exertion of the climb.

He forced his mind to work as it had once been trained, to live in the present and face problems as they arose. They were going to be outnumbered and outgunned, that much was certain. Following the trade route across the Nangpa-la to Tibet was the only option. There were other passes but they were either too far away or too dangerous for such an unprepared expedition. That meant they wouldn't be able to outflank the enemy and set an ambush for them to walk into. They would have to catch the soldiers but then keep their distance and an element of surprise until they came to a place they could either overtake them unseen or attack.

Philip smiled grimly. If his Gurkhas got close enough they'd be able to dispatch the Chinese with their knives before they realised what'd happened. That's how they stood a chance. In addition to himself, Corporal Prem and the nine men, he also had Mingma who would be able to supervise the cooking and camp, as well as help guide with Lhamu. He glanced up ahead but they were already well strung out and she was out of sight. They'd decided the previous evening that she and Prem would push ahead to pick up the trail of the soldiers and try to establish their exact position. They were to rejoin the rest that evening, hopefully at the snout of the Nangpa Glacier where they intended to camp. Anything they managed to learn would be invaluable.

He estimated that, if they were careful, they had food for

three days. Mingma hoped to buy some from the villages they'd pass through that day, so that might give them an extra day or two. He'd selected food that could be eaten cold if necessary. They were carrying no fuel and when they got up above the snowline firewood would be hard to find. It should take two days to cross the pass; everything depended on what lay on the other side.

Lhamu knew of several settlements that she'd visited and stayed at on trips with her father, but the people on the Tibetan Plateau were nomads and they could have moved off if the grazing was poor this year. They'd just have to hope that they or some other settlers were there. Failing that, they would have to eke out the food out until they reached the monastery at Rombuk. The Gurkhas had, Philip thought grimly, survived for much longer on much less.

When he'd first been told of his assignment to Everest, Rombuk had been the place that had flashed into his mind. The stories of Mallory and Irvine's attempt to climb the mountain from Tibet had filled the boys' adventure books he'd read when he was young; whether or not they'd made it to the summit before dying in the storms that engulfed the peak. They'd started their climb from Rombuk, as in those days Nepal had been closed to all foreigners.

From these stories, and from his evening chatting to Lhamu and her father Karma, he knew that there was still a large monastery there, despite the Chinese persecution. They, at least, would be able to offer shelter and food if needed. Monks from Thangboche who'd been there recently had told Lhamu that there were still many monks there, with large herds of mountain sheep and yaks.

He'd settled into a good rhythm, walking steadily and in pace with his breathing. He felt fitter now; three weeks of constant exertion had made his body stronger. Excess fat had been burnt away and muscles built up so that he felt as if he'd be able to keep up with the rest of the men who all walked these mountains for their livelihood.

Slowly he became aware that there was somebody following behind, the occasional sound of a dislodged stone or of a boot scraping on rock carrying up to him. He thought he heard a cough and the sound of someone hacking and spitting. It was lighter now, the sun's rays striking the very tips of the tallest mountains. As he watched it fell to the highest points of the valleys eastern ridge, bathing them in a morning light that glowed orange. Looking back down the trail he could now see the outline of a man catching him quickly, almost jogging as he sprang from rock to rock. As he got nearer and the light got brighter he recognised Tashi.

A minute or so later the Indian caught him, nodding in greeting as he panted for breath.

"You're up early," Philip remarked laconically. "Come to enjoy the sun rise?"

Tashi stood hands on hips and shook his head with a grimace. "I didn't want you to have all the fun," he wheezed. "Anyway, whenever I'm not around you get into such trouble."

Philip shook his head, holding Tashi's eye. "Why didn't you say you wanted to come last night?"

Tashi shrugged. "By the time I returned last night you were all sleeping. The police had been uncooperative so I'd thought I'd be more use in Namche, pestering away at them.

But this morning, after you'd left, I changed my mind." He paused, still breathing heavily. "I realised that those flatfoots weren't going to take any notice of a creep like me, whatever I showed them." He reached into his trouser pocket and pulled out the ring, passing it to Philip. "Here," he said smiling. "Take this. I don't want you thinking I've sold it."

Philip took it and stood looking at the Indian. "You do realise it's going to be dangerous, don't you?" he said at last. "There's at least twice as many soldiers as there are of us and they're all armed."

Tashi nodded. "Another reason for me to come. Even up the numbers a bit."

Philip continued. "Crossing the pass is going to be cold and exhausting and we haven't even got enough food to get back. If we don't find some friendly people over there we'll freeze and starve."

Tashi reached back and tapped his rucksack. "I've bought food for myself which I'll either keep separate or throw into the communal pot."

Philip studied Tashi's face. "Why would you want to come?"

The Indian stood silently, considering his response. "I've seen some bad things in my life, many of which I've try hard to forget." He stopped to compose himself for a few moments before continuing. "I've told you my two brothers were killed in fighting between the Chinese and Tibetans. They didn't deserve to die. They were good men, caring and peaceful. I was too young to help them. My two elder sisters were taken and my youngest sister died on the journey to Sikkim. She froze to death. I woke one morning to find she had rolled from our blankets during the night. Her face was so peaceful

I tried to wake her for a while until I touched her shoulder and felt she was solid. She was only seven."

He looked at Philip. "Those monks didn't deserve to die either. My brothers were Tibetan. I was Tibetan until we were forced to India. Seems to me that this is my battle as much as anyone's." He rubbed his mouth. "Anyway, I speak Chinese. I learnt it as a boy and have used it many times for my work. I think I might well be of use at some point."

There was silence, the men standing looking at each other, the eastern horizon behind them lightening to a pale yellow that merged with the growing blue of the sky.

At last Philip nodded. "You can come but on one condition. You follow my orders. We'll need to pull together if we're to stand any chance." He smiled at Tashi. He liked him and he had to admit that he'd been useful the previous day. "And remember," he held up his finger, "this isn't a trading trip. So forget any ideas you've got of buying the Dalai Lama's prayer beads if we run into him!"

Tashi held out his hands and looked shocked. "The very thought is outrageous," he replied good-naturedly. "I'm here only to help." He smiled. "If they happen to reward me however I wouldn't want to turn down a gift and offend them." He continued walking up the trail, Philip turning back up the slope and following on behind.

They walked on in silence until they reached the village of Thamo, where Philip stopped and joined Mingma who was busy bartering with the villagers for supplies. They sat outside a large stone house, drinking some of the saltiest tea Philip had yet tasted. He had to stop himself gagging after every sip.

They soon had enough potatoes and onions for a meal and Mingma hired a local man to carry them up to that night's campsite, hoping they'd arrive in time for supper that evening. They lingered for a few more minutes, questioning the villagers about what they knew about the events of the last few days. They'd all heard rumours of the massacre and of the soldiers marching through the higher villagers.

Mingma spent several minutes questioning a man who'd returned from Khunde that morning to see if they could learn anything more. When he'd finished he turned to Philip looking worried.

"This man was in the high street when the soldiers came through. He says there were more than twenty and they had big guns." Mingma stopped and looked at the man. "There was one man in charge, with a different uniform, and shouting a lot at the others. They were walking fast but two of them were injured and being helped." He turned towards Philip. "That's good. The injured will slow them down and give us more of a chance to catch them."

Philip nodded. "Let's hope so. Did he see a prisoner?"

Mingma nodded. "A young monk who was tied and being dragged along. His face was swollen and bruised but otherwise he looked well."

They stood to go, the villagers crowding around them, shouting angrily.

Philip looked at them, nervously. "Why are they yelling at us?" he asked over his shoulder, "We've done nothing wrong."

"They are angry with the soldiers. They don't know who the prisoner is but they are angry because he was a monk and should not be treated like that," Mingma replied. "They are urging us to catch them and get him back."

As Philip pushed through the throng a child grabbed his hand and pushed something into it. It was an apple, small and shrivelled from its long winter storage. The child scampered back to a Sherpani standing on the other side of the street, who smiled at Philip's nod of thanks. Small packets of sugar and rice were pushed into their pockets until they got free and walked briskly out of the village. Once clear of the houses they stopped and stowed the gifts in their rucksacks.

"They want to help. It will help their karma to assist in the release of the holy man," Mingma said.

They moved off at a brisk pace, soon catching up with Tashi whose earlier exertions seemed to be taking their toll. He fell into line and didn't complain as Mingma set a strong pace up the valley, glancing back suspiciously every now and again at the Indian. They didn't stop for lunch, just a few minutes resting beside a small stream and sharing some cold potatoes and dried fruit. Philip also cut the apple into three with his penknife and passed the segments round, savouring its sweetness.

They set off again, the sky now leaden with cloud that had closed in over the peaks. A breeze had got up that blew into their faces, making them stop to pull on windcheaters and gloves. Their progress had slowed, mainly due to the altitude which was making their breathing more laboured. Finally, after a couple of hours of steady progress, they emerged from around a small spur jutting out into the valley and could see the camp ahead. The Gurkhas had erected the tent in which they were to sleep, but looking up the valley, from where they stood, it looked like a tiny speck against the vastness of the glacier that tumbled its way down the mountainside. Enormous blocks of ice towered over the valley floor, some as white as snow, others with dark fissures and crevasses slicing through them. It stretched away up the valley, in places covered with rock and scree which had slid down the slopes and come to rest on the icy surface.

Philip felt the cold cut through him as a gust of wind stung his face with ice particles from the glacier, and without needing to say anything the three men moved off towards the camp before they froze. Small streams bisected their route, roaring down from the snow-covered ridge high above them. Some were bridged using spindly tree trunks that were propped over the water on neat piles of stone. On one Tashi almost lost his balance as the wood shifted under his weight, making him jump hastily to the far bank.

Smaller streams had no such bridges, the three men leaping from boulder to boulder to cross. The water tumbled beneath them as it swept small stones and pebbles down the mountain side. With their laden rucksacks it was hard to spring and Philip soon found himself sitting on a rock emptying a boot of freezing water. He wrung out his sock miserably, wriggling his toes to get some heat back into them before grimacing as he forced them back into the sodden garment.

When they finally arrived at camp, over an hour after first spotting it, they headed straight for the large fire that crackled and spat in the cold late afternoon air. They'd met the village porter heading back down the valley earlier, happy that his load was delivered and with the cash he'd been paid.

Prem had two of the men busy preparing the potatoes and a large pot of water steaming over the fire. They all pulled their mugs from their bags and were given tea, which they nursed in their hands, enjoying the sensation of the heat through their gloves. The drink steamed into the chill air but when Philip cautiously sipped at the liquid he found it almost tepid and drank it down gratefully. He remembered that the altitude made things boil at lower temperatures, as he held out his mug for a refill.

He looked up and smiled, seeing Lhamu walk from the tent and giggling at the sight of Philip's wet foot, still in the sock, wiggling by the fire. "Got a bootful on the way up," he said ruefully. "I think my toes are about ready to drop off."

She sat down beside him on a boulder and they were joined by Prem, squatting down with his hands outstretched before him and almost being licked by the flames.

"How did the recon go?" Philip asked, pulling his leg in slightly as the sock started to steam.

"Good," Lhamu replied, glancing at Prem, who nodded in agreement. "We walked hard and reached this place by late morning. We approached it carefully as we could see it had been their camp last night." She pointed towards the fireplace. "Their fire had been here also, the stones were still warm. We tracked them up the side of the valley. It was easy. They are not mountain people and had dislodged stones and trampled through wet ground as they went. "

"There was blood too," added Prem. "One or more of them is still bleeding. There was some here and then nothing until quite a way up the trail. I think someone's wound opened up again with the exertion of the climbing."

Philip nodded.

"We tracked them for a couple of hours. It was even easier by then as we were on snow. The trail soon turns east towards the pass and is always in shadow, so it is icy and cold. Soon after, we saw them. They were towards the top of the ridge, just specks of black against the snow. They were moving very slowly."

"Did you manage to count them?" Philip asked, looking between Lhamu and Prem.

"I counted twenty-two," answered Prem.

"And I saw twenty-one," said Lhamu. "They were far away and some were walking very close together, helping each other. It was hard to be sure."

There was a pause as Philip took in the information. "So they'll have crossed the Pass today." He scratched at the stubble on his chin. "We must cross over quickly tomorrow and close up on them. They'll be exhausted after all the exertions of the last few days, so we should be fresher and faster. If we catch and surprise them then we might stand a chance."

Prem nodded. "We'll break camp early and be off before dawn. If we can get up to the top of the pass by late morning the snow will be firmer and we won't sink in to it as much as they did. By the time they got there this afternoon the sun had melted the crust and made it soft. It makes the going very slow." He stood up. "I'll go and tell the men. Supper will be ready soon and when it's eaten we will prepare for the early start."

There was a silence as Lhamu and Philip sat awkwardly side by side.

"It's a good thing to be getting up early," Lhamu said at last. "None of us will sleep well. The ground will be hard and cold, the tent will be freezing and everybody will snore."

Philip looked at her and smiled. "Does the snoring include you?"

"Definitely," she replied. "My brothers have compared my snoring to that of the Yeti. They believe it keeps our sheep safe as it scares away the wolves."

Philip laughed. "In which case, it's a blessing you came along. I'll sleep easier, if less well, knowing you're keeping us all safe."

There was another silence. "When was the last time you crossed over the pass?" he asked, looking at Lhamu.

She stared into the flames. "Two years ago. There were some of our monks heading to Lhasa and I travelled with them over the border. As soon as we arrived at the road I was sent back." She picked up a piece of wood from the pile lying to one side and started poking the fire to open it up, throwing it on top when she'd finished in a cloud of sparks. "The first time, however, was many years ago with my father. He was strong then and made his living trading over the pass to get salt."

She smiled, speaking slowly as she worked on translating the right words. "He used to put me on the back of one of the heavily laden yaks so I could get to the top of the pass. I used to stroke and pat them as we climbed up and up, thanking them for carrying me and worried that it would make them too tired to continue." She started giggling, looking at Philip. "Now I realise that they wouldn't even have felt the weight of a little girl."

Philip laughed back, his eyes captivated by Lhamu's face as it glowed with the happy memories in the flickering light of the fire. Daylight was going, making it seem as if they were in their own tiny world.

"It was rare to see a young child travelling so high, especially a girl," Lhamu continued, occasionally slowing as she thought for a word. "Everywhere I went I was spoilt. The Tibetan women always took me off when we stayed near their camps, scolding my father for bringing me and making me sleep in their warm yurts, wrapped in thick blankets. I loved it. I was the centre of attention and given fresh sheep milk to drink every morning."

She fell silent for a moment, lost in her thoughts. "But the last time I went things were different. The herdsmen were scared, not even willing to give shelter to monks on a pilgrimage. They sold us food but were suspicious and would not talk. I think they were worried that we were Communist spies come to take their land. After the invasion in the east many people were displaced and everybody fears that the Chinese will now take the whole country. Their spies are everywhere, so nobody trusts anyone."

She looked at Philip. "This is why we must not fail. If the Chinese capture the Rinpoche and bring him to Peking then they can control Tibet by ruling in his name." She leant forward and grasped Philips forearm. "If the Rinpoche is not free then Tibet will fall. And if Tibet falls, the Dalai Lama, the monasteries, our religion will all be destroyed."

Philip stared at her and then cautiously reached out and took her hands, squeezing them gently. "We'll do our very best. All I can say is that it's a miracle that Prem and the men were in Namche. I cannot think of anyone I'd trust more. I'm not a great believer in religion, but in this instance there certainly seems to have been a God from somewhere looking out."

He fell silent, feeling awkward. She withdrew her hands, clasping them together on her lap as if trying to make them disappear and nodded, gazing up the valley. "That's not our only good fortune. Prem has told me what a brave leader you are." Cautiously, she glanced back at him. "And my father, he likes you. "The corners of her mouth twitched into a small smile. "You do not realise how unusual that is."

Philip blew out his cheeks and nodded, relieved the awkward moment had passed. "Gosh, I am honoured!" He looked at Lhamu and smiled. "And from what he said when we were talking in your house, he's obviously very proud of you."

Lhamu sat in silence for a few moments before replying. "He loved my mother very much and I think I remind him of her. I was always his favourite, my brothers could never do anything right. They had to work long hours on our land while I travelled with him and learnt what he could teach me. My mother's brother was a monk at the monastery and my father got him to teach me to read and write Tibetan and Nepalese, and then pestered him to get me work with the abbot. He wants me to live the life I want rather than the one I was born to, not die in child birth like my mother."

She shook her head. "Any boy I met was never good enough and any suitor, well he told you how he gets rid of them." She laughed, a sound that dissolved the last awkwardness between them. "Usually he pleads poverty, claiming I have no dowry to bring. Any that still remain are frightened off by his demand for a bride-price. He's old but he's still clever. Sometimes I think I will spend my whole life working at the monastery. I am already the oldest unmarried woman in the village. He tells me to be patient but sometimes I worry. He is old and if he were to die my brothers would get rid of me on the first man who asked. And yet I fear that if the opportunity to leave does come I'll be too scared to take it."

Philip sat in silence, his turn to be struggle for the right words. He turned to where Parul had set up the radio set and was busy trying to get a message down to the police at Namche. There was no reply to his repeated calls, just bursts of static.

He looked at Philip and shrugged. "Nothing."

"Turn it off," Philip replied. "Save the batteries in case we need it later."

Parul nodded and had just started dismantling the set when Prem came hurrying back into camp.

"You must come," he said to Philip, looking grim. "Lalit was collecting firewood and has found a body."

Philip quickly shoved his feet back into his boots and without bothering to tie the laces followed the Gurkha up behind the camp. They walked a couple of minutes, crossing a tumbling moraine of boulders and ice, until they came to a huge boulder the size of a house. Philip could see a pile of wood dumped beside it and as he slowly walked around its side a body came into view.

It was lying on its back, wearing the tattered remnants of a thin green uniform. There was no sign of any baggage or weapons but the way stones had been placed around the body made it obvious that someone had tried to bury it by placing it hard up against the boulder and piling rocks over the top. They certainly wouldn't have been able to dig into the frozen ground for a proper grave or had enough wood for a cremation.

Philip grimaced as he looked at the body. The face had gone, torn away to leave exposed bone and gaping cavities. The stomach had been ripped open, intestines strewn over the legs and the body cavity empty.

"Wolves," said Lalit, anticipating Philips question. "They will have smelt the blood on his clothes from a wound in his back. They would not care that the man is dead, meat is scarce up here and this is a feast to them." He kicked one of the stones. "They would move stones much bigger than these to get meat as fresh as this."

Philip took his eyes away from the mutilated body and looked to where Lalit was now pointing. Three wolves sat on the far side of the glacier, a couple of hundred yards away, patiently waiting to resume their meal. He shuddered. "OK, back to camp. Let's keep that fire well banked up tonight and warn everybody not to stray too far from its light."

CHAPTER 13

Nepal/Tibet border, 1953

The night was hell. All fourteen were squeezed into the tent making it impossible to lie out straight. The gain in altitude had given Philip a headache which a couple of aspirins could only reduce to a dull but constant ache. Snoring and coughing merged with the wind that whined through the seracs and ice pinnacles of the glacier and the occasional groaning of moving ice. The place had a cruel and sinister feel, reinforced by the occasional howling of the wolves back feasting on the body of the dead soldier. Philip shuddered every time he heard them.

After a supper he'd gone to bed warm, but after a few hours of tossing and turning he could feel the cold creeping back into his body. Sometime after midnight he'd had to climb out of his sleeping bag in order to relieve himself. He'd tried hard not to disturb the others and was rather annoyed to see that everybody else seemed to be enjoying a deep, dreamless sleep. Having untied and crawled through the tent flap, he walked down the valley to the designated toilet area, watching nervously for the wolves, he could still hear, not far away. Having fumbled though his many layers of clothing he stood looking at the huge glacier climbing up to his right. A thin moon occasionally broke through the clouds, its light glinting off the ice. There was a beauty to it, but as a blast of frozen wind cut through him, he buttoned his fly as best he could and stumbled back to the tent.

The interior felt positively tropical after his exposure to the elements and he pulled himself gratefully back into his bag. He lay there, panting heavily from the exertion in the thin air and for a few minutes enjoyed the luxury of space as the other occupants pulled away from his cold form. He was just cursing that he'd never get back to sleep when he was woken by Prem gently shaking his shoulder.

"It's time to go," the Gurkha said. "There will be fried potatoes in a few minutes and then we go straight off when we get the first light."

Philip groaned, rubbing his face and wincing as his dried lips cracked when he mumbled a reply. He pulled a battered tube of thick zinc cream from his bag and started rubbing it into his face in an effort to protect it from the sun and wind of the day ahead. A mug of tea arrived, making him feel guilty that despite the shared hardships, the men were still trying to look after him. As he sipped he sighed with pleasure, letting the hot liquid flow into him, its heat radiating warmth through his body.

Reluctantly he crawled from his bag and shoved it into his rucksack, which had been serving both as a pillow and a barrier from the other occupants. There was no need to dress as he was already wearing everything he had with him except his goggles and boots. The snow goggles he took from the rucksack and shoved into a pocket. His boots he retrieved from where he'd left them after his night time excursion. As he pushed his feet into them he grimaced, the leather had frozen solid in the dawn dip of early morning, so he shuffled out of the tent and towards the fire.

He emerged just in time. No sooner had he reached the fire than the tent was down and the various poles, ropes, groundsheets and canvas distributed amongst the men. Philip was handed a few guy ropes which seemed a bit light to him but after the night he'd had he didn't feel like querying it.

He sat down on a boulder and took off his boots, holding them over the rekindled fire, working at the leather to get some flexibility back into them. The laces, wet from the snow the night before, were like twigs, so he crushed and squeezed them between the thick material of his gloves. After a minute or so, he pushed his feet back into them, feeling their coolness against his warm woollen socks. He wiggled his toes. At least there was a little flex in them now.

Breakfast was called by the cook, sticking his head out from what served as the kitchen, a small canvas sheet draped over a rock overhang, and held down by rocks. He pulled his plate and mug from his bag and walked over, insisting that the men in front were served first when they tried to usher him through. A pile of crispy, fried potatoes, coated in dried chilli and with a fried egg on top was put on his plate, together with a refill of tea. Returning to his place he tried to force it down despite a complete lack of appetite, knowing he'd need the energy later. The kitchen roof was folded and the frying pan washed in the river using ashes from the fire to scour it clean. By the time Philip had finished and rinsed his plate the party was ready to move out.

They all stood around the fire, bathed in its flickering light as the first glimmer of dawn silhouetted the mountains around them. The moon was still in the sky, but only as a faint glow hidden behind fast moving cloud. Everybody looked at Philip expectantly, several stamping their feet and banging their arms to keep warm.

"We must move fast today," Philip said with as much conviction as he could muster. "We want to be well over the pass by the time we camp tonight, hopefully somewhere with a nice hotel and decent restaurant."

The men laughed grimly.

"It will be safest if we stick together. It'll be steep and slippery as we get higher so we may need to rope up in places. Everybody needs to look out for everybody else. Remember," he stared around the group, "it's cold and treacherous up there. This is our chance to catch up on the soldiers. Yesterday they were struggling and we reckon they'll have spent a freezing night high up on the pass. They'll be cold and exhausted. If we can catch them soon, they'll be weak and no match for us. Then," he pointed back down the valley, "we can all get home. Right, let's get going before we all freeze."

He nodded to Mingma, who turned and set off up a rough trail to the side of the valley, the rest falling in behind. Philip joined about half way back and noticed Tashi walking close behind. "Sleep well?" he asked with raised eyebrows.

The Indian grunted. "Thanks to the winning combination of snoring and the howling wolves, I'm beat." He rubbed his eyes. "Are you sure it's a good idea to go on? That tent seemed a bit dicey to me. If it gets damaged up on the pass we'll freeze to death."

Philip looked over his shoulder as he walked. He'd noticed that Tashi had been the last to be ready that morning, and wondered whether he would slow them down. "It's not too late to go back you know?" he said. "You could be back in Namche this evening in a nice warm lodge."

The Indian shook his head. "Or inside a wolf," he muttered grumpily. "I'm here now so I may as well carry on, but I still reckon you lot are nuts to be trying this."

Considering how remote they were the trail they were following was surprisingly good, trodden flat by centuries of traders and their caravans of yaks. It zigzagged its way up the side of the small valley, climbing steeply and keeping to the edge of the vast grey glacier. In some places the path disappeared, swept away by avalanches of monsoon snows or the floods of the thaw. Where these had happened, the path had been diverted or re-established depending on what had happened to the original terrain. Sometimes it climbed high to pass round an earth slip, other times down to the glacier's edge to skirt round rock falls.

Philip was breathing hard, the thin air and heavy load making him feel sluggish and listless. He was grateful for the steady pace, with Mingma setting a speed that would get them over the pass in good time and keep them together. It was a race that would be won by being sensible, not spectacular. After only half an hour Philip was hot, his body sweating under the thick layers he was wearing to keep out the gusting wind blowing down the valley. His face however was numb, his ears aching with cold and he kept flexing his fingers within his mittens to keep some circulation going.

The morning was getting brighter as dawn grew and they

climbed to meet the sunrise. After an hour Mingma stopped, allowing the men to pack away the heavy woollen blankets they'd been swathed in since camp and Philip took the opportunity to strip off a couple of tops, which he tied to the outside of his rucksack in the hope that they might dry out before evening.

Soon they were off again and Philip understood why they'd stopped when they had. The sides of the valley closed in, two sheer walls of rock rising on either side of the glacier, climbing to become the snowy upper slopes of the surrounding peaks. He glanced nervously upwards, hoping that the snow held back this year as if an avalanche came down while they were in Tibet it could block the valley for days.

The trail picked its way along the southern flank of the glacier, using the tonnes of debris that had fallen onto the ice. The going got slower as they picked their way through, following a series of small cairns and tattered prayer flags that has been crudely built to mark the route. Philip was relieved to see that these still stood undisturbed, indicating that the soldiers didn't suspect that they were being followed.

As they climbed Philip studied the huge glacier, a vast frozen waterfall cascading down the valley. In places tall pillars of ice, many over fifty feet tall, looked as if they needed only the slightest touch to bring them crashing down. Huge boulders the size of cars sat perched on thin columns of ice, sheltered by their bulk from the heat of the scorching high altitude sun. The occasional boom reverberating around the valley told when one had finally shattered under the weight.

He could feel his feet chilling, the cold from the ice

beneath them slowly creeping through his boots and into the soles of his feet. He tried to wriggle his toes but found them restricted by the two pairs of thick socks he had on, so stamped his feet whenever they reached a tricky portion of trail and had to wait until the man in front had cleared it.

They'd been going a couple of hours when glancing up he saw Lhamu holding up her hand, bringing them to a halt. He watched for a few moments, swinging his arms in an attempt to get some circulation going, before slowly working his way forward up the column. As he went he checked on the men, patting them on the back as he passed and receiving grins in return. No one else seemed to be breathing heavily he noticed, trying his best to look relaxed. Glancing up ahead he saw Mingma looking back towards him and beckoning him forward. It was only twenty or so yards but the effort of getting there quickly made him so breathless he was unable to talk.

No words were needed. Mingma pointed in the direction of a large rocky overhang that jutted out from the valley wall. Underneath it, a rough wall had been built with uneven stones, a barrier on which to lie saddles and rugs to create a basic wind break. The rock roof was blackened with soot from centuries of campfires as traders had used it as an overnight camp on their journeys. Inside, leaning with his back against the rock sat a soldier; cap pulled low over his face and huddled in a thin blanket. Philip started and instinctively reached down to where his pistol hung.

Momentarily he was confused as to why Mingma and Lhamu had brought him forward rather than getting everybody under cover but it quickly dawned on him why. He walked forward, cautiously glancing around the open shelter and entered through an opening in the low wall. There was a pungent smell of yak dung and the dried remnants of it covered the floor. Animals were obviously allowed to shelter here too in bad weather, probably just the young, and in the fireplace he could see the remains of the last fire that had used this dung as its fuel.

Crossing over to where the soldier sat, on a flat rock beside the fire pit, he crouched down. The man's eyes were open, staring down at where the last flickers of light they'd ever have seen would have burnt. His face was white, like a diluted whitewash covering a deep blue. Philip pulled off his mitten and glove and reached forward, feeling that he should at least feel for a pulse. When his fingers made contact with the soldiers skin they recoiled back and he shuddered, quickly standing and putting his hand back inside his glove.

"Christ," he said, looking down at the corpse. "He's frozen solid."

Mingma nodded, glancing across to Prem who'd moved up from the rear and was entering the shelter.

The Gurkha moved forward and using a fair amount of force managed to prise the frozen blanket away from the body, it retaining the shape of the soldier as he tossed it aside. Prem studied the corpse and then turned to face them. "He was injured," he said. "Looks like a stab wound in the stomach. One of the monks must have wounded him with a knife during the ambush." He turned back and looked at the soldier again. "Perhaps he was slowing them down too much so they left him here." He bent down and felt the ashes in the fire. "This has been out for some time. He must have burnt all he could find and then..." He shrugged.

"Poor sod," said Philip quietly, slowly shaking his head. "I bet the last place he wanted to be was here, traipsing through the Himalayas. What a terrible way to die," he said, studying the soldiers face. "He looks so young, hardly out of school. I wonder if his family will ever find out what happened to him?"

There was a silence as they all imagined the horrific death he must have suffered; injured, alone, cold and scared. Prem picked up the man's rifle which stood leaning against the rock wall and pulled some ammunition from a bag that lay by its side. He checked its mechanism, and satisfied that it was in working order, handed it to one of the Gurkhas.

It was Philip who pulled them all back to the present. "Let's get going," he said abruptly, turning and leaving the rough shelter. "We don't want to get stuck up here as well or we'll end up suffering the similar fate."

The walked on, the valley gradually widening again and the trail climbing away from the glacier. A series of switchback corners meant they were ascending rapidly, zigzagging up the steep slope and the pace slowed, not helped by the fact they were now walking on old, icy snow that made their footing more treacherous. The sun was now high enough to clear the ridge but remained hidden behind thick cloud that blew down the valley. He tried treading in the steps that Mingma and Lhamu were kicking into the hard surface, but on several occasions he felt himself slip, only just managing to catch his balance in time.

Occasionally they came across abandoned equipment that had been jettisoned by the exhausted Chinese soldiers. Ammunition lay beside the trail and Philip wondered whether it had been quietly abandoned by exhausted men or dumped as the result of a direct order. Whichever way, he didn't care. It meant fewer bullets to be shot at them when they did catch up. He picked some of it up, others following suit without breaking stride. Within a short stretch, they'd accumulated over 200 rounds of ammo and a hand grenade, while many other items like mess tins were left lying frozen into the snow.

The higher they climbed, the stronger the wind became, blasting into their faces. Philip had his hood tied tight around his face and thick scarf pulled up over his mouth and nose. When they'd started walking on the snow he'd pulled out the snow goggles from his pocket and slid them on, although he had to stop frequently to clear their lens from mist. Despite this he could feel his cheeks going numb and every few minutes rubbed at them vigorously with his hands. His fingers and toes were dead and yet he could feel sweat running down between his shoulder blades, his silk vest plastered to his back.

A flurry of snow blew past, flakes caking themselves onto his face and goggles. As he wiped them off he looked ahead, trying to work out whether it was a fresh snow fall or simply spindrift being picked up and driven by the wind. Another flurry hit him, the flakes bigger and more persistent.

"Bugger it," he muttered under his breath. He glanced around and saw that visibility had dropped considerably. Unless they were careful it would be all too easy to lose someone in these conditions. Mingma and Lhamu had stopped and he caught them up.

"How far to the top?" he yelled into the wind, peering up the pass.

"Soon," Lhamu replied, her voice emerging from within a heavy hood that completely covered her face. "It is hard to be sure, but at this pace we should be over in less than an hour."

Philip nodded. "We must keep moving." He turned and faced the rest of the men. "Quickly, gather in close." The men huddled in, leaving Mingma, Lhamu and him with their backs acting as a barrier to the worst of the weather. "We've made good time," he yelled, trying to make himself heard over the roar of the wind. "Less than an hour and we'll be over and on our way down. It's important we stick close and don't get lost in this snow. Whoever else is carrying guy ropes get them out and pass them around."

He slipped off his pack and pulled out the ones he'd been given, replacing them with the tops he'd hung on the outside to dry and which were now flapping around annoyingly. Two of the men untied the neat bundles of cord that hung from their packs and passed them around. "Tie them to the man in front, off his bag, and get the other tied to your belt. That way we won't lose anybody if the snow gets thicker and becomes a white out."

There was a burst of activity as goggles were pushed up and gloves removed. With a silent efficiency the cords were tied in place and an order worked out. Philip found himself behind Lhamu and when she saw him fumbling to tie a knot with his cold hands she came over and tied it to his belt for him.

"You must work your hands," she said, feeling how cold his fingers were. "Rub them together and keep them tight together inside your glove. Otherwise you will have a problem with them later. What is it you say?" She looked up at his face. "They will have frost-bitten."

Philip grimaced and nodded, pulling on his gloves and mitts and silently cursing that they'd lost any semblance of heat they'd contained before.

"Let's go," yelled Mingma, trudging forward and the column slowly moved off.

If Philip had thought it had been tough going before, now it felt impossible. The wind blasted the snow directly into his face, plastering his skin and freezing in his stubble. His goggles constantly steamed up making it all but impossible to see. Being tied in a long line meant that when one person stumbled he would pull against the person in front or behind. Often the whole column ground to a halt, only to start forward again when the tautness went from the cord. It was hard enough keeping your own balance without this constant pulling and tugging. It felt as if their progress had pretty much stopped.

To Philip, everything was white except the blurred outline of Lhamu in front. He concentrated on her footsteps, trying to step in the exact same spot and keep them open for those behind. It was impossible. The whiteout was complete, meaning there was no shadow to show where her feet had gone and through misted goggles everything was a uniform white.

For what felt like hours they trudged forward. His head was pounding, a point of throbbing pain sitting behind his eyes that pulsed in time with his racing heart. His breathing was ragged and breathless, trying to gasp oxygen into his lungs that just wasn't there. His legs felt like jelly, his feet and hands had no feeling and he felt on the point of collapse.

Something in the featureless white caught his eye, initially a dark blur until he got closer. It was a body, dressed in green with its legs drawn up close to its chest. Snow had drifted behind it, mercifully covering the man's features. His back and buttocks were taking the full brunt of the gale, the material of his clothes frozen by the bitter wind. Beside him lay a large bag, a solid lump of canvas and ice. He watched Prem stoop to clumsily rip it's flap open and peer inside, before retrieving a rifle that lay frozen to the icy ground. As he wrenched it free Philip saw that beneath it was black rock. A few more steps and they were walking on bare stone, blasted so smooth that no snow could cling to its surface.

Squinting ahead Philip noticed the blurry outline of colourful prayer flags flapping wildly off a small, bent pole wedged into a pile of rocks and realised that they weren't climbing any more. He looked around. The snow was easing and he glimpsed jagged white peaks towering over them as the cloud momentarily lifted. They pressed on, their speed picking up considerably now they were off the snow. After a few minutes Mingma came to a large boulder left from an old rock fall and halted. Without being told they untied the ropes and stowed them away. Already the strength of the wind had decreased and it was possible to talk again.

Philip tried to remove his goggles but found his hands too cold to grip them. Clumsily he pushed them up with his gloves, blinking in the brilliant light. He looked around, squinting and trying to ignore the pounding headache. It was a relief to see the world in focus again, if only for a few moments. They were standing in an area of bare rock, dotted with small patches of frozen snow that lay protected from the prevailing winds behind small rocks and boulders. The glacier they'd been following had vanished, left behind in the valley as they'd climbed up to the pass in the storm. Ahead he could see a new glacier tumbling down the far side of the valley. It was different from the dirty, grey ice they'd been following that morning. This was pristine white, covered in a dazzling layer of fresh snow. He fumbled for his goggles and slid them back over his eyes. This ice flow fell from a small hanging valley down into the one they were now following, tumbling off ahead of them towards Tibet. Its beauty made him momentarily forget his exhaustion.

Lhamu pulled back her hood and smiled at him. "We are over the pass. It will be easier now." She stepped closed and took his hands, pulling the outer mittens off and rubbing them hard between her own gloved hands. "We must get these working again." She looked at him sternly. "As we walk you must work them constantly. Keep them moving and rub them."

Despite the pain in his head he smiled at her weakly. "You sound like my mother!" he said, wincing as his dry lips split and he tasted blood in his mouth.

"Someone has to look after you while you are here," she replied, not looking at him as she carefully slid his hands back into his mittens. "We will descend quickly now, mostly on the rocks beside the glacier. There is little snow from now on. It all falls on the Nepal side from the Monsoon rains. The mountains prevent it from reaching Tibet, which is why the plateau is so dry. Apart from occasional storm there is little rain on this side."

"We must now be alert for the soldiers," added Prem.

"You saw the dead man on the pass?" he asked, indicating with his head back up the slope. "They must have been in a bad way when they got here and I don't think they would have been able to go much further yesterday. It was their radio in that bag and if they were not able to retrieve that they must have been exhausted."

Philip nodded. "You and Mingma scout ahead so we don't stumble into them. When you locate them, follow until they camp and come back and report." He winced as he dabbed more cream onto his lips. "We'll keep moving until we meet up with you. Then we'll decide on a plan of attack."

Prem nodded and had a brief conversation in Nepalese with the Sherpa.

"If we're not back by nightfall, camp when you find a suitable place," Prem said. "We will find you."

Philip and Lhamu nodded and watched as the two men pulled on their packs and head off down the slope, walking strongly and springing from rock to rock.

Philip turned to the men and explained what was happening. "We must keep going as long as we can. It's going to be tough on the knees for the rest of the day but at least the air will be getting thicker and the temperature warmer the more we drop. It everybody OK?"

There was a murmur of assent and some nodding heads.

"Good," he continued. "Let's get going and get out of this cold before bits start dropping off."

They set off down the valley, Lhamu setting a pace that everybody seemed comfortable with except Tashi, who was struggling at the rear. Philip slowly dropped back, checking on the men as he passed and offering an encouraging word.

When he finally reached Tashi, his face was white with exhaustion and cold.

"Are you OK?" Philip asked, resting a hand gently on his shoulder. He could feel the Indian shaking beneath his hand.

"I … I've never been this God damned cold in my life," he replied at last, his jaw shivering. "Can't we just camp and get a big fire going. I need a hot drink or I don't think I'll make it."

Philip shook his head. "If we stay here we'd be as good as dead come nightfall. We've no fuel and there's not going to be any firewood this high."

"How about a proper rest then," the Indian asked desperately. "Just for an hour or so until we've all recovered and had something to eat. I'm sure everybody feels the same."

"No," Philip replied firmly. "The only option is to push on and get down as quickly as possible. Don't worry, the worst's over. We should have left the snow behind on the other side." He reached back into a side pocket of his pack and pulled out a half-eaten bar of chocolate.

"Here," he said, handing it to the Indian. "Eat this; it'll give you some energy. I'm afraid it's frozen solid," he added with a smile, "so you'll need to suck it until it softens."

Tashi took the chocolate and ripped off the wrapper, pushing a chunk into his mouth.

"Didn't you have weather like this when you were growing up in Tibet?" Philip asked, trying to keep Tashi's mind distracted.

He nodded, moving the chocolate into a cheek to reply. "The winters were bitter," he said. "There was rarely snow but the wind blew across the steppe and stripped it bare.

When I was sent out to fetch wood it would cut through my clothes as if they weren't there." He smiled weakly. "At least they couldn't send me to get the water. It was frozen so thick that I was too weak to break through so my older brothers had to go."

"What about when you had to flee?" Philip asked, intrigued by the past of the trader. "Were you allowed to bring your possessions with you?"

Tashi shook his head, his face bitter. "We took only what we could salvage after they burnt our home. They said they wouldn't kill us as we were fellow Buddhists but they might as well have done. My brothers had died trying to defend us, my grandparents and younger sister died as we fled to India." He spat a small piece of wrapper from his mouth that had been frozen on to the chocolate. "My mother never recovered. She died soon after reaching Darjeeling, broken by the journey and the betrayal. My elder sisters I've never seen again, despite searching on my trading trips. That's why I'm still here and not sauced up in Kathmandu right now. Someone is going to pay for what happened to my family and however tough, this is my chance."

They continued in silence, trudging along lost in their own thoughts. The path here was easier, a frozen crust of small stones and pebbles that their feet crunched into and gripped. Although breathless from the thin air he didn't feel the need to stop so often but without the exertion of climbing, he could feel himself getting colder and colder. The wind still blew into his face making his sinuses ache from the frozen air.

After an hour they left the stony terrain and snaked down

onto the side of the huge glacier that tumbled down from a mountain to the north, filling the valley they were descending. After several hundred yards of scrambling along its surface, leaping small crevasses that cut across the trail, they climbed off its ice and picked up a small trail that followed the loose moraine to its side. Giant boulders lay scattered around; some perched precariously on smaller ones, with others occasionally blocking their progress, making them detour around them.

It slowed progress considerably, every footstep needing careful attention as the scree was loose and liable to slip away. Several of the men fell and slid down the slope to where the glacial ice started, its outer edge melted by the warmth of the rocks to create a menacing black void that seemed to fall away deep into its core. Philip felt his feet slide away at one point, grasping desperately for a stable handhold as he slithered down the slope. When he finally stopped himself some fifteen feet below the trail, he lay on the ground panting, face down on the cold rock with his heart beating wildly.

They stopped after another hour in the lee of a small cliff. Within minutes the men had a small fire burning and some water boiling for tea. Philip had always marvelled in the jungle how quickly the men could conjure a brew, however wet the weather. He sat watching with his back against the rock. He'd carefully removed his gloves and was now working on his fingers in an attempt to get some circulation back. He blew on them, flexing each finger, rubbing and wringing them in turn before sitting with hands squeezed tightly together as the agony of returning blood made the bones in the fingers ache.

Mani came over with a mug of strong, sweet tea which he gratefully took, nodding his thanks and sitting with it clasped in his hands. He could feel the heat burning into his palms, the tips of his fingers throbbing. He raised the mug to his lips and gulped the liquid greedily, ignoring the pain from his lips. He felt it searing his mouth and tongue, relishing the sensation of heat. Gulping down the rest of the drink he returned the mug to the men tending the fire.

He felt stronger, the sugar from the tea strengthening his body and resolve. Stamping his feet he tried to restore some feeling in them but without success. They'd have to wait, he thought grimly, until there was time to examine and warm them properly. He had, he noticed, been served his drink first and not wanting the men to feel hurried he turned and slowly made his way up a moraine slope that ran up the side of the valley. Since crossing the Nangpa la the snow had stopped and the cloud lifted, giving better visibility, even if the wind still blew bitterly into their faces.

He'd gone about fifty feet up the valley side when he found a small outcrop of rock he could perch on, glad to have found somewhere stable to prop him up as he tried to catch his breath. Looking around he was amazed at how the terrain had changed. On the Nepal side there'd been forest and scrub high up the valley until it was finally buried by the ice of the glacier and the thick snows that blanketed the entire upper valley. Here there was nothing but ice and rock. Looking down the valley he could see the tumbling glacier of white and blue, framed as far as the eye could see by the black and grey of the valley walls on either side. This was Tibet, its high plateaux kept barren by the freezing temperatures and the bitter winds that swept across its endless, arid plain.

He squinted, looking down the valley for any sign of movement. He could see nothing, partly because his eyes filled with tears as the breeze blew fine dust into his face. After rubbing his eyes clear he scrambled back down the slope to where the men had finished their brew and were packed to depart. Without a word they moved out, moving at a faster pace that, invigorated by the tea, Philip was comfortable with for a while. But he knew he was getting tired. His concentration kept wandering which resulted in a couple of stumbles he only just managed to recover. He'd always been amazed by the stamina of Gurkhas, they seemed to just keep on going, accepting and adapting to whatever situation they were in. He'd often wished for the same strength during his time in Burma and he did again now.

Without warning the trail contoured around a small ridge that jutted out into the valley and down below they could see Mingma and Prem. Their packs were lying on a silt beach beside a large pool fed by a stream that tumbled down the mountain side, before overflowing and disappearing under the glacier. They were both searching around, looking he guessed for anything that would burn. There was already a small pile of dead scrub and yak dung neatly stacked in the lea of some rocks. The weary column dropped down to join them and as soon as they arrived the Gurkhas collected the pieces of the tent from everyone's baggage and started to erect it. Mingma set about creating a stone hearth and dispatched any spare men off to find more fuel.

Philip, Prem and Lhamu rolled three rounded boulders

over to where it was going to be and sat wearily upon them, Tashi collapsing exhausted onto the beach beside them.

"Did you spot them?" Philip asked, trying to sound interested when all that he could really think about was removing his frozen feet from his sodden boots.

Mingma nodded, lighting some dry kindling he'd taken from his pack. "They are less than an hour ahead and already camped." He looked at his watch. "That was a couple of hours ago so they must have been exhausted to camp so early. They must have spent last night high on the pass. It will have been freezing."

"They have several men in a bad way," Prem added. "I saw a couple using their rifles as crutches and one was lying down being bandaged."

Philip sat starring into the small crackling fire that Mingmo was coaxing into life, almost too weary to think.

"So they're within striking range. We just have to decide on what's the best way to tackle them." He grimaced as he rubbed his feet and felt blood slowly forcing its way back into them.

He looked at Lhamu. "Where do you think they're headed?"

She shrugged. "It is hard to say. I think they will continue north. The trail gets easier as you drop out of the mountains. In three days they will hit the main caravan route between Kathmandu and Lhasa. I think they will have some transport waiting there or will steal some ponies."

Philip nodded. "We'll start before dawn and attack them while they're still asleep. They'll be exhausted and disorientated, and in the dark their guns won't be as effective as our knives."

He glanced at Prem. "Can you tell the men?" He nodded towards his feet. "If I stay here all night they might just about be thawed in time for the fun tomorrow."

Prem stood up and smiled. "Makes a change from tropical sores and leeches."

CHAPTER 14

Burma, 1943

Philip cautiously approached the hut. It seemed deserted, not a sound to be heard above the noises of the jungle that had started again after the shooting. Perhaps the villagers had fled when they heard the gunfire. He hoped not. They still needed food and without them they'd never find out where it was hidden.

There was a flash and the air by his left cheek fizzed, followed by the shark crack of a gunshot. He threw himself down, landing with a thump on the hard, dusty ground and rolling forward. He gasped in a couple of breaths, spitting out the dust that had clogged his mouth and rubbing it from his eyes. Peering back he realised that he was the nearest to the hut, his dive having taken him close enough to be out of the line of fire.

"Stay down," he hissed back into the night before squirming his way forward on his belly, keeping as low as possible.

More shots rang out. Looking back he could see how exposed Prem and the other Gurkhas were. They'd been caught in the open, with only the darkness of the night preventing them from being easy targets. It fell silent again and he could hear them scrambling back to safety behind the tall stone shrine which was the nearest cover. A short burst of machine gunfire rattled out and tiny plumes of dirt were kicked up as the bullets danced around them, others ricocheting off into the night from the stone shrine walls.

The moon slowly emerged from behind some heavy storm clouds that had been building all day. It bathed the village in an eerie light strong enough to throw ghostly shadows all around and Philip realised that the others were pinned down, unable to move without being seen. He was the only one who could act.

He scrambled to where a thick teak post was driven into the earth, one of the main supports for the hut that loomed over him. The pungent smell of pig muck stung his nose and he could hear panicked squealing from the darkness beneath the building. Leaning against the wood he fumbled for his belt, groping for the smooth metal texture of a grenade. Wrenching one free he clasped it to his chest, removing the pin while keeping the spoon held tightly down. It was a five second fuse. If he threw it immediately there was the chance that it might be picked up and thrown back. He spun up onto his knees and released the spoon.

He took deep, steady breaths to calm himself. He was standing deep in the outfield of a manicured cricket pitch, the ball racing towards him. In one movement he would stoop, pick it up and throw it back like an arrow. It would smack into the wicketkeepers gloves, hitting their toughened leather exactly as he counted five. He was good at this. He'd done it thousands of times on the pitches at school.

On two he stood and peered over the veranda. It was about level with his head and set back about ten feet was the front wall of the hut itself. There was a small window, no more than a gap in the matting, through which two rifles protruded. In one fluid flick of the arm he threw the grenade as he reached three. One of the rifles fired and in the flash he glimpsed the dull sheen of the grenade as spun past the barrel and disappeared into the void of the window. Too late he turned to throw himself down as the blast of the explosion lifted him and drove him hard into the dirt, winding him with the impact. Debris rained down, a bamboo rafter landing painfully across his back, followed by smaller pieces of wood and then stems of dried grass and leaves that smouldered and glowed.

His ears were ringing, his lungs clogged once more with dust and now smoke. He pulled his knees up under his body, trying to pull air back into his lungs. He could smell burnt flesh, pork meat he guessed, and made a note to get some of it before they left the village. He shook his head to clear his ears and wiped his mouth on his sleeve, blood smearing across the material.

A hand grasped him under the arm and hauled him to his feet. He turned and saw Prem looking at him, glancing him up and down to check for injuries. Satisfied there were none, the Gurkha nodded and turned back to the others who'd emerged from behind the shrine and surrounding bush. They lifted the ladder back in place and climbed silently into the shell of the hut.

Philip looked around, still dazed, and stooped to retrieve his revolver which lay on the ground. He climbed the log ladder after his men, almost falling as it shifted sharply to one side but managing to scramble onto the platform. The hut had almost totally gone, its light construction obliterated by the explosion. A few hard teak posts still stood, some connected by beams from which hung fragments of the woven leaf matting that had made up the walls.

He walked to where the door had been, its broken frame now the only thing remaining, and stepped inside. The interior was still thick with smoke but to his left he saw the bodies of two Japanese soldiers, thrown forward by the blast, which looked to have happened while the grenade was still tumbling through the air. Half buried in the debris, their legs stuck out naked where their trouser legs had been ripped away, twisted into unnatural angles. One boot had been blown off, taking the foot with it and leaving a bloody stump clogged with dust.

The smoke and dust were slowly clearing, and as Philip turned to look it revealed a scene of utter devastation. Philip stood paralysed, unable to comprehend what was before him, before turning and vomiting over the legs of the dead soldiers. The retching had cleared his ears of the pressure of the explosion and the sounds of moaning and weeping swept over him. He slowly turned back, his chest so tight he couldn't breathe. There were bodies everywhere. It looked as if the whole village had been crammed into this one hut by the Japanese, presumably to stop them slipping away to warn them of their presence.

Looking down he saw the body of a young Burmese boy, little more than six or seven years old. His left leg was twisted back on itself at the knee. His arms were thrown back above his head with several fingers missing from each hand. Blood slowly seeping from the torn stumps and disappeared through gaps in the rough wooden floor. His eyes were still open, staring blankly up at the moon whose rays fell through the non-existent roof and caught the smoke still rising from his singed and burnt hair. Philip knelt, fearing that his legs might give way beneath him, and reached out his trembling hand gently closed the boys eyes. He felt himself going numb, his mind detaching itself from his consciousness as shock washed through him.

Glancing around he saw the bodies of other villagers, who must have been standing directly under the blast. The bodies were a jumble, an unrecognisable mass of flesh, cloth and bone. Others sat or lay on the floor, perforated with small shrapnel wounds to their faces and necks or with splinters of jagged wood protruding from their bodies. Most bled from their ears after the enclosed blast had shredded their ear drums.

He watched as Prem made his way through the bodies towards him and crouched beside him.

"We've found Balbir. He was in a room at the back. He should be strong enough to come with us. The villagers had bound his wounds before," he looked around, "before the explosion. He'll be able to walk when he gets circulation back into his legs. The Japs had tied him up tight."

Philip nodded, trying to think. "Help him out and then get back to where we left the packs. Rana will show you the way." He looked around the hut. "We know they'd radioed their HQ and after this I expect every Jap in Burma is heading this way."

Prem nodded and stood, ordering the Gurkhas out of the hut with a curt order in Nepalese. They left quickly, one of them supporting Balbir, keen to leave the carnage. They carefully lowered him off the edge of the veranda into the waiting hands of those who'd been on watch outside, before jumping down and disappearing off into the darkness.

Philip stood alone. The flames were now subsiding and everything was fading into darkness. The villagers who'd escaped the worst injuries were starting to wander around, staring in disbelief at what surrounded them. He heard a woman cry out in anguish and run over to the boy at his feet, collapsing onto it and hugging the broken body to her. Her weeping and torrent of desperate words made Philip despair, holding his head in his hands.

Why had he tossed the grenade? His men had scrambled to safety and he could have climbed onto the veranda unnoticed and shot through the opening. He could have joined the pigs under the hut, looking silently up from the darkness beneath to shoot through the uneven flooring at the guards. For Christ's sake he could just as easily have killed Balbir as the Japs as he'd no idea where the injured man had been in the hut. All he could hear was silent weeping and the moaning of the wounded. It was his fault. He had to get out. He couldn't bear to listen any longer to the consequences of what he'd done.

As he turned towards the door he heard a small whimper of pain. Taking a couple of faltering steps, towards a pile of singed grass thatch laying in the corner, he gingerly pushed it aside. In the moonlight a beautiful young woman lay motionless, staring up at him. Her long black hair fanned out behind her head on the floor and framed the pale white of her skin. Her face was perfect, unblemished, with large brown eyes and a small, full mouth. She reminded Philip of one of his sisters china dolls she'd used to carry everywhere when still young; delicate, as if she could shatter at any moment. The eyes focused on his face and he saw the face crease with a combination of pain and fear. Glancing down at her body he could see no sign of an injury but noticed a large stain of blood spreading on the floor beneath.

"Hello," he said quietly, kneeling by her side. "You seem to have been in the wars. Will you let me have a look at you?"

The woman didn't move, only her eyes following Philips movements.

Gently he felt the woman's shoulders and head, trying to find the source of the bleeding. Nothing. The front of her abdomen looked fine so he carefully ran his fingers behind her shoulders and sides. As he felt beneath her upper arm he could feel the flow of hot, sticky blood, pumping rhythmically onto his fingers.

"I'm just going to move you slightly to see where it is that you're hurt," he said, trying to make his voice sound reassuring and sliding his hands beneath her shoulder and waist, gently raised her up. He knew immediately it was hopeless. In the centre of her back was a hole; protruding from it a huge splinter of hardened bamboo. It was half embedded in her spine, the rest lost in a bloody pit from which blood pumped. She hadn't moved when she'd seen him because she hadn't been able. She was paralysed. He could see air bubbling through the wound and knew it'd pierced her lungs.

He reached into his pocket and pulled out a dose of morphine, ripping it from its wrapping. He'd been trained before the campaign had started in giving lethal injections, knowing that there'd be no evacuation possible for seriously injured men and a quick end was a better than a painful, lonely death in the jungle.

"Here we go," he said, his voice cracking. "This will take away the pain." A tear ran from his eye, landing on her tiny hand. Lifting the woman's arm he searched for a vein and quickly stabbed in the drug. Throwing the empty container away he stayed, gently squeezing the woman's hand. After a few moments she felt her weakly grasp his back. "I'm not going anywhere," he said quietly, "I'll stay with you."

The morphine acted quickly but to Philip it felt like an eternity. Finally her eyes started to lose their focus and slowly close. Gently he placed her hand on her chest and lowered his head, his eyes clamped shut to prevent more tears. He felt he should pray but had no words to use. It seemed wrong to pray for someone you'd just murdered.

His mind lurched as a bright light flashed through his eyelids. Forcing them open he watched bemused as a thin beam of light moved around the hut, shining through the rips and holes in the shattered walls. Glancing out, he could see a wall of distant torches sweeping towards the village. Japs. He struggled to his feet, trying to think what to do. It must have been at least a couple of minutes since Prem had left with the men. He could jump down behind the hut and run for the forest. He glanced out again and realised that his chances of getting away, unspotted, were slim. Even if he did, it would take him time to work his way around the village and fields back to the rendezvous, time his men could better use.

He glanced around the hut. He couldn't stay here. If he fired they would pinpoint his position and god knows how many more villagers would be killed when they returned fire. For the first time in days he felt calm, certain of what he had to do to save his men.

Moving to where the dead Japanese lay he searched the floor, groping with his hands until they felt the hot barrel of the machine gun. A quick examination showed it to be undamaged, shielded from the blast by the body of its user. Scrabbling around he found a couple of belts of ammo and slung them around his shoulders. Crossing to the furthest wall he crouched and waited out of sight behind some debris. For a moment the torches swung away and seizing the moment he leapt through a shredded wall and ran in a crouch towards the shrine, diving behind it just as a beam swept back across the clearing.

He lay there panting, listening for any indication that he'd been spotted. When none came he clambered up onto the first ledge, then the next of the stepped structure until he was ten feet or so above the ground. Sitting with his back to the shrines rock pinnacle he loaded the gun. It felt good to have it in his hands. After all the skulking around of the previous weeks it was a relief to finally have an enemy you could see.

Rolling onto his stomach he slid along the ledge until he could just see around the side of the shrine. Its stone felt cool and solid, a relief after the rotting decay of the forest floor. In the moonlight he could make out a line of thirty or so soldiers walking slowly into the top end of the village, spread out every five yards or so. They all had their guns at the ready, pointing ahead. Many had torches and were sweeping them around the deserted village, looking for signs of life.

Philip took a deep breath and clenched his fists, trying to force the shaking from his hands. If he couldn't escape at least he could buy more time for the men. He slowly slid the barrel forward, until its tip peeped around the stone at the enemy. He closed his eyes, forcing himself to breathe deeply and smoothly. Taking aim at a Jap in the middle of the line he gently squeezed the trigger, slowly swinging the gun round as it exploded into life. Several of the men fell to the ground.

His world exploded. Noise enveloped him and the very air seemed to be sucked from his lungs as the stone on which he lay started to disintegrate under the barrage of fire. Pain seared through him; something burnt into his shoulder, physically knocking him back a few inches. He laid his head down on the rough masonry, not to shelter his head but to rest. He was so tired. He'd failed his men. He'd led them into ambushes and led ridiculous river crossings. He'd killed innocent villagers. They would all have been better off without him. This was the end he deserved. At least in death he'd achieve what he'd been unable to give them alive; the chance to survive and see their families again.

The deafening noise had left him stunned, his ears ringing and blinded by the dazzling muzzle flashes. He wasn't sure where he was anymore. He was walking through a wood, his father beside him. They were laughing, his father's arm draped over his shoulder with its hand up tousling his hair. He felt so proud, so grown up. He was enveloped in an embrace, warm, comforting, secure. He couldn't see who it was but he knew it was his mother. The smell of lavender filled his nostrils, her hair tickled the side of his face. She was crying, he could tell, her breath coming in quiet sobs. They were thousands of miles away in a different world yet somehow they'd come to him, to help him through.

It was a shame. He felt angry. There was so much he'd wanted to do, so much left to see. The silence was almost as shocking as the chaos had been, as every creature in the jungle seemed to have fallen silent in anticipation of his death. Philip tilted his good wrist and looked at the small luminous hands on his watch. Three more minutes had passed, his men should be clear, warned away by the shooting. His eyes fell on the date that was displayed on the dial. It showed a two. It was the second of April. He pushed the gun forward again and fired blindly into the night. A storm of bullets spat back out of the night at him as his strength slipped away. He'd forgotten. It was his twentieth birthday. He hoped his family found out how he died.

CHAPTER 15

Tibet, 1953

They were up well before dawn. Despite his exhaustion Philip had slept fitfully. A combination of the biting cold, the constant ache in his feet and the rest of the men coughing and turning all night made him grateful when the time finally came to stir. There seemed to have been a constant procession of men leaving the tent to relieve themselves, a consequence of the altitude. He winced as he pushed his feet into his stiff boots, pain from his damaged toes shooting painfully up his legs. He's slept with his boots inside his sleeping bag in an attempt to keep them from freezing, another factor in his bad night.

The Gurkhas quickly collapsed and dismantled the tent and within minutes they were packed and heading off along the rough trail that lead down the valley. At least the wind had died during the night but the temperatures were still well below freezing and seemed to cut right through Philip's clothing. The sky had also cleared and a waxing moon shone down at them, its light reflecting off the snow and ice of the glacier and illuminating their path in a pale, silvery light.

Philip stopped as the person in front of him stumbled and fell, landing heavily upslope on his hip. Leaning down, he took the arm of the man, who was now struggling to get up, pulling against the weight of his rucksack. It was Tashi.

"Thanks," the Indian said weakly. "I seem to be short on gas this morning."

Philip smiled. "I know the feeling." He stopped short as the light fell on his face. He looked terrible. His eyes were sunken and hollow, black rings dark beneath them. He could feel him trembling where he still grasped his arm.

Tashi must've noticed his expression and pulled his arm free. "I didn't sleep well," he said defensively. "Too damn cold." He continued down the path, walking determinedly but unsteadily.

They trudged on, each lost in their own world of pain. Philip winced every time one of his boots caught a rock, a searing pain replacing the dull ache that emanated from his feet. His hands had gone numb again and the rough stubble that covered his chin was now encased in ice, the moisture from his breath freezing to it as it hit the icy air. Now his eyes had grown used to the eerie light he could see quite well. The moon was high overhead, bright enough for him to follow his lunar shadow as it mirrored his laboured actions on the broken terrain.

Glancing down the valley he could see that they'd swung eastwards, turning a bend which had hidden them from the Chinese camp. He realised that they'd slowed, and mustering energy he didn't really think he had, he moved forward along the line to the front. When he reached Prem, the Gurkha had stopped and was climbing onto a huge glacial boulder lying beside the trail. Philip followed, trying to pull himself up with his arms to save his toes scraping on its rough surface.

Prem glanced at him as he crawled along side, lying flat on the icy surface.

"Can you see them?" Philip whispered, scanning the valley for signs of a fire.

"No. Their camp was only a few hundred yards on from here." He tapped the boulder with his gloved hand. "I used this rock as a marker." He pointed to a spur of rock that jutted far out into the valley below, squeezing the glacier into a narrow gorge. "They were using that for shelter from the wind and had a big fire going. I don't understand why they wouldn't keep it burning. There is enough fuel down here. I'm sure they don't know we are following them. They were relaxed and hadn't set any guards." He looked up at the sky. "Even if they had let the fire die, they should be up by now making it again. It'll be dawn in less than an hour and they will want to get down from this glacier as soon as they can."

There was a silence as both men peered intently down the valley.

"Perhaps they've decided to stay in their tents until the sun rises and brings some heat?" Philip suggested but Prem shook his head.

"Their tents have gone. We could see them from here and even in this light we should still be able too."

They were silent again. "Well, there's only one way to know for sure," Philip said at last. "We'll have to get closer."

They slithered back down to the trail where Lhamu was waiting anxiously.

"Wait here," Philip whispered. "They seem to have moved out so we're going to take a look. Can you tell the rest so they know what the delay is?"

"Of course," she said with a nod. "And Philip," she added, catching his sleeve as he passed. "Take care."

Philip smiled back, trying not to wince as the ice on his face cracked and pulled at his raw skin. He turned and followed Prem, trying to keep up with the Gurkha as they quickly climbed up the steep side of the valley, gaining height over the trail as it dropped steadily down towards the camp. In a couple of minutes they were looking down onto a small area of flat ground nesting behind the shelter of the rocky spur. There was nothing there. They scrambled on a short distance until the slope from the ridge rose so steeply they could climb no further. From this vantage point they could just see over the ridge and down towards the lower valley. There was nothing to be seen, the only sound was that of a river far below drifting back up to them.

"They've gone," said Prem, standing up and scrambling down towards the abandoned camp. Philip followed and started searching for any signs of life while Prem signalled with his torch for the rest to join them. He soon found the extinguished fire, with a pile of wood beside it, and pulling off his thick mitten, held his exposed hand to the ashes. Nothing. Carefully he picked up a piece of half-burnt wood and knocked the charcoal from the end. When he touched it to his skin there was a faint trace of heat. He turned as Prem walked over to him.

"They must have left before we were up." He shook his head. "I don't understand it. Why get up at the coldest time of night when you are tired, have firewood and don't need too?"

Prem dropped the wood back into the hearth, shaking

his head. "Perhaps they did spot us yesterday, or one of them came back up the trail and saw our camp." He looked around at the valley walls looming over them. "They must have had a good reason."

Philip stood up, pulling his mitt back over his fingers. The rest had caught up and were now standing watching, moving from leg to leg, stamping their feet on the ground and swinging their arms. "As you can see, they've moved on, some time ago we believe." He rubbed at his face to dislodge some of the ice from his stubble. "I suggest we keep moving to stay warm until the sun rises, then we'll halt for some breakfast." He looked into the group of men. "Tarun?"

A small, squat man stepped forward and nodded. Ten years earlier, Philip recalled, they used to joke that he could track a termite in the jungle.

"Time to see if those skills you had are still there. You and Prem lead us and track them. We need to know where they're going."

They walked on, initially climbing up onto the glacier itself to get through the narrow gorge created by the ridge. It was only for a few hundred yards but Philip didn't like it at all. It had a claustrophobic feel, with the rock walls seeming to hang in over you. Beneath his feet the ice groaned and creaked as it was forced through the narrow opening. It was with some relief that the valley opened up once more and they climbed back down onto the rocky valley floor, picking up the snaking path that dropped away in front of them.

As they descended, Philip could hear the roar of a river getting louder and louder and suddenly, without warning, the glacier ended. From its snout rushed a torrent of water, spewing from its bowels. It cascaded off down the valley, surrounded by wide boulder fields and the occasional patch of brown, crisp grass.

Dawn rose about them, the eastern skyline with a deep blue that highlighted every gulley and ridge on a towering mountain in crystal detail. Philip watched in wonder, for a few minutes forgetting the aching in his legs and throbbing feet. It was Everest. Somewhere high up there were the men he'd met only a few days before. James was there, perhaps at that very moment eating eggs and bread and drinking tea. It already felt like another world. The skies colour changed to a deep orange, slowly lightened to a yellow from which burst the first rays of the sun, cutting across the valley to light the tips of the western peaks. Slowly it crept down, shadows shortening, until at last it kissed the men's heads with its warmth.

The whole atmosphere changed. There was laughing as thick scarves and hoods were pulled off freezing faces. Philip spotted a small area of ground bathed in the sun and dropped his bag, indicating for the others to do the same. Tea was brewed, food shared out and feet exposed and massaged around a fire that had been lit. Prem and Tarun set off again as soon as they'd finished their breakfast to pick up the trail of the soldiers but after only twenty minutes they were back.

"Anyone could follow them," Tarun said dismissively. "They left a trail like a herd of yaks. They turn east where the valley splits rather than continuing north."

Prem looked at Lhamu. "I think they're exhausted and need somewhere to rest up for a while. What is the nearest village they could head for?"

"It is not a village," Lhamu replied. "It is the monastery at Rombuk. It is an easy trail used by the Thangboche monks when they visit. They will be there by nightfall."

"Can we catch them?" Philip asked.

Lhamu shook her head. "There are no faster ways I know of, and if they left early I doubt they will stop until they get there."

"Damn it," said Philip. "Now they'll be able to rest and eat while we're the ones who'll be cold and exhausted." He rubbed at his stubble which was itching now that the ice had melted. "What will the monks do when they turn up?"

Lhamu shrugged. "They will not be happy. The Chinese army has destroyed many monasteries in Tibet. But what can they do if the soldiers are armed?"

"What about the Rinpoche. Won't they recognise him?" Philip asked.

"Maybe. They will have seen photos of him but I think the Chinese will keep him disguised or hidden."

There was silence, except for the roaring of the river and the occasional calls high above from a flock of chuffs, soaring in the morning sun.

Finally Philip spoke. "Right, we need to get there and layup. If we can get a message to the Head Lama explaining the situation then I'm sure the monks will help. Let's head off once we've all thawed out a bit. We can make the monastery by nightfall and then try to make contact with the monks under cover of darkness."

Philip stood up and wandered around the rest of the men, most of whom were lying on the ground, heads resting on their packs and dozing in the warm sun. He could see the exhaustion in their faces. They all had cracked lips, many with blood oozing from between the dried, damaged skin. Their faces were burnt and blistered from the snow-reflected sun, with panda eyes from where their goggles had protected the surrounding skin. Their hair was dishevelled and rigid, caked to their heads and running into the beginnings of wispy beards. A couple of the men started to get up as he passed but he put his hand on their shoulders to keep them from doing so, smiling at them as he moved on.

His own feet were in a bad way. The tips of his toes, especially the smaller ones, were a deathly white which no amount of massage seemed to change. He returned to his bag and after a quick rummage around pulled out a pair of dry socks. As soon as they were on he felt better, sitting down and toasting them by the flames until he could feel the painful prickling as blood fought its way back in. He felt his eyes close as the heat rippled through him, relaxing knotted muscles. He was just starting to doze when he felt somebody gently lift his foot and start massaging it. Opening his eyes he saw Lhamu concentrating on his foot as she firmly squeezed and stretched his toes.

She looked up at him and smiled. "I think a rub now will be painful but for the best. My father lost two toes when he was on Everest." She raised her eyebrows. "I am sure that would hurt more."

Philip winced as one of the toes gave a sharp crack but she continued undeterred. He thought of something to say to distract himself. "So what's Rombuk like?"

"It is a hard place to live," she replied. "The winters are

dark and cold, and the summers are hard and long as they try to gather food for themselves and their animals."

"Is it a large monastery?"

"Yes," she nodded. "When I was last there they had over 500 monks living there, as well as a good number of traders passing through and many, many pilgrims who'd come for blessings and the festivals. I remember the men in the caves most." She smiled. "They frightened me when I was young. I do not know the word for them in your language."

"Men in caves?" Philip asked. "You mean hermits? Monks who live by themselves?"

Lhamu nodded. "That's right. They are considered very holy because their life is so harsh but still they meditate for inner peace. It is the most isolated and highest of all monasteries so they are much respected."

"Is there a big central building like at Thangboche?" Philip tensed as searing pain sliced through his foot.

"Not really," Lhamu replied, switching her attention to his other foot. "It is too cold for big rooms. Mostly the monks live in small dormitories or the caves. The central shrine is the largest building, set high above the others."

They chatted on about her memories, of the floors being so slippery from butter spilt from the lamps she could hardly stand, of breaking the ice from the storage barrels of water in the mornings to boil. The time passed quickly and nearly an hour had gone when he saw Prem get up and nod towards him.

He started putting his boots on, trying not to show Lhamu how painful his feet now were. "Thank you," he said with a rather forced smile. "That's feels much better."

She laughed. "You are a very bad liar," she replied, "but they will be fine in a day or two."

They all stood and having pulled on their packs, fell into line and head off stiffly down the trail. They soon came to the fork in the valley and struck off east, following a path that meandered its way along beside a small stream. After the terrain of the last few days it was easy going. There was no ice or glaciers to traverse or climb, occasional snow patches were compacted and easy to cross and as they descended the oxygen returned and made their breathing less laboured.

They walked on for several hours, Philip dropping up and down the line to chat with several of his old platoon that he hadn't had the opportunity to catch up with. He still found it hard to believe that they all here. It was mid-afternoon, just as the sun was dropping behind the mountains that he spotted a small light ahead of them down the valley. He hurried forward.

"Is that the monastery?" he asked when he caught them.

"No," Lhamu replied. "It is a lamp in one of the hermit caves. This side valley drops into the main valley and the monastery is situated down to the left, we cannot see it yet."

"Is it far?" he asked, scanning the horizon for any signs of habitation or people.

"No more than thirty minutes," she replied.

They'd stopped walking and Philip scanned around. At some point the stream must have run close up against the valley wall as it had cut into it and formed a shallow cave facing back towards them.

"We'll camp there," Philip said, pointing at the overhang.

"We'll be shielded from view if anyone looks back up this way. We can light a fire."

They crossed to the cave, keen to get set up before they lost the last of the light. He looked at Prem. "Let's establish camp and some get some hot food cooked. Then get the men to rest for an hour or so. It's going to be a long night."

The corporal nodded and headed off.

Philip looked at Mingma and Lhamu. "We'll need to do a reconnaissance, work out where the soldiers are and what the monks are doing. I'd like the three of us to go." He looked at Lhamu. "You're the only one who's been before and has got any idea of where to go. I wouldn't normally ask but …"

She shook her finger. "I am a Sherpani, not some fine English lady. Of course I will go."

Mingma nodded. "There will be confusion there and we must take advantage of it before things quieten down. The monks have dogs to protect their sheep. If we go too late, it will be impossible to get past them without being detected."

Philip nodded. "And the Chinese will post guards. We need to discover where the soldiers are sleeping and where they've put the Rinpoche." He rubbed his aching eyes. "If we can convince the monks to help us it would certainly help even the numbers up as well."

He glanced up as Prem returned and quickly outlined the plan to him. The Gurkha wasn't happy.

"You should take us with you, you will not be protected," he said, glaring at Philip.

Philip shook his head. "We're not there to fight, and having me there will add weight to Lhamu and Mingma when they talk to the monks. You'll bring the men down at the same time but stay hidden until we send word. We need to know more about the monastery before we all go piling in."

Prem nodded, his face serious. "We'll leave Parul here. He can keep the fire going and the water hot. We may need it if we decide to delay any attack until morning"

"Good idea," Philip said. "And we'll leave Tashi as well. The man looks exhausted and he'll be more of a hindrance than a help. He can help Parul here at the camp."

He looked at Lhamu and Mingma. "While we wait for the food Lhamu can tell us what she remembers of the monastery layout."

They rolled some boulders to one side of where the fire was now crackling into life and Lhamu, having levelled the dusty surface of the ground with her hand, took a thin stick from the pile of firewood.

"The monastery is different from Thangboche. It is harsher and colder here so it is made of many smaller buildings rather than the one big one. It is easier for the monks to keep warm." She drew a rectangle in the dirt. "This is the main shrine. It contains a large statue of the Buddha and many other images and offerings. It is just one big room and the main entrance is here. It is built on the end of a," she paused a moment, searching for the word, "a large rock that sits out into the middle of the valley. It is why it was selected many years ago as it has an unbroken view of Everest which is a sacred mountain."

Quickly she added a line through one of the rectangles sides, then drew a series of smaller buildings and the shrine's other end.

"Here there is the cook house and several store rooms, as well as some Stupas with prayer wheels the monks can use while doing their everyday jobs."

She leant forward and drew a larger square with wavy edges on the far side of the shrine. "These are the animal enclosures. At night they put the herds in these to keep them safe from wolves and yetis. There is also a stone building here where they keep the guard dogs locked in during the day."

Finally she drew some large blocks opposite the shrine entrance. "There is a large courtyard in front of the shrine that is used for dancing during the festivals. On the far side of this are the dormitories where the monks sleep."

Philip nodded, staring down at the rudimentary plan and trying to fix it in his mind. "So from which direction will we be coming from?" he asked at last.

Lhamu drew an arrow. "We will be coming from the south, here. There will be no cover between us and the main shrine as this is the direction of Everest."

The food arrived, brought over by Lalit and they ate hungrily, plain rice washed down with sweet tea. Philip rummaged in his bag and produced a battered bar of Mint cake he'd been saving since leaving London. "Seems like a good moment to share this," he announced with a smile, carefully dividing the crushed pieces and crumbs into three small piles. It tasted divine. The sugar bringing an instant hit of energy that brought strength flooding back into Philip and with it an optimism he'd been lacking.

It all seemed so horribly familiar. An attack on a settlement to free a prisoner. An unknown enemy, miles from safety in a hostile environment. He glanced at Lhamu. She looked so beautiful, her face glowing with excitement and the absolute belief that what they were doing was right. God, he wished he still had such strength. He felt a sharp twinge from his old wounded shoulder and reached up to massage it through his clothing.

Whatever happened tonight, the life he'd lived for the last decade was over. So many people had died because of and instead of him, it was time he started to make retribution for all that had transpired. He'd somehow lived to get home, to see his mother rush down the long, gravel drive to meet him, engulfing him in an embrace he'd never expected to feel. He'd finished his studies and moved to London, drinking in pubs with friends, dancing at balls and dining at fine restaurants. He'd even got to go to the chiropodists, whose look of horror as he'd revealed his scarred, nail less feet had made him almost collapse with laughter. If he was to die it was at the end of time given, not cut short. He looked at Lhamu again whose eyes met his and smiled, glowing in their shared, private moment. For the first time in many years he realised he wanted to truly live.

It had now grown dark, the clear sky dropping the temperature quickly. He could feel his back chilling despite the fact that his face and chest were warm in the heat of the fire. Glancing up he saw that the moon had yet to rise. It was going to be tricky to get to the monastery but at least without it there was less chance of being seen.

Prem appeared, swathed in a thick blanket in preparation for a cold vigil. Philip slapped him on the shoulder and offered him his last piece of mint cake.

"Go on, take it," he said. "It'll help keep you warm."

The Gurkha suspiciously took it and popped it into his mouth, before smiling and sucking at the same time. The rest of the men appeared, all suitably wrapped, and glancing at his watch Philip saw it was time to go. He looked around and saw Tashi huddled up on the far side of the campfire. He walked round to him and the Indian nodded his head in greeting.

"Keep the fire going and the water hot. I'm not sure how long we'll be but we may be back at any time and we'll be cold. If things go well I'll send somebody back to get you and Parul." He paused, glancing out into the dark night. "If you hear shooting and we haven't returned by first light then pack up and head back over the pass. Parul can use the radio, so keep trying until you get a message through to Namche or anywhere in Nepal requesting assistance."

Tashi shrugged. "I understand," he replied, glancing up at Philip. "But I think you should wait for the morning or it could be one mighty screw up. The men are exhausted and you'll be blundering into a place you know nothing about. What's the hurry? They won't be going anywhere, not now they've found food and somewhere warm. No one's going to rescue them."

Philip looked at the Indian and could see the exhaustion etched on his face. "You might be right, but I just think we need to get it done while they're still exhausted from the journey. Hopefully the heat and food will make them sleepy and we can surprise them."

The Indian shook his head, ignoring Philip by staring into the flames. Philip returned to where the men were waiting. He drew the revolver from its holster, checking it was loaded and shoved his hand into a pocket to feel for the spare ammo. Reaching into his pack he took the hand grenade they'd found on the pass and clipped it onto his belt. The weight of it on his hip made him feel nauseous.

"Ready?" he asked, smiling weakly at Mingma and Lhamu. They both nodded back.

CHAPTER 16

They started off down the trail, walking in silence. Stars filled the sky, more than Philip had ever imagined, and the thick belt of the Milky Way glowed overhead and gave them enough light to find their way. Lhamu led, halting every now and again to look around and check her position. They reached the point that the valleys merged and she stopped. They huddled in close, aware that on such a still night any noise would carry a long way.

"That is the main monastery," she whispered, pointing to a tall, square building whose outline was just visible about 400 yards down the valley. It sat on the top of a rocky knoll, its walls seeming to merge with the rock and give the impression of an impenetrable fortress. Faint light came from cracks around wooden shutters that covered a small window in its side.

She pointed towards a maze of low buildings slightly to the east. "And those are the houses for the monks, and behind are the pens where the sheep are kept. Hopefully the buildings will shield us from the dogs that guard them or they will give us away with their barking if they hear or smell us."

Philip nodded and turned to Prem. "You remain here with

the men. We'll return or send for you when we've made contact with the monks and discovered where the soldiers are."

The Gurkha nodded and using hand gestures commanded the men to get themselves hidden behind some of the moraine that littered the ground.

Philip turned back to Lhamu. "Let's get a look at the main building first. There's light coming from inside and it's the obvious place for the soldiers to be."

They crept forward, ears straining for any sound that might indicate danger. The noise from a rushing river filled the valley, a distant rumble disturbed only by the occasional bleating of a goat or bark from the tethered dogs. Philip felt happier, sure that it was enough to cover the sound of our footfalls.

They ran at a crouch, crossing a barren area of ground covered in a thin, weedy grass that had been grazed down to its roots. It seemed to take forever and there was little cover for them to use. Philip could feel his heart thumping, both from the exertion in the thin air, and from memories that preyed at him. He was back in Burma, the noises of the valley momentarily changing to a night time chorus of the jungle. He shook it from his mind.

At last they reached the bottom of the hill, tight up against a small rock face and he fell to his knees, resting his head on the cold stone as he caught his breath and swallowed down his fear. Leaning back, he looked up. The sides were higher than he'd anticipated, rocky crags jutting out from steep slopes of small, loose stones. It certainly wasn't impossible to climb but it would be impossible to climb quietly.

Having recovered his breath, Philip stood and moved

slowly round to the left, circling the base of the hill while studying its slope. It was, he estimated, about fifty feet up to the shrine walls and he could just see the window from where he'd spotted the light escaping earlier. Continuing on, he moved around to the back of the shrine and noticed, to his satisfaction, that there were no windows in this wall. The hill here was less steep and in the faint starlight he could just make out the start of a small path meandering its way upwards, little more than a rough trail made by grazing animals as they climbed up looking for food.

He beckoned the others to join him and they slowly started to climb, treading carefully so as not to dislodge any loose rocks. The path turned back on itself halfway up, dropping slightly to skirt around a rock outcrop, before continuing its rambling climb to the top and a narrow paved ledge that ran around the foot of the shrine.

Philip quickly walked to the corner and cautiously peered around, Mingma and Lhamu crouching behind him. Everything looked still and he could hear no sound coming from inside the building.

Mingma tapped him on the shoulder, indicating that he was going to move along to the nearest window to look inside. Philip shook his head and pointed to himself, edging forwards around the corner. It was no more than a timber-framed square in the rough masonry. Leaning forward he could see a wooden shutter pushed shut against the opening and behind it what seemed to be a heavy drape of filthy black cloth. He raised himself onto tiptoe and saw a small pool of light falling onto the sill, and when he glanced along saw a small rip in the cloth.

He slowly moved his eye towards the tear and looked inside. Several butter lamps cast a flickering light inside of the shrine. He recoiled as a face turned towards him, eyes staring at him, teeth flashing white in a leering smile. He breathed out slowly when it swung away and he recognised it as a festival mask similar to the ones he'd seen in Thangboche, hanging on a cord from the rafters.

He peered back inside. He could see several figures lying on the floor, some propped against the walls or the bases of large gilded statues of the Buddha. Others were lying on the floor in an exhausted sleep. He heard a raised voice, and shifting his position looked around to where three men, all dressed in filthy uniforms, were berating an old monk. The tallest of them was shouting and Philip winced as he struck the monk a stinging blow to his face. The old monk staggered back, regained his balance and bowed to the man. The soldier called something over his shoulder and two of the sitting figures got wearily to their feet and walked over, shouldering rifles as they did so. Orders were barked at them to which they nodded and walked over to the door, pushing the monk along in front of them.

Philip ducked down. "Quick," he hissed. "Back."

They scrambled around the rear of the building, diving into its shadows. They heard a creaking as a large door swinging open, followed a few moments later by talking. Philip cautiously looked back round the corner. The two soldiers and monk had appearing around the front corner of the building. One of them lifted his boot and kicked the backside of the old man, who fell forward into the dust. He pulled himself to his feet and scurried away, down what

Philip assumed must be the steps at the front of the building, reappearing a few moments later skirting around the base of the hill and disappearing into a long, low stone building.

The two soldiers lit cigarettes, their heads huddled together around a match. Sliding back, he turned to the others. "They've set guards. That seems strange. I'd have thought they'd feel secure now they're back over the border." He thought for a moment. "Perhaps they want to keep an eye on the monks." He looked across at Lhamu. "Make your way down and go to the building where the monk went. See if you can find and talk to him."

Lhamu nodded. "It is the cook house," she replied in a voice he could hardly hear. "I remember it from when I was young." She started to move away and Philip grabbed her arm.

"Be careful," he whispered. "Keep to the shadows and watch for the soldiers." She smiled and was gone.

He turned to Mingma. "Return to Prem. Tell him to bring the men and to wait behind the cook house. I'll stay here and keep an eye on things. They seem to be settling in so this is our best chance to catch them unawares."

Mingma nodded and disappeared silently down the slope.

Philip leant back against the wall, his knees drawn up against his stomach. Despite the exertions of the last few days his body felt surprisingly good, aches vanishing now that adrenalin was pumping around his body. He'd forgotten the feel of danger, the knowledge that any moment could be your last was something he'd once lived with daily.

He opened the pistol and checked again that all the chambers were full. Quietly he slid it back into place, leaving the holster unclipped. Holding his breath so that it wouldn't be visible in the freezing night air he cautiously looked around the corner again. The soldiers were standing where they'd been before, collars raised up over hunched shoulders. In the glow of their cigarettes he could see their faces lined by fatigue, a low babble of chat coming between deep drags.

They finished and ground out the butts underfoot. With a final word, he saw one of them turn and slowly start walk down the side of the shrine towards him. Trying to keep still he waited until the soldier glanced out across the valley and before pulling his head back round the corner. He glanced around, desperately looking for somewhere to hide, but only the smooth white-washed wall of the monastery ran away from him.

Philip cursed as the moon chose that moment to rise over the surrounding ridge. With his eyes now adjusted to the dark, it seemed as bright as day. He had no choice but to run for it. As quietly as he could he scrambled back to the path, taking small, precise steps in an effort to be silent. Loose stones kicked out of the slope and bounced after him, their noise echoing off the surrounding walls. Some hit him on the back of his legs as he dived behind the jagged outcrop halfway down and pressed himself against its rough surface, pulling his revolver free.

He sat there, trying to keep his ragged breathing quiet, staring back up at the small section of the path he could see, willing the last few pebbles to stop rolling. Everything fell silent, only a gently rustling from prayer flags on a nearby chortern and distant running water disturbed the night. He strained his ears, trying to catch any noise that would give away the position of the soldier. He heard the rustling of cloth and then the sharp metallic click as a bullet was pulled through into the breach of a rifle.

He sat holding his breath, praying for the moon to disappear. He could hear soft footsteps walking along the top of the slope. Slowly lifting his left hand he placed it on the pistol which was pointing back up at the slope, ready to flick back the hammer and fire. He heard loose stones rolling down the slope, flinching as the first ones bounced into view on the path. The soldier had to appear at any moment and he started breathing slowly to steady his aim. The tip of a rifle emerged around the rock, followed by a hand, grasping its stock. Philip slowly pulled the hammer back, his hands trembling, when the gun suddenly swung away and disappeared from view. He froze, his pistol on the point of firing, not daring to move. He heard voices calling and the sound of the soldier's footsteps climbing away. He gently eased the pressure on the trigger and shifted his position so he could peer around the edge of the outcrop.

Down below the monk had re-appeared from the kitchen, the light from the open door silhouetting him. The other soldier, who'd presumably been patrolling the bottom of the hill, walked over to him and helped himself to some of the food he'd been carrying to the main shrine. Having filled his pockets he said something and roughly pushed the monk away, happy that he'd enough to fill himself.

Philips head spun around as he heard someone behind him and he sighed in relief as he recognised Lhamu creeping towards him.

"Are you good?" she asked him, laying a hand gently on

his sleeve. "I saw the soldier coming towards you from the kitchen. I sent the monk out to distract him."

Philip grasped her hand, squeezing its warm fingers in his. "Thank you. Another couple of steps and he'd have seen me." He glanced back towards the kitchen and saw the other guard arrive. The two soldiers stood, rifles hanging from their shoulders, sharing the food that the first one had taken. "If I'd had to shoot him we'd have had the whole lot of them after us, which would rather have spoilt our element of surprise."

Lhamu shook her head, her face serious. "I am afraid we do not have that anyway."

Philip stared at her. "What do you mean?"

"The monks told me," she whispered. "The soldiers arrived this afternoon totally exhausted. They left their camp last night because someone woke them and told them they were being followed."

Philip shook his head, confused. "But how? Everybody was in camp last night." He tried to think. "Perhaps they saw us higher up on the pass."

Lhamu shook her head. "No, they definitely said that they were warned by somebody. The monk with the food is the only one who speaks Chinese, that is why they have him as a go-between. It was he who overheard them talking. Whoever it was came down from our camp."

Philip blew out his cheeks and sighed, stealing a quick glance back towards the soldiers. Now they'd finished the food they were lighting more cigarettes.

"Damn it," he whispered, turning back. "It was going to be tricky enough anyway." He looked at Lhamu. "Did you find out how many there are?"

Lhamu nodded. "There are eighteen. Two are injured by bullets and others have frostbitten feet. The good news is that there is a prisoner with them and he does not appear to be injured."

Philip felt his heart beat faster. "Have the monks recognised him?"

Lhamu shook her head. "No, he has a cloth sack over his head. And I did not tell them. When they find out they will rush straight in and attack the Chinese with their bare hands, Buddhists or not."

They sat in silence, Philip trying to take everything in. "Right, let's fall back to behind the cook house," he said at last. "That way we can keep out of sight until Prem gets here with the men."

He started to get up and realised he was still holding Lhamu's hand. They glanced at each other and Philip gently squeezed it before releasing his grip. As quietly as they could they scrambled down the loose path and behind the chortern, soon hidden in the deep shadows of the moonlit night.

In less than a minute they reached the cookhouse and were squatting in the dark alley behind it. A smell of decomposition and dung mingled with the smoke that was escaping through cracks around the door.

"Christ," he muttered, trying to breathe as shallowly as possible. "What a stink."

"It is where they feed the dogs," Lhamu replied, a scarf pulled up over her nose. "They throw the scraps out here in the morning and the dogs come to get them after being out all night guarding the sheep. It's how they catch them to shut them up again."

Philip looked around nervously. "Where are they now?"

Lhamu chuckled at his voice. "They are still shut up," she replied. "You can hear them barking occasionally. They will be released when the soldiers are fed and the monks all inside for the night. They are vicious in the dark."

Philip nodded, feeling reassured. "It's a good thing we came early." He grimaced as he felt his boots sticking in something greasy. "I don't suppose we could wait inside," he asked, nodding towards the door. "It would be a damn sight warmer and a lot less smelly."

Lhamu moved over to the door and after listening intently for a few moments gently opened it and looked inside. Beckoning Philip she slipped through.

He followed and found himself in a long room centred around a large central fire, raised on a low stone hearth. Over this stood several metal tripods, off which hung large three cauldrons. The walls were lined with shelves, on which large copper and clay pots stood in rows. Beneath them on the floor were open sacks of rice, potatoes and other foodstuffs, with thin wooden benches running in front of them. The smoke was acrid, his eyes stinging and he coughed into his sleeve. Glancing up he could see that the stone roof was black with soot, smoke billowing beneath it as it slowly filtered through into the clean night air.

He could hear Lhamu quietly talking to someone and rubbing his eyes saw three young monks, their faced grubby with soot, staring solemnly at him.

He tried to smile. "Namaste," he said, hands held together.

The boys hesitated, but after glancing at each other nervously and then at Lhamu, returned the greeting.

There was an awkward silence, the monks staring at Philip and his clothes.

"Ask them how many monks are here?" Philip said, looking at Lhamu. "Especially how many young, fit ones."

He watched the monks, noting their reactions as Lhamu spoke to them in a flow of Tibetan. They answered her thoughtfully, each adding something to what had been said before until they seemed to arrive at a number they all agreed upon.

"About 120," Lhamu replied. "That is not including the hermits in the caves and the young boys. There used to be more but many have fled, frightened of what will happen if the Chinese army comes here."

Philip whistled. That was more than he'd hoped. He was convinced he could get them on their side, he just had to mention the Rinpoche. It was just how to do it without causing a riot.

"Do they have any weapons?" he asked again. "Guns, knives, staffs, things like that."

Again he waited until Lhamu had an answer. She shook her head. "They have sticks to defend themselves from wild animals, as well as some machetes that are used for cutting crops in the summer. Other than that, nothing. This is a sacred valley and nothing is allowed to be killed in it."

"And where are all these monks?"

The monks were more confident now and enthusiastic in their replies.

"They are in their dormitories, which are on the other side of the main Shrine, across the courtyard," she replied at last. "There are three buildings but each has a guard outside its door to stop them escaping."

Philip nodded and sat down on one of the benches, stretching out his legs towards the fire and watching as some ice crystals melted off his glistening boots.

Lhamu was busy giving orders to the monks, who now seemed completely under her spell. One went to the main door to keep watch for the soldiers, while a second was stationed at the back door to intercept Prem when he arrived with the men. The third busied himself at the fire and soon Philip was holding a scalding cup of greasy Tibetan tea.

He felt himself relaxing. With the hot drink and heat from the fire it was the first time in days he'd been truly warm. In an effort to stay alert he took a slug of the tea, scalding the roof of his mouth as he did so and grimacing as his cracked lips stung. He sat forward and placed the cup on the floor. He had to keep alert in order to work out what to do now. If the soldiers knew they were being followed they'd be more alert, which made it even more vital to strike as soon as possible.

Also, one of their group was a traitor who'd tipped off the Chinese. His mind ran through other possibilities, that perhaps one of the Chinese had dropped back, either through exhaustion or to collect firewood, and had seen them following. But if that was the case why would they have camped at all, surely they'd have pushed straight on to the monastery?

He'd trust any one of the Gurkhas with his life. He'd done so frequently. They'd been through things together that he'd never been able to even talk about to others, not even his family. They were tied by blood and memories.

Lhamu and Mingma were both devout Buddhists, he'd watched them at the monastery at Thangboche and they would never hurt the Rinpoche. That only left one man. Tashi. But he seemed, of all of them, to have the strongest reasons to want to stop the Chinese, to punish them. Philip sighed, thoughtfully picking at flaking skin on his upper lip, and a realisation dawning. They only had Tashi's word for what had happened all those years ago. Unlike everybody else, there was no one to corroborate his story.

He looked up, hearing muffled whispers and saw Prem enter the room, his khukri drawn and flashing in the firelight. The Gurkha glanced around the room, taking everything in, and after acknowledging Philip kept his eyes fixed on the young monk at the main door, who shifted uncomfortably under his gaze.

"The men are ready."

Philip nodded. "There are eighteen of them. We've seen two guards outside. They're smoking so we should be able to take them out easily enough. There're three more guarding the three dormitories on the far side of the courtyard. That leaves thirteen inside the main shrine. Two seem badly injured and several others are exhausted and asleep." He ran his hand through his hair which had started itching in the warmth of the kitchen. "I guess that when they're fed they'll release the dogs and barricade themselves in for the night. We need to get to them before then."

Prem nodded in agreement.

Philip continued. "We need to get rid of the five guards first without alerting those inside. If they realise something's going on they could use their hostage as a shield and that could be dangerous." He stood up. "We'll take out the guards by the dorms first. We'll need three teams. I'll lead one, you another and the third can be with Mani. We'll all take one man; you can assign the three best knifemen, and one of these monks. They can lead us there."

He glanced at Lhamu. "The rest will stay here, watching the doors. When we've dealt with the guards we'll return and start the main assault. I want to talk to the monks first and get them to create some sort of diversion. Mingma, you'll come with us but stay well back until the guards have been dealt with. Then I'll need you to explain what's happening and to tell them what to do."

Mingma nodded and he and Prem turned and disappeared back into the alleyway.

Philip turned to Lhamu. "Can you explain to these monks what I want them to do. We need to get to the dormitories without being spotted, circling around to approach them from the rear. And they must be quiet, *really* quiet."

Lhamu turned to the three boys and started talking, their eyes growing wider as she spoke. They glanced at each, shuffling their feet on the packed earth floor. At last one of them replied, his eyes downcast and avoiding Lhamu's.

She shrugged. "They are scared," she said. "They say the soldiers have told them that they will go tomorrow and leave them alone if they give them food and let them rest."

Philip sighed, shaking his head in frustration. "Tell them who the hostage is and for Christ's sake make sure they keep quiet."

Lhamu turned back to the monks and started speaking in a slow, deliberate voice. As she spoke he reached inside a pocket and pulled out the ring of the murdered abbot, holding it up for the monks to see hanging on an old lace he'd tied it too so as not to lose it.

There was a chorus of disbelief, and angry hands waved at Lhamu. One of the monks was arguing with her, pointing at Philip accusingly until he glanced over and froze. Slowly he crossed the room and stared at the gold ring twinkling in the light. As the Coral seal swung to face him and his face paled. He said something quietly in Tibetan and Philip looked at Lhamu to translate.

"He recognises it. It is the Seal Ring of the Head Abbot of Shigatze Monastery. He was here last year on pilgrimage," she said

"Well," replied Philip sternly. "Tell them they can't help him anymore but they can help the Rinpoche. If they don't he might die." He looked at the three monks. "We need their help to get us round to the dormitories."

Lhamu said something quickly and he was relieved to see them nod their heads in agreement.

Mingma hurried back into the room. "Prem has the men ready outside. He doesn't want them to come inside as it will damage their night vision."

Philip turned and beckoned the monks to follow. He walked out into the alley, catching his breath as the cold enveloped him and taking a few moments to allow his own eyes to adjust. The men slowly became visible in the shadows.

Philip spoke quickly and quietly. "Someone tipped off the Chinese last night that we were tracking them. That's why they'd broken camp so early this morning." He looked around the shocked faces. "It means they know we're coming."

There was muttering as the men took this in, glancing amongst themselves.

"I trust everyone here so, if it's true, it must have been the Indian Tashi." Philip continued. "What's important is that he doesn't get the chance to warn them again now that we're about to attack."

Prem nodded, understanding immediately. He turned to Balbir. "Take Tarun and go back to the camp. Tie him and bring him here. If he tried to flee, cut him but keep him alive. We will need to speak to him."

Philip shook his head, unable to believe how trusting he'd been of the Indian. It was obvious now, he'd been in the right place at the right time too many times for it to be a coincidence. But why would an exiled Tibetan want to help the Chinese? He pushed it from his mind, watching as the two Gurkhas disappeared off into the night. They were outnumbered already, without losing two more men, but what choice did he have? He couldn't risk Tashi turning up and either attacking them from behind or shouting a warning to the Chinese in the shrine.

Prem had already briefed the men and those who were staying behind silently disappeared into the kitchen. He heard a hissing as the fire was extinguished. A small squat Gurkha called Nandan walked up to him and smiled. Philip nodded back, remembering how he'd always sat in camp in the jungle lovingly sharpening his blade. He'd once seen him drop a leaf onto its upturned edge and watched as it fell to the ground, sliced cleanly in two.

Without another word they set off, following the young monks into a small, dark alley.

CHAPTER 17

The moon was still bright, flooding the valley in a white light that helped them navigate quickly through the maze of buildings and giving everything a ghostly appearance.

"Make sure they keep us well back and out of sight," he whispered to Mingma, who nodded and caught up with the boys as they paused at a small junction. He heard a short, muffled conversation and they moved off again. They were now on the very edge of the monastery complex, the valley dropping off below them in a wide sweep of stony pastures. Pens of sheep and goats flanked the buildings, built from thick bushes of dead thorn and crudely built dry stone walls.

The animals stirred as they passed; a low chorus of nervous bleating starting as mothers called out to their kids and lambs. Philip jumped in fright as the rough wooden door of the building they were passing rattled on its hinges as it was hit by a strong blow from within, accompanied by a frenzy of snarling and frantic barking. Hurriedly they moved on, wanting to get past the caged dogs before they caught the attention of the Chinese. It only took another minute until they were on the far side of the settlement, crouching behind the first of the dormitory buildings.

"We'll split up here," Philip whispered. "I'll take this

block, the rest move onto the other two and get in position. Take the guards out as silently as possible and then get inside the buildings. Use the monks to explain the situation and then wait for us. I'll come round once we've secured this one and Mingma can explain things further."

He glanced at his wristwatch. "Okay, let's go. Get in position and we'll attack in exactly two minutes from … now."

The others disappeared into the shadows. He turned to Nandan. "I'll go down this side, you skirt round the other. I'll distract the guard and when he moves towards me you take him from behind."

Nandan nodded, the handle of his crooked bladed khukri already in his hand, and disappeared around the far side of the building.

Philip turned to the remaining monk and held his finger to his lips. He pointed to a large boulder that lay a few yards behind them and whispered to Mingma. "Wait with him behind that, I'll come for you when it's over." He checked his watch and started creeping along the side of the dormitory.

There wasn't much cover. The rough stone wall was whitewashed and against it Philip felt completely exposed in the moonlight. At the front, a low wall ran off at an angle, part of the barrier that surrounded the large courtyard in front of the main shrine. As quietly as he could he crouched down behind it. The dogs were now howling, desperate to be released and he was grateful for it. That, combined with the distant roar of the river, created a background of noise that covered any sounds they were making on what was otherwise a silent night.

He looked at his watch again, the faded fluorescent paint on the dial dimly glowing back at him. It was nearly time. He picked up a fist-sized stone in one hand and filled the other with gravel, returning his eyes to the watch. At the exact moment the second hand reached the top he threw the gravel along the wall, away from the dormitory, listening as the small stones bounced and rolled along its surface. He heard the shuffling of footsteps coming towards him.

Quickly he lobbed the larger stone further away. It landed with a sharp crack, rolling along the wall and falling with a dull thud into the yard. He heard a frantic scuffing of feet and the rattle of air bubbling through liquid. Nandan's head appeared around the corner and signalled to him that it was clear.

Philip nodded and ran back to where Mingma and the monk were hiding, the latter quietly chanting a mantra. "Let's go," he hissed, grabbing the monk's arm and dragging him back towards the door of the building. After a quick glance across the deserted courtyard they dodged inside and Nandan closed the door behind them.

They were met by a sea of faces staring fearfully at them, and the crumpled body of the Chinese guard lying in a growing pool of blood that glistened in a dull light thrown out by several butter lamps. The monks were dressed in purple and yellow robes, many wrapped in rough, brown blankets and wearing lumpy woollen hats.

He held his hands together and bowed. "Mingma," he whispered out of the side of his mouth. "Explain what's going on. Quickly."

The Sherpa stepped forward and started to talk. Philip

watched the monks as they listened, their eyes moving from Mingma to him and back again as he explained the story, a couple of times interrupting to ask questions.

Philip had returned to the doorway, and was looking through a small crack in the frame. All seemed silent until after a minute or so he recognised the dark outline of Prem and opened the door to let him in.

"We've secured the other buildings," he said as he entered. "The guards were fools. One of them was asleep."

Philip smiled grimly. "Luckily for us. That's three down but the rest won't be so straight forward. Have the young monks explained what's happening to the others?"

Prem nodded. "Yes. And I've left the men at the doors to stop them running out to help the Rinpoche immediately. They were not happy with the news."

"When he's finished here, Mingma will go to make sure they understand what we need them to do. One wrong move and the soldiers will kill the Rinpoche rather than risk losing him. It's vital they keep quiet until everything's ready."

Mingma turned to them. "These monks understand and will help us. They will not kill, but will charge with us and try to overpower the Chinese. They agree that their religion and their country have been attacked and that some violence cannot be avoided to follow the correct path. I have instructed them to wait here until told what to do,"

"Excellent," replied Philip, nodding towards the monks. "Let's go and check on the others."

They darted out of the building, leaving Nandan guarding the door, and quickly entered the next building situated about twenty yards away. Philip could see that the young cook was doing a good job. The monks were all listening to him quietly, shock on their faces but no with panic visible. After a few words from Mingma they headed off to the last dormitory.

They arrived just in time. Philip could hear the raised voices as they crossed the rough paving outside, and as they opened the door a scene of chaos greeted them. Several older monks were arguing with the young cook, held back by a Gurkha who stood beside him menacingly, his hand holding his bloodstained khukri. Everything fell silent as Philip entered, the shock of seeing a westerner in their doorway too much for the monks.

Philip pushed Mingma forward who started to berate the occupants in a stern but low voice. Prem was standing by the door, looking out up the complex when suddenly he held up his hand.

"Shh," he hissed. Mingma immediately fell quiet and the monks, picking up on the tension stood in silence. "The two guards are coming," he whispered, still looking through the gap. "I can see their cigarettes moving this way."

"Damn it," Philip cursed. The sound of the arguing voices must've carried over to where the guards were standing. He turned to Prem. "We must get them inside. We'll never be able to take them out quietly in the open."

He crossed to where the crumpled body of the Chinese soldier lay and picked up his cap which had been thrown down on top of him. It wasn't too blood soaked so he put it on. Looking up he saw an old beer bottle standing on a stone ledge, full of butterfat with which to top up the lamps. He picked it up he walked back to Prem.

"If they call out, I'll open the door and beckon them in.

You and Giri must take them when they enter. The lamps in here will silhouette me so they won't be able to make out my face."

Prem nodded and gestured to the other Gurkha. They took up positions as close to the wall as possible, their knives drawn.

Everything fell silent. Philips ears strained to hear any movement outside. He breathed slowly and deeply, preparing himself. Everything became clearer and sharper. The dull lamplight now filled the room and he could hear Prem slowly scrapping his finger across his the blade, back and forth repeatedly, as he waited to strike. He could hear the dogs, even the river seemed to have become a torrent. Finally he heard footsteps on stone that stopped abruptly.

He could feel a draft of cold night air coming through a gap in the door, chilling a line of skin down the back of his neck. A voice called out.

"Nï shentï häo ma?"

There was silence for a few seconds.

"Nï zài nä li?

Philip took a final, calming breath. He turned and opened the door so the soldiers could only see his head peering around it. He'd stooped down, so he looked smaller than he was and swayed slightly, his right hand enthusiastically waved the beer bottle towards them.

There was a short silence as the two soldiers stared back and then he heard them laugh and lower their guns. Something was called out but Philip had, with a final flourish of the bottle retreated behind the door, leaving it ajar. He heard them laugh again and talking quietly to each other as they walked the final few steps and pushed in through the entrance. As the first one entered he reached up to remove the cigarette from his mouth, his eyes squinting from the sudden light and smoky interior. As the foot of the second man appeared in the doorframe the Gurkhas struck.

Prem, who was standing nearest to them, threw himself behind the first man, hitting him in the back and throwing him forward. Giri lunged at the soldier behind, grabbing his rifle barrel and pushing it up into the air. With one upward slash of his knife the man's throat was cut. He crumpled to the ground, blood spurting from the wound and his eyes and mouth open, screaming a silent cry of terror.

Prem had grabbed the first soldier's hair, trying to pull back his head to expose the throat but the man's stumble had thrown him off balance. Seeing the danger Philip flung himself at the rifle, trying to wrestle it away from him and keep his fingers away from the trigger. The soldier tried to shout but Philips shoulder knocked the air from his lungs and as Prem's knife bit into the back of his neck his body convulsed and a deafening roar filled the room. Philip felt himself crash to the floor, his senses scrambled by the explosion.

He tried to get up, his ears ringing, but was pinned to the ground. He pulled his knees up under his chest to give himself some leverage and pushed, struggling harder as he felt hot, viscous liquid running down his neck. He couldn't feel any pain, he was sure he hadn't been hit. The weight on top of him was lifted off, and he turned to see Mingmo pulling the body of the soldier away. Blood poured from a gaping wound where the khukri had almost sliced through his neck.

He looked up, forgetting the stickiness of his neck. Prem was crouched at the door, looking out across the courtyard towards the shrine. Philip scrambled to his feet and joined him.

"Bang goes our surprise attack," he said, letting his eyes adjust to the darkness. He tried to shake the buzzing from his head.

He glanced around. "At least that's five of them out of the way." He looked down at the bodies. "Let's get their guns and ammo together and see what we've got."

Prem nodded at Giri who finished wiping his knife on the soldier's uniform and slipped out of the hut door. A burst of gunfire tore into the night, echoing around the valley, bullets smacking into the wall of the building. Prem and Philip dived for cover as chips of wood flew off the wooden doorframe.

"Shit," exclaimed Philip, looking round at the monks who were now all cowering on the floor. "Mingma, ask them if there's another way out."

Mingma nodded and after a brief conversation with the nearest monks nodded. "There is a small window at the back we can get through. It cannot be seen from the shrine."

Philip looked at Prem. "You stay here. Keep a rifle and try to keep them pinned down. If you can keep them all inside until we get back round to the cook house we'll be able to come at them from behind." He paused, rubbing at the congealing blood on his neck with the hat of the dead soldier.

"I'll leave another man in one of the other dormitories to help you. I'll also leave Mingma." He turned and looked over towards the Sherpa. "I need you to organise the monks. Get them to arm themselves with anything they can find; sticks, rocks, anything. When you hear us start to attack, we'll be drawing the fire and I need these monks charging, screaming across the courtyard to the shrine. If we're to prevent the Rinpoche being killed we'll need to cause as much confusion as possible. A hundred angry monks screaming out of the night towards the Chinese could just do the trick.

He watched as Prem checked the rifle and started searching through the dead soldiers pockets, pulling out any ammunition he found. Soon he had a decent quantity and looked at Philip.

"I understand. I will keep them in there. When we hear you, we will charge immediately."

Philip put his hand on the Gurkha's soldier and squeezed, before striding across the room after a young monk who'd stood up to show him the way out. The sleeping quarters were dark and he stumbled his way over the lumpy grass mattresses and heavy woollen blankets that littered the door. Some of the monks had already pulled down the filthy drapes and shutters that covered a small window, through which Philip could see the moonlight now streaming through.

It was quite high, but a chest had been dragged over and by standing on this it was fairly straight forward to climb up and drop to the ground the other side. He carefully worked his way around the side to the next dormitory and keeping just out of sight called out as loudly as he dared. A shot rang out, aimed blindly at his voice and Philip heard it fizz harmlessly overhead. Almost immediately it was answered by a shot from Prem and Philip heard his round ricochet off the stonework of the shrine. It all fell quiet again.

He called again and on hearing a reply told them to get out the back through the window. In less than a minute they were all reunited behind the first building. Giri, it was agreed, would stay as the second gun. He'd been winged in the shoulder by a round from the initial burst and while it didn't seem serious, Philip was concerned it may affect his mobility.

He quickly outlined his plan to him and told him to ensure the other two dormitories were ready when the signal came.

Without having to worry about the guards, Philip quickly led them back around the complex, avoiding the dogs this time, and within a couple of minutes they entered the cook house.

There was one lamp burning and by its light he saw Lhamu gasp and come hurrying over.

"What happened? Are you injured?" she asked, her hand reaching up to the back of his head, concern in her eyes.

Philip nodded. "I'm fine. It's not my blood." He looked around to see who was there and quickly described what had happened. "Did you find Tashi?" he asked when he'd finished, looking at Balbir.

The Gurkha nodded and said something in Nepalese to two of the men, who turned and left the room. "We were almost back at the camp when we heard someone hurrying towards us. When we saw it was the Indian we tackled him and tied him up. Back at camp we found Parul unconscious, I think he will be OK, he came round while we were there and we left him by the fire."

The Gurkha paused as the door opened and Tashi was pushed roughly into the room.

"The radio set had been set up and was turned on."

Everyone was watching Tashi, who cut a forlorn figure in the pale light. His hands were tied behind his back and his face was bruised and scratched from falling on the way to the monastery, no doubt assisted by being pushed along by the Gurkhas behind. Philip walked up to him and stood looking into his eyes, one of which was puffy and starting to close.

"Balbir," he said in a quiet voice, his eyes not moving. "Stand behind him. If you even think he's going to shout a warning, cut his throat."

The Gurkha walked over and stood behind him, the silent whisper of his Kukri being drawn just audible in the silent room. Reaching up, Philip pulled down the filthy gag that covered his mouth.

"Last night, you crept down and warned the Chinese about our planned attack." He paused momentarily, watching as Tashi started to deny it. He cut across him, holding up his hand and continuing in a calm voice. "Please don't deny it. We've learnt it from the monks who overhead the Chinese talking. It explains why you were so exhausted this morning."

Tashi stood still for a few moments, seemingly torn as to whether to defend himself or not. After a few seconds, he took a deep breath and pulled himself up as tall as he could, his face hardening.

"I meant no harm to you or these men," he said in a steady voice, nodding around the room. "I could have knocked off your radio man tonight if I'd wanted to, or any of you guys on numerous occasions."

"So why didn't you?" Philip replied.

"It was the Rinpoche I wanted," he spat out. "No one else."

"But you're a Tibetan by birth," Philip said, confused. "You fled the Chinese. They threw you off your farm for Christ sake and killed most of your family. Why the hell would you want to help them?"

Tashi laughed bitterly. "I'm afraid your history is a little bit goofed up. It wasn't the Chinese who threw us off our lands. That year the Tibetan army invaded disputed lands that had been under Chinese control for decades. They exiled people like us, accusing us of being collaborators and confiscated our lands for their own estates. My father pleaded with them, saying that we were Tibetan like them, that we'd had no choice but to live under Chinese rule but they wouldn't listen. That's when they killed my brothers and I vowed that one day that somehow, somewhere I would avenge them."

There was a stunned silence, Philips head reeling. "But, but they're your own people ..."

"They threw us out, they killed my family," Tashi spat. "They are ignorant tyrants who deserve to die and be replaced by the people whose country it really is."

Philip shook his head. "Enough, I haven't time for this now. I just need to know who you were trying to contact on the radio. Do the soldiers have a receiver in the monastery?"

Tashi sat for a few moments looking at him before slowly he shaking his head. "They don't have a radio, which is why I had to warn them on foot last night."

Philip looked hard at him. "So who were you calling?"

"I tried to send a message to the main force they were

planning to join. They are camped waiting for them a few days north of here on the main route to Lhasa. If it hadn't been for your persistent little chase getting too close they'd have been well on their way there by now. As it was, when I told them you were coming and they decided to head for the monastery for protection. They've sent a man off to get the reinforcements, but when I saw the radio I thought I'd try to speed things up a bit." Tashi stopped talking for a moment, keeping his stare fixed on Philip. "I shouldn't tell you this but I don't want innocent people hurt and I've got no beef with you. You've been good to me, not judging or looking down on me. You must leave now while you've got a chance. If the main force arrives while you are still here you'll be annihilated."

Philip slowly reached out and pulled the gag back into place.

"Balbir, tie him to that column," he said quietly, nodding towards the corner. "We've more important things to do. He can wait. We know the radio's useless in these mountains so the time the messenger gets there and they hurry back here we'll be long gone. We've time enough." He watched as the Gurkha roughly pulled Tashi away, thinking about what they must do next.

"We'll climb back up to the rear of the shrine. There are no windows there. If we then keep close to the side walls they won't see us until we reach the front and rush the main door." He stopped, his mind running through his visit to the monastery at Thangboche. An idea came to him and he looked at Lhamu.

"Ask the monk if there's an open courtyard inside the shrine."

She turned to the old monk, who'd delivered the food earlier, and asked something in Tibetan, listening intently to his reply. "No," she replied, shaking her head. "It is too cold in winter to have an open courtyard."

Philip thought for a moment. "So how does the smoke from all the lamps and incense escape?" he asked, looking at the monk.

Lhamu translated again. "There is a hole in the roof, covered by a thin stone slab that can be slid closed if the weather is bad."

Philip nodded. "And how do they get on the roof to move the stone?"

"There is a ladder," confirmed Lhamu after a brief conversation with the monk.

"OK," he replied and looked at the nearest Gurkha Eknath. "Take him with you and fetch the ladder. We'll meet you beside the chortern at the foot of the hill."

The man nodded and beckoning the old monk disappeared out of the door.

Philip turned to the rest. "We'll put two men on the roof with rifles. They'll be able to shoot down into the shrine and add to the confusion. At the same time I'll use the hand grenade we found to take out the doors. We'll use those few seconds of smoke and confusion to get inside. I've organised it that Prem will lead the monks on a charge across the yard when they hear our attack, which will add to the general chaos, so we need to get inside before they do." He looked around at the men. "It's going to be knife work so I don't think I need to tell you what to do."

The men all nodded, several lifting their knives for him to see.

"Right then, you two." He pointed at Balbir and Ram. "Take a rifle each. I want you up on the roof as quietly as possible so they don't know you're there. I'll give you two minutes from when you start climbing the ladder to get in position. When the time is up try to take out a couple of soldiers at the front. If they are running back from the door it will confuse them even more. Remember though," he held up his finger. "Don't shoot towards the back of the shrine. That's where the Rinpoche is and we don't want to injure him."

The two Gurkhas nodded and took a rifle each, checking their actions and that they were loaded.

Philip looked around at the men, a flutter of panic welling inside him as he realised he was about to lead his first action for years, something he'd sworn never to do again. He turned to the door, trying to disguise it. "Lhamu, you stay here and watch the prisoner. The rest of you, let's go."

He led them out of the door, flinching as he heard the crack of a rifle shot coming from the other side of the yard. Prem was doing his job well.

When they reached the chortern they found Eknath and the monk waiting with the ladder, a spindly tree truck with footholds hacked roughly into its sides. Philip quickly turned away from it, forcing old memories away. He led off, taking them up the rough trail to the rear of the hill. The noise they made, despite their best efforts to be quiet, seemed to echo back to them from the surrounding buildings; the crunching of stone underfoot, small rocks bouncing down the slope and the occasional scraping of the ladder catching a protruding rock. At least, Philip reasoned to himself, the Chinese are trapped inside the shrine and distracted by Prem.

They reached the top and the ladder was silently lifted into position. Philip pointed to his watch and held up two fingers. Balbir nodded and clambered up the ladder, followed close behind by Ram.

Philip glanced around the remaining men. He pointed at three of them and indicated for them to go round the opposite side of the building.

"Keep behind the corner of the wall until the grenade explodes," he warned. "That's the signal for the charge. I don't want to kill you lot by mistake."

They nodded and moved off.

Philip looked at the remaining two Gurkhas and tried to smile reassuringly at them. The tension in his face made him feel as if he was scowling.

He turned and edged his way along the side wall of the shrine, making sure that they all kept as low as possible when passing under the small window. He thought he heard low voices as he ducked past, mingling with the groans of a wounded man.

At the front corner he stopped and checked his watch. Twenty seconds to go. He carefully placed his pistol on the ground and unclipped the grenade from his belt. It felt like a block of ice in his hand and he wiggled his fingers to reassure himself that the freezing metal wouldn't stick to his flesh. With five seconds to go he looked cautiously around the corner.

It was about ten yards across a paved terrace to the door.

An easy throw. He just had to ensure that the grenade didn't roll off the front edge and down the wide flight of steps that dropped to the main courtyard. If it did that it would deflect the blast and probably leave the doors intact. Slowly he raised his other hand to the grenade and slid his finger through its pin, ready to rip it out and lob it towards the target.

His hands were trembling, his mind filling with bloody memories that threatened to overcome him. He forced his mind to visualise the inside of the shrine, of Chinese soldiers preparing for their attack. An image of young monks came into his head. He stopped breathing. He hadn't checked that the shrine was clear of monks. Perhaps the Chinese had some inside that they were using as human shields. Perhaps the Rinpoche had been moved up to be by the door. If he threw the grenade, he would kill him, kill them.

He glanced at his watch. It was time.

CHAPTER 18

Calcutta

15th February 1945

Dear Mr and Mrs Armitage,

I enclose a copy of a letter I was entrusted with by your son Philip with whom I was a prisoner in Rangoon. When I last saw him he was as alive as anyone else incarcerated there and we exchanged letters when I was moved up country to work on the railway. From here I managed, more by luck than judgement, to escape to our lines. I hope the letter brings you some comfort and that one day you are reunited.

With best wishes,

Capt. John McMillan
13th Kings Liverpool Regiment

Rangoon Central Jail
3rd November 1944

Dear Mother and Father,

I hope that you're well? I often think of your lives continuing unchanged at home and in many ways it's this that gives me strength to continue. With so much time on my hands I seem to remember every detail, every conversation from my past that a normal, busy life drives from your memory. And yet other things are confused and blurred. Sometimes I don't know whether the faces I see in my mind are truly you or what I've now imagined them to be.

You wouldn't believe the number of times I've reread your last letter. The paper is so worn that the writing has almost gone. It matters not as I know every word, every mark on the paper. I used to hold it to my nose, inhaling deeply to try to catch a smell of home. Sometimes I thought I caught your lavender water or fresh scones or the Labradors panting from a rummage in the woods. The grief I felt at the news of Will's death has passed away to nothing but fond memories of our childhood running wild on the estate. Sometimes I even envy him.

I now wake in the morning thinking that my old life was a glorious dream that evaporates slowly in the dawn light. The St. Christopher you sent out deserted me long ago. It's for the best. There are some things even god shouldn't see. Sometimes, when everybody is settled in the huts for the night, I lie awake in the darkness and silent tears run down to soak the rough sacking that serves as bedding, weeping for the boy who stepped from the ship in Bombay.

We exist here only to try to survive. After what I've seen and done, I think it would be better to die rather than live my life with the images that fill my mind. The life I had is over and can never come back as the man, the boy, who lived it has died. It's strange. I can actually remember his passing. I remember you coming to comfort him at the last and I can see a million stars dazzling high above the jungle fading to darkness through failing eyes.

So I was born again to this. The smell of rotting flesh and dysentery, of death and desperation. When I came round my wounds had been treated by the Jap field doctors. Without them I would have died as in a camp there is no medicine and no compassion from the guards. We live our lives waiting. Waiting to see what, if any, food arrives. Waiting for the next concert or reading that we have seen or heard a thousand times. Waiting for the next death so we can move to a better bunk or wear better boots. Waiting for our lives to start again.

When I first arrived it was wounds and disease that did for most men. They marched us from camp to camp, with no time to dress injuries that festered in the tropical heat. To this day I've no idea why the wound in my shoulder healed quickly and cleanly when that of the man who slept next to me went bad and gave him an agonising death. Now we're at Rangoon it's starvation and illness we fear. Flies are so numerous that you can kill four or five with one swat and still they cover your hand before you can lift it. It's no wonder dysentery is rife, many die as skeletons in skin, while beriberi taunts us with fat, swollen bodies and peaceful resignation. The thing I fear most are the sores. A small scratch can turn into a hole the size of your hand, eating to the bones and oozing a foul green discharge. Men die of them frequently, usually desperate for the release death will bring.

As an officer I've presided over more funerals than Reverend Fisher will ever be called on to perform. Bodies sewn into old rice sacks, saluted by their friends and buried in a crammed piece of scrubland, marked only by a brittle cross of bamboo or twigs. I try to remember words from our Sunday Services in Norfolk, but they and god seem so far away. I use the Lord's Prayer, a mantra I can repeat without having to think about what I'm doing or having to say.

The rations are never enough and I've run out of things to trade with the Burmese. The "wage" the Japs pay us for the slave labour they make us do is taken by them to pay for our board and to buy Japanese War Bonds. The few rupees that are left I use to buy myself one egg a week. Our bodies are little more than bones, my teeth are loose and hair falls out in clumps.

What keeps me going and yet terrifies in equal measure is watching the Americans over Rangoon most nights. I hope the bombing means that the war is finally drawing to a close. But I lie awake petrified that after all we've endured I'm to be killed by a trigger-happy Yank at the very end of it all. Two downed airmen were brought in last week, with terrible burns and wounds seething with maggots where they'd been locked up in this heat without treatment. They died badly but bravely, but gave us hope with what they told us of the war.

One day Father, I hope to sit with you in those deep, leather chairs in your study, whiskeys in hands, staring in companionable silence into the glowing embers of the fire. I understand at last. We'll never need to speak about our experiences but I think it will bring comfort to us both.

I've written several letters that have been entrusted to those I think strongest and the most reliable. Should I escape through death, I want you to know that I loved you both dearly. I don't have the strength to pray anymore, but my thoughts are always and always will be, with you both, Kim and Mary.

Your loving son,
Philip

CHAPTER 19

Tibet, 1953

Shots echoed out from inside the shrine as the Gurkhas on the roof opened fire exactly two minutes after Philip had given them the signal. A scream came from through the door to show they'd successfully found a target. A second later a roar erupted from across the courtyard and glancing up Philip saw a wall of purple and yellow monks screaming towards him, Prem at the front.

He realised he was too late. The grenade would have a fuse several seconds long and if he pulled it now the monks might be there when it exploded. He dropped it to the ground and threw himself around the corner, sprinting for the door. It was ajar so that the Chinese could keep watch on the dormitories and occasionally shoot across the yard. In the initial confusion of the attack he saw that it hadn't been closed and through the opening, lying on the ground, was the outstretched arm of a shot Chinese soldier. It started to disappear as the body was dragged out of the way and he launched himself at the heavy wooden planking. The force of his dive crashed the doors back, knocking two soldiers flat on the ground who'd been trying to secure the entrance.

Before they could recover Philip rolled over and shot single rounds into their scrambling bodies, hearing cries of pain as the bullets hit home. The Gurkhas had been left flat-footed as they waited for the grenade explosion to signal the attack and the next instant the monks, led by Prem, slammed through the door, packing the shrine in a matter of moments. He lay watching as their sticks rained blows on the rest of the soldiers who'd collapsed in terror, cowering on the ground to protect their heads and bodies. In less than a minute it was over. An eerie calm descended and then, starting from the back of the shrine, the monks started prostrating themselves on the ground.

As the last of the monks lay themselves down on the paved floor the Gurkhas stepped around them, knives raised and ready. They tied the hands of those Chinese soldiers who were still conscious, dragging them to the corner of the shrine and tying them to the base of a large seated Buddha. Others – they cautiously prodded with their boots before kneeling to check for pulses. Those who were unconscious were next tied and dragged away. In total five were dead, including the Chinese Commander who'd been taken out by the sniper fire from the roof which probably explained why their resistance had crumbled so quickly.

Philip looked around, shocked, his heart still racing. He hadn't realised that the monks would be so devastating, but looking at them now, as they lay prostrate on the floor he could see why they were. They lived a tough life, working tirelessly to survive in an unforgiving environment. Before arriving at the monastery many would have come from the families of nomads who'd worked hard from the moment they could walk. They were hardened and fit and outraged that the Chinese had captured the Rinpoche.

Philip pushed himself up and walked carefully through them, moving towards a young man who stood by himself at the back of the shrine, rubbing his wrists which were raw from where the binding had cut into him. He stopped in front of him and gave a small bow, unsure what to do.

The man stepped forward and offering his hand. "I believe this is how you greet friends in your country," he said in a clear voice. "Thank you." He looked around the shrine, his eyes stopping on the bodies of the dead soldiers. "Death, even of an enemy, is a terrible thing." He looked back at Philip. "But what is done had to be done and I thank you for it."

Philip moved forward and took the hand and they stood for a few moments studying each other. He was tall for a Tibetan, their eyes almost level. His face was open and strong, his hair, originally shaved, was now a black stubble streaked with dried blood. He was young, but not, Philip suspected, as young as people had suggested. His eyes were old, betraying a depth of experience beyond the age of his body. Philip felt calm, completely at peace. He'd only felt it once before, such complete acceptance but this time he felt a surge of hope. They stood, hands clasped together, until Philip became aware of Prem standing beside him. He reluctantly released the Rinpoche's hand and turned to the corporal.

"The room is secure," the Gurkha said, bowing his head to the Tibetan as he spoke. "We have no casualties, except two monks who got hit by blows from other monks. The soldiers are all tied up and secure."

Philip nodded, looking down at the monks who still lay prone on the floor. "Well done Prem. That was quite a charge! " He turned back to the Rinpoche. "If you'll excuse me I have something I must attend to in the cook house." He nodded over his shoulder. "I'll leave you to address your monks."

He turned and walked with Prem out of the shrine into the cold night air, sucking it deep into his lungs. He walked over to where the grenade lay abandoned on the ground and picked it up, handing it to Prem. "You should take this. I failed again, I just couldn't throw it. Memories …"

"It didn't need to be thrown," replied Prem, shrugging. "The attack was successful. We had no losses."

"But we could have," Philip snapped back angrily. "Some of the monks could have been shot or our men injured. It's better you take it."

He watched as the Gurkha clipped it to his belt and they turned and quickly strode down the steps, heading towards the kitchen. As they walked Philip filled the Gurkha in about what they'd learnt from Tashi.

As soon as he entered he knew something was wrong. Where Tashi had been tied was deserted and the door into the back alley stood wide open. He glanced around and saw Lhamu's feet sticking out from behind the raised hearth. He rushed over. She was lying face down, arms up above her head. Discarded beside her lay a long thin piece of firewood, its end covered in congealing blood. Philip fell to his knees, unable to breath. Gently he laid a trembling hand on her shoulder and whispered her name.

"Lhamu?"

There was no reply. He carefully rolled her over so her

head and shoulders were resting on his lap. He could see an ugly cut on her scalp, her hair plastered to it as it oozed blood down her face. Some of it had run down into her eyes, which he gently wiped away with his sleeve. Taking her wrist he felt for a pulse and a shiver of relief ran through him.

"Lhamu," he said again, tenderly rubbing her cheek, and was rewarded by a small groan and movement of her head. Slowly she opened his eyes, unfocused and objecting to the dull light that the one remaining lamp threw out. Then they suddenly snapped open and stared at Philip.

"Tashi …" she gasped, trying to pull herself up.

"Easy," interrupted Philip, gently holding her down. "Don't get up yet. You've had a nasty bang to the head and will be dizzy for a while. Tell me what happened as you lie here."

Prem, who'd run to the open door and checked in alley returned, shaking his head.

Lhamu spoke slowly, her mind still fuzzy and slow. "He must have had a knife hidden in his sleeve. I was looking out of the door to watch what was happening and when I turned I saw he had nearly cut through the ropes. Before I could reach him he had freed himself and hit me with some wood from the fire."

She grimaced, the mention of the blow seeming to flood the pain from the wound into her.

"It's alright," Philip reassured her. "It doesn't matter he escaped. We've captured the shrine and the Rinpoche is safe. The men and monks are all safe."

Lhamu shook her head, struggling from his grasp and sitting up.

"But we are not. Before he escaped he was taunting me.

He said that when he was on the radio, he was successful. He managed to contact the main Chinese force."

Philip looked at her, slowly shaking his head. "That's impossible, he must have been lying to you, trying to upset you. The radio won't work here, it's got no range in these mountains."

"I know," Lhamu replied, grasping Philips hand, "but it does not need to. The Chinese are only a day's march up the valley and he has told them about our attack. They are already on their way."

Philip glanced up at Prem. "Go and find the abbot. He must know if there are any other soldiers around camped around here." He turned back to Lhamu, just as several monks rushed in and started to relight the fires. "Let's get you over to the shrine and get that cut in your head seen to."

Thirty minutes later and they were sitting around a roaring fire in a large hearth at the centre of the shrine, its smoke snaking out through the uncovered hatch in the roof. Philip had carefully cleaned Lhamu's wound, which had turned out to look much worse than it was. Two wooden benches had been dragged up to the fire and he found himself describing the last few days to the Rinpoche, who sat watching him intently through eyes over the rim of a large bowl of butter tea.

On the Rinpoche's other side sat the Head Abbot of Rombuk, an old man who'd been woken in his private chamber by the fighting and had been brought straight over to them by Prem. When he'd arrived, Philip had immediately asked him if he knew of any other Red Army in the area.

There'd been a pause as Lhamu translated but Philip felt his heart sink as the old monk started pointing down the valley.

Lhamu looked at Philip. "He says some traders came through a couple of days ago and said there was a large camp of soldiers about a day's journey to the North. "

Philip looked at the old man. "Does he know how many?" he asked.

There was a brief conversation.

"About fifty," she replied.

"Damn it," cursed Philip, looking into the fire and running a blood stained hand through his filthy hair. "In which case we'll have to assume that Tashi was telling the truth and that he got a message through to them. If they received it a couple of hours ago they still won't be here until dawn, even if they set off straight away. Let's eat and rest here where it's warm." He looked around at the men. "Everybody's exhausted. A few hours good sleep and a hot meal will make a big difference on the return."

Philip had soon discovered that the Rinpoche spoke excellent English, so there was no need for Lhamu or Mingma to translate. Despite the reverential way he was treated by everybody he soon put Philip at his ease.

"Please, call me Dawa," he said, lightly resting his hand on Philips wrist. "You've rescued me and given me the opportunity to continue my mission. It's our last hope. If we cannot get help from the United Nations then I fear my country will be overrun by the Chinese."

They chatted on, Philip describing their discovery of the ambush by the river and the pursuit through the mountains. The Rinpoche often nodded and added his own comments.

It was about their last campsite that Philip was particularly interested in.

"I remember," the Rinpoche had replied. "It was the middle of the night. They'd removed my blindfold as I'd just been out to the toilet. I saw a man come into camp whom the guards were very wary of. They fetched the commander who initially wasn't pleased to have his sleep disturbed. There was a brief conversation and then everybody was woken." He shook his head. "I didn't hear what they said but we set off fast down the valley."

"It was a man from our camp who'd come with us as a translator. We know now that he's a spy and has fled. Before he went though he used our radio to warn the main Chinese force who were waiting to meet you, presumably with transport to take you away in."

At that moment some of the younger monks appeared carrying trays laden with plates of small, boiled potatoes cooked with some kind of green leaf vegetable and covered in thick melted butter. The smell was delicious and Philip realised just how hungry he was. There was silence as they all ate ravenously and drank their tea which was constantly topped up by a nervous monk who hovered behind them.

Philip had just finished when he saw Prem hurrying into the shrine.

"There's no sign of the Indian," he reported. "We've checked every building in the monastery. But there is a pony missing from the stable. I think he's taken it and fled. The two monks in charge of the guard dogs have taken them to see if they can pick up a trail. I wouldn't like to be him if they get onto it. They are savage."

Philip nodded, quickly filling the corporal in about the soldiers.

"We'd have had no chance if they'd reached them and we'll struggle now if they catch us. They'll be well armed and rested." He looked at the Rinpoche.

"Your Holiness, we need to get back to Nepal as quickly as possible. Could you ask the abbot to spare us some supplies as we've nothing left for the return journey."

The Rinpoche nodded.

"One other thing," Philip continued. "We need to get rid of the prisoners. If the Chinese find them here then I dread to think what they'll do to the monastery."

The two Tibetans had a conversation and after a minute or so the Rinpoche turned back to Philip. "He will confine the prisoners inside one of the many caves in the valley until the army has gone. Then he'll get some of the traders whose caravans pass through to take them far away across the plateau and release them. They won't be able to cause any harm from there and by the time they eventually return to Lhasa nobody will remember. The bodies of the dead with be put out with respect for sky burials, releasing their spirits."

He paused, keeping his eyes fixed on Philip. "And now I have a favour to ask of you. With your permission I will travel back with you. If I'm caught here I will be taken to China and the monastery razed. It would be as if you'd never come." He fell silent.

"Of course," said Philip. "We'll do our very best to get you to safety." He looked at the young man. "May I suggest one thing. We should disguise you as one of us. I'm sure we can find some spare clothing. That way, if we're pursued, they're less likely to recognise you. Also, they'll be warmer than the ones you have and easier to travel fast in."

The Rinpoche waved his hand dismissively. "I am the Rinpoche of Tibet and will not try to hide that for fear of my enemies. My faith makes me strong and I will not deny it. As for the cold, I spent the first seven years of my life living on the Steppe with my parents, herding and following the pasture. I'm used to it."

Philip nodded and turned to Prem. "Get yourself fed and everybody warm and settled. We need to be off at first light and I want them as rested as possible."

Prem hurried from the shrine and they sat talking, the Rinpoche asking about Britain. "I've heard many things about your country," he said. "They say it is the Great Britain, so magnificent that the sun never leaves it." He looked at Philip. "Do you think they will help Tibet?"

Philip shrugged. "I don't know. We've always tried to help those who need it but the war changed things. Then there were people who needed our help, people who'd relied on us for many years and we were unable to save them." He looked at the young man. "But I'm sure you'll find many supporters on your mission. The most important thing is to let the world know what's happening."

They settled down for the night on bedding that was carried in by some aged monks, each of whom then fell to the floor and prostrated themselves before the Rinpoche and had to be almost dragged up by the young llama before they'd leave. The bedding looked filthy, greasy to the touch and reeking of smoke. It didn't matter for as soon as Philip's head was on it he fell into a deep, untroubled sleep.

CHAPTER 20

It was still dark when they roused themselves next morning. The moon had set and the sky was now covered by thick cloud that blotted out the morning stars. Philip shivered as he walked out behind the complex to relieve himself. A wind was blowing, whipping up dust that stung his face and whining its way through the rocks and moraine that littered the valley.

They ate breakfast in silence; a thick tsampa mash and were on the trail before the first tinge of morning touched the eastern horizon. Two monks came with them, guiding them along the trails they used when grazing their sheep, and they made fast progress, lit by several hand-held lamps supplied by the monastery.

Prem was keen to get back to the main valley to the Nangpa la as soon as they could, worried that the Chinese reinforcements might march directly down this trail and cut them off from the pass. When they finally reached the junction the sun had long risen, although hidden behind a featureless slab of thick grey cloud. Climbing a small outcrop, they gazed down cautiously into the main valley.

The glacier that tumbled down from the pass looked enormous from their vantage point, towering seracs of ice teetering above gaping crevasses that slashed their way across the ice flow. The trail they'd followed was a tiny line zigzagging its way along the valley's rocky edge. Where the glacier finally ended Philip could see the raging torrent of melt water pouring from its snout, tumbling in a series of frothing rapids beneath them and on down the valley. He scanned along it, briefly removing his snow goggles, to see if he could see any movement. It looked clear and he was just starting to relax when one of the guides grunted and pointed down the valley.

Philip followed his finger, squinting to cut out some of the glare. In the distance, perhaps two or three miles away, he could make out a line of small black dots slowly moving across a large boulder field. It was the soldiers.

"How long do you think we have?" he asked, replacing his goggles.

"About an hour," Prem replied, his eyes scanning the terrain between them. "We won't be able to outrun them," he added.

Philip looked back up the valley. "We need to find somewhere where their numbers cannot be used against us." He ran over in his mind the terrain from the previous few days. "What about just below their last camp? There are boulders there to give us cover and they'll have to funnel through the gorge where the path climbs up onto the glacier."

"Get the men moving," he ordered Prem. "We must give ourselves time to prepare before they arrive." He called to Mingma. "Thank the guides and send them back. Tell them to inform the abbot that the soldiers are after us on the pass but that we've got in front of them." He thought for a moment. "Suggest that they leave the monastery for a day or two in case the soldiers turn their attentions to them. Perhaps they should all become hermits for a while."

They moved out, dropping quickly to the main valley floor and turning south towards the pass. As they started climbing the trail beside the glacier Philip felt a large snowflake land on his face. He wiped it away but it was immediately replaced by another and then more.

"Keep close together," he yelled at the men. "Mingma and Lhamu, you lead. Prem and I will follow at the rear. Don't lose sight of the person in front otherwise you'll lose your bearings."

They maintained a decent pace, the men climbing strongly and without complaint despite having had little rest over the previous few days. As the snow grew heavier he was grateful that he was at the rear and not having to kick steps in the soft white blanket that was already building underfoot.

They didn't stop for rests, but ate dried fruit given to them by the monastery as they went. They were apricots, tough to chew but giving a burst of delicious sweetness as they softened in the mouth. He wondered how far they'd travelled, from some distant orchard, to end up in this inhospitable place.

He lost track of time, marching through a white, featureless landscape. Occasionally he was aware of the path switching back as it climbed remorselessly upwards, but otherwise his mind kept wandering, dreaming of armchairs and woollen slippers. Occasionally he noticed Prem stopping to check behind, but as you could see no further than ten yards it was more a case of keeping their ears open for any sounds not muffled by the heavy fall. Other than the squeaking of their boots in the snow and the sound of laboured breathing there was nothing.

They seemed to walk for days. Other than cold feet Philip felt surprisingly warm, the exertion of the climb making him sweaty and itchy inside his warm wool clothing. It made him drowsy, so it was with a start that he became aware of the rising cliffs pushing in around them as they entered into the bottleneck of the gorge, scrambling up onto the glacier to reach the upper valley. This was it, he realised, the campsite wasn't much further. He made his mind focus, taking care that he didn't slip into one of the many small crevasses that yawned open beside the rough trail. Occasionally they were slowed when one cut across the path, making it necessary to leap over its black void that fell away beneath.

He tried to plan what they needed to prepare. It was, he was relieved to see, an excellent ambush site. There were fourteen of them, although the Rinpoche and Lhamu wouldn't be fighting and Giri had the minor shoulder wound he'd picked up at Rombuk. If they were to hold off a force four or five times their size then they needed to be set out right and know what they were doing. Another ten minutes and they'd reached the old camp site. It was unrecognisable. The snow had eased as they'd dropped off the glacier and had now all but stopped. Everything was buried in a layer of snow well over a foot deep.

"You two," Philip said, nodding at two of the Gurkhas. "Clear the snow by the rock face and get a fire going. We'll need some tea to keep warm."

The men nodded and, dropping their packs to the ground, started unpacking the dried dung they'd been carrying from the monastery as fuel. He walked off up the valley, followed by Prem, searching for positions that offered the best lines of fire back towards the narrow ravine.

They stood and surveyed the valley from a small outcrop of rock, panting from the exerting of scrambling up through the soft powder.

"That snows done us a favour," Philip exclaimed, looking up at the valley sides. "It's made it impossible for them to try to climb and outflank us. It would be suicide going up there, they'd slip and fall."

Prem followed his gaze and nodded grimly. "They'll have to come up the glacier like us," he agreed. "They won't know the layout of the valley either which helps us." He scratched at his chin. "Unless that Indian is with them."

Philip stood thinking. Tashi did know this part of the valley as he'd climbed down through it to warn the soldiers. It would, however, have looked different at night and after all the snow they'd have to hope he'd be disorientated.

They continued on and selected three more decent positions before returning to the fire. The men were gathered around, the Rinpoche amongst them, drinking black, sweet tea. In the freezing air a column of steam rose from each mug. Philip watched it rise, his eyes drawn up to the leaden blanket of cloud that sat over the valley, hiding the surrounding ridges and peaks. It was like being in a tunnel, claustrophobic and smothering, as if their world had shrunk to this one small bubble.

Philip gratefully accepted a mug himself. Between mouthfuls, which made his teeth ache from the heat, he briefed the men.

"We'll be in four groups of three, each with an equal split of the ammo." He pointed at a nearby rifle. "After Rombuk we now all have guns and about fifteen rounds each. You must be sparing. There's over fifty of them and we've less than 200 rounds in total. Only shoot when you have a clear shot. From our positions we'll be able to pick them off as they come over the glacier. But first I want to draw them in a bit, let them get closer and hit as many as possible with the first volley. That way we'll be able to scavenge their guns and ammo." He looked around the men. "Nobody shoots until I shoot, is that understood?"

The men nodded, a determination etched on their faces that gave Philip a glimmer of hope and a welling of pride.

"We've got to finish this here, we've no other choice. If we try to fall back up the pass they'll pick us off as we climb. At worst we need to hold them off so we can retreat when it's dark." He tried to smile. "Good luck everyone. Now follow Corporal Prem. He'll put you in your positions."

The men retrieved their packs and head off behind Prem. Philip turned to Mingma and Lhamu who, along with the Rinpoche, were the only ones left by the fire.

"I want you all to stay here. There are no more weapons and little you can do in the fighting. Keep close to the cliff face and you'll be out of the line of fire. Try to keep the fire going and water hot. If this thing drags on we're going to need to keep warm. Lying in the snow is going to be cold."

They nodded, immediately starting to kick snow out of the way, clearing a place to sit and building a wall of snow behind which they'd be hidden. Philip turned and looked up at where the men were bedding in. He could see them clambering into their positions, two groups behind rocky outcrops on the ridge that he and Prem had climbed earlier, the others behind piled debris that had slid down to the valley floor in rock falls. As the men settled down they vanished into the landscape.

Philip grunted contentedly. If he couldn't see them, there was no way the Chinese would. He'd just taken a couple of steps towards where he was to fight when he felt a hand catch his sleeve. He turned and saw Lhamu staring up at him, her mouth open as if trying to say something but with no words coming out. Slowly he turned to face her, taking both her hands in his. They stood motionless for a few second and then, without warning, she threw herself into his arms. He could feel her squeeze him tightly, despite the thick layers of clothes they each wore. He held her, nuzzling his mouth and nose into the exposed crown of her head, feeling its warmth radiate onto his cold face.

Nothing was said. They stood, holding each other for a few moments until she let him go, turning away and walking back to the cliff without a backwards glance. Philip watched her go, wanting to call after her and reassure her. He realised it was more than that but still nothing came, his mind confused by emotions he'd never felt able to experience before. He turned and slowly walked to where Prem had positioned them, lying behind a large boulder that gave an excellent field of fire back towards the glacier. He looked up and saw Prem nod at him. They were ready.

Time passed so slowly. Philip fought the urge to constantly glance at his watch, not wanting to take his eyes off the fringe of the glacier or to allow cold air up his sleeve.

The thick cloud blotted out all traces of the sun, throwing a dull pall that gave no hint of the time. It must be afternoon; breakfast seemed a distant memory. Not too late though, he hoped. He didn't want the Chinese camping before the gorge. Every few minutes his goggles misted up and he had to put down his rifle to clear them.

He'd just replaced his goggles when he saw a movement on the crest of the glacier. He picked up his rifle and resting it against the boulder to steady his aim, he looked down the sights towards the gorge. A figure was emerging about 200 yards away, cautiously following their footsteps which, now the snow had stopped, lay uncovered along the trail. He was the point, Philip was sure of it. He moved steadily but warily, watching his footing while constantly checking what lay ahead. As if to confirm this he stopped, raising his hand as a signal to those who must be following behind. He crouched and stayed there unmoving for several seconds.

Philip was holding his breath, willing his men to remain motionless. After what felt like an eternity the man stood and beckoned those behind him forward. Another soldier appeared and then another, all carrying their weapons at the ready. His body tensed as he recognised the figure of Tashi appear on the crest of the glacier, stumbling on the rough ice and sitting down heavily on a half-buried boulder to adjust a boot. The dogs obviously hadn't got him. Philip made himself relax, a grim smile coming to his face. He was glad they'd brought him. There was a debt to pay.

Philip's eyes moved to the next man who'd appeared carrying something more bulky than the rest, a large tube that was resting casually across his shoulders. A bazooka.

Christ, he thought, if they got the chance to use that then they'd be annihilated. By now there were about twenty men in view, the first of which was no more than a hundred yards away. He forced himself to breathe steadily, long, slow inhalations followed by a steady release. When the lead man was no more than fifty yards away, he'd emptied his lungs, paused and squeezed his trigger.

The shot seemed deafening and was immediately followed by a volley from the Gurkhas that reverberated around the gorge, a wall of sound that enveloped their world. Soldiers fell, some dead, others throwing themselves down into the soft snow for cover. He swung his rifle around, pointing it to where Tashi had been. The rock he'd been sitting on was now empty. A few of the Chinese were trying to return fire, but whenever they did they were being picked off by the Gurkhas, who calmly waited for the muzzle flashes before firing.

Looking around Philip searched for the soldier with the bazooka and saw him crouching low in some loose moraine. With the help of another soldier he was setting up the weapon. Philip pivoted round and fired. The second man fell to the ground, this head exploding in a spray of red. Seemingly unperturbed by this, the handler calmly shouldered his weapon, steadying it with his left hand. With his right he pulled out the sighting mechanism and settled into a firing position.

Philip swore and quickly aimed again, pulling at the trigger in his desperation to fire. The Chinese soldier ducked as the bullet fizzed past his head but quickly got back in position. Philip knew he didn't have time to fire again when a shot rang out. The man's body shuddered with the bullet's impact, before slowly pitching forward into the snow. He glanced to his left and caught Prems eye, who was reloading, nodding his approval.

There was no time to say anything. The Chinese had regrouped and were attempting a charge through the gorge. He could see the Gurkhas were slowing them down with their accurate shooting but it was only a matter of time until they ran out of ammo and were overwhelmed. Tashi would have told them their strength so the Chinese commander must know he just had to bide his time. More men ran over the glacier and this time they were met by fewer guns. Some of the men, he realised, had finished all their ammo.

A soldier appeared, unarmed and running at full pelt to where the bazooka lay in the snow. Philip aimed and fired, seeing a plume of snow fly up just behind him as he raced down the slope. Other shots rang out, but he kept going unscathed. Philip was just aiming again when he noticed a shadow flash over him. Glancing up he saw Balbir had broken cover and was racing down the valley towards the soldier.

"Cover him," Philip screamed and was answered by a crackle of fire towards the glacier. He watched transfixed. The Chinese soldier had reached the fallen bazooka, falling to his knees as he picked it up. His back was turned to them so he didn't see Balbir hurtling towards him. He stood and swinging the weapon round, aimed at where Lhamu and the Rinpoche were hiding. They must have been spotted in their hiding place by one of the first wave. The soldiers must have decided that it would be better to kill him if they couldn't recapture him.

Philip started to scream a warning but before he could utter a sound the soldier was hit square in the stomach by the thick-set Gurkha. Even at that distance Philip heard the air knocked from the soldiers lungs as he was lifted from the ground and thrown several yards back into the soft snow.

The men were rolling around, fists flailing at each other, when Philip heard a shot and saw Balbir's body convulse and fall away. The soldier pushed himself to his knees turned and dropped a revolver to the ground, bending to retrieve the bazooka from where it had fallen. He was balancing it on his shoulder once more when Philip noticed Balbir drag himself up, his clothes drenched in blood. With a roar the Gurkha grabbed the man from behind in a bear hug that pinned his arms to his side. Balbir dragged him backwards, shuffling on his knees as the soldier kicking furiously. Without warning Balbir threw himself backwards into some untouched snow on the lip of a large crevasse. The soldier screamed but was powerless as the body of the Gurkha slipped into the black void and dragged him in after, his scream fading as they fell with the bazooka into the deepest bowels of the glacier.

There was total silence as everybody looked on aghast.

"He always believed he'd been spared for a reason," Prem said at last. "He felt the cost of his life in Burma deeply. He is released."

Before Philip could reply more soldiers appeared on the crest of the glacier, just visible through the first flurry of a new snow storm. He knew they wouldn't be able to repulse this attack, that they'd reached the end. He put his hand out.

"Give me the grenade," he said to Prem.

The Gurkha unquestioningly unclipped it from his belt

and passed it across. Philip looked at the glacier. If he threw it towards the trail he might, at best, be able to take out two, maybe three of the enemy. It wasn't enough. He looked around the valley and noticed a small slip of fresh snow landing lightly on the glacier, running off the ridge that thrust out to create the gorge. He looked up into the thick grey cloud that hid the valley walls.

Pulling himself to his feet he raced down the slope, trying to keep in the footsteps left by Balbir to give himself more speed. He heard rifles and then a burst of automatic fire that kicked up grit and ice as they peppered the ground around him. As he approached the glacier he veered to the right, using his momentum to carry him some way up the side of the valley.

The grenade was in his hand. He knew he needed a perfect throw if there was to be any chance. A gulley ran down into the valley, its mouth just below the ridge that jutted out and created the gorge. He needed to land it just there. He glanced ahead, picking out a low, flat boulder and deciding that was the best place to throw from. He traced the footfalls that would take him there, each chosen to maintain his momentum and add to the weight of his throw.

As his foot hit the boulder he ripped the pin from the grenade and launched it with all his strength. He knew he should move. He was a sitting target for the enemies' guns but he stood transfixed as the grenade arced high into the air, tumbling over and over. It wasn't going to clear the ridge. His muscles tensed as he urged it upwards. He'd stopped breathing, wanting to turn away but unable to move, completely spellbound. He felt something sting his shoulder, momentarily knocking him forward but regained his balance he glanced up just in time to see the grenade clear the top of the ridge with no more than an inch to spare. He breathed, relief washing through him, and was blown backwards down into the valley.

The roar was deafening. Magnified by the naked rock, the explosion ripped through the air, its flash lighting the clouds above and bathing their entire world in a fiery orange. The whole valley shook, loose stones jolted free and crashing down the slopes. Philip listened through his ringing ears as the noise echoed away until only a distant rumble was left.

"Please God, please," he mumbled, picking himself up. Everywhere was silent but after a few seconds of peace he heard the noise returning. Elation ran through him. He listened as the explosion raced back towards them. He felt someone grab his arm. It was Mingma.

"Run," the Sherpa screamed, pulling him along. "Avalanche."

They stumbled up the valley for thirty yards or so. The noise was now overwhelming, the ground moving so violently it was virtually impossible to even stand. They reached the cliff and threw themselves at its base, burying their heads in their hands. A wall of freezing air hit them, slicing through their clothes and blasting their skin. Philip could feel himself being buried, weight pushing down on him until he could hardly move. A noise like an Express train ripping past them, as the seconds passed its noise diminishing as the snow settled deeper on top.

As quickly as it had arrived, it was over and the valley was left in a shocked silence. Philip could feel the others struggling around him and added his strength to theirs, ignoring the pain in his shoulder and pushing upwards with all his might. He could feel the snow moving, the weight of it reducing and suddenly he was free. He saw Mingma, coughing and spitting the snow from his mouth and lungs, kneeling nearby. Reaching down he grabbed the coat of Lhamu who was lying beside him and pulled her free, hooking the ice from her mouth and nostrils with his fingers. She spluttered and coughed, hacking icy mucus from deep inside her and gasping for air.

Turning his head he looked out at the scene behind. The avalanche had struck down the valley, just below the crest where the Chinese had been climbing over the glacier. Snow now covered the trail to a depth of fifty feet or so, stretching out across the glacier to the far side of the gorge. The snow that had buried them had only been a small side flow pushed over the outcrop by the volume of snow beyond. God knows, the Chinese would've had no chance, their lungs filled with ice particles and bodies crushed by the wall of snow hitting them at over 200 miles per hour.

Glancing up the valley he could see the Gurkhas emerging from their hiding places, smiles on their faces and waving their khukri overhead in triumph. His ears were slowly clearing and he became aware of a voice. He turned to see the Rinpoche standing behind him, head bowed and chanting in prayer. He sat watching him, the gentle flow of his voice filling the still valley like a gentle breeze.

"He is praying for the dead," Lhamu said from behind him. "Making sure that their souls can be found and go forward to their rebirth."

He crawled beside her and took her in his arms, holding her as tightly as his painful arm would allow.

CHAPTER 21

It was soon apparent that the Chinese force had been swept away and buried by the avalanche. It had been huge and stretched several hundred yards down the valley. Those Chinese who'd already advanced over the glacier lay stunned and half buried, bewildered by the change in fortune and the Gurkhas quickly dispatched them with their knifes. When they regrouped by the cliff a few minutes later the fight was over.

As well as losing Balbir, Ram had also been killed by a bullet in the initial fire fight and a couple of others were cut and bruised from debris of the avalanche. Everyone was dazed; the silence that surrounded them contrasting completely with the deafening chaos of a few minutes before.

"We'll camp here," Philip ordered, sitting exhausted in the snow. "Dig out the equipment and let's get the tent up and some food cooked." He glanced up the valley at the gun positions. "We must get Ram buried as well."

He tried to push himself to his feet but in doing so felt a sharp pain sear through his left shoulder. Lhamu noticed and pushed him back down. Opening his jacket and shirt she discovered a bullet wound in his upper shoulder.

Philip winced as she gently probed around it. "Ouch!" he said through gritted teeth, looking down at it in surprise. "I thought I'd been hit by some debris from the avalanche."

Lhamu pulled down his clothes at the back and nodded approvingly. "It has gone right through," she said, looking at the exit wound." She smiled. "And it does not seem to have hit any bones." Her fingers traced the scar tissue of an older wound. "It is an unlucky shoulder, it has been shot before."

The men, who'd been watching with concerned faces turned and moved off, satisfied that he wasn't going to die. They wearily followed Prem up to where Ram's body lay. Mingma had dug out and relit the fire and had started melting some snow. At the altitude they were at the water boiled quickly and Lhamu used it to wash the wound, dressing it with bandages from the First Aid kit before fashioning a sling with a length of material ripped from the uniform of one of the dead soldiers.

"You are lucky," she said, "the muscles will heal. Your arm will be fine."

"Thank you," he said as he gingerly got to his feet. He caught her hand as she wiped it on some spare cloth and bringing it to his lips he kissed it.

They looked at each other in silence and then both smiled. Philip took a couple of steps backwards, his eyes lingering on Lhamu's until her hand dropped from his and he turned and carefully climbed to join the men.

There was no place to dig a grave. The side of the valley was a jumble of boulders and rock that fell into the ice of the glacier. When he reached them the men had taken Ram over to a deep crevasse in the ice and were preparing the body, washing it with water from their bottles.

Philip stood beside Prem. "It seems a cold and lonely place to be left," he said, sadness washing through him.

Prem glanced over at him. "Our people believe that his body will go back to the earth and his spirit will join those of his ancestors. It is a good place to lie." He turned and pointed to a large boulder that stood at the side of the glacier. "His name will be remembered there for the man he was."

Ram was carefully redressed in his clothes and then swathed and tied in his large woollen blanket. When he was prepared the Gurkhas stood back and started reciting a prayer, a mournful chant that left tears on Philip's cheeks. He looked at the wrapped corpse, remembering the cheerful young man of years before. How cruel it seemed to escape that hell only to die here. At least he'd have Balbir for company in the cold heart of the glacier.

He realised the prayer was over and Prem gently took his good arm and led him forward to Ram. Together they all lifted the small body and gently slid it over the lip of a dark, bottomless crevasse. There was no noise; no catching on the sides or distant thump as it hit the bottom. It was as if he'd slipped peacefully into the next world.

Returning to camp they started to dig their bags from the snow. Most were undamaged but the radio had been shattered by the force of the avalanche. The tent was erected in silence and after a hot meal Philip crawled exhausted into his sleeping bag. He was worried that his wound may keep him awake but he fell into a deep sleep.

The sun was warm on his face, bringing the smell of hot earth into his nostrils as he tried to cool himself with a small rattan fan. In his other hand was a rough clay bowl from which he took a swig of toddy juice, grimacing as the rough palm alcohol burnt the back of his throat. There was laughter and glancing up he saw Balbir and Ram sitting cross-legged opposite, swigging at their drinks. Village women were serving them sticky rice, fat lumps of meat poking from it, meat juice running from the side of the wooden platter on which it was served.

He smiled up at the girl who'd just brought his food. Her long black hair was in a thick plait hanging behind her, the flower from a deep purple orchid woven into it. Her face was perfect, unblemished, with large brown eyes and a small, full mouth. She reminded Philip of one of his sister's china dolls she'd played with when young; delicate, as if it could shatter at any moment. Her eyes fixed on his. She placed a tiny hand on his shoulder and leant forward, gently kissing him on his cheek. He lay back into a soft bed of silken cushions and fell, at last, into a dreamless sleep.

The next morning dawned bright and still, a strip of unbroken blue sky over the valley. It was a leisurely morning, a breakfast of millet tsampa at dawn, before breaking camp and moving out up the valley. Compared to their journey in the other direction, it would have felt easy had it not been for Philip's wound. Every step he took jarred it, causing the dressings to rub on the scab and shoot pain down his left side.

Fortunately the weather held, keeping fine and warm, allowing them to make good progress. As they climbed up they met a trading caravan travelling back from Namche. Prem and the men greeted the grizzled looking Tibetans as old friends.

"We do business with them," Prem explained as they stood together, communicating in a mixture of Tibetan and Nepali. "We took much of their salt on this very trip." He looked at Philip. "They'll trust us. If you would like to ride from here I'm sure we could borrow one of their yaks."

Philip looked up at the Gurkha, indignant that they though him in such a bad state, but before he could reply Prem erupted with laughter. When he and the other Gurkhas had recovered, he leant on Philips good shoulder to prop himself up. "No, I'm sorry, when they saw you they offered but I have already said no."

They said their farewells and the traders continued, warned but unconcerned about the avalanche lower down the valley and hopeful, Philip thought, of scavenging abandoned equipment scattered around the scene.

Prem and Philip continued up the trail, walking in companionable silence until, after a hour or so, they finally reached the small rock cairn covered in tattered prayer flags that marked the top of the pass. They stopped to drink and sat enjoying the heat of the sun on a large flat rock, the place unrecognisable from a couple of days before. Looking back down the valley they could see the brown plains of the Tibetan Plateau stretching far away into the distance.

"How did you get back?" Philip asked, shielding his eyes with his good hand as he looked up at the towering form of Everest to their left.

There was silence as Prem screwed the top back onto his water bottle and clipped it onto his pack.

"We had just arrived at the baggage when the shooting started." He rubbed at some dirt on his palm with the thumb of the other hand, staring into the distance. "The whole valley was flashing with the light from the guns and torches. I could see the trees black against the light, every leaf showing clearly. Then we heard shouting and recognised Japanese. I knew there was no way we could go back. We grabbed our bags and I took the map case from your pack before heading off on the bearing you'd set earlier. After a couple of miles we stopped and waited but you didn't come. At daybreak we moved off again."

The Gurkha sighed. "It took us another nine days to get to the border. We were very weak with hunger and Balbir was slowed by the beatings the Japanese had given his feet." He smiled grimly. "We were found by a platoon of British soldiers patrolling the west bank of the Chindwin river. They couldn't believe it. At first they thought we were ghosts but when they realised who we were they gave us food and took us to HQ."

Prem looked at Philip. "We waited and hoped. So many men wandered in alone after many weeks in the jungle. We prayed you might suddenly appear. Back in Calcutta we met up with others from the column but nobody had news of you. The war ended and still we heard nothing. We came home to our lives in the foothills, to our families and farms but we always remembered the officer who'd died so we could escape that village." The Gurkha put his hand on Philips shoulder. "I came to accept that you died that day, that you'd been broken by what happened to those villagers in that hut."

Philips head bowed and turned away, trying to keep composed. When he did speak his voice cracked. "You're right. I didn't care what happened to me that night, I just wanted to make amends in some way for what I'd done. Giving you a chance seemed to be all I could offer. It seemed the only way out for me too. I grabbed a gun and kept firing until I thought I died. When I came to I was in the back of a truck, I'd been shot in the shoulder and had passed out. My wound had been cleaned and dressed. The first Japs treated me well." He laughed grimly. "They believed I'd fought bravely and to the death. It wasn't my fault I'd fallen unconscious." His voice caught and he cleared his throat. "That changed when I reached Rangoon Jail."

He looked again at the towering peaks all around. "In a hell like that it's impossible to believe that places like this can exist in the same world. Two years I was there. No news in or out. Treated worse than animals. When I was liberated and brought home everything had changed. My father had died, a cancer he hadn't wanted to bother anyone with." He leant forward, elbows resting on his knees, head bowed. "He never knew I'd survived. Letters I'd sent had never got through and when one finally did it was too late, he'd gone. I often think that he'd have been the one who'd have understood, who could have taught me to live with all that happened. But he wasn't there. I'd always wondered why he was never still, up at first light and late to bed. Now I knew it was to keep the memories away, to always be doing something rather than remembering." Philip slowly shook his head. "I finally understood my own father and I couldn't put my arms around him and tell him. It would've been the first embrace we'd ever have had but it would've been worth the wait."

He sighed and look up. "I decided that I didn't want to

know the truth about you in case you'd all died and what little comfort I could take from my actions was taken from me. It was easier not to ask. I just wanted my old life back again, free of the memories of what happened."

He rubbed his eyes, pushing his fingers beneath his goggles so the Gurkha couldn't see his tears. The relief, the joy he'd felt at meeting them in Namche a few days before finally forced its way out. Prem reached up and undid the top fastening of his jacket. Taking hold of a worn cord that hung hidden around his neck he pulled it out and, unsheathing his khukri , cut through its leather. In his hand lay a tiny gold St. Christopher medal.

"It was in with the maps. When I looked in the wallet next morning I found it. I didn't know what it was but vowed to keep it and return it one day." He looked down at the image, of a man carrying a child across the water. "It seemed to show me what we all owed you, helping us to escape." He held it out to Philip. "I never thought I would get this chance."

Philip took it, his hand trembling. Reaching into his own shirt he pulled out the charm he'd been given by the old Tibetan woman on the trail in to Everest. Slipping it over his head he held it out to Prem. "We'll swap. This has served me well over the last few weeks. I hope it brings you the good luck and peace it's brought me."

The Gurkha placed it over his head, as Philip tied the medallion around his. He jumped down from the rock and head off up the trail, his vision still blurred. He'd walked no more than fifty yards when he saw the Rinpoche standing by the trail, admiring a wall of weathered mani stones that had been carried up to this desolate spot by devout travellers. Wiping his face he quietly walked over and stood beside him. He was studying a large stone in the centre of the wall, on which intricate text had been beautifully carved around a large relief image of the Buddha.

"The Buddha told us that everybody has free will and is responsible for their actions," he said in a calm voice, his eyes not moving from the stone. "But that doesn't make actions good or evil simply because of their consequence. It depends on the circumstances of the person when the action is done. A bad ending when an action was done for good reasons should not bring shame."

With this he turned and walked off in silence along the trail.

They continued on and late the next day they finally dropped in the fading light back into Namche. Wearily they trudged to the house of Mingma's family where, after a large meal of chicken and rice, Philip slept on the hard earth floor as if it was a feather mattress.

The next morning they sat around the hearth with large mugs of warm chang in their hands. Mingma had been to the Police Post at first light to report the avalanche and had returned shaking his head.

"When I spoke to them they said you had never reported the dead monks by the river." He looked at Philip. "The officer said that when you visited them last week you'd simply said that a monk was missing down by the river. That is why he did not act, thinking that the man would turn up later and it would be a waste of time sending his men. It was only after we'd left next day that he heard of the massacre from porters coming from Thangboche and realised they must be linked."

Philip shook his head. "It's my fault. I should have brought someone else with us to the Police Post to check what he was saying. Strangely enough, in the end it probably worked out better thanks to him. If it hadn't been for him telling us about the main Red Army force we may well have been caught by them at Rombuk. They'd have massacred us."

He looked around the group. "What are everybody's plans?"

"I shall return to Thangboche," the Rinpoche announced, looking around the faces of the men who'd risked their lives for him. "Lhamu and Mingma have offered to take me. I want to pray for those who were killed and to get a message sent to the Dalai Lama in Lhasa telling him what's happened and that I'm well enough to continue." He looked around the faces of the Gurkhas. "I can never thank you or your dead friends for what they have done for me and Tibet."

He looked at Prem. "I will speak to the Abbot of Thangboche. Should the families of your dead comrades wish it, their sons will be welcomed there to study. Should they need it, alms will be given. They have only to ask, their names will be remembered and revered."

Prem bowed his head. "I will tell them. Balbir always believed he'd been saved by the Lieutenant for some purpose. When the sahib appeared again he knew that the time had come and he went gladly to his fate. I will make sure their army pensions are changed to their widows so they do not suffer more hardship."

Prem stood and the other Gurkhas followed his lead, draining their mugs and crossing to the bunks to fetch their possessions. Philip slowly stood, his shoulder still painful, and followed the corporal out of the door. He squinted in the bright morning light, sunlight bathing the small lane in a warm light that reflected off the white washed walls. He breathed in deeply, enjoying the sensation of the cool air in his lungs after the smoky lodge.

The two men stood facing each other awkwardly, unsure what to say. Prem slowly saluted. Philip smiled and nodded, sharply returning the salute before stretching out his hand. Prem lowered his salute and reached out to grasp the hand. The men stared at each other.

Philip faltered, trying to find words. There were none.

The Gurkha smiled and nodded, and with their hands still grasped they embraced.

The other Gurkhas had emerged and came over, hugging him, smiling faces he would now remember with fondness and pride. And with that they were gone, off down the small cobbled street and around the corner.

It was a beautiful day. Sunlight streamed down through a canopy of rhododendron, leaving pools of dappled light on the trail that contoured its way up the valley. The flowers were now in full bloom, huge splashes of pink and white that sat framed by the vivid green of the foliage. Ahead, high up on a spur, stood the gold pinnacled roof of Thangboche Monastery, glistening in the morning light.

Philip walked steadily along the trail, his body rested after a day of being fed up by Mingma's mother back in

Namche Bazaar. The only exertion he'd done the previous day was to take a short afternoon stroll up to the radio station, where he'd enjoyed a very pleasant hour drinking tea with the charming Indian operator, who'd been delighted to have a visitor in such a remote place. It would, he'd been assured, be an honour to relay any messages for the expedition. When Philip had enquired about the radio's performance with the new parts he'd had to walk to collect, the man had looked at him bemused and informed him with a shrug that he hadn't been out of Namche for nearly two months.

They rested for half an hour at the river, Philip finding it impossible to believe that such a tranquil place had been the scene of such horror only days before. The Rinpoche knelt and said prayers for the spirits of those who'd been killed, before they shared some dried fruit from their packs.

It was several hours later that they wearily crested the ridge and found themselves walking through the village of Thangboche once more. The chickens still scurried around, mangy dogs still lay sleeping in the shade and grubby children chased them gleefully. As they approached the monastery the great horn boomed its welcome, its note seeming to settle under the normal noise of the valley to lift everything upwards.

The monastery doors opened and the Head Lama scurried out, followed by a group of senior monks. They were followed by Mingma, who'd gone ahead with Lhamu, to warn the monastery of the arrival of their visitor. They all prostrated themselves before the Rinpoche, who acknowledged them with hands pushed together and told them to rise.

The abbot turned to face Philip and taking his hand pressed it to his head. He said something Philip didn't understand.

Lhamu stepped forward smiling. "He says that you must eat with them tonight in thanksgiving."

Philip smiled, rather embarrassed by the fuss. "Please tell him it would be an honour," he replied, looking at Lhamu. "Although I have a very important appointment planned for later this evening so tell him to keep the prayers short."

Lhamu giggled and translated the first part of the reply to the abbot, who smiled happily and turned his attention back to the Rinpoche, who was being ushered inside the monastery.

Before leaving Namche they'd arranged to meet up that evening at Lhamu's family house where he was to stay as a guest. He smiled and winked at her. "I'll see you later." He nodded in the direction of where the expedition tents had been. "I'd better go and visit the Expedition and see if I still have a job. There should be a message or two by now."

Lhamu waved as he turned and briskly set off across the small meadow. The camp was much smaller than it had been on his last visit. Most of the tents had gone and many of the crates of supplies had also been carried, he guessed, up the valley to the Base Camp. As he approached he saw a man busy unpacking what looked like oxygen bottles and using a screw-in gauge to check their pressure.

He walked over. "Major Roberts?" he enquired, recognising him from an introduction from James on his previous visit. "Philip Armitage, from *The Times*."

The man stood up, wiped his hands on a cloth that had

been draped over his shoulder and shook his hand. "Oh yes, hello again," he replied with a smile. "James told me you'd probably appear at some point. Good to see you. You've timed your arrival very well," he continued, walking over to a table that stood outside in the sun. He rummaged through a mound of papers and pulled out an envelope.

"This came in for you this morning with James runner. He dropped it before heading off again at full gallop for Kathmandu. He said things seemed to be going as planned." He pointed at the desk. "There's a party of porters heading up in the morning with some of this oxygen. If you want to send a reply, write it now and I'll seal it in the dispatch bag."

Philip thanked him and sank gratefully into a canvas camp chair that stood beside the desk. After satisfying himself that James seal was intact he ripped open the envelope and started reading the message;

"Base Camp, 3rd May

Philip, Base Camp established. Climbing started up the Ice-flow. Need to know that messages are secure. Any news on Izzard? Got a stinking cold. Wish I had my feet up in cosy Namche like you. Hope you're not too bored! Best James."

He smiled to himself and looking up, pulled over a sheet of plain paper from a pile on the desk being held down by a small lump of quartz. He picked up a pencil and started to write.

"James. Izzard no longer a threat and reports say has returned to Kathmandu. Dispatches can be sent with confidence, I suggest important messages are coded as planned and sent via the Namche radio who seem delighted to assist. I'll head back to Kathmandu, checking for other reporters as I go." He looked up, his eyes falling on the summit of Everest that was just visible above the huge snow ridge of Lhotse. It was a black pyramid of inhospitable rock, snow blasting from it as high altitude winds battered it from the north. On the other side of the mountain lay Rombuk, geographically so near and yet part of a different, turbulent world. He looked down at the paper and added. "Don't worry about me. I'll find something to pass the time."

He sealed the note in an envelope and left it on the desk under the rock. He walked over to where Roberts was busy testing another oxygen cylinder, carefully noting its serial number and pressure before placing it in a porters load ready to be carried up the mountain.

"Did Hunt have anything interesting to say?" Philip asked after they'd chatted amicably for a while about the equipment.

Roberts looked at him. "I don't suppose there's any harm in telling you since James will have written about it in that dispatch that's just gone. He's told them whose going to be going for the summit. Tom Bourdillon and Charlie Evans are having first crack and apparently they're looking strong. If they fail then it'll be Tenzing and Ed Hillary's turn."

They chatted a bit longer until the sun dipped beneath the western wall of the valley and Philip excused himself, walked slowly back towards the monastery. He was welcomed at the door and given some ornate yellow slippers and a long white scarf to wear, before being solemnly led up to the banqueting room. He was embarrassed to see that he'd been placed on the top table, next to the Rinpoche, and blushed brightly when the room fell silent and the monks bowed as he was led to his place.

This time the meal went quickly, mainly because he was able to talk to the Rinpoche. He asked about the mission the Llama had been given.

"Our country has been defending itself against China for many years. The eastern border has moved back and forward on numerous occasions." He looked at Philip. "That was the cause of your friend Tashi's hatred for us."

"I still find it hard to believe that he'd help the Chinese," Philip said. "He was a Tibetan, surely they could have settled elsewhere in Tibet?"

The Rinpoche shook his head. "If the Tibetans took their lands they would have been exiled and the Chinese would not have taken them in. They want their own people in these areas to make their grip on the land stronger. Any ill will he bore the Chinese would have been lost in the great revolution, when he must have thought that at last the people would have their say. The Kuomintang ruled China when his family were refused entry, but in 1949 they were beaten by the Communists under Mao Tse-tung." He shrugged sadly. "It was the Communists Tashi thought were his allies, as they'd beaten his Chinese enemies and then invaded his Tibet ones.

"His father must have brought him up to remember the wrong we Tibetans had put their family through and at some point, perhaps under the guise of trading on the High Plateau, he must have contacted the Communists and started working for them."

Philip interrupted. "He told me that he used to fly into Southern China during the war with the American planes. Perhaps that was the start of it?"

The Rinpoche nodded. "The Communists were fighting with the Kuomintang against the Japanese at that point, he may well have come across them. They were recruiting their network of spies to help them seize control of China after the war. They were paranoid that Tibet would gain the support of India and that they would come to our aid. He was a useful agent for them to recruit if he was living in Calcutta."

He shook his head. "I don't know how the Chinese discovered my trip to the UN, but they must have contacted him and told him to get to Nepal. I guess it was he who located me and then guided the soldiers to where they could ambush us."

Philip sighed. "It's a great shame he couldn't put his early life behind him. From what I gathered he'd done rather well for himself in Calcutta." He scratched the back of his head. "For all the time we spent together I don't even know if he had a wife and family."

"You shouldn't feel bad," the Rinpoche replied, placing his hand on Philip's. "You were right to see the good in him rather than dwell on the dark. You couldn't know about his past."

The Rinpoche was distracted by the abbot and Philip sat picking at his meal, his anticipation growing about seeing Lhamu again. Soon the abbot stood and escorted the Rinpoche from the room, marking the end of the evening. He turned to see Lhamu walking up behind him and beckoning him to follow. He stood stiffly, his legs numb after sitting cross-legged for so long, and descended the steps before crossing to the monastery entrance.

They slipped on their shoes and stepped outside. The whole valley was bathed in moonlight, the snow-covered mountains glowing in the distance under a dazzling array of stars. They descended the steps in silence and as they did so Philip felt Lhamu's hand slide tentatively into his. He forced his body to relax and when they reached the gate they stopped and turned to face each other.

"It's been a strange way to get to know someone," she said quietly. "Normally in Nepal, a potential suitor would bring food so their families could eat together and get to know each other."

"Sorry," replied Philip, laughing nervously, "I didn't realise, I'm a bit out of practice. I thought rescuing a kidnapped Llama would be more impressive than a bunch of flowers and box of chocolates."

They stood in the freezing night air together, and Philip could feel himself relaxing, enjoying the pleasure of simply being with a woman for the first time in many years. Lhamu giggled and turned away, pulling Philip by his hand along the small street.

"We had better hurry," she laughed over her shoulder. "My father will wonder what you are doing with me out here in the dark. He might start demanding a large dowry!"

CHAPTER 22

Philip woke to the sound of the dawn chorus, every bird in Kathmandu seemingly outside his window. He tried rolling over, covering his ears with the heavy bolster that served as a pillow, but even that couldn't muffle the hungry roar of a tiger.

The first time he'd heard it a few weeks before he'd been out of bed in a single leap, convinced in his half-asleep state that a wild animal had got into the grounds of the hotel. He now knew, thanks to Hutch who'd told him once he'd stopped laughing, that a Nepalese nobleman kept a small zoo in the grounds of his palace next door, the inhabitants of which could often be heard.

He'd arrived back into Kathmandu at an opportune time. Hutch was ill. He'd been feeling feverish for several days but with Philip back in town he took to his bed, weak and exhausted. The Embassy had sent their doctor over and it was diagnosed as Glandular Fever with a period of bed rest prescribed. Being an old hand on the subcontinent and used to bouts of Malaria he'd insisted on carrying on, so continued receiving the dispatches from James on Everest and transcribing them for onward transmission. But it was left to Philip to shuttle between his room, the telegraph office and the Embassy, as well as keep an eye on the other papers.

On his first few days back in the city he'd been surprised and alarmed by the number of journalists who'd descended on Kathmandu in an attempt to get the story. As well as the main British papers, there were reporters from various European countries, several from India and all of the major news agencies. As the Government had stopped issuing permits to trek up to Everest, they were all milling around the Embassy and City trying to unearth any news from the mountain.

Not long after he'd returned they'd received a dispatch bag from James that had obviously been opened, the seal was broken and the small lock that held the neck of the canvas closed was gone. He was relieved when he'd read it to discover that it was only an article about life on the mountain, rather than containing any important news, but the runner was paid off and not used again.

The Times had an agreement that the Embassy would send articles for them using their transmitter and Philip was a regular visitor to the Radio room. It was during one such visit, while he was waiting for the latest dispatch on establishing Camp Four high on the Lhotse ridge to be sent, that he discovered something alarming. He was chatting to the Second Secretary who shared the office.

"I suppose I'd better take you gentlemen out for a meal next time you're back in London," he'd suggested light heartedly. "You've saved me a lot of time and effort hanging around the Public Telegraph Office. Christ," he laughed and shook his head. "I don't think I'd have survived. I'd probably have been ripped to shreds by the pack of hacks that hangs about outside!"

The Second Secretary, a young, enthusiastic man on his first overseas posting, had smiled back. "You'd better throw in a decent bottle of claret as well," he'd replied. "We've had quite a few offers that would have make us a few quid if we'd taken them up."

Philip looked at him, perplexed. "What do you mean?"

"Well, without naming names, let's just say that one of your Fleet Street chums has offered us £400 for copies of certain messages we might be asked to send." He widened his eyes and nodded to where the Radio Operator was busy transmitting the dispatch. "That would pay for a pretty decent hotel next time I'm back on leave to Blighty!"

Philip was stunned. That was the best part of six months' salary and if some of the papers were prepared to spend that much then they'd certainly be willing to obtain information in any way they could. He'd become even more careful.

All messages to him and Hutch from *The Times* in London weren't allowed to be sent to the Embassy in case the other papers complained of preferential treatment. Instead they went to the Public Telegraph Office just off Durbar Square in the heart of Kathmandu. When he'd gone there to check for any new correspondence on his first day back, to his surprise, he'd been handed the entire pile of all incoming messages to check, regardless of who they were for. He'd immediately warned his editors not to send anything sensitive there and made a point of arriving at opening time every day to ensure he could check them before anyone else.

He'd also made a point of visiting and introducing himself at the Indian Embassy, wanting to ensure that if and when the coded message arrived from Namche they'd know exactly where to forward it to by runner. Once every week he popped round, usually with a box of fresh cakes he'd picked up from a little bakery near the hotel, and enjoyed a tea and chat with the Indian High Commissioner.

Interest in the Everest climb was reaching fever pitch in Nepal. Now that the population of Kathmandu knew that a Sherpa was going to be one of those attempting to reach the summit, the excitement had grown and with it an insatiable desire for news on how Tenzing Norgay was doing. People crowded around battered radios set up in shops and offices, listening to the daily updates from the state radio network. Others crowded around as someone read reports from the local paper, shaking their heads in wonder at the vivid accounts copied from James dispatches in *The Times*.

Life settled down into a routine that swung from complete boredom to frenzied activity when a runner arrived in Kathmandu. He now avoided the cafes of Durbar Square, fed up of being cross-examined by other journalists who congregated there and he spent more time out at the Buddhist shrine of Boudha. There were few other Westerners here and he found he could escape and relax. He'd gone there the day after he'd arrived back in Kathmandu and sought out the Tibetan Zigsa.

Zigsa had greeted him politely, leading him to a tiny tea house frequented only by Tibetans where you sat on old, upturned crates. When they'd both taken a sip of their drinks and exchanged pleasantries, Philip reached down and pulled something from a bag he'd brought with him. He passed it to the Tibetan.

"I've brought you something you might been interested in," he said with a smile, watching Zigsa's eyes widen.

"Where … where did you get it?" Zigsa asked in a stunned voice, looking down at the black pages and golden ink of the Kanjur that lay on his knees.

"It's a long story and I'm afraid it got a bit damaged on the way."

The Tibetan shook his head, running his fingers gently over the damaged cover with its embedded precious stones. Philip sat in silence, letting him enjoy the beauty of what he was holding. He'd left the book at Mingma's house while they'd been off pursuing the Chinese, his mother locking it in an ancient chest that sat in the corner of the family's room.

After the fight at Rombuk, Mingma had carefully searched all the soldiers bags until he'd found the missing cover in the pack of the commander, plundered and hidden to be sold off later. The Sherpa had carefully wrapped it in his blanket and carried it back to Namche where he'd reunited the two pieces. Other than the ripped binding and a few loose stones, it had survived remarkably well. They'd offered it to the Rinpoche but he'd shaken his head.

"This manuscript needs to be taken to safety in Kathmandu and the safest way I can think of is for it to go with a westerner. Nobody will think you have a sacred book with you and as part of the expedition the authorities will not search your baggage. In any case I will give you a signed letter of authority that explains your possession of it."

Philip had felt uneasy at first, worried about the responsibility and potential risks. The book, the Rinpoche had explained as he flicked through the beautifully illustrated pages, had been written in the 1450's and been in Ganden Monastery ever since. It was sacred to all Buddhists as the original translation of the Buddha's word. But he realised that what the Rinpoche said made sense and as he'd predicted he'd encountered no problems or awkward questions. The only downside had been a crick in the neck he'd developed as he slept every night with it safely stowed in his pack, which doubled as his pillow.

"We must take this straight to the Chinia Lama at the shrine," Zigsa had whispered, standing up and leaving the tea beside him untouched. "He is the Dalai Lama's representative here and will know what to do. It must be placed somewhere safe from the traders and given to the monks so they can repair it. They are very skilled at restoring such items."

Philip followed him through the warren of tiny alleys that criss-crossed the refugee shelters and up a short flight of stairs to the ornate doors of the shrine. Zigsa strode in without even acknowledging the main golden statue and led Philip up more stairs to a small room where an old monk sat writing at a desk.

The Tibetan nodded towards him. "This is the Chinia Lama." The two men spoke briefly and then fell upon examining the book. After several minutes the old monk came around his desk and took Philip's hand, raising to his forehead and saying something.

"He is thanking you," Zigsa translated. "For saving such an important item and restoring it to us. He asks where you got it from as he is concerned that other such works have been lost as well."

Philip retrieved his hand. "Tell him not to worry. This book was being smuggled out by some Tibetan monks when they encountered some problems. It was the only manuscript they had with them and nothing was lost." He paused and looked at the abbot. "You must warn him that he has an important guest on his way. It was he who was originally escorting the Kanjur. He'll be here in a few days' time."

He'd taken his leave, declining to reveal the identity of the traveller, feeling that after all that had happened the fewer people who knew about the mission the better.

Since that visit Zigsa had always welcomed him warmly and now even offered him black tea with sugar rather than butter. It felt like a tranquil refuge where Philip could recover from the exertions, both physical and mental, of the previous few weeks.

On one occasion, a week or so later, he'd been led by the Tibetan, whom Philip could see was bursting with excitement, straight over to the shrine. Here he'd been delighted to find the Rinpoche, who'd arrived a couple of days before, and spent an enjoyable afternoon with him. His attempt to visit the UN was looking promising. He'd managed to obtain the necessary visas for India, Britain and the US and was just awaiting for his travel arrangements to be confirmed.

He'd looked worried and Philip had tried to reassure him that he'd be well received and treated.

"To be honest it's not that," the Llama had confided. "It's the travelling in the aeroplanes that I'm apprehensive about. Tell me," he asked, leaning forward in his chair, "What is it like?"

Philip thought of the flight into Kathmandu, of the updrafts buffeting the plane as it wove between the forested peaks of the Himalayan foothills. He wasn't sure what to say as he didn't want to lie to a highest incarnation of Buddhist Llama. "It's easier than climbing over a Himalayan pass and more comfortable than camping in the mountains," he replied tactfully. "The only thing is it can get a bit bumpy as the plane bounces around in the air."

The Rinpoche nodded. "Before I was a monk I used to enjoy breaking in young ponies on the Steppe. If it gets too rough I will close my eyes and imagine I'm there once more, the wind in my face and sun on my back."

It was the last time he saw him. By the time of his next visit, he was gone.

In his spare time Philip hadn't been idle. On his last night in Thangboche, staying with Lhamu's family, he'd listened to her father's stories and reminiscences of the earlier climbing expeditions, taking copious short-hand notes into his battered notebook. The old Sherpa had loved it, arms waving as he relived his memories in front of a new, enthralled audience. Philip had explained his plan to Lhamu as they'd sat alone by the dying fire later that night, her eyes sparkling with an enthusiasm he prayed was more than the reflected glow of the embers.

Back in Kathmandu he'd used the notes to outline a series of articles about the Everest attempts of the 1920's, including the mystery of the disappearance of Mallory and Irvine and whether or not they'd managed to reached the summit before vanishing in a storm. If accepted by his editor he'd be able to invite Old Karma, accompanied by Lhamu, to Kathmandu to interview him in more detail. He hoped that after spending so much money on the exclusive rights to the current climb, *The Times* would be keen to cash in. His proposal went further than this, but he'd not dared mention all of it to her in case it didn't come off.

It was with some trepidation that he'd sent through the proposal to the Features Editor and he then waited nervously for several days for a response. When it came, sitting in the pile of incoming messages at the Public Telegraph Office one morning, he couldn't bring himself to read it but had shoved it in a pocket, not retrieving it until he was sitting in the gardens of the hotel with a large pot of coffee before him. Taking a deep breath he unfolded the flimsy telegraph paper.

"Attn. Philip Armitage, *Times* Correspondent. Proceed with old Everest articles x 3. Reasonable expenses only please for Sherpa in Kathmandu. Re. your second proposal. We agree so long as the current climb is successful . Best Jack ."

Philip leapt to his feet bursting with excitement and spilling most of his coffee in the process. Lhamu was going to be coming to Kathmandu to look after her father. He felt a surge of hope now that he'd be able to spend time with her and get to know her better, away from the mountains. More exciting was the second proposal. If Hunt's expedition managed to climb Everest then the amount of interest in the mountain worldwide would be huge. Philip had suggested a series of lectures at the Royal Geographical Society, where the old Sherpa, in tandem with Philip, could talk about Everest past and present. If Lhamu came to Britain with him, he'd have the chance to show her more of his life.

He smiled to himself. His sister Mary had married an American during the war, meeting him while he was on leave in London and happened to shelter in the same tube station as her during an air raid. That had, by all accounts, caused quite a stir back in Norfolk when people found out. Imagine if he turned up there with a Sherpani. He laughed out loud. Damn it, who cares, he thought to himself.

He walked quickly through the streets to the Indian Embassy, where his cultivation of their good will came into its own as his brief message was happily transmitted by their radio operator to their station in Namche.

They arrived just over two weeks later, a period that dragged interminably to Philip, with the old Sherpa revitalised by his journey on pony to the capital. They stayed in the same small hotel as Mingma and the young Sherpa did everything he could to ensure that the old man's stay was comfortable.

That evening Karma had gone to bed early, tired from the journey and Philip had seized the opportunity to take Lhamu out to a nearby restaurant. Initially they were like teenagers, tongue-tied and smiling shyly at each other again but slowly the awkwardness passed. They sat at a rickety table at the back of the dimly lit restaurant where there was no menu and no choice. The rice and lentils sat untouched in front of them as soon they were chatting and laughing together.

When the conversation finally died down, Philip took a deep breath, wondering whether his heart had ever worked as hard on the march to Tibet.

"I'd like to spend more time with you," he blurted out at

last. "If the Everest climb is successful, my paper have offered to bring you and your father to London for a lecture tour. I'm sure your father would enjoy seeing England and it would, well, it would give us more time to get to know each other."

He paused, fumbling for words. "If the climb doesn't succeed I could try to get a posting out here, perhaps with Hutch in Delhi. That way we can be near to each other, assuming that is what you'd like …" He stopped, finally exhausting all the words in his mind and responding to a gentle squeeze on his hand.

Looking up at her he saw her smiling. "I have spent my life being told about the world outside the mountains; of the great cities and railways and the sea. It always excited me but was frightening, so big and hard to understand. I often thought that if I ever had the opportunity to go I would probably not have the courage to take it up. Now that moment is here I've never been more certain of anything. I would love to go to your country," she replied quietly. "In London, in Delhi, in Khumbu, I'm sure we could be happy."

They toasted their future in chang which, at that moment, Philip thought tasted better than any champagne he'd ever drunk. They left and started walking slowly back to the hotel, stopping outside and, after arranging to meet the following morning, he kissing her goodnight gently on the hand.

It was still early and Philip, too elated to sleep, walked slowly back through Durbar Square. Hawkers were carefully tending their corn cobs as they cooked on glowing charcoal embers. Saddhus sat cross-legged on the bases of monuments, their faces smeared white with ash and bronze bowls placed before them in which to collected alms for their supper. Monkeys performed acrobatics, hanging off bars and jumping through hoops as laughing children watched wide-eyed. The western sky was still tinged orange from a fast fading sunset that still silhouetted the dark outline of the High Himalaya. It felt so good to be alive.

He didn't hear the voice at first, his name alien and out of place in such an exotic place.

"Armitage, sahib?" it said again and this time he turned. It was the runner from the Indian Embassy holding out a folded note.

He reached into his pocket and without looking shoved a handful of rupees towards the boy, snatching the message from his hand and ripped open the light air-mail envelope.

It contained one small piece of paper, on which was written:

"Snow Conditions bad... Abandoned Advance Base... Awaiting Improvement. All well."

Philip fumbled for his wallet, dropping more bank notes on the ground as he pulled out the folded sheet of paper that James had given him at Thangboche all those weeks before. His heart was pounding as he translated the code, checking it carefully before daring to believe.

"Summit May 29th, Hillary. Tenzing. All well." He looked at his watch. If he got the message off tonight there was a chance it would reach London in time for the story to be broken in *The Times* on Coronation day. He turned and started running towards the Embassy. Everest was conquered.

Notes

The characters in this book are mostly fictitious, created to tell a story against the backdrop of two historical events; the first Chindit Expedition into Burma in 1943 and the British Mount Everest Expedition of 1953. While I have tried to convey the atmosphere and feel of these two events, neither is represented historically accurately either in terms of timescale or the actions of the characters within them.

The characters in *Sacred Mountain* who are journalists, with the exception of the main character Philip, and mountaineers do use the names of the climbers and correspondents who were there in 1953, but all their characteristics and actions are completely fictitious, created for the story.

The Times correspondent on Everest in 1953 was James Morris (now Jan Morris, the famous writer). My thanks go to her for responding to my requests for information and for her encouragement in the project. Over the years the conspiracy theorists have suggested that news of the expeditions success was held back so that it would arrive in London on Coronation Day. Anyone who has read Morris' *Coronation Everest* (1958) and spoken to her will realise that this was not the case, and indeed she nearly died descending the mountain in time to get the dispatch off.

The Mail correspondent Ralph Izzard did leave Kathmandu and trek towards Everest, but did not have a transmitter or interfere with Expedition communications. This is fiction added to create the story. His book *An Innocent on Everest (1954)* is an excellent account of the whole episode, giving more flavour to the expedition than the rather functional accounts of the climbers. He returned to Nepal a couple of years later with the *Mail* in search of the Yeti, recounted in his book *The Abominable Snowman Adventure* (1955).

The *Telegraph* correspondent Colin Reed and *Times* correspondent Arthur Hutchinson did remain in Kathmandu for the duration of the climb. Their actions and words within the book are fictitious.

There are several meetings and conversations with members of the Everest Expedition in the book. These are all fictitious, albeit in places that they should have been at the time. The climbers did stay at Thangboche to acclimatise and, while there, were invited to the monastery for a blessing.

As well as the books mentioned above, I also used several accounts of the Expedition written by the climbers to help get an understanding of it. There were *The Ascent of Everest* (1953) by John Hunt, *South Col* (1954) by W.Noyce and *High Adventure* (1955) by Edmund Hillary.

Everest – The Swiss Everest Expeditions (1954) and *The Mount Everest Reconnaissance Expedition 1951* (1952) by E. Shipton gave excellent descriptions of the landscapes, countryside and high passes, the former particularly good for details of the peoples, monasteries and villages encountered.

For general details of Tibet and the Tibetans I used *Seven*

Years in Tibet (1953) by H.Harrer and *Through Forbidden Tibet* (1936) by H.Forman.

To get an understanding of the North side of Everest I used the accounts of the three British Expeditions there in the 1920's, alluded to in the book. They were *Mt. Everest – The Reconnaissance 1921* (1922) by C. Howard-Bury, *The Assault on Everest 1922* (1923) by C. Bruce and *The Fight for Everest 1924* (1925) by E. Norton.

For details on Kathmandu and Nepal in general I referred to *The Forgotten Valley* (1959) by K. Eskelund, *The Sherpa and the Snowman* (1955) by C. Stonor, *Nepal Himalaya* (1952) by H. Tilman and *Tiger for Breakfast* (1966) by M. Pleissel.

For the Burma story, I used *The Burma Campaign* (2010) by F. McLynn, *Forgotten Voices of Burma* (2010) by J. Thompson and *War in the Wilderness* (2011) by T. Redding.

My main inspiration came from *Return via Rangoon* (1994) by Philip Stibbe, a memoir of his time as a Chindit and POW in Rangoon. He was my old school Headmaster.